T0007815

EXTENUATING CIRCUMSTANCES

Also by Joyce Carol Oates

EXTENUATING CIRCUMSTANCES

STORIES OF CRIME AND SUSPENSE

JOYCE CAROL OATES

THE MYSTERIOUS PRESS

NEW YORK

EXTENUATING CIRCUMSTANCES

Mysterious Press
An Imprint of Penzler Publishers
58 Warren Street
New York, N.Y. 10007

Library of Congress Control Number: 2022900855

ISBN: 978-1-61316-425-9
eBook ISBN: 978-1-61316-316-0

10 9 8 7 6 5 4 3 2 1

Printed in the United States of America

Distributed by W. W. Norton & Company

CONTENTS

THE DEATH OF MRS. SHEER

One afternoon not long ago, on a red-streaked dirt road in the Eden Valley, two men in an open jalopy were driving along in such a hurry that anyone watching could have guessed they had business ahead. The jalopy was without species: it bore no insignia or features to identify it with other cars or jalopies, but many to distinguish itself in the memory—jingling behind was a battered license plate, last year's and now five months outdated, hanging down straight from a twist of wire, and other twists of this wire (which was not even chicken fence wire, but new shiny copper wire), professional and concise, held the trunk door nearly closed and both doors permanently closed. Dirty string and clothesline laced important parts of the car together too, notably the hood and the left front fender the only fender remaining. Though parts here and there creaked and the lone fender shuddered, everything really moved in harmony, including the men who nodded in agreement with the rapid progression of scrubland. Their nods were solemn prudent, and innocently calculating. They looked vaguely alike, as if their original faces had been identical and a brush stroke here, a flattening as with a mallet there, had turned them into Jeremiah and Sweet Gum.

Jeremiah, who drove, was about thirty-four. He was a tall thick-chested man, with a dark beard ragged about his face and pleased-looking lips shut tight as if he had a secret he wouldn't tell, not even to Sweet Gum. His forehead was innocent of wrinkles or thought. It was true that his hair was matted and made him look something like one of the larger land animals—most people were put in mind of a buffalo, even those who had never seen buffaloes but had only looked at pictures of them. But his eyes were clear and alert and looked intelligent, especially when anyone was talking to him. Jeremiah, years ago, had passed up through all grades except seventh, his last, just by gazing at his teacher with that look and sometimes nodding, as he did now. They were approaching an old wooden bridge and Jeremiah nodded as if he had known it was coming.

Sweet Gum's throat jumped at the sight of that bridge: Sweet Gum was only twenty and had never been this far from home, except to the Army and back (he told the story that he had decided against the Army, even after they gave him supper there, because he didn't like all the niggers around). He had a fair roundish face, that of a cherub dashed out of his element and so baffled and sullen for life. His hair, bleached by the sun, grew down shabby and long on his neck, though the ridge where the bowl had been and his mother had stopped cutting was still visible, jutting out two or three inches up his head, so that he looked ruffled and distorted. He had pale eyes; probably blue, and soft-looking eyebrows that were really one eyebrow, grown gently together over his nose. His cheeks were plump, freckled, his lips moist and always parted (at night there was wet anywhere he put his head, after a while). Like his cousin Jeremiah he wore a suit in spite of the heat—it was about ninety-eight—with a colored shirt open at the throat. Sweet Gum's suit was still too big for him, a hand-down that was wearing out before he grew into it, and Jeremiah's suit, a pure, dead black, was shiny and smelled like the attic. Ever since Jeremiah had appeared wearing it, Sweet Gum had been glancing at him strangely, as if he weren't sure whether this was his cousin Jeremiah or some other Jeremiah.

They clattered onto the bridge. "Whooee," Jeremiah laughed without enthusiasm, as boards clanked and jumped behind them and the old rusted rails jerked up as if caught by surprise. The bridge spanned nothing—just dried-up, cracked ground with dying weeds—and both men stared down at it with all their features run together into one blur of consternation. Then Jeremiah said, "All passed. All passed," and they were safe again.

"*God* taken hold of us there," Sweet Gum said, so frightened by the bridge that he forgot Jeremiah always laughed at remarks like that. But Jeremiah did not seem to notice. "God's saving us for our promise," he muttered, so that Jeremiah could hear it or not, just as he wanted. Back in his mind, and even coming out when his lips moved, was the thought: "First promise to do. First promise." If the Devil himself were to come and take Sweet Gum out into the desert with him, or up on a mountain, or pyramid, or anywhere, and tempt him to break his promise to his uncle Simon, Sweet Gum would shout "No!" at him— "No!" to the Devil himself.

As if to mock Sweet Gum's thoughts, Jeremiah twitched and rubbed his nose suddenly. "Christ, boy," he said, "I got a itch— Am I going to kiss a fool all the way out here?"

Sweet Gum turned red. "You keep your goddamn kissing to yourself!" he snarled, as if Jeremiah were no one to be afraid of. Had the duty of fulfilling a promise already begun to change

him? He felt Jeremiah's surprise with pride. "Nobody's going to
kiss *me*," Sweet Gum said with venom.

Probably no one on Main Street in Plain Dealing saw Jeremiah
and Sweet Gum leave, though many would see them leave for
the last time a few days later. By now Sweet Gum sat in a real
sweat of anticipation, his suit drenched and his eyes squinting
past a haze of sweat as if peering out of a disguise. As soon as the
startling sign PLAIN DEALING appeared by the ditch, Jeremiah said
quietly, "Now, I don't want no upstart rambunctiousness ruining
our plans. You remember that." Sweet Gum was embarrassed
and angry, yet at the same time he knew Jeremiah was right.
Behind Jeremiah his family stretched out of sight: all the Coke
family, grandfathers and fathers, sons, cousins, brothers, women
all over; it made Sweet Gum and his mother and little brother
look like a joke someone had played. Of course maybe someone
had played a joke—Sweet Gum's mother was not married, and
through years of furious shame he had gathered that his father,
whoever he was, was not even the father of his brother. *That*
bothered Sweet Gum as much as not knowing who his father was.

They drove through town. It was larger than they had expected. The main street was wide and paved; at either side long
strips of reddish dirt stretched out to buildings and fields far from
the road. There were open-air markets for vegetables and fruit
and poultry, a schoolhouse (without a flag on its flagpole), a gas
station and general store and Post Office put together (groups of
boys and young men straggled about in front of this building,
and Sweet Gum stared at them as if trying to recognize someone), houses (all built up on blocks, perched off the ground),
and, even, catching the eye of both men, a movie house—in

a Quonset hut with a roof painted shiny orange and a bright, poster-covered front. Sweet Gum stared as they drove by.

Jeremiah shortly turned the car into a driveway. Sweet Gum wanted to grab his arm in surprise. "This place is where *he* stays, you found it so fast?" he said faintly. "Hell, no," Jeremiah said. "Can't you read? This is a 'hotel.' We got to stay overnight, don't we?" "Overnight?" said Sweet Gum, looking around. "You mean in a room? Somebody else's room?" "They fix them for you. You get the key to the door and go in and out all you want," Jeremiah said. He had parked the car on a bumpy incline before an old, wide-verandaed house—peeling white, with pillars and vines and two old men, like twins, sitting in chairs as if somebody had placed them there. "Why are we staying overnight? *That's* what I don't like," Sweet Gum said. "It ain't for you to like, then," Jeremiah said with a sneer. He had climbed with elastic energy out of the car and now began smoothing his suit and hair and face. Out of his pocket he took a necktie: a precise-striped, urban tie, of a conservative gray color. "You ain't going to leave me, are you?" Sweet Gum said, climbing awkwardly out of the car.

They went to the counter inside and stood with their hands out on it, as if waiting to be fed. A middle-aged woman with a sour face stared back at them. "No luggage, then pay in advance," she said. "Pay?" said Sweet Gum. Jeremiah jabbed him in the ribs. "How much is it?" Jeremiah said carefully, making a little bow with his head. "Three for the two of you," the woman said. Sweet Gum hoped that Jeremiah would roar with laughter at this; but instead he took out of his pocket a billfold and money, and counted it out to the woman. One dollar bill and many coins. "Might's well sleep in the car as pay all that," Sweet Gum muttered. No one glanced at him. Jeremiah was staring at the woman strangely—standing at his full height, six foot three or so—so that when the woman turned to give him the key she froze and stared right back at him. Jeremiah smiled, dipped his head as if pleased. The woman withdrew from the counter; little prickly wrinkles had appeared on her face. "Ma'am," Jeremiah said formally, "maybe I could put to you a little question? As how we're guests here and everything?" "Maybe," said the woman. Jeremiah paused and wiggled his short beard, as if he were suddenly shy. Sweet Gum waited in an agony of embarrassment, looking at the floor. But finally Jeremiah said, rushing the words out: "Where's *he* live? Where's *his* house?"

His words vibrated in the hot musty air. Jeremiah's face was wet with new perspiration as he listened to them with disbelief. The woman only stared; her lips parted. Sweet Gum, sensing error, wanted to run outside and climb in the car and wait for Jeremiah, but his legs were frozen. Finally the woman whispered "*He?* Who do you mean, *he?* My husband? My husband's right—" "No, hell!" Jeremiah said. "I mean *Motley.*" With a clumsy try at secrecy he leaned forward on the counter, craned his neck, and whispered: "Motley. Nathan Motley. *Him.*" "Why, Nathan Motley," stammered the woman, "he lives around here somewheres. He— You relatives of his, back country? Why do you want to see him?"

Sweet Gum could bear it no longer. "Who says there's a why about it?" he snarled. "Why? Why what? What why? *You* said there was a why about it, we never did! We just drove into town five minutes ago! Where's there a *why* about—"

Jeremiah brought his arm around and struck Sweet Gum in the chest. Not with his fist or elbow, but just with his arm; somehow that was degrading, as if Sweet Gum were not worth being hit properly. "That'll do," Jeremiah said. The woman was staring at them. "Get outside and get the *things*," he whispered to Sweet Gum contemptuously, "while I see to this woman here, you scairt-like-any-goddamn-back-country bastard."

Outside, four or five young men of Sweet Gum's age stood around the jalopy. They had hands pushed in their pockets, elbows idle, feet prodding at lumps of dried mud. Sweet Gum, glowering and muttering to himself, walked right down to the car. They made way for him. "How far you come in this thing?" one boy giggled. Sweet Gum leaned over and got the satchel out of the car. He pretended to be checking the lock, as if it had a lock. "Going to lose your license plates back here," somebody said. "This making way to fall off. Then the cops'll get you." Sweet Gum whirled around. "Cops? What the hell do I care about cops?" He lifted his lip. The boys all wore straw hats that looked alike, as if bought in the same store. Sweet Gum had the idea, staring at them, that their deaths—if they should fall over dead right now, one after the other—would mean no more than the random deaths in a woods of skunks and woodchucks and rabbits and squirrels. Somehow this pleased him. "Ain't worrying my young head over *cops*," Sweet Gum said. He knew they were watching as he strode back up to the hotel. Someone yelled out daringly, "Backwoods!" but Sweet Gum did not even glance around.

In a tavern that night Sweet Gum had to keep going back and forth to the outside and stand trembling on the seashell gravel, waiting to get sick; then if he did get sick, good enough, it was over for a while; if not, he went back inside. Each time the fresh air revived him and made him furious at Jeremiah, who sat slouched at the bar talking to a woman, his big knees out in opposite directions. Sweet Gum wanted to grab Jeremiah and say it was time they were about their business. But when he did speak, his voice always came out in a whine: "Ain't we going to locate him tonight? What about that room they got waiting for us? That woman—" Jeremiah turned away from the conversation he was having—with a strange thick black-haired woman, always smiling—and, with his eyes shut tight, said, "You see to your own bus'ness. I'm finding out about *him*." "But—" "Find out some yourself, go over there," Jeremiah said, his eyes still shut, and waving vaguely behind Sweet Gum. Then he turned away. Sweet Gum drank beer faster and faster. Once in a while he would sniff sadly, wipe his nose, and take out the black cloth change purse in which he had put the money Uncle Simon had given him for "food." Despair touched him: had he not already betrayed his uncle by drinking instead of eating, by wasting time here, by getting sick so that by now people laughed when he got up to hurry outside? If he *did* have a father, maybe that man would be ashamed of him; and what then? Sweet Gum sometimes dreamt of this—a strange man revealing himself to be his father, and then saying plainly that he was disappointed in his son. A man back from the Navy, or from a ranch farther west. Sweet Gum wanted to begin, to go to Motley, to find him somewhere—where would he be hiding, up in an attic? crawled under a house?—and get it over with and return home, have his uncle proud of him and give him the reward, and turn, in two days into a man. His chest glowed with the thought: he would become a man. But his inspiration was distracted by Jeremiah's big, sweating indifferent back and Sweet Gum's own faint, sickish gasey feeling. "Goin' outside, ain't comin' back," he muttered,

purposely low so that Jeremiah would not hear and would wonder, later; where he was. He stumbled down from the stool
and wavered through the crowd. Someone poked him, Sweet
Gum looked around expecting to find a friend, found nothing
instead—faces—and someone laughed. A woman somewhere
laughed. Sweet Gum's stomach jerked with anger and he had
to run to the door.

When Sweet Gum woke, lying flat on his stomach in the
gravel, he could tell by the smell of the night that it was late.
Everything was quiet: the tavern was closed and looked dark
and harmless, like an abandoned house. Sweet Gum spat and
got up. A thought touched him, really a recollection; and, with
sweet memories of abandoned houses, he groped for a handful
of seashells and pebbles and threw them at the window nearest
him. It did not break and he threw again, more energetically:
this time the window shattered. Sweet Gum nodded and went
out to the road.

He went back to the hotel but found the door to the room
locked. He could hear Jeremiah snoring inside. Yet instead of
being angry, he felt strangely pleased, even pacified, and lay down
on the floor outside. As he fell asleep he thought of Jeremiah,
one of his many cousins, a Coke rightfully enough—a Coke who
had killed a man before he was twenty-five and whose clever
talk made all the girls whoop with laughter and look around at
one another, as they never did with Sweet Gum.

After breakfast the next morning Jeremiah and Sweet Gum and
the black-haired woman drove in Jeremiah's car through town.
The woman sat by the door, where Sweet Gum wanted to sit,
and as they drove up and down Main Street she shrieked and

waved and roared with laughter at people on the street. "Don't know 'em!" she yelled at someone, a man, and shrugged her shoulders high. "Never seen 'em before!" Even Jeremiah thought that was funny. But after a while, when they had driven back and forth several times, Jeremiah announced that they had to be about their business: they were on a proposition and their time wasn't all their own. "Hell, just one more time around," said the woman loudly. She had a broad, splendid face, so shiny with lipstick and makeup and pencil lines that Sweet Gum's eye slid around helplessly and could not focus on any single part. "Ain't got time for it," Jeremiah said, "we got to be about our business. Which way is it?" "Drive on. Straight," the woman said sullenly. She had a big head of hair, a big body, and a hard, red, waxen mouth that fascinated Sweet Gum, but whenever he looked at her she was looking at something else; she never noticed him. All she did was push him away with her elbow and thigh, trying to make more room for herself but doing it without glancing at him, as if she didn't really know he was there. "Keep straight. A mile or two," she said, yawning.

A few minutes later, out in the country, they stopped in front of a house. It was a small single-story house, covered with ripped brown siding, set up on wobbly blocks. "He don't do no work that *I* know of," the woman said. "He's got his finger in some backwoods whisky—y'know, whisky from the backwoods." She winked at Jeremiah. Sweet Gum's heart was pounding; Jeremiah kept jiggling his beard. In the cinder driveway an old brown dog lay as if exhausted and watched them, getting ready to bark. There was a wild field next to the house on the right, and an old decaying orchard—pear trees—on the left. Across the road, a quarter mile away, was a small farm: Sweet Gum could see cows grazing by a creek. "All right, honey," Jeremiah said, "you can start back now." "Walk back?" said the woman. "Yes, we got bus'ness here, between men. Ain't I explained that?" "What kind of bus'ness?" said the woman. "Men's business," Jeremiah said, but kindly; and he reached past Sweet Gum and put his big hairy hand on the woman's arm. "You start walking back and like's not we'll catch up in a few minutes and ride you back. Don't worry Jeremiah now, honey." The woman hesitated, though Sweet Gum knew she had already made up her mind. "Well," she said, "all right, if it's men's bus'ness. But don't . . . maybe don't tell Nathan it was me put you on him." "We won't never do that," Jeremiah said.

Jeremiah wasted more time by waving at the woman and blowing kisses as she walked away, but finally he calmed down and got out of the car and straightened his clothes and pressed down on his hair; he took out the necktie once more and tied it around his neck. Sweet Gum, carrying the satchel, climbed over the door on Jeremiah's side and jumped to the ground. The dog's ears shifted but the dog itself did not move. On the porch of the house sat a child, and behind him were piles of junk—firewood, old boxes, barrels, coils of rusted wire. The screen door opened and another child came out, a boy of about eight. He wore jeans and was barefoot. He and the smaller child and the dog watched Jeremiah and Sweet Gum arrange their clothing, slick down their hair by spitting into their palms and rubbing their heads viciously, and stare straight before them as if each were alone. Finally it was time: they crossed the ditch to the house.

The dog whimpered. "Son," cried Jeremiah to the older boy, "is your pa anywheres handy?" The boy's toes twitched on the edge of the steps. He began stepping backward, cautiously, and the other boy scrambled to his feet and backed up too, retreating behind the piles of junk. "Tell your pa we're here to see him," said Jeremiah. He walked ahead; Sweet Gum, hugging the satchel, followed close. Faces appeared at a window, another child or a woman. Then the screen door opened cautiously and a man stepped out.

He was about forty, gone to fat now, with a reddish apologetic face. The way he scratched the underside of his jaw made Sweet Gum know that he was apologetic about something. "You Nathan Motley?" Jeremiah cried. "What's that to you?" the man said, clearing his throat. Behind the piles of junk the two boys crouched, watching. "Here, boy," Jeremiah said to Sweet Gum, "open it up." Sweet Gum opened up the satchel and Jeremiah took out his pistol, an old rust-streaked revolver that had belonged to his father. He aimed it at the man and fired. Someone screamed. But when Sweet Gum could see again, the porch was empty even of children—the screen door had fallen shut. "Goddamn," said Jeremiah, still holding the pistol aloft, "you spose I *missed* him?"

Sweet Gum had his pistol now—not his own yet, but it would be when he returned home. "I'm going around here," Sweet Gum said. He ran around the house. In the driveway the dog had drawn its muddy feet up to its body and lay watching them with wet alert eyes. Sweet Gum had just rounded the back corner when be saw someone diving into a clump of bushes in the wild field behind the house. Sweet Gum let out a yodel: this was all familiar to him, nothing frightening about it, it was exactly like the games he had played as a child. "Here! Back here!" he yelled. He fired wildly at the clump of bushes. Behind him, in the house, there were screams and shrieks—Jeremiah was stomping through the house, bellowing. When he appeared running out of the back door his tie was thrown back over his shoulder as if someone had playfully pulled it there, and he still looked surprised. "This is hot weather for a hunt," he said when he caught up to Sweet Gum. They ran through the stiff grass, in brilliant sunshine, and about them birds flew up in terror. The field smelled of sunburned grass. "I'm headed this way, you keep straight," Jeremiah grunted. Sweet Gum ran on, slashing through bushes, pushing aside tree branches with his gun. "You, Motley!" he cried in despair. "Where you hiding at?" Something stumbled on the far side of a clump of bushes; Sweet Gum fired into it. In a moment Jeremiah appeared, mouth open and sucking for breath, as if he were swimming through the foliage. "Where's that bastard? He ain't over on my side, I swear it," Jeremiah said.

"If he gets away it ain't my fault," Sweet Gum cried. He was so angry he wanted to dance around. "He was standing there for you and you missed! Uncle Simon asks me, I got to tell the truth!" Jeremiah scratched his head. "I got a feeling he's over this way. Let's track him over here." "I never seen him on my side," Sweet Gum said sullenly. "Nor me on *mine*," Jeremiah answered. They walked along, slashing at the tops of weeds with their guns. Birds sang airily about them. After a minute or two they slowed to a stop. Jeremiah scratched his beard with the barrel of the gun. "Spose we went back to the house," he said suddenly. "He's got to come back for supper, don't he? Or to sleep tonight?" Sweet Gum wished he had thought of that, but did not let on. "Hell of a idea," he grumbled. "First you miss him at that close, then want to quit tracking him." "You track him, I'll go back alone," Jeremiah said. "Naw," said Sweet Gum, hiding his alarm, "I ain't staying back here alone." They turned and followed their paths back through the field.

Then something fortunate happened; Sweet Gum happened to see a hen pheasant start up in a panic, off to their left in a big long stretch of high grass. Sweet Gum fired into the grass. "There he is, he's hiding in there! He's hiding in there!" Jeremiah started forward, yelling, "Where do you see him? Do you see him?" He pushed past Sweet Gum, who fired again into the weeds. "He's laid flat," Sweet Gum said, "crawling around on the ground—" In the silence that followed, however, they heard only the usual country noises, insects and birds. "Motley, are you in there?" Jeremiah asked. His voice had a touch of impatience. "Where are you?" They waited. Then, incredibly, a voice lifted—"What do you want?" Sweet Gum fired at once. Both he and Jeremiah ran forward. "Which way was it? Was it this way?" Sweet Gum cried. He and Jeremiah collided. Jeremiah even swung his gun around and hit Sweet Gum, hard, on the chest. Sweet Gum sobbed with pain and anger. "*I* found him! *I* saw the pheasant go up!" he snarled. "Shut your mouth and keep it shut!" Jeremiah said.

"But what do you want?" the voice cried again. It was forlorn, a ghostly voice; it seemed to come out of the air. Sweet Gum was so confused he did not even fire. "Let's talk. Can't we talk?" Jeremiah stood, staring furiously into the grass. His face was red. "Ain't nothing to talk about," he said sullenly, as if he suspected a joke. "We got a job to do." "Somebody hired you?" the voice said. Sweet Gum lifted his gun but Jeremiah made a signal for him to wait. "Hired us for sure. What do you think?" Jeremiah said. "Somebody wants me kilt, then?" said the voice. "Somebody paying you for it?" "I just explained that!" Jeremiah said. "You having a joke with me?" And he lifted his pistol and took a step into the high grass. "No, no," the voice cried, "I'm not joking—I . . . I want to hire you too—I got a job for you to do . . . both of you—I'll pay—" "*How* can he pay, if he's dead?" Sweet Gum yelled furiously. "He's making fun of us!" "He ain't either, you goddamn backwoods idiot," Jeremiah said. "Shut your mouth. Now, mister, what's this-here job you got for us?"

The patch of weeds stirred. "A job for two men that can shoot straight," the voice said slowly. It paused. "That take in you two?" "Takes in me," Jeremiah said. "Me too," Sweet Gum heard his voice say—with surprise. "How much you paying?" said Jeremiah. "Fifty dollars a man," the voice said without hesitation. "Hell, that ain't enough," Sweet Gum said, raising his pistol. "No, no, a hunnert a man," the voice cried. Sweet Gum's arm froze. He and Jeremiah looked at each other. "A hunnert a man," Jeremiah said solemnly. "Uncle Simon's giving us fifty both, and a gun for Sweet Gum—that's him there—and a horse for me that I always liked; spose you can't thow in no horse, can you?" "And no gun neither!" Sweet Gum said in disgust. "Can't thow in no gun, and I'm purely fond of this one!" "But you can have the gun," said the voice, "after he's dead—and the horse too— Why couldn't you keep them, after he's dead? Didn't he promise them to you?"

Jeremiah scratched his nose. "Well," he said.

The patch moved. A man's head appeared—balding red hair, pop eyes, a mouth that kept opening and closing—and then his shoulders and arms and the rest of him. He looked from Jeremiah to Sweet Gum. "You two are good men, then?" His arms were loose at his sides. What was happening? Sweet Gum stood as if in a dream, a daze; he could not believe he had betrayed his uncle. "Aw, let's shoot him," he said suddenly, feverishly. "We come all this ways to do it—"

"*Shut* your mouth."

"But Uncle Simon—"

There was silence. The man brushed himself calmly. He knew enough to address Jeremiah when he spoke. "You two are good men, then? Can be trusted?"

"Ain't you trusting us now?" Jeremiah said with a wink.

The man smiled politely. "What experience you got?"

At this, Sweet Gum looked down; his face went hot. "*I got it,*" Jeremiah said, but slowly, as if he felt sorry for Sweet Gum. "Got put on trial for killing two men and found Not Guilty."

"When was this?"

"*Few* years," Jeremiah said. "I'm not saying whether I done it or not—was cautioned what to say. I don't know if the time is up yet. Two state troopers come and arrested me that hadn't any bus'ness in the Rapids—where we're from—and I got jailed and put on trial; for killing two storekeepers somewhere and taking seven hundred dollars. Was put on trial," Jeremiah said with a sigh, "and different people come to talk, one at a time, the jury come back and said Not Guilty for robbery; so it went for the other too—murder too. *But* they didn't let me keep the seven hundred dollars; they kept that themselves and fixed up the schoolhouse. New windows and the bathrooms cleaned and something else. Makes me proud when I go past—I got lots of cousins in the school."

"You were Not Guilty? How was that?"

Jeremiah shrugged. "They decided so."

The man now turned to Sweet Gum. But Sweet Gum, ashamed, could hardly look up. He could see his uncle, with that big wide face and false teeth, watching him and Jeremiah as they stood in this field betraying him. "What about you, son?" the man said gently. "This ain't your first job, is it?" Sweet Gum nodded without looking up. "Well, I like to see young people given a chance," the man said—and Sweet Gum, in spite of his shame, did feel a pang of satisfaction at this. "I like to see young ones and experience go together," the man said.

He turned to Jeremiah and put out his hand. Jeremiah shook hands with him solemnly; both men's faces looked alike. Sweet Gum stumbled through the grass to get to them and put his hand right in the middle. His eyes stung and he looked from man to man as if he thought they might explain the miracle of why he was acting as he was. But Motley, with color returning unevenly to his face, just grinned and said, "Let's go back to the house now."

An hour later Jeremiah and Sweet Gum were heading out of town. Jeremiah drove faster than before and kept twitching and shifting around in the seat, pressing his big belly against the steering wheel. "No one of us mislikes it more than me," he said finally, "but you know Uncle Simon ain't much expecting to live too long. Three-four years." With his mouth open, Sweet Gum stared at the road. There was a small dry hole in the side of his head into which Jeremiah's words droned, and Sweet Gum had no choice but to accept them. Inside, the words became entangled with the shouting and cursing with which Uncle Simon blessed this ride. The old man sat in his rocking chair on the porch, stains of chewing-tobacco juice etched permanently down the sides of his chin, glaring at Jeremiah and Sweet Gum who, thirty and forty years younger than he, were rushing along hot dirt roads to hurry him out of his life. And his teeth were new: not more than five years old. Sweet Gum remembered when Uncle Simon had got the teeth from a city and had shown the family how they worked, biting into apples and chewing with a malicious look of triumph. Uncle Simon! Sweet Gum felt as if the old man had put his bony hand on his shoulder.

"Boy, what's wrong with you?" Jeremiah said nervously.

"Sent us out after something and we ain't preformed it," Sweet Gum said. He wiped his nose on the back of his hand.

Jeremiah considered this. Then he said, after a moment, "But kin don't mean nothing. Being kin to somebody is just a accident; you got to think it through, what other ones mean to you. Uncles or what not. Or brothers, or grandmas, or anything."

Sweet Gum blinked. "Even a man with his father? If he had a father?"

That was the thing about Sweet Gum: he would always get onto this subject sooner or later. Usually whoever it was he spoke to would shrug his shoulders and look embarrassed—but Jeremiah just glanced over at him as if something had shocked him. "A father's maybe different," Jeremiah said, and let Sweet Gum know by the hard set of his jaw that he was finished talking.

They made so many turns, followed so many twisting roads, that the sun leaped back and forth across the sky. Sweet Gum could always tell the time at home, but out on the road it might as well be nine o'clock as three o'clock; nothing stayed still, nothing could be trusted, The old car was covered with dust and it got into their noses and mouths, making them choke. Sweet Gum wondered if his punishment for betraying his uncle had already begun, or if this wouldn't count because the murder hadn't taken

place yet. "Remember this turn, don't you?" Jeremiah said, trying
to be cheerful. Sweet Gum showed by his empty stare that he
did not remember having seen this patch of hot scrubby land
before—he recognized nothing on the return trip, as if he were
really someone else.

As soon as they crossed the bridge to the Rapids, Sweet Gum
gulped, "I can't do it."

Some boys were running in the road after the car, shouting and
tossing stones. "Hey, you, Jeremiah Coke, you give us a ride!"
they yelled. But Jeremiah was so surprised by Sweet Gum that
he did not even glance around. "Hell, what's wrong now? Ain't
we decided what to do?"

Sweet Gum's lips trembled. "Sent us out and we ain't preformed it for him," he said.

"Goddamn it, didn't you shake hands with Motley? Come
loping acrost the weeds to stick your hand in, didn't you? Hired
yourself out for a hunnert dollars. Do you do that much bus'ness
every day?"

"No," said Sweet Gum, wiping his nose.

"Ain't a man his own bus'ness? Christ Himself was a bus'ness;
he was selling stuff. Wasn't He? He never took money for it,
wanted other things instead—more important things—a person's
life, is that cheap? Everybody's a bus'ness trying for something
and you got to farm yourself out to the richest one that wants
you. Goddamn it, boy," Jeremiah said, "are you going back on
Motley when you just now gave him your word?"

"Gone back on Uncle Simon," Sweet Gum said.

"That'll do on him. I'm asking you something else. The least
thing you do after you break one promise is to keep the next
one. A man is allowed one change of mind."

Sweet Gum, already won, liked to keep Jeremiah's attention so fiercely on him. When Jeremiah looked at him he felt warm, even hot: but it was a good feeling. "Well," said Sweet Gum, sighing. They were just then turning off onto their uncle's lane.

There the old house was, back past a clump of weedlike willows, with the old barns and the new aluminum-roofed barn behind it. Sweet Gum was surprised that he didn't feel frightened: but everything seemed familiar, as it did when he was chasing Motley, and strangely correct—even righteous—along with being familiar.

The car rolled to a stop. Jeremiah took his pistol out of the satchel and shoved it into the top of his trousers, past his big stomach; it looked uncomfortable but Jeremiah wouldn't admit it by taking it out. Sweet Gum climbed over the door and stood in the lane. The dirt quivered beneath his feet; he felt unreal. He giggled as he followed Jeremiah back the lane. They crossed to a field, half wild grass, half trees. When Jeremiah got down on his hands and knees, Sweet Gum did the same. They crawled along, Sweet Gum with his head hanging limply down, staring at the bottoms of Jeremiah's boots. If Jeremiah had wanted to crawl back and forth all day in the field Sweet Gum would have followed him.

Jeremiah stopped. "There he is. Sitting there." He pulled some weeds aside for Sweet Gum to look out, but Sweet Gum nodded immediately; he did not have to be shown. His brain was throbbing. "Here, aim at him," Jeremiah whispered. He pulled Sweet Gum's arm up. "I'll say the word and both fire at once. Then lay low; we can crawl back to the car and drive up and ask them what-all went on." Sweet Gum saw that Jeremiah's face was mottled, red and gray, like Motley's had been. Jeremiah aimed through the weeds, waited, and then, queerly, turned back to Sweet Gum. "You ain't aiming right! Don't want to shoot, do you? Have me do it all, you little bastard!"

"I ain't one of them!" Sweet Gum screamed.

The scream was astounding. A mile away, even, a bird must have heard it and now, in the following silence, questioned it—three bright notes and a trill. Sweet Gum was so numb he couldn't think of the name of that bird. Jeremiah was staring at Sweet Gum; their faces were so close that their breathing surely got mixed up. That was why, Sweet Gum thought, he felt dizzy—old dirty air coming out of Jeremiah and getting sucked into him. Rocked in inertia, dazzled by the sunshine and the silence, the two men stared at each other. "No, I ain't one of them," Sweet Gum whispered. "Please, I ain't." Then a voice sailed over that Sweet Gum recognized at once.

"Who's over there? Who's in the field? Goddamn it if I don't hear somebody there." There was a furious rapping noise: Uncle Simon slamming the porch floor with his old-fashioned thick-heeled boots, angry enough to break into a jig. Jeremiah and Sweet Gum crouched together, sweating. They heard the old man talking with his wife, then his mutter rising without hesitation into another series of shouts; "Who is it? Stand up. Stand up and face me. Who's hiding there? I'll have my gun out in a minute.—Get the hell out of here, Ma, go back inside. I *said*—"

Jeremiah, sighing mightily, got to his feet. "Hiya, Uncle Simon," he said, waving the pistol. "It's Sweet Gum here, and me." He helped Sweet Gum get to his feet. Across the lane the old man stood on the edge of his porch with one fist in the air. Was that the Uncle Simon who had cursed them all day, hovering over the car like a ghost? The old man looked younger than

Sweet Gum remembered. "Just us over here," Jeremiah said, smiling foolishly.

"What the hell are you up to?" Uncle Simon yelled. At this, the old woman came out again, her hands wiping each other on her apron as always. "Jeremiah himself and Sweet Gum hiding over there, playing at guns with their own Uncle Simon," the old man said viciously. "A man with three-four years to go and not a month more. See them there?"

The old woman, almost blind, nodded sullenly just the same. Sweet Gum wanted to run over to her and have her embrace him, smell the damp clean odor of her smooth-cracked hands, be told that everything was all right—as she had told him when two cousins of his, boys hardly older than he, had been arrested for killing a government agent one Hallowe'en night. And that *had* turned out all right, for the judge could not get a jury— everyone liked the boys or were related to them—and so the case was dismissed. "Like niggers in a field! Look at them there, crawling around like niggers in a field!" Uncle Simon yelled.

Jeremiah was the first to break down. Big hot tears exploded out of his eyes, tumbled down his face and were lost in his beard. "*He* talked us into it," he said, "me and Sweet Gum was trapped by him. *He* talked us all kinds of fast words, and long sentences like at church; and explained it to us that he would tell the state police. I had enough trouble with them once, Uncle Simon, didn't I?—And he tole us it would be a hunnert a man and we could keep the horse and the gun anyways. We got so mixed up hearing it all, and them police at the back of my mind—" Jeremiah's voice ran down suddenly. Sweet Gum stared at his feet, hoping he would not be expected to continue.

"Who? Motley? A hunnert a man?" What was strange was that Uncle Simon stared at them like that—his rage frozen on his face, and something new taking over. "A hunnert a man?"

"And to keep the horse and the gun anyways," Jeremiah said in a croaking voice.

The old man put his little finger to his eye and scratched it, just once. Then he yelled: "All right. Get back in that car. God-damn you both, get in it and turn it around and get back to Plain Dealing! I'll plain-deal you! I'll ambush you! Use your brains—tell that Motley bastard you took care of it out here—shot your poor old uncle—and want the reward from him now. Say you want your reward, can you remember that? Jeremiah, you stay back; don't you come on my lane. You stay back in the field. I don't want to see your goddamn faces again till you do the job right. Do I have to go all that ways myself, a man sixty-five or more years old, would be retired like they do in the city if I was a regular man? Yes, would be retired with money coming in, a check, every month—Ma, *you* stay back, this ain't anything of yours! And say to Motley you want your reward, and let him give it to you—one hunnert a man—then fire at him and that's that. How much money you make from it?"

Sweet Gum said, so fast he surprised himself, "A hunnert a man."

"*How* much?"

Sweet Gum's brain reeled and clicked. "A hunnert-fifty a man and a gun for me. And a horse for Jeremiah."

"Put in a horse for you and another one for Jeremiah. That's that." The old man spat maliciously toward them. "Now, get the hell back to the car. You got some work to do with Motley."

"Yes, thank you, that's right, Uncle Simon," Jeremiah said. He gulped at air. "We're on the way to do it. Two horses? Which one is the other? The red mare or what?"

"Your pick," the old man said. He turned sullenly away as if he had forgotten about them. Sweet Gum wanted to laugh out loud—it had been so easy. He did laugh, he heard himself with alarm, and felt at the same time something begin to twitch in his face. It twitched again: a muscle around his eye. Nothing like that had ever happened to him before, yet he understood that the twitch, and probably the breathless giggle, would be with him for life.

Jeremiah's jalopy broke down on the return trip, without drama: it just rolled to a stop as if it had died. Jeremiah got out and kicked it in a fury and tore off the fender and part of the bumper; but Sweet Gum just stood quietly and watched, and by and by Jeremiah joined him. They strolled along the road for a while. Sweet Gum noticed how Jeremiah's fingers kept twitching.

Though they were on a U.S. highway, there was not much traffic—when a car appeared Sweet Gum would stand diffidently by the road and put up his hand, without apparent purpose, as if he were ready to withdraw it at any moment. After an hour or two an automobile stopped, as if by magic; the man said he was driving right through Plain Dealing.

When they arrived in front of Motley's house it was suppertime. Sweet Gum and Jeremiah went up the driveway; Jeremiah took out his pistol and looked at it, for some reason, and Sweet Gum did the same—he noticed that he had one bullet left. Hiding a yawn, Jeremiah approached the porch and peered in the window: there the family sat, or at least the woman and children, arguing about something so that their faces took on slanted, vicious expressions. Jeremiah stood staring in the window until someone—the oldest boy—happened to see him. The boy's face jerked, his features blurred together, his bony arm jerked up as if he were accusing Jeremiah of something. Then the woman caught sight of him and, pulling her dress somehow, straightening the skirt, came to the door. "Whatcha got there? He's in town right now. You them clowns come out here before, ain't you?" The woman looked ready to laugh. "Nat told me about you; says you were kidding him with play-guns. How come I don't know you? Nat says—"

"Where is he?" said Jeremiah.

"In town," the woman said. "He's at the club, probably. That's the Five Aces Club, acrost from the bank. He tole me not to wait on him tonight so I didn't, but he never tole me to expeck some guests for supper. As a fact, he never tells me much," she laughed. "Bet you tell your wife where you are or whatcha doing or who's coming out for supper. Bet you—"

"How do you spell that?" Jeremiah said patiently.

"Spell it? Huh? Spell what?"

"The place he's at."

"Acrost from the bank, the Five Aces—I don't know, how do you spell five? It's a number five, they got it on a sign; you know how five looks? That's it." Both Jeremiah and Sweet Gum nodded. "Then 'Aces,' that's out there too—begins with A, A S or A C, then S on the end—it's more than one. Acrost from the bank. But why don't you come in and wait, he'll be—"

"We surely thank you," Jeremiah said with a faint smile, "but we got bus'ness to attend to. Maybe later on."

It took them a while to walk back to town. Jeremiah's fingers were busier than ever. Most of the time they were scratching at his head, then darting into his ears or nose and darting back out again. Sweet Gum walked behind so that his giggling would not annoy Jeremiah. They passed houses, farmers' markets; a gas station with an old model-T out front filled with tires. They passed a diner that was boarded up, and the movie house, in front of which the boys with straw hats stood around smoking. When Sweet Gum and Jeremiah passed, the boys stared in silence; even the smoke from their cigarettes stiffened in the air.

Town began suddenly: a drug store, an old country store on a corner. In a clapboard shanty, a dentist's office advertised in bright green paint. There were no sidewalks, so Jeremiah and Sweet Gum walked at the side of the road. "Down there looks like the bank," Jeremiah said, waving his pistol at something ahead; Sweet Gum did not see it. They walked on. "We come a long way," Jeremiah said in a strange remote voice, like a man embarking on a speech. "Done a lot this past week or however long it's been. I never known till now that I was born for this life—did you? Thought it'd be for me like anyone else—a farm and cows maybe and a fambly to raise up and maybe chickens, the wife could take care of them; I mostly had the wife picked out too. Won't tell you which one. But now I know different. Now see it was in me all along, from before I kilt them two men even—I thought I done that by *accident,* had too much to drink—something in a dream—but no, now I know better; now I got it clear." A few cars passed them; people out for after supper rides. A girl of about two, with thin blond hair, leaned out a window and waved sweetly at Sweet Gum. "Now I know," Jeremiah said, so strangely that Sweet Gum felt embarrassed in spite of his confusion, "that there isn't a person but wouldn't like to do that, what I did. Or to set a place afire, say—any place—their own house even. Set it all afire, house and grass and trees alike, all the same. Was there ever a difference between a house people live in and trees outside that they name? Them trees *make* you name them, think up names for them as soon as you see them, what choice does a man have! Never no choice! Get rid of it all, fire it all up, all the things that bother you, that keep you from yourself and people too—and people too— Sweet Gum, I got to tell you now, with us both coming so far like we did, that I'm your pa here, *I* am, Jeremiah your pa after all these years, all the way from the beginning!"

They continued walking. Sweet Gum blinked once or twice. Jeremiah's words bored through that tiny hole in the side of his head, flipped themselves around right side up to make sense: but Sweet Gum only hid a sudden laugh with his hand, stared at the sweaty back of Jeremiah's old funeral suit, and thought aloud, "Is that so." "That so, boy, all the way from the beginning," Jeremiah said, stifling a yawn. "This-here is your own pa walking right in front of you."

Sweet Gum should have said something, but he could not think of it and so let it pass. They were approaching the 5 Aces Club now, heading toward it as if it were a magnet. Sweet Gum heard voices behind him and glanced around: the group of boys was following them, idly and at a distance; a man in overalls had joined them, looking sour and disapproving. Sweet Gum forgot them as soon as he turned again. They passed a laundromat with orange signs: OPEN 24 HOURS EACH DAY WASH 20¢ DRY 10¢. A few people were inside in spite of the heat. In the doorway children kicked at one another and did not even glance up at Jeremiah and Sweet Gum. Then there was a 5¢ 10¢ 25¢ AND $1.00 STORE, gold letters on a red background, windows crowded and stuffed with merchandise; but it was closed. Then the club itself, coming so fast Sweet Gum's eye twitched more than ever and he had to hold onto it with his palm to keep it from jumping out of his head. "Spose he's in there," Sweet Gum whimpered, "spose he gets to talking. Don't let him talk. Please. Don't let him. Shoot him right off. If I hear talk of horses or gun or twice as much money—"

The club had had a window at one time, a big square window like something in a shoe store, but now it was completely hidden by tin foil. There were advertisements for beer and cigarettes everywhere: beautiful pink-cheeked girls, men with black hair and big chests and clean white gleaming teeth. Long muscular thighs, smooth legs, slender ankles, silver-painted toenails, tattooed arms and backs of hands; and curly-haired chests and dimpled chests, chests bare and bronze in the sun, chests demurely proud in red polka-dot halters—everything mixed together! Faces channeled themselves out of blue skies and rushed at Sweet Gum with their fixed serene smiles. "That *there* is heaven," Sweet Gum thought suddenly, with a certainty he had never before felt about life—as if, about to leave it, he might pass judgment on it. His stomach ached with silent sobs, as much for that lost heaven as for the duties of this familiar, demanding world.

Jeremiah had opened the door to the tavern, "You, Motley, come out here a minute." Someone answered inside but Jeremiah went on patiently, "Motley. Some bus'ness outside."

Jeremiah let the door close. Sweet Gum clutched at him, "Is he coming? Is he? Was that him inside?" he said. "Don't let him talk none. Shoot him first or let me—shoot him—"

"We ain't going to shoot him yet."

"But what if he talks of more horses or another gun? What if—"

"He ain't. Get back, now—"

"I'm going to shoot him—"

"Goddamn you, boy you stand back," Jeremiah shouted. "Why's it always you at the center of trouble? Any goddamn thing that bothers me these days, *you're* in the middle!"

"Don't let him talk none. If he—"

"We got to talk to him. Got to tell him we come for the reward."

"Reward?" Sweet Gum's sobs broke through to the surface. "Reward? I don't remember none, what reward? What? He's going to talk, going to—"

Jeremiah pushed him away and opened the door again. "Motley!" he yelled. Sweet Gum's head was so clamoring with voices that he could not be sure if he heard anyone answer. "He's coming, guess it's him," Jeremiah said vaguely. "Stand back now, boy, and don't you do no reckless shooting your pa will have to clean up after—"

"I'm going to shoot him," Sweet Gum cried, "or he'll talk like before— If he talks and we hear him we got to go back and be in the field again. We got to hide there. And Aunt Clarey, I always loved her so, how it's for *her* to see us hiding there? Even if she can't see much. If he comes out and talks we got to—"

"Boy, I'm telling you!"

"Don't you call me boy!"

The door opened suddenly, angrily. Sweet Gum raised his pistol, took a giant step backward, and was about to shoot when a stranger appeared in the doorway, a big pot-bellied bald man with a towel used for an apron tucked in his belt. "What the *hell*—" the man roared.

Sweet Gum, shocked, staggered back. Inside his head the clamoring arose to a mighty scream and, in defense, he turned to Jeremiah. Everything focused on Jeremiah, the sun itself seemed to glare on his bulging eyes. Sweet Gum cried: "*You!* It was *you* I been hunting these twenty years!" But somehow in his confusion he had turned around, or half around, and when he fired he did not shoot Jeremiah at all, or any man at all, but instead a woman—a stranger, a stocky woman with a sunburned, pleasant, bossy face, dressed in jeans and a man's dirty white shirt. She fell right onto the basket of damp laundry she was carrying. Blood burst out of nowhere, onto the clothes, and also out of nowhere appeared two children, shrieking and screaming.

Sweet Gum backed away. A crowd, an untidy circle, was gathering about the fallen woman. Sweet Gum, dazed, put the barrel of the pistol to his lips and stared, still backing away, stumbling. He had been cheated: he could not get things clear: his whole life had flooded up to this moment and now was dammed and could not get past, everything was over. He could have wept for the end of his young life (mistakenly, as it turned out, for in less than three years he would be working downriver at the tomato canning factory, making good money), spilled here on the dirt road, splashing and sucked away, while everyone stood around gawking.

IN THE WAREHOUSE

"Why does your mother do that to her hair? Does she think it looks nice or something?"

"Do what to her hair?"

"Frizz it up or whatever that is—she's such a ugly old bag! If I looked like that I'd stick my head in the oven!"

The two girls are standing out on the sidewalk before a house, at twilight. The taller one makes vast good-humored gestures in the air as she talks, and the other stands silently, her lips pursed. She has a small, dark, patient face; her brown hair falls in thick puffy bangs across her forehead. The taller girl has hair that is in no style at all—just messy, not very clean, pulled back from her big face and fixed with black bobby pins, which are the wrong color for her dark blond hair. She has a lot to talk about. She is talking now about Nancy, who lives a few houses away. Nancy is eighteen and works uptown in a store, she thinks she's too good for everyone—"I could show her a thing or two, just give me a match and let me at that dyed hair of hers"—and her mother is grumpy and ugly, like everyone's mother, "just an old bitch that might as well be dead."

It is autumn. Down the street kids are playing, after supper, running along between houses, or all the way down to the open area that is blocked off because of an expressway nearby. "You don't want to go in already do you?" the taller girl whines. "Why d'ya always want to go in, you think your house is so hot? Your goddam mother is so hot? We could walk down by the warehouse, see if anybody's around. Just for something to do."

"I better go in."

"Your mother isn't calling you, is she? What's so hot about going in that dump of a house?"

I am the short, dark girl, and my friend Helen is laughing into my face as she always does. Helen lives two houses away. Her mother has five children and no husband—he died, or ran away—and Helen is the middle child, exactly, thirteen years old. She is big for her age. I am twelve, skinny and meek and incredulous as she jumps to another subject: how Nancy's boy friend slapped her around and burned her with his cigar just the other night. "Don't you believe me? You think I'm lying?" she challenges me.

"I never heard about that."

"So what? Nobody'd tell you anything. You'd tell the cops or something."

"No I wouldn't."

"Some cop comes to see your father, don't he?"

"He's just somebody—some old friend. I don't know who he is," I tell her, but it's too late. My whining voice gives Helen what she needs. It's like an opening for a wedge or the toe of Helen's worn-out old "Indian" mocassins. She pinches my arm and I say feebly, "Don't. That hurts."

"Oh, does it hurt?"

She pinches me again.

"I said don't—"

She laughs and forgets about it. She's a big strong girl, like a boy grown up and not like a girl. Her legs are thick. Her face is round and her teeth are a little crooked, so that she looks as if she is always smiling. In school she sits at the back and makes trouble, hiding her yellowish teeth behind her hand when she laughs. One day she said to our teacher—our teacher is Mrs. Gunderson—"There was a man out by the front door who did something bad. He opened up his pants and everything." Mrs. Gunderson is always nervous. She told Helen to come out into the hall with her, and everyone tried to listen, and in a minute she called me out too. Helen said to me, "Wasn't that Mr. Whalen out by the front door? Wasn't it, Sarah?" "When?" I said. "You know when, you were right there," Helen said. She was very excited and her face had a pleasant, high color. "You know what he did." "I didn't see anything," I said. Mrs. Gunderson wore ugly black shoes and her stockings were so thick you couldn't see her skin through them. Helen wore her mocassin loafers and no socks and her legs were pale and lumpy, covered with fine blond hairs. "Mr. Whalen stood right *out there* and Sarah saw him but she's too afraid to say. She's just a damn dirty coward," Helen said. Mr. Whalen was the fifth grade teacher. Nobody liked him, but I had to say, "There wasn't any man out there." So Mrs. Gunderson let us go. Helen whispered, "You dirty goddam teacher's pet!"

That day at noon hour she rubbed my face in the dirt by the swings, and when I began crying she let me up. "Oh, don't cry, you big baby," she said. She rubbed my head playfully. She always did this to her little brother, her favorite brother. "I didn't mean to hurt you, but you had it coming. Right? You got to do what I say. If we're friends you got to obey me, don't you?"

"Yes."

Now she talks faster and faster. I know her mother isn't home and that's why she doesn't want to go in yet—her mother is always out somewhere. No one dares to ask Helen about her mother. In our house my mother is waiting somewhere, or maybe not waiting at all but upstairs doing something, listening to the radio. The supper dishes are put away. My father is working the night shift. When he comes home he will sleep downstairs on the sofa and when I come down for school in the morning there he'll be, stretched out and snoring. When my father and mother are together there are two currents of air, like invisible clouds, that move with them and will not overlap. These clouds keep them separate even when they are together; they seem to be calling across a deep ditch.

"Okay, let's walk down by the warehouse."

"Why do you want to go down there?"

"Just for the hell of it."

"I got a lot of homework to do—"

"Are you trying to make me mad?"

The first day I met Helen was the first day they had moved into their house, about two months ago. Helen strolled up and down the street, looking around, and she saw me right away sitting up on our veranda reading. She was wearing soiled white slacks that came down to her knees and a baggy pull-over shirt that was her brother's. Her hands were shoved in her pockets as she walked. She said to me, on that first day: "Hey, what are you doing? Are you busy or can I come up?"

Now she is my best friend and I do everything she says, almost everything. She keeps talking. She likes to touch people when she talks, tap them on the arm or nudge them. "Come on. You don't have nothing to do inside," she says, whining, wheedling, and I give in. We stroll down the block. Nobody sits outside anymore at night, because it is too cold now. I am wearing a jacket and blue jeans, and Helen is wearing the same coat she wears to school: it used to be her mother's coat. It is made of shiny material, with black and fluorescent green splotches and tiny white umbrellas because it is a rain coat. As we walk down the street she points out houses we pass, telling me who the people are. "In there lives a fat old bastard, he goes to the bathroom in the sink," she says, her voice loud and helpful like a teacher's voice. "His name is Chanock or Chanick or some crappy name like that."

"How do you know about him?"

"I know lots of things, stupid. You think I'm lying?"

"No."

We walk on idly. We cross the street over toward Don's Drug-store. A few boys are standing around outside, leaning on their bicycles. When they see us coming they say, "Here comes that fat old cow Lay-zer," and they all laugh. Helen sticks out her tongue and says what she always says: a short loud nasty word that makes them laugh louder. When she does this I feel like laughing or running away, I feel as if something had opened in the ground before me—a great gaping crack in the sidewalk. The boys don't bother with me but keep on teasing Helen until we're past.

This street is darker. The houses are older, set back from the sidewalk with little plots of grass that are like mounds of graves in front of them. There are "boarders" in these houses. "Dirty old perverts," Helen calls them if we ever see them. One of the houses is vacant and kids come from all over to break windows and fool around, even though the police have chased them away. "In this next house is a man who does nasty things with a dog. I saw him out in the alley once," Helen says, snickering.

I have to take big steps to keep up with her. We're headed out toward the warehouse, which is boarded up, but everyone goes in there to play. I am afraid of the warehouse at night, because bums sometimes sleep there, but if I tell Helen she'll snort with laughter and pinch me. Walking along fast she says, "I sure don't want to miss that show on Saturday. You and me can go early," and she says, whistling through her teeth, "One of these days that big dumpy warehouse is going to burn down. Wait and see."

Helen once lit a little fire in someone's garage, but it must have gone out because nothing happened. She wanted to get back at the people because she didn't like the girl who lived there, a girl ahead of us in school. At noon hour Helen and I sit alone to eat our lunches. If she is angry about something she can stare stare me down, with her cold blue eyes that are like plastic caps fitted over something; but other times she has to wipe at her eyes, saying, "This bastard who came home with her last night, he—he—" Or she talks bitterly of the other girls and how they all hate her because they're afraid of her. She has wild, reckless hair, a dirty neck, and her dresses are just—just old baggy things passed down from someone else. At noon she often whispers to me about kids in the cafeteria, naming them one by one, telling me what she'll do to them when she gets around to it: certain acts with shears, razors, ice picks, butcher knives, acts described so vividly and with such passion that I feel sick.

Even when I'm not with Helen I feel a little sick, but not just in my stomach. It's all through my body. Ma always says, "Why do you run out when that big cow calls you? What do you see in her?" and I answer miserably frightened, "I like her all right." But I have never thought about liking Helen. I have no choice. She has never given me the privilege of liking or disliking her, and if she knew I was thinking such a thought she would yank my hair out of my head.

Light from the street lamp falls onto the front and part of the side of the old warehouse. There is a basement entrance I am afraid of, because of spiders and rats. Junk is stored in the warehouse, things we don't recognize and never bother to wonder about, parts from machines, rails, strange wheels that are solid metal and must weigh hundreds of pounds. "Let's climb in the window," I say to Helen. "The cellar way's faster," she says. "Please, let's go in the window," I beg. I have begun to tremble and don't know why. It seems to me that something terrible is waiting inside the warehouse.

Helen looks at me contemptuously. She is grave and large in the moonlight, her mother's shiny coat wrinkled tight across her broad shoulders. The way her eyes are in shadow makes me think suddenly of a person falling backwards, falling down— onto something hard and sharp. That could happen. Inside the warehouse there are all kinds of strange, sharp things half hidden in the junk, rusty edges and broken glass from the windows that have been smashed. "Please, Helen, let's climb in the window," I beg.

She laughs and we go around to the window. There is an important board pulled out, which makes a place for your foot. Then you jump up and put one knee on the window ledge, then you slide inside. The boards criss-crossing the window have been torn down a long time ago. Helen goes first and then helps me up. She says, "What if I let you go right now? You'd fall down and split your dumb head open!"

But she is just kidding. She helps me crawl inside. Why do we like the warehouse so much? During the day I like to explore in it, we never get tired of all the junk and the places to hide and the view from the upstairs windows. Machines—nails and nuts and bolts underfoot—big crates torn apart and left behind, with mysterious black markings on their sides. The moonlight is strong enough for us to see things dimly. I am nervous even though I know where everything is. I know this place. In my bed at night I can climb up into the warehouse and envision everything, remember it clearly, every part of it—it is our secret place, no growns-ups come here—I can remember the big sliver of glass that is like a quarter-moon, a beautiful shape, lying at the foot of the steps, and the thing we call the "tractor" and a great long dusty machine that is beside the stairs. When you touch it you feel first dust, then oil; beneath the dust there is a coating of oil. Three prongs rise out of one end like dull knives.

Helen bumps into something and says, "Oh Christ!" She is always bumping into things. It flashes through my mind that one time when she hurt herself—fooling around with some bricks—she got angry at me for no reason and slapped me. She was always poking or pinching or slapping. It occurs to me that I should kill her. She is like a big hulking dead body tied to me, the mouth fixed up for a grin and always ready to laugh, and we are sinking together into the water, and I will have to slash out at her to get free—I want to get free. So I say, beginning to shiver, "Should we go upstairs?"

"What's upstairs but pigeon crap?"

"We can look out the window."

"You and your goddam windows—"

She laughs because I like to look out of the windows, and she likes to grub around instead in corners, prying things loose, looking under things for "treasure." She told me once that she found a silver dollar in the warehouse. But now I go ahead of her to the stairs, a strange keen sensation in my bowels, and she grumbles but comes along behind me. These old steps are filthy with dust and some of the boards sag. I know exactly where to step. Behind me, Helen is like a horse. The stairs are shaking. I wait for her at the top and in that second I can see out a window and over to the street light—but past that is nothing, there is nothing to see at night! The street light has a cloudy halo about it, something that isn't real but seems real to my eye. Helen bounds up the stairs and I wait for her, sick with being so afraid, my heart pounding in a jerky, bouncy way as if it wanted to burst—but suddenly my heart is like another person inside me nudging me and saying, "Do it! Do it!" When Helen is about four steps from the top I reach down and push her.

She falls at once. She falls over the side, her voice a screech that is yanked out into the air above her, and then her body hits the edge of that machine hard. She is screaming. I stand at the top, listening to her. Everything is dry and clear and pounding. She falls again, from the edge of the machine onto the floor, and now her scream is muffled as if someone had put his hand over her mouth.

I come down the stairs slowly. The air is hard and dry, like acid that burns my mouth, and I can't look anywhere except at Helen's twisting body. I wait for it to stop twisting. What if she doesn't die? At the base of the stairs I make a wide circle around her, brushing up against something and getting grease onto my jeans.

There is this big girl half in the moon light from the shattered window, and half in the dark. Dust rolls in startled balls about her, aroused by her moans. She is bleeding. A dark stain explodes out from her and pushes the dust along before it, everything speeded up by her violent squirming, and I feel as if I must walk on tiptoe to keep from being seen by her . . . Blood, all that blood!— it is like an animal crawling out from under her, like the shadows we've walked around with us for so long, broken loose now and given its own life, twisting out from under her and grappling with her, big as she is. She cries out, "Sarah! Ma!" but I don't hear her. I am at the window already. "Ma!" she says. "Ma!" It does not seem that I am moving or hearing anything, but still my feet take me to the window and those words come to me from a distance, "Ma, help me!" and I think to myself that I will have to get to where those words won't reach.

At home our house is warm and my head aches because I am sleepy. I fall asleep on my bed without undressing, and the next day we all hear about Helen. "Fooling around in that old dump, I knew it was going to happen to somebody," my mother says grimly. "You stay the hell out of that place from now on. You hear?"

I tell her yes, yes. I will never go there again.

There is a great shadowy space about me, filled with waiting: waiting to cry, to feel sorry. I myself am waiting, my body is waiting the way it waited that night at the top of the steps to pounce down upon my friend. But nothing happens. Do you know that twenty years have gone by? I am still dark but not so

skinny, I have grown into a body that is approved of by people
who glance at me in the street, I have grown out of the skinny
little body that knocked that clumsy body down—and I have
never felt sorry. Never felt any guilt. I live in what is called a "colonial" house, on a lane of colonial houses called Meadowbrook
Lane. Ours is the sixth house on the right. Our mailboxes are
down at the intersection with a larger road . . . I am married and
have children and I am still waiting to feel guilty, to feel some
of Helen's pain, to feel the shock of that impact again as I felt it
when she struck the prongs of the machine—but nothing happens. In my tedious pleasant life when my two boys are at school
I write stories I hope might be put on television someday—why
not, when everything I see on television is so stupid? But my
stories are more real than my childhood; my childhood is just
another story, but one written by someone else.

BY THE RIVER

Helen thought: "Am I in love again, some new kind of love? Is that why I'm here?"

She was sitting in the waiting room of the Yellow Bus Lines station; she knew the big old room with its dirty tile floor and its solitary telephone booth in the corner and its candy machine and cigarette machine and popcorn machine by heart. Everything was familiar, though she had been gone for five months, even the old woman with the dyed red hair who sold tickets and had been selling them there, behind that counter, for as long as Helen could remember. Years ago, before Helen's marriage, she and her girl friends would be driven into town by someone's father and after they tired of walking around town they would stroll over to the bus station to watch the buses unload. They were anxious to see who was getting off, but few of the passengers who got off stayed in Oriskany—they were just passing through, stopping for a rest and a drink, and their faces seemed to say that they didn't think much of the town. Nor did they seem to think much of the girls from the country who stood around in their colorful dresses and smiled shyly at strangers, not knowing any better: they were taught to be kind to people, to smile first, you never knew who it might be. So now Helen was back in Oriskany, but this time she had come in on a bus herself. Had ridden alone, all the way from the city of Derby, all alone, and was waiting for her father to pick her up so she could go back to her old life without any more fuss.

It was hot. Flies crawled languidly around; a woman with a small sickly-faced baby had to keep waving them away. The old woman selling tickets looked at Helen as if her eyes were drawn irresistibly that way, as if she knew every nasty rumor and wanted to let Helen know that she knew. Helen's forehead broke out in perspiration and she stood, abruptly, wanting to dislodge that old woman's stare. She went over to the candy machine but did not look at the candy bars; she looked at herself in the mirror. Her own reflection always made her feel better. Whatever went on inside her head—and right now she felt nervous about something—had nothing to do with the way she looked, her smooth gentle skin and the faint freckles on her forehead and nose and the cool, innocent green of her eyes; she was just a girl from the country and anyone in town would know that, even if they didn't know her personally, one of those easy, friendly girls who hummed to themselves and seemed always to be glancing up as if expecting something pleasant, some deliberate surprise. Her light brown hair curled back lazily toward her ears, cut short now because it was the style; in high school she had worn it long. She watched her eyes in the mirror. No alarm there, really. She would be back home in an hour or so. Not her husband's home, of course, but her parents' home. And her face in the mirror was the face she had always seen—twenty-two she was now, and to her that seemed very old, but she looked no different from the way she had looked on her wedding day five years ago.

But it was stupid to try to link together those two Helens, she thought. She went back to the row of seats and sat heavily. If the old woman was still watching, she didn't care. A sailor in a soiled white uniform sat nearby, smoking, watching her but not with too much interest; he had other girls to recall. Helen opened her purse and looked inside at nothing and closed it again. The man she had been living with in the city for five months had told her it was stupid—no, he had not used that word; he said something fancy like "immature"—to confuse herself with the child she had been, married woman as she was now, and a mother, an adulterous married woman . . . And the word *adulterous* made her lips turn up in a slow bemused smile, the first flash of incredulous pride one might feel when told at last the disease that is going to be fatal. For there were so many diseases and only one way out of the world, only one death and so many ways to get to it. They were like doors, Helen thought dreamily. You walked down a hallway like those in movies, in huge wealthy homes, crystal chandeliers and marble floors and . . . great sweeping lawns . . . and doors all along those hallways; if you picked the wrong door you had to go through it. She was dreamy, drowsy. When thought became too much for her—when he had pestered her so much about marrying him, divorcing her husband and marrying him, always him!—she had felt so sleepy she could not listen. If she was not interested in a word her mind wouldn't hear it but made it blurred and strange, like words half heard in dreams or through some thick substance. You didn't have to hear a word if you didn't want to.

So she had telephoned her father the night before and told him the 3:15 bus and now it was 3:30; where was he? Over the telephone he had sounded slow and solemn, it could have been a stranger's voice. Helen had never liked telephones because you could not see smiles or gestures and talking like that made her tired. Listening to her father, she had felt for the first time since she had run away and left them all behind—husband, baby girl, family, in-laws, the minister, the dreary sun-bleached look of the land—that she had perhaps died and only imagined she was running away. Nobody here trusted the city; it was too big. Helen had wanted to go there all her life, not being afraid of anything, and so she had gone, and was coming back; but it was an odd feeling, this dreamy ghostliness, as if she were really dead and coming back in a form that only looked like herself. . . . She was bored, thinking of this, and crossed her bare legs. The sailor crushed out a cigarette in the dirty tin ashtray and their eyes met. Helen felt a little smile tug at her lips. That was the trouble, she knew men too well. She knew their eyes and their gestures—like the sailor rubbing thoughtfully at his chin now, as if he hadn't shaved well enough but really liked to feel his own skin. She knew them too well and had never figured out why: her sister, four years older, wasn't like that. But to Helen the same man one hundred times or one hundred men, different men, seemed the same. It was wrong, of course, because she had been taught it and believed what she had been taught; but she could not understand the difference. The sailor watched her but she looked away, half closing her eyes. She had no time for him. Her father should be here now, he would be here in a few minutes, so there was no time; she would be home in an hour. When she thought of her father, the ugly bus station with its odor of tobacco and spilled soft drinks seemed to fade away— she remembered his voice the night before, how gentle and soft she had felt listening to that voice, giving in to the protection he represented. She had endured his rough hands, as a child, because she knew they protected her, and all her life they had protected her. There had always been trouble, sometimes the kind you laughed about later and sometimes not; that was one of the reasons she had married John, and before John there had been others—just boys who didn't count, who had no jobs and thought mainly about their cars. Once, when she was fifteen, she had called her father from a roadhouse sixty miles away; she and her best friend Annie had gotten mixed up with some men they had met at a picnic. That had been frightening, Helen thought, but now she could have handled them. She gave everyone too much, that was her trouble. Her father had said that. Even her mother. Lent money to girls at the telephone company where she'd worked; lent her girl friends clothes; would run outside when some man drove up and blew his horn, not bothering to get out and knock at the door the way he should. She liked to make other people happy, what was wrong with that? Was she too lazy to care? Her head had begun to ache.

Always her thoughts ran one way, fast and innocent, but her body did other things. It got warm, nervous, it could not relax. Was she afraid of what her father's face would tell her? She pushed that idea away, it was nonsense. If she had to think of something, let it be of that muddy spring day when her family had first moved to this part of the country, into an old farmhouse her father had bought at a "bargain." At that time the road out in front of the house had been no more than a single dirt lane . . . now it was wider, covered with blacktop that smelled ugly and made your eyes shimmer and water with confusion in the summer. Yes, that big old house. Nothing about it would have changed. She did not think of her own house, her husband's house, because it mixed her up too much right now. May she would go back and maybe not. She did not think of him—if she wanted to go back she would, he would take her in. When she tried to think of what had brought her back, it was never her husband—so much younger, quicker, happier than the man she had just left—and not the little girl, either, but something to do with her family's house and that misty, warm day seventeen years ago when they had first moved in. So one morning when that man left for work her thoughts had turned back to home and she had sat at the breakfast table for an hour or so, not clearing off the dishes, looking at the coffee left in his cup as if it were a forlorn reminder of him—a man she was even then beginning to forget. She knew then that she did not belong there in the city. It wasn't that she had stopped loving this man—she never stopped loving anyone who needed her, and he had needed her more than anyone—it was something else, something she did not understand, Not her husband, not her baby, not even the look of the river way off down the hill, through the trees that got so solemn and intricate with their bare branches in winter. Those things she loved, she hadn't stopped loving them because she had had to love this new man more . . . but something else made her get up and run into the next room and look through the bureau drawers and the closet, as if looking for something. That evening, when he returned, she explained to him that she was going back. He was over forty, she wasn't sure how much, and it had always been his hesitant, apologetic manner that made her love him, the odor of failure about him that mixed with the odor of the drinking he could not stop, even though he had "cut down" now with her help. Why were so many men afraid, why did they think so much? He did something that had to do with keeping books, was that nervous work? He was an attractive man but that wasn't what Helen had seen in him. It was his staring at her when they had first met, and the way he had run his hand through his thinning hair, telling her in that gesture that he wanted her and wanted to be young enough to tell her so. That had been five months ago. The months all rushed to Helen's mind in the memory she had of his keen intelligent baffled eyes, and the tears she had had to see in them when she went out to call her father. . . .

Now, back in Oriskany, she would think of him no more.

A few minutes later her father came. Was that really him? she thought. Her heart beat furiously. If blood drained out of her face she would look mottled and sick, as if she had a rash . . . how she hated that! Though he had seen her at once, though the bus station was nearly empty, her father hesitated until she stood and ran to him. "Pa," she said, "I'm so glad to see you." It might have been years ago and he was just going to drive back home now, finished with his business in town, and Helen fourteen or fifteen, waiting to go back with him.

"I'll get your suitcase," he said. The sailor was reading a magazine, no longer interested. Helen watched her father nervously. What was wrong? He stooped, taking hold of the suitcase handle, but he did not straighten fast enough. Just a heartbeat too slow. Why was that? Helen took a tissue already stained with lipstick and dabbed it on her forehead.

On the way home he drove oddly, as if the steering wheel, heated by the sun, were too painful for him to hold. "No more trouble with the car, huh?" Helen said.

"It's all right," he said. They were nearly out of town already. Helen saw few people she knew. "Why are you looking around?"

her father said. His voice was pleasant and his eyes fastened
seriously upon the road, as if he did not dare look elsewhere.

"Oh, just looking," Helen said. "How is Davey?"

Waiting for her father to answer—he always took his time—
Helen arranged her skirt nervously beneath her. Davey was her
sister's baby, could he be sick? She had forgotten to ask about
him the night before. "Nothing's wrong with Davey, is there,
Pa?" she said.

"No, nothing."

"I thought Ma might come, maybe," Helen said.

"No."

"Didn't she want to? Mad at me, huh?"

In the past her mother's dissatisfaction with her had always
ranged Helen and her father together; Helen could tell by a
glance of her father's when this was so. But he did not look
away from the road. They were passing the new high school,
the consolidated high school Helen had attended for a year. No
one had known what "consolidated" meant or was interested in
knowing. Helen frowned at the dark brick and there came to
her mind, out of nowhere, the word *adulterous*, for it too had
been a word she had not understood for years. A word out of
the Bible. It was like a mosquito bothering her at night, or a
stain on her dress—the kind she would have to hide without
seeming to, letting her hand fall over it accidentally. For some
reason the peculiar smell of the old car, the rattling sunshades
above the windshield, the same old khaki blanket they used for
a seat cover did not comfort her and let her mind get drowsy,
to push that word away.

She was not sleepy, but she said she was.

"Yes, honey. Why don't you lay back and try to sleep, then," her father said.

He glanced toward her. She felt relieved at once, made simple and safe. She slid over and leaned her head against her father's shoulder. "Bus ride was long, I hate bus rides," she said. "I used to like them."

"You sleep till we get home."

"Is Ma mad?"

"No."

His shoulder wasn't as comfortable as it should have been. But she closed her eyes, trying to force sleep. She remembered that April day they had come here—their moving to the house that was new to them, a house of their own they would have to share with no one else, but a house it turned out had things wrong with it, secret things, that had made Helen's father furious. She could not remember the city and the house they had lived in there, but she had been old enough to sense the simplicity of the country and the eagerness of her parents, and then the angry perplexity that had followed. The family was big—six children then, before Arthur died at ten—and half an hour after they had moved in, the house was crowded and shabby. And she remembered being frightened at something and her father picking her up right in the middle of moving, and not asking her why she cried—her mother had always asked her that, as if there were a reason—but rocked her and comforted her with his rough hands. And she could remember how the house had looked so well: the ballooning curtains in the windows, the first things her mother had put up. The gusty spring air, already too warm, smelling of good earth and the Eden River not too far behind them, and leaves, sunlight, wind; and the sagging porch piled with cartons and bundles and pieces of furniture from the old house. The grandparents—her mother's parents—had died in that old dark house in the city, and Helen did not remember them at all except as her father summoned them back, recalling with hatred his wife's father—some little confused argument they had had years ago that he should have won. That old man had died and the house had gone to the bank, somewhere mysterious, and her father had brought them all out here to the country. A new world, a new life. A farm. And four boys to help, and the promise of such good soil. . . .

Her father turned the wheel sharply. "Rabbit run acrost," he said. He had this strange air of apology for whatever he did, even if it was something gentle; he hated to kill animals, even weasels and hawks. Helen wanted to cover his right hand with hers, that thickened, dirt-creased hand that could never be made clean. But she said, stirring a little as if he had awakened her, "Then why didn't Ma want to come?"

They were taking a long, slow curve. Helen knew without looking up which curve this was, between two wheat fields that belonged to one of the old, old families, those prosperous men who drove broken-down pickup trucks and dressed no better than their own hired hands, but who had money, much money, not just in one bank but in many. "Yes, they're money people," Helen remembered her father saying, years ago, passing someone's pasture. Those ugly red cows meant nothing to Helen, but they meant something to her father. And so after her father had said that—they had been out for a drive after church—her mother got sharp and impatient and the ride was ruined. That was years ago. Helen's father had been a young man then, with a raw, waiting, untested look, with muscular arms and shoulders that needed only to be directed to their work. "They're money people," he had said, and that had ruined the ride, as if by magic. It had been as if the air itself bad changed, the direction of the wind changing and easing to them from the river that was often stagnant in August and September, and not from the green land. With an effort Helen remembered that she had been thinking about her mother. Why did her mind push her into the past so often these days?—she only twenty-two (that was not old, not really) and going to begin a new life. Once she got home and took a bath and washed out the things in the suitcase, and got some rest, and took a walk down by the river as she had as a child, skipping stones across it, and sat around the round kitchen table with the old oilcloth cover to listen to their advice ("You got to grow up, now. You ain't fifteen any more"—that had been her mother, last time), then she would decide what to do. Make her decision about her husband and the baby and there would be nothing left to think about.

"Why didn't Ma come?"

"I didn't want her to," he said.

Helen swallowed, without meaning to. His shoulder was thin and hard against the side of her face. Were those same muscles still there, or had they become worn away like the soil that was sucked down into the river every year, stolen from them, so that the farm Helen's father had bought turned out to be a kind of joke on him? Or were they a different kind of muscle, hard and compressed like steel, drawn into themselves from years of resisting violence?

"How come?" Helen said.

He did not answer. She shut her eyes tight and distracting, eerie images came to her, stars exploding and shadowy figures

like those in movies—she had gone to the movies all the time in
the city, often taking in the first show at eleven in the morning,
not because she was lonely or had nothing to do but because
she liked movies. Five-twenty and he would come up the stairs,
grimacing a little with the strange inexplicable pain in his chest:
and there Helen would be, back from downtown, dressed up
and her hair shining and her face ripe and fresh as a child's, not
because she was proud of the look in his eyes but because she
knew she could make that pain of his abate for a while. And
so why had she left him, when he had needed her more than
anyone? "Pa, is something wrong?" she said, as if the recollection
of that other man's invisible pain were in some way connected
with her father.

He reached down vaguely and touched her hand. She was
surprised at this. The movie images vanished—those beautiful
people she had wanted to believe in, as she had wanted to believe
in God and the saints in their movie-world heaven—and she
opened her eyes. The sun was bright. It had been too bright all
summer. Helen's mind felt sharp and nervous, as if pricked by
tiny needles, but when she tried to think of what they could
be no explanation came to her. She would be home soon, she
would be able to rest. Tomorrow she could get in touch with
John. Things could begin where they had left off—John had
always loved her so much, and he had always understood her,
had known what she was like. "Ma isn't sick, is she?" Helen said
suddenly. "No," said her father. He released her fingers to take
hold of the steering wheel again. Another curve. Off to the side,
if she bothered to look, the river had swung toward them—low
at this time of year, covered in places with a fine brown-green
layer of scum. She did not bother to look.

"We moved out here seventeen years ago," her father said. He cleared his throat; the gesture of a man unaccustomed to speech. "You don't remember that!"

"Yes, I do," Helen said. "I remember that."

"You don't, you were just a baby."

"Pa, I remember it. I remember you carrying the big rug into the house, you and Eddie. And I started to cry and you picked me up. I was such a big baby, always crying. . . . And Ma came out and chased me inside so I wouldn't bother you."

"You don't remember that," her father said. He was driving jerkily, pressing down on the gas pedal and then letting it up, as if new thoughts continually struck him. What was wrong with him? Helen had an idea she didn't like: he was older now, he was going to become an old man.

If she had been afraid of the dark, upstairs in that big old farmhouse in the room she shared with her sister, all she had had to do was to think of him. He had a way of sitting at the supper table that was so still, so silent, you new nothing could budge him. Nothing could frighten him. So, as a child, and even now that she was grown up, it helped her to think of her father's face—those pale surprised green eyes that could be simple or cunning, depending upon the light, and the lines working themselves in deeper every year around his mouth and the hard angle of his jaw going back to the ear, burned by the sun and then tanned by it, turned into leather, then going pale again in the winter. The sun could not burn its color deep enough into that skin that was almost as fair as Helen's. At Sunday school she and the other children had been told to think of Christ when they were afraid, but the Christ she saw on the little Bible bookmark cards and calendars was no one to protect you. That was a man who would be your cousin, maybe, some cousin you liked but saw rarely, but He looked so given over to thinking and trusting that He could not be of much help; not like her father. When he and the boys came in from the fields with the sweat drenching their clothes and their faces looking as if they were dissolving with heat, you could still see the solid flesh beneath, the skeleton that hung onto its muscles and would never get old, never die. The boys—her brothers, all older—had liked her well enough, Helen being the baby, and her sister had watched her most of the time, and her mother had liked her too—or did her mother like anyone, having been brought up by German-speaking parents who had had no time to teach her love? But it had always been her father she had run to. She had started knowing men by knowing him. She could read things in his face that taught her about the faces of other men, the slowness or quickness of their thoughts, if they were beginning to be impatient, or were pleased and didn't want to show it yet. Was it for this she had come home?—And the thought surprised her so that she sat up, because she did not understand. Was it for this she had come home? "Pa," she said, "like I told you on the telephone, I don't know why I did it. I don't know why I went. That's all right isn't it? I mean, I'm sorry for it, isn't that enough? Did you talk to John?"

"John? Why John?"

"What?"

"You haven't asked about him until now, so why now?"

"What do you mean? He's my husband, isn't he? Did you talk to him?"

"He came over to the house almost every night for two weeks. Three weeks," he said. Helen could not understand the queer chatty tone of his voice. "Then off and on, all the time. No, I didn't tell him you were coming."

"But why not?" Helen laughed nervously. "Don't you like him?"

"You know I like him. You know that. But if I told him he'd of gone down to get you, not me."

"Not if I said it was you I wanted. . . ."

"I didn't want him to know. Your mother doesn't know either."

"What? You mean you didn't tell her?" Helen looked at the side of his face. It was rigid and bloodless behind the tan, as if something inside were shrinking away and leaving just his voice. "You mean you didn't even tell Ma? She doesn't know I'm coming?"

"No."

The nervous prickling in her brain returned suddenly. Helen rubbed her forehead. "Pa," she said gently, "why didn't you tell anybody? You're ashamed of me, huh?"

He drove on slowly. They were following the bends of the river, that wide shallow meandering river the boys said wasn't worth fishing in any longer. One of its tributaries branched out suddenly—Mud Creek, it was called, all mud and bullfrogs and dragonflies and weeds—and they drove over it on a rickety wooden bridge that thumped beneath them. "Pa," Helen said carefully, "you said you weren't mad, on the phone. And I wrote you that letter explaining. I wanted to write some more, but you know . . . I don't write much, never even wrote to Annie when she moved away. I never forgot about you or anything, or Ma. . . . I thought about the baby, too, and John, but John could always take care of himself. He's smart. He really is. I was in the store with him one time and he was arguing with some

salesmen and got the best of them; he never learned all that
from his father. The whole family is smart, though, aren't they?"

"The Hendrikses? Sure. You don't get money without brains."

"Yes, and they got money too, John never had to worry. In a
house like his parents' house nothing gets lost or broken. You
know? It isn't like it was at ours, when we were all kids. That's
part of it—when John's father built us our house I was real
pleased and real happy, but then something of them came in
with it too. Everything is s'post to be clean and put in its place,
and after you have a baby you get so tired. . . . But his mother
was always real nice to me. I don't complain about them. I like
them all real well."

"Money people always act nice," her father said. "Why
shouldn't they?"

"Oh, Pa!" Helen said, tapping at his arm. "What do you mean
by that? You always been nicer than anybody I know, that's the
truth. Real nice. A lot of them with those big farms, like John's
father, and that tractor store they got—they complain a lot.
They do. You just don't hear about it. And when that baby got
polio, over in the Rapids—that real big farm, you know what I
mean?—the McGuires. How do you think they felt? They got
troubles just like everybody else."

Then her father did a strange thing: here they were, seven or
eight miles from home, no house near, and he stopped the car.
"Want to rest for a minute," he said. Yet he kept staring out the
windshield as if he were still driving.

"What's wrong?"

"Sun on the hood of the car. . . ."

Helen tugged at the collar of her dress, pulling it away from
her damp neck. When had the heat ever bothered her father

before? She remembered going out to the farthest field with water for him, before he had given up that part of the farm. And he would take the jug from her and lift it to his lips and it would seem to Helen, the sweet child Helen standing in the dusty corn, that the water flowed into her magnificent father and enlivened him as if it were secret blood of her own she had given him. And his chest would swell, his reddened arms eager with muscle emerging out from his rolled-up sleeves and his eyes now wiped of sweat and exhaustion. . . . The vision pleased and confused her, for what had it to do with the man now beside her? She stared at him and saw that his nose was queerly white and that there were many tiny red veins about it, hardly more than pen lines; and his hair was thinning and jagged, growing back stiffly from his forehead as if he had brushed it back impatiently with his hand once too often. When Eddie, the oldest boy, moved away now and lost to them, had pushed their father hard in the chest and knocked him back against the supper table, that same amazed white look had come to his face, starting at his nose.

"I was thinking if, if we got home now, I could help Ma with supper," Helen said. She touched her father's arm as if to wake him. "It's real hot, she'd like some help."

"She doesn't know you're coming."

"But I . . . I could help anyway." She tried to smile, watching his face for a hint of something: many times in the past he had looked stern but could be made to break into a smile, finally, if she teased him long enough. "But didn't Ma hear you talk on the phone? Wasn't she there?"

"She was there."

"Well, but then . . ."

"I told her you just talked. Never said nothing about coming home."

The heat had begun to make Helen dizzy. Her father opened the door on his side. "Let's get out for a minute, go down by the river," he said. Helen slid across and got out. The ground felt uncertain beneath her feet. Her father was walking and saying something and she had to run to catch up with him. He said: "We moved out here seventeen years ago. There were six of you then, but you don't remember. Then the boy died. And you don't remember your mother's parents and their house, that goddamn stinking house, and how I did all the work for him in his store. You remember the store down front? The dirty sawdust floor and the old women coming in for sausage, enough to make you want to puke, and pigs' feet and brains out of cows or guts or what the hell they were that people ate in that neighborhood. I could puke for all my life and not get clean of it. You just got born then. And we were dirt to your mother's people, just dirt. I was dirt. And when they died somebody else got the house, it was all owned by somebody else, and so we said how it was for the best and we'd come out here and start all over. You don't remember it or know nothing about us."

"What's wrong, Pa?" Helen said. She took his arm as they descended the weedy bank. "You talk so funny, did you get something to drink before you came to the bus station? You never said these things before. I thought it wasn't just meat, but a grocery store, like the one in . . ."

"And we came out here," he said loudly, interrupting her, "and bought that son of a bitch of a house with the roof half rotted through and the well all shot to hell . . . and those bastards never looked at us, never believed we were real people.

The Hendrikses too. They were like all of them. They looked through me in town, do you know that? Like you look through a window. They didn't see me. It was because hillbilly families were in that house, came and went, pulled out in the middle of the night owing everybody money; they all thought we were like that. I said, we were poor but we weren't hillbillies. I said, do I talk like a hillbilly? We come from the city. But nobody gave a damn. You could go up to them and shout in their faces and they wouldn't hear you, not even when they started losing money themselves. I prayed to God during them bad times that they'd all lose what they had, every bastard one of them, that Swede with the fancy cattle most of all! I prayed to God to bring them down to me so they could see me, my children as good as theirs, and me a harder worker than any of them—if you work till you feel like dying you done the best you can do, whatever money you get. I'd of told them that. I wanted to come into their world even if I had to be on the bottom of it, just so long as they gave me a name. . . ."

"Pa, you been drinking," Helen said softly.

"I had it all fixed, what I'd tell them," he said. They were down by the river bank now. Fishermen had cleared a little area and stuck Y-shaped branches into the dried mud, to rest their poles on. Helen's father prodded one of the little sticks with his foot and then did something Helen had never seen anyone do in her life, not even boys—he brought his foot down on it and smashed it.

"You oughtn't of done that," Helen said. "Why'd you do that?"

"And I kept on and on; it was seventeen years. I never talked about it to anyone, Your mother and me never had much to say, you know that. She was like her father. You remember that first day? It was spring, nice and warm, and the wind came along

when we were moving the stuff in and was so different from that
smell in the city—my God! It was a whole new world here."

"I remember it," Helen said. She was staring out at the shallow muddy river. Across the way birds were sunning themselves
stupidly on flat, white rocks covered with dried moss like veils.

"You don't remember nothing!" her father said angrily. "Nothing! You were the only one of them I loved, because you didn't
remember. It was all for you. First I did it for me, myself, to
show that bastard father of hers that was dead—then those other
bastards, those big farms around us—but then for you, for you.
You were the baby. I said to God that when you grew up it'd be
you in one of them big houses with everything fixed and painted
all the time, and new machinery, and driving around in a nice
car, not this thing we got. I said I would do that for you or die."

"That's real nice, Pa," Helen said nervously, "but I never . . . I
never knew nothing about it, or . . . I was happy enough any
way I was. I liked it at home, I got along with Ma better than
anybody did. And I liked John too, I didn't marry him just
because you told me to. I mean, you never pushed me around.
I wanted to marry him all by myself, because he loved me. I
was always happy, Pa. If John didn't have the store coming to
him, and that land and all, I'd have married him anyway—You
oughtn't to have worked all that hard for me."

In spite of the heat she felt suddenly chilled. On either side
of them tall grass shrank back from the cleared, patted area,
stiff and dried with August heat. These weeds gathered upon
themselves in a brittle tumult back where the vines and foliage
of trees began, the weeds dead and whitened and the vines a
glossy, rich green, as if sucking life out of the water into which
they drooped. All along the river bank trees and bushes leaned

out and showed a yard or two of dead, whitish brown where the water line had once been. This river bent so often you could never see far along it. Only a mile or so. Then foliage began, confused and unmoving. What were they doing here, she and her father? A thought came to Helen and frightened her—she was not used to thinking—that they ought not to be here, that this was some other kind of slow, patient world where time didn't care at all for her or her girl's face or her generosity of love, but would push right past her and go on to touch the faces of other people.

"Pa, let's go home. Let's go home," she said.

Her father bent and put his hands into the river. He brought them dripping to his face. "That's dirty there, Pa," she said. A mad dry buzzing started up somewhere—hornets or wasps. Helen looked around but saw nothing.

"God listened and didn't say yes or no," her father said. He was squatting at the river and now looked back at her, his chin creasing. The back of his shirt was wet. "If I could read Him right it was something like this—that I was caught in myself and them money people caught in themselves and God Himself caught in what He was and so couldn't be anything else. Then I never thought about God again."

"I think about God," Helen said. "I do. People should think about God, then they wouldn't have wars and things. . . ."

"No, I never bothered about God again," he said slowly. "If He was up there or not it never had nothing to do with me. A hailstorm that knocked down the wheat, or a drought—what the hell? Whose fault? It wasn't God's no more than mine so I let Him out of it. I knew I was in it all on my own. Then after a while it got better, year by year. We paid off the farm and the new machines. You were in school then, in town. And when we went into the church they said hello to us sometimes, because we outlasted them hillbillies by ten years. And now Mike ain't doing bad on his own place, got a nice car, and me and Bill get enough out of the farm so it ain't too bad, I mean it ain't too bad. But it wasn't money I wanted!"

He was staring at her. She saw something in his face that mixed with the buzzing of the hornets and fascinated her so that she could not move, could not even try to tease him into smiling too. "It wasn't never money I wanted," he said.

"Pa, why don't we go home?'"

"I don't know what it was, exactly," he said, still squatting. His hands touched the ground idly. "I tried to think of it, last night when you called and all night long and driving in to town today. I tried to think of it."

"I guess I'm awful tired from that bus. I . . . I don't feel good," Helen said.

"Why did you leave with that man?"

"What? Oh," she said, touching the tip of one of the weeds, "I met him at John's cousin's place, where they got that real nice tavern and a dance hall. . . . "

"Why did you run away with him?"

"I don't know, I told you in the letter. I wrote it to you, Pa. He acted so nice and liked me so, he still does, he loves me so much. . . . And he was always so sad and tired, he made me think of . . . you, Pa . . . but not really, because he's not strong like you and couldn't ever do work like you. And if he loved me that much I had to go with him."

"Then why did you come back?"

"Come back?" Helen tried to smile out across the water. Sluggish, ugly water, this river that disappointed everyone, so familiar to her that she could not really get used to a house without a river or a creek somewhere behind it, flowing along night and day: perhaps that was what she had missed in the city?

"I came back because . . . because . . ."

And she shredded the weed in her cold fingers, but no words came to her. She watched the weed-fragments fall. No words came to her, her mind had turned hollow and cold, she had come too far down to this river bank but it was not a mistake any more than the way the river kept moving was a mistake; it just happened.

Her father got slowly to his feet and she saw in his hand a knife she had been seeing all her life. Her eyes seized upon it and her mind tried to remember: where had she seen it last, whose was it, her father's or her brother's? He came to her and touched her shoulder as if waking her, and they looked at each other, Helen so terrified by now that she was no longer afraid but only curious with the mute marblelike curiosity of a child, and her father stern and silent until a rush of hatred transformed his face into a mass of wrinkles, the skin mottled red and white. He did not raise the knife but slammed it into her chest, up to the hilt, so that his whitened fist struck her body and her blood exploded out upon it.

Afterward, he washed the knife in the dirty water and put it away. He squatted and looked out over the river, then his thighs began to ache and he sat on the ground, a few feet from her body. He sat there for hours as if waiting for some idea to come to him. Then the water began to darken, very slowly, and the sky darkened a little while later—as if belonging to another, separate time—and he tried to turn his mind with an effort to the next thing he must do.

QUEEN OF THE NIGHT

I

This is how Claire Falk's marriage of twenty-six years, which accounted for more than half her life, ended one humid Saturday afternoon in June: she blundered into overhearing a conversation.

It was one-sided, only one-half of a conversation because her husband was on the telephone. And there were no words to it, no distinct recognizable words, because she was nearly out of earshot. She heard only sounds. Her husband's voice, curiously raw and aggrieved, a young man's voice, and yet *his*. She would know it anywhere.

He was arguing with someone. And then begging. His voice rose and dipped and went silent. Then began again: strident, passionate, craven, exasperated, frightened. A harsh, jagged, dissonant music Claire had never known in her own lifetime.

Or, if she had known it—it had been long ago, many years ago.

She shrank back against a wall, listening. Though she did not want, *really*, to eavesdrop. Even in this moment of shock, of sickening apprehension, she did not want to violate another person's privacy. But who was her husband talking with in that angry, intimate tone, why was he so upset, why so suddenly and uncharacteristically abject. . . . Claire half-wanted to go to him, to comfort him. It had been many years since she had had to comfort him.

He was silent awhile. Then began again, this time more evenly. He was trying to convince someone, his manner was more familiar; half-jocular, ironic, bullying. Yet he was still begging. It was the begging that was so ugly, so final: Claire knew what it must mean.

She knew, and retreated.

After all she was a woman of principle. Her instinct turned her away from what she might discover, what she might precisely discover, if she drew nearer, if she pressed her ear against the closed door: it would be *degrading* to eavesdrop now that she knew her husband was quarreling with a woman. She did not at that time think exactly of betrayal, in the sense in which she had been "betrayed," their marriage "betrayed." Her husband's passion excluded her. It had nothing to do with her at all.

She left the house. Retreated. He had not expected her home for another hour, she had made a miscalculation, a fatal blunder. Consequently nothing would be the same again. Now is life very real, is it very convincing—so Claire Falk queried herself, half ironically. When she was alone she often spoke to herself in silence and her voice, her tone, at such times was oddly cynical, even impersonal; not exactly a woman's voice. It was frequently reproachful as if it considered her something of a fool, yet it was sympathetic, good-humored, forgiving, if she stayed with it long enough. How much reality can you credit to all this?—so the voice drawled, referring to the street, the busy intersection which she was approaching, a child pedaling energetically on a bicycle, the filmy sky, the day, the world itself. But despite the voice's smug cynicism Claire was trembling, she was really in a state of mild shock, she hardly knew what she was doing. Afterward, when such extreme emotions, centered on her first husband, were to seem merely curious, she was to remember that blind panicked walk that would take her some three miles from home. She did not know what day of the week it was, what time of the day, what she had been doing all afternoon, why she had imagined it important. Her life had come to a stop.

She survived the blow, barely. How must she have looked that afternoon, a woman in her fifties, well-dressed, very pale, blind and disheveled and in a great hurry. . . . She must have been a spectacle, people must have stared at her. But she saw nothing. She saw no one. There was a wide street busy with traffic, and the corner of the park there were a number of people playing tennis, there was the cemetery where for weeks now the groundkeepers had been on strike and weeds grew abundantly. She found herself huddling in the doorway of the little stone chapel in the cemetery. It was raining, when had it begun to rain? The drops were cool on her overheated face.

You had no idea that your husband was in love with another woman, they would ask, watching her closely.

I had no idea.

There wasn't anything . . . strange . . . ?

I had no idea.

Stubbornly, angrily. But then her jaw would quiver, her voice shake.

In the doorway of the chapel she crouched like an animal, her back against the heavy oak door. Now you can cry if you must, the voice instructed her, impatiently, but nothing happened. Her forehead and cheeks were damp, it was only the rain, which was now being flung against her. An indignity. But somehow consoling.

Such things are blows, after all, people would say. There were many divorced women now. There was a small army of divorced women in this very part of the world, in the wide circle of friends and acquaintances and business associates Claire and her husband knew. A kind of death, people said. Losing a loved one in any way—it's a kind of death. A terrible blow to one's ego, to one's sense of self. So the familiar words went, the litany of clichés. She would hear them all many times, she would not turn away in contempt or anguish or amusement. Chagrined, she would recall that she herself had mouthed such platitudes in the past before she had known what they meant—before she had even guessed at their incontestable truth.

You had no idea, Claire . . . ? Really? So her sister would inquire, staring at her.

I had no idea.

With Ronald it was so obvious, you know, you remember all that year I was calling you late at night, I must have made your life miserable, you must have dreaded picking up the phone. . . . But *you* hadn't any idea, any suspicion?

Nor had she wept. Weeks after that Saturday, months afterward, on the morning of the divorce, on the evening of the divorce, she had been grim and subdued and even a little ravaged but tearless. Not out of defiance or rage but out of a queer impersonal conviction that had come to her . . . that had come to her from nowhere, as she crouched in the stone doorway, her face streaming with rain, her clothes soaking. The conviction had to do with the fact that tears were pointless. What had happened was an event, it was out of her control, in a sense not her responsibility, not her fault. Her husband had evidently fallen in love with another woman. A younger woman, of course. Younger by twenty-five years. *He* had acted, he had turned from her, he had not so much violated their marriage as simply forgotten it. And of course it was not true, as Claire told her friends, that she had "no idea": she had known very well that the two of them were emotionally estranged, no longer really intimate, uninterested in sexual love, uninterested in seeking out the causes of their indifference. She had known very well that they were friends rather than lovers, they were courteous with each other, but not *always* courteous. . . . Yet the marriage had seemed to Claire an absolute unalterable fact, an impersonal condition in which she was to continue to live, neither happy nor unhappy: simply as Claire Falk.

The divorce proceedings were impersonal too. And tedious. Even with the reformed divorce law Claire found the experience tedious, and any emotions she might have felt—after all, the Falks were dissolving not only a marriage but what added up to a small but complicated business partnership involving property, investments, works of art, two cars, a son in his mid-twenties who was studying international law in London—were flattened, drained away. There were too many details, too many fussy points, her husband's attorney and her own were better suited to deal with them, let them deal with such things while she went her own way. She would acquire an apartment, of course the house must be put on the market and sold quickly; though her husband—guilty, embarrassed, proud—had very generously offered it to her, without qualifications. Once she was out of the house and living in an apartment, perhaps one of those large, airy, very modern high-rise apartments along the river . . .

Her son flew home, to comfort her. To accuse his father. But the drama did not really interest her, she found herself embarrassed in her son's presence, as if he were mistaking her for someone else: another, weaker, far less intelligent woman. Has he always thought of me like this, she wondered. His mother. A woman who is his mother, and that only. . . . With him she managed to be "hurt," to express the usual ritual bewilderment. (Why, when things have been going so well, when we've been so happy together, twenty-six years together after all. . . .) He had her long blunt nose and squarish chin and somewhat bold, intimidating stare, and that pronounced widow's peak that had caused her grief as a young girl but which, in later years, she was rather vain about. Unlike her he was tall, and his complexion was coarse. Still he was an attractive young man. Too fussy, too solicitous of her feelings, in a way too inquisitive (for there were private matters Claire would never discuss with anyone, not even members of her family), but an attractive man, a boy who had turned out well.

Could you call him off me? her husband pleaded.

Amused, Claire assured him that their son wouldn't stay long. He had made plans to spend a month with her but of course he would grow restless, he'd soon return to London, they had only to be patient with him. He thinks I am grief stricken, Claire said with an ironic twist of her mouth. Eventually I will convince him otherwise.

Twenty-six years, now being put behind them. And apart from the burden of the legal problems, and certain flashes of memory that evidently overtook them both (neither Claire nor her husband were sentimental people but they were susceptible, at times, to queer unanticipated painful stabs of nostalgia), the experience of closing off that passage of time, declaring it no longer valid, was not a very difficult one. One lives, after all, day by day; petty problems are more exasperating than large ones; there was no time for Claire's skeptical voice to quiz her about love, the meaning of love, whether it *had* any meaning, when she was arranging with a realtor to put their house on a crowded and grotesquely inflated market.

It *did* hurt, of course, to learn—by way of an acquaintance— that her husband believed he was in love "for the first time in his life." This, at the age of fifty-five. After those twenty-six years. But was the statement, the flamboyant deluded hope, very original . . . ? Claire laughed her infrequent ribald laugh, and said that adultery must have unhinged him. The illicit meetings, the scrambling in corners, the deceit, the silly tiresome guilt. The physical exertion involved in keeping up with a woman that young, and no doubt very experienced.

But even that hurt, that wound, faded. In the judge's chambers she and her husband were polite with each other, they made every effort to smile when smiles were not inappropriate, they were very civilized and responsible adults. Their attorneys, the judge, the recording clerk, the young woman whom Claire's husband was to marry the following week—all must have been impressed with the Falks' behavior,

In truth, Claire had been strangely hopeful about the young woman. Her initial resentment had long since faded, she felt only a curious hope that . . . that her husband would not shame himself, make a fool of himself. For she too was involved. Intimately, and publicly. If the young woman were a disappointment, if everyone talked about them, her husband's new bride, the folly of the alliance, what it must mean about Claire herself as a wife, as a woman . . .

But the girl was not a disappointment. She was not extraordinary, certainly no beauty, Claire could not reasonably feel a tug of envy of her, not even of her youth, which seemed merely shallow; she was attractive and soft-voiced, and obviously ill at ease, and probably not *very* bright—but she wasn't a disappointment, to Claire's relief. The new Mrs. Falk would not publicly shame her.

And yet—how flattering it would have been, she said, joking, to friends, to her sister, if he had managed to set himself up with a truly beautiful, a truly remarkable woman. A politician friend of theirs had done exceptionally well, though he was in his late fifties. . . . On the other hand, another friend, newly divorced from *his* wife, had made an utter fool of himself by marrying a vulgar simpering divorcée with two small children, who quite clearly wanted only his money. So Claire's husband had not done *too* badly. At least I don't have to feel sorry for him, she said. I can begin the process of forgetting him.

As a young girl Claire had not been especially attractive. The bones of her face were strong, her nostrils flared as if she were impatient, thinking her own rebellious thoughts, cryptically amused, censorious. Her thick dark hair and her deep-set intelligent eyes were her most striking features. As she matured, however, the very uniqueness of her appearance came to have a value; she was set apart from other women, conventionally pretty women, and dependent upon her mood she was sometimes exceptionally beautiful. Who can say, who can judge, she often queried herself, studying that face she was linked to for life, examining it for blemishes or signs of aging, idly, without the anxiety other women commonly feel. By a quirk of fate she was photogenic, and a little vain; but not *really* vain, since she measured such things as a woman's sexual attractiveness against other, more abiding qualities, or were they achievements, or possessions—marriage, family, friends, a home, a fairly busy life, flexible bonds with the community. She did volunteer work for the symphony, for St. Patrick's General Hospital, for the Art Students' Guild; for a while she had been thinking quite seriously of buying into an unusual clothing boutique with the wife of her husband's most frequent golfing companion, but in the end the project had fallen through, no one knew quite why. She handled many of their finances, prepared a good deal of their income tax information for their accountant and tax lawyer, did research on certain investment properties, even wrote, from time to time, freelance articles for her suburban newspaper. (She had hoped while in college to become a journalist, not knowing at the time how difficult, how exhausting, and how ill-paid such jobs were.) Now is all this relevant to your present situation, she quizzed herself, or is it to be brushed away, forgotten with all the rest . . . ? She stared at herself unsmiling. It was remarkable how little the divorce had affected her, how alert, even youthful she still looked. (And another birthday drew near: another!) She had a very pale, opaque skin, a certain heavy and slumberous look, disturbingly erotic; or so someone had told her. Her husband, perhaps. Or a half-drunk admirer. Though she was not overweight there was a solidity, an almost leaden substance to her, as if she were not flesh—not entirely. Something sculpted. Marble. Alabaster.

As a young wife, newly pregnant, she had been eerily lethar-
gic, slow-moving, given to long periods of daydreaming. Her
husband would call her back. Sometimes rudely, she thought.
Jealously. What are you thinking of, where has your mind gone,
he wanted to know. But she could not answer, she could not
say. In later years, particularly in the year before the telephone
conversation, she had found herself drifting off again. . . . She
would stand immobile, as if listening to sounds in the distance,
or to a near-inaudible music. Claire, what are you thinking
about? her husband would inquire. When you stand like that,
staring off like that, what are you thinking of?

Nothing, she said, roused, and a little embarrassed.

But it isn't possible to think of nothing, her husband said.

Now he was good-natured about her moods, her habits. They
were harmless, after all. Hardly a threat or a challenge to him. Of
course he was in love, and like a young besotted lover he could
think no one else but his love, though he made an attempt to
be attentive, even generous; Claire had not understood at the
time but she had felt the force of his good-humored, somewhat
distracted curiosity.

My mind just slipped away, she said.

Yes, but where?

An immobile, impassive woman, with a striking profile, a
head of thick dark hair wildly streaked with gray. Something
glacial about you, something remote and forbidding, the young
man who was to be her second husband said, shyly, yet half-
mockingly. It was clear that he was in awe of her. Fascinated by
her. ". . . Queen of the Night," he whispered.

"What? What did you say?"

He caught his lower lip between his small crowded-together teeth.

"Oh nothing. Some nonsense that crossed my mind."

Queen of the Night. She had of course heard him perfectly well. And her heart expanded as though it would burst, flooded with a sudden violent knowledge of her power.

His name was Emil. Which was, or was not, his real name.

On a private stretch of beach in Hollywood, Florida. Between Christmas and New Year's. That busy merciless time of the year that Claire had always disliked, and now positively dreaded. To fill it up, to squander it as brainlessly as possible, she had accepted her sister's invitation to fly south and stay with her. There are some fascinating people here, her sister bragged. Friends of mine. In politics, real estate, show business. And the children too—*their* friends. Wait till you meet them!

Nearly every afternoon there were cocktail parties, nearly every evening beach parties, or parties around lighted pools. Since her divorce Claire's sister had blossomed, but gaudily: a trim nervous woman in her late forties, she had tanned her skin dusky, and bleached her hair, and wore amazing eye makeup—luminous eye shadow, water-repellent mascara. In her flowing robes and ankle-length skirts she *did* look attractive, Claire thought.

"But *you*," her sister exclaimed, squeezing Claire's face between her hands, studying her almost rudely, "*you* look marvelous. And after all you've gone through. . . . Do you know, Ted dropped me a line when he was back in the States, he said you were in a state of shock, you were very depressed, he was half-tempted to break off his studies. . . . But I didn't *think* so, myself, I mean every time we talked on the phone . . ."

Claire winced, blushing angrily. Her son, gossiping about her with her sister! It was insupportable.

"Ted has always exaggerated things," she said.

"Oh yes—don't they? Children, I mean. And then your Ted is, you know, something of a prig."

She met Emil on the fourth night of her visit though she had seen him, without knowing who he was, or that he was a friend of her niece's, on the very first night. He was "something in the theater." Or was it in music. Mime? Dance? A tall, painfully thin young man, in his late twenties, perhaps, not at all suntanned. He wore snug white trousers and a close-fitting white jersey shirt and a red scarf knotted carelessly about his throat. His blond hair was very pale, almost white, and fell nearly to his shoulders in languid, spent curls. When Claire first happened to see him, quite by accident, he was at the center of a noisy, hilarious group of young people in a sidewalk café near the ocean. Their laughter and outrageous high spirits drew Claire's attention, though she was, at the time, tired from her plane flight, and not terribly interested in her sister's excited chatter (She was showing Claire around, walking arm in arm with her, pointing out restaurants, nightclubs, Christmas decorations, the high-rise apartments of acquaintances of hers. "This part of the world is so much *alive*," she kept telling Claire. "It's nothing like—you know—back north.")

If Claire had been a more self-conscious woman she might have imagined that the young people were laughing at her and her sister. But of course they were not. They were interested only in one another. It was the holiday season, they'd been drinking together for some time, they were all young and fairly attractive and . . . One of them drew her eye involuntarily: the willowy young man in the white trousers and jersey, with the bold red scarf about his neck. There was something both mocking and plaintive about him. His eyeglasses caught and reflected light as if he were blinking compulsively. His chin receded delicately, he was far too thin, the laughter that burst from him seemed raw and painful. And his companions: Claire saw with disapproval that they were not really so attractive. One was muscular and very tanned, a good-looking young man, but brash and pushy, with too-red lips. He appeared to have a severe limp. Another, a skinny short-haired girl in a silver halter top and near-transparent black trousers, was giggling shrilly, her eyes shut.

"It's like this every night during the season, isn't it wild?" Claire's sister said, steering her along the crowded sidewalk.

"It's very . . . it's very colorful," Claire said faintly.

Three evenings later she saw the young man again, and it seemed to her that he half-recognized her. We know each other, she thought calmly.

So long as the sun shone one might imagine it was summer, but as soon as the sun dropped away the air became uncomfortably cool. It was winter, after all. It was nearly New Year's. Claire was wise enough to dress prudently, even to wear stockings. She had no intention of catching cold. But the other party guests dressed lightly, the women especially. A number were even barefoot. And the young blond man who watched her so closely, had he kicked off his shoes too? Yes, she saw with a small inexplicable thrill of concern that he was barefoot despite the chill.

His long slender feet danced bluish-white in the dusk.

There was a party of "adults" and a party of "young people," some of them very young indeed—fifteen or sixteen. Claire did not approve, really. The two parties overlapped awkwardly, as if by accident. Her sister, vodka martini in hand, introduced her to the guests: a Democratic congressman, someone in the hotel business, an editor for the *Miami Herald*. "My sister is a freelance journalist," Claire's sister said before Claire could silence her.

The party had no center. There must have been hosts—the couple who owned the enormous sprawling stucco-and-glass house—but Claire never met them.

Her niece Maryanna appeared, hair loose to her waist. She was nineteen years old and had dropped out of the University of Miami in order to join an amateur theatrical group; she was training to be a mime. A pert, pretty girl with small high breasts and small buttocks snug in a pair of bleached blue jeans, Claire's only niece, at one time quite a favorite of hers. But all that had changed. Why it was that Maryanna didn't care for her Aunt Claire, why she never smiled *quite* warmly enough, Claire could not fathom. Certainly she had always been kind to the girl, especially since her sister's divorce, and generous with gifts.

"How nice you look tonight, Aunt Claire," the girl said, raising her droll eyebrows.

Maryanna's friends hung back, as if conscious of being obtrusive at the party. Certainly they had not been invited—but then who *had* been, in this confusion? The young blond man edged forward, barefoot, graceful. The lenses of his eyeglasses were round and fairly thick, and magnified his beautiful eyes. He stared at Claire openly, taking in her fashionable new gown, which was coarse-knit, ivory and cream-colored and a pale russet-orange. The skirt was made of several layers which fell unevenly, rather rakishly, about her ankles.

"My name is Emil," he said softly, licking his lips.

His hand was small-boned, light as a bird; the flesh was un-commonly soft. Though their two hands joined for the space of some seconds during which they gazed raptly at each other, there was little pressure, hardly any force at all.

He introduced himself as a "polymath." His pale hair stirred in the ocean breeze, his eyelids and his fingers fluttered, Claire found him charming—though rather absurd of course—as he elaborated his talents: he was a poet, a playwright, a composer of "musical theater," a linguist, an economist, an actor, a direc-tor, a historian, a former track star (in high school—long ago, in Paris, Illinois), a watercolorist, a potter, a flautist, a pianist. He was to have been a concert pianist, and the piano was still his first love, but the designs and blackmailing tactics of his parents and various instructors had forced him to reject the entire business; it was sordid, the competition was sinister and antimusical. Did Claire agree?

Delighted with him, Claire found herself laughing in agreement.

Some minutes later the two of them were strolling along the beach, carrying their drinks. Emil had even offered to carry Claire's heavy purse of glazed wicker into which she'd thrown, earlier that day, all sorts of things—hand lotion, moisturizer, a bottle of Bufferin, a four-ounce bottle of expensive French perfume, her checkbook, her traveler's checks, a pair of plastic sunglasses with oversized blue frames. As they walked Emil kept up a constant stream of chatter: anecdotes about a few of the people at the party, speculations on the future of Florida, and of the United States, and of Western civilization in general, his theories of art and culture and morals and religion. Evidently we are in the "Tin Age," the last of the cycles before the entropic collapse of the universe. Languages begin to fail. The gestures of affection and love begin to fail. Individuals take to shouting at one another but still cannot make themselves heard. Frustrated, they take refuge in the senses, they attempt to communicate through the body—through love, or brutality; but of course they fail. And all subsides into its original chaos.

"Really?" Claire laughed.

Then he was complaining bitterly about the poor public and critical reception he and his group had received back in October when they had presented their own production of Webster's *The White Devil,* conceived in a Brechtian style, with appropriate music. Tickets had been only one dollar, yet very few people had come; and some rude, ignorant fools had even left during the performance, which badly upset certain of the actors. Including Emil. ". . . just don't make the *attempt* to hear what we're say-ing," he mumbled, edging around in front of Claire, gazing at her appealingly. "Then they wonder why we shout, they wonder why we're forced to behave like children. And it's very difficult, you must realize, to retain a child's innocence and arrogance at the age of twenty-nine!"

His pale jester's face was drawn up into a look of—was it sorrow, was it a small boy's naughty glee—and there was a hint of complicity too. Claire grinned at him, refusing to be moved, to be obviously "charmed."

She sipped at her drink, which she no longer tasted. "If the universe is running down," she said, raising her voice gaily to be heard over the sound of the surf, "none of this matters, does it?"

"Oh hell," Emil said flatly, his shoulders slumping, "the uni-verse *won't* run down. It never *has* and it never *will.*"

They had walked some distance, the party was far behind them, Claire's feet in her expensive sandals were wet and sandy, the moon had become filmy, eerily beautiful, nothing mattered and everything mattered. The palm tree leaves made papery, restless sounds in the wind, and of course the surf pounded and pounded spilled itself frothily up onto the beach. Am I drunk, Claire asked, allowing her attentive, admiring young escort to slide an arm through hers when she stumbled in the sand, is any of this real, does it *matter* . . . ? Emil's daring made him tremble. She could feel him trembling. But her own body was suffused with a sudden vitality, an uncanny strength that had lain in trance for many years. The body's life is a matter of power, she saw, and one of the manifestations of this power is—simply—to recognize it and pay homage to it.

Emil was dissatisfied with the Miami area and had plans, tentative plans, to hitch a ride out to Key West. Where he had friends. Someone to put him up for a few weeks. Though possibly he might go elsewhere—he really didn't know.

"Emil—you hear such stories about him," Maryanna said.

"What kind of stories?" said Claire.

The girl's limbs were covered with soft brown-blond down, like the down of a baby animal. Except for her lower legs, which she had shaved, and which were hard and muscular and very tan. She did not like her aunt, that was clear. And now she had a reason for not liking her.

"What kind of stories?" Claire persisted.

"Oh—drugs and dealing and—that kind of thing—" Maryanna said irritably. "Borrowing money and not paying it back.

Lying. Playing people off against one another. That kind thing."
But then she added, glancing at Claire, as if she suddenly feared
this information might find its way back to Emil, "I don't know:
you hear stories about everyone. Most of it's bull. I really *don't*
know, you'll have to ask him yourself."

Claire laughed in surprise. "But I won't be seeing him again,
I'm leaving next Monday."

"Next Monday?" her niece said, raising her eyebrows. "Oh,
that soon? Are you leaving that soon? . . . But it's so cold back
north isn't it?"

She bought a car, one of the smaller models (she had, of course,
a car back home), and she and Emil took turns driving. It was
not a difficult trip—a few nights on the road, interstate highways that were dry well up into southern Pennsylvania, and after
that adequately plowed. Emil had drawn up a "verbal contract":
though she was paying for his meals and lodging and the gas for
the car, he fully intended to repay her within six months, as soon
as he was settled with a job. He had connections in Boston. But
he wouldn't mind even manual labor, for a while.

In a Sheraton Hilton "motor hotel" somewhere in the hills
of Virginia they shared a bed for the first time. (They had taken
adjoining rooms.) Claire in an ivory negligee—a beautiful thing,
and rather costly, bought as a Christmas present for herself back
in a Miami Nieman-Marcus—opened the door to Emil's timid
knocking, and saw with pleasure the awe, the confused love,
in the young man's eyes. "Oh God," he whispered, as if for an
invisible audience. And she *was* beautiful at the moment—her
own reflection had startled her. Calm and impassive and hard
and yet lovely, classically lovely, with her dark eyes and strong

bones and pursed, contemplative lips. She felt no passion herself but might gaze upon it, unjudging, tolerant.

"Do you think—? Is it—? I mean—Could I, just for a while—"

He began to stammer. Claire touched his lips with her forefinger.

As a lover he was quivering and self-conscious and far too quick, too clumsy. Claire held him, feeling unashamedly maternal: she murmured words of love and encouragement and praise to him, and stroked his shuddering sides, and his sweat-slick back. Ah, the poor boy was so thin!—so painfully thin. His ribs protruded, his collarbone protruded, his grinding pumping hips were hardly larger than a child's. Though his shoulder and arm muscles were hard. And his thighs. Claire held him, and laughed with delight of him, and told him she had never been so happy in her life—which was, of course, untrue: but then such things are uttered, at such times.

"Do you love me?" he whispered.

His body still trembled he had to press himself against her, burrowing his face into her shoulder. He was very warm, and slender as a fish, quivering with life, altogether delightful. While making love to her he had whimpered, like a child in pain, or a child terribly frightened, and Claire had found herself excited by the sounds, the high-pitched half-conscious sounds, which stirred a memory she could not grasp.

"Do you love me?" he whispered.

II

They were married the first week in March, at a private ceremony, and celebrated alone afterward with a champagne breakfast at the city's most elegant hotel. And then on their honeymoon: to Nassau: which was supposed to be different enough from Miami to make the effort worthwhile. (It was not *very* different, but then what can one expect from a winter resort?) Emil was an energetic, attentive, high-spirited young bridegroom, apt to mock his very enthusiasm by droll grins and self-mimicking routines, though it was obvious that he loved Claire very much, and was still somewhat intimidated by her. He liked to attribute to her certain not-quite-natural powers: she could "read" his thoughts, she could pitch him out of a black mood by "focus-ing" on him, she could draw him to her, to make love to her, by her gaze alone, fixed on the back of his head. On the wide white beach he never tired of oiling her body, or arranging the beach umbrella so that the shadow fell over her face; he never tired of running little errands—getting lemon ices for them at midmorning, and drinks at noon, and beer at odd times. (Claire developed a taste for beer, it must have been because of the sun and the beach, a certain dryness in her mouth, a near-perpetual thirst. They discovered a very interesting Japanese beer, new to them both, which was expensive but well worth the price.)

The only problem was, Emil could not tan: his pale, near-translucent skin simply pinkened and began to smart.

"Just look at you!" he wailed, sitting slump-backed beneath the umbrella. "You're so dark! You're dark as a native! Perfect! You radiate heat and warmth and health and sanity, your body is obviously *wiser* than mine though you don't belong to the daylight any more than I do. . . . Oh God, how I envy you, it just isn't *fair*."

His nose was burned, and began to peel. Which humiliated him. Which he would not allow her to joke about.

"I feel like a freak. I *am* a freak. Go to the dining room by yourself, you obviously can't want a creature like me to accompany you," he said.

She overheard him speaking in a peremptory way to one of the tennis instructors, a young man his own age, and was startled at first—and then rather thrilled—by the tone of his voice. He could be firm, even somewhat bullying, out of her presence. Though with her, of course, he was always puppyish, boyish, tremulous, uncertain.

"You *do* love me, you *do* love me?" he asked repeatedly.

"I'm your wife now, of course I love you," Claire laughed, stroking his hair, his shoulders, his sides.

"You won't throw me aside someday, the way you snatched me up?"

"Don't be absurd."

"I'm not absurd," he said petulantly. ". . . Am I absurd, Claire?"

"Hush. Why don't you sleep."

"Will you sleep too?"

"Of course."

"You won't stay awake, will you?—and look at me?"

"Hush now. It's very late."

"You *won't* stay awake, will you? After I've gone to sleep?"

"No. Of course not."

"Shall we fall asleep at the very same moment?"

"That's rather difficult, isn't it, Emil?"

"But don't you even want to try!"

Then he would drift off into sleep, his eyelids only partly closed, his pale, almost white eyelashes fluttering with the nervous intensity of unwilled sleep. At such times her heart would expand with love of him—of his awkward, almost crude innocence; and she would kiss his parted lips gently, and murmur a blessing.

"*Love, love, love. . . .*"

Though her realtor had received an offer of $275,000 for her house and the 2.3 acres that went with it Claire decided not to sell after all. Emil saw the house and exclaimed, "Oh Jesus. Is *that . . .* ?" And so she decided not to sell.

Why bother with the fuss of locating an apartment, and moving her things, and selling much of her lovely furniture? She could not even remember the reason she had wanted to move, had it had something to do with her grief over her first husband's adultery, and her wish to put all memories of him behind . . . ? But now all memories of him *were* behind.

When Emil questioned her about him—lightly, playfully, not at all jealously—Claire had to think before replying. What sort of man was he, this Falk? "Oh, I think basically—basically he was a man of limited imagination," Claire said slowly. "But very solid. Very reliable."

Emil snickered. "He wasn't worthy of you, obviously!" he said.

"He didn't exactly *know* me."

Her husband's closet, empty; and filled now, or partly filled, with Emil's clothes.

"We'll have to buy you some things," Claire said. "You seem to own only summer clothing."

"Yes, it *is* winter up here, isn't it? I'd almost forgotten what winter was."

A houndstooth English jacket, a pale orange blazer, a camel's-hair coat, fur-lined leather gloves made in Hungary, fur-lined leather boots made in Italy, a half-dozen sweaters, a dozen shirts.

A smart plaid vest. A suede suit. Trousers of various textures, various hues. A blue terry-cloth bathrobe to slip into when he was still wet from his shower.

Clowning, he went to stand in the plate-glass window of the men's shop in the Fairway Hotel, positioning himself like a manikin. He was wearing the suede suit, without a shirt. His slightly hollow hairless chest shone.

The salesman managed to laugh but Claire, unamused, spoke sharply.

Whereupon her young husband turned away at once, flushing, hurt, and fled—simply ran out the front door. Claire called after him but he didn't look back.

He was gone, that time, overnight. She stayed up until two and then decided that she would sleep, she wouldn't martyr herself for him; she made herself a rum toddy and fell asleep on her bed, beneath a quilted afghan. Where Emil found her the next morning and awoke her with a wet puppyish kiss.

He crept under the afghan, burrowing into her arms.

"Forgive, forgive. Forgive little Emil."

His breath stank, there was an odor of something dry and harsh in his hair, perhaps smoke; and the stubble on his chin chafed her sensitive breasts. But she held him, and rocked him gently, and forgave him.

There were temper tantrums, there were shouting matches. Claire had never guessed herself so easily enraged. Once she even began to strike Emil's tear-stained face, screaming at him, and he tried to catch her wrists, ducking backward in alarm. He *was* frightened of her, she saw with amusement. But how silly! . . . As if she didn't love him more than life itself.

After the quarrels there were drinking sessions, occasionally. And frequent bouts of lovemaking. And once Emil fished out of a knapsack in his closet something for them to smoke in a pipe—hashish, it was: but Claire demurred. She had read somewhere . . . No, she was afraid.

"But don't you trust me, Claire, dear?"

"It isn't that, Emil."

"Yes. But *don't* you trust me?"

"I simply don't want to. I don't want to."

"You hold yourself back from me, judging me. You're always judging. You don't *trust* me."

"Of course I trust you. I love you."

"But you hold yourself off from me, behind a glass case!"

Once, after the most protracted and childishly abusive of their quarrels—he called her a witch, she called him a male slut—they made love on the first-floor landing, gasping and clutching at each other. It was the first time Claire allowed herself to feel passion, to draw the tiny spark of pleasure up, upward, into something resembling a flame, and by the time she came to her climax she was groaning and shouting and tearing at him, her face distorted, her mouth gaping and ugly as a fish's—and still the sensation billowed onward, higher and higher, more and more violent, until she thought she would lose consciousness. *I love you, I love you, I love* . . .

Afterward, dazed, she hardly knew where she was, who this thin shuddering creature was lying on top of her, dripping sweat. Who, why . . . What had led her to . . .

She began to cry. Her body shook. Everything was naked, exposed: her soul, her brain, her nerves: she had been destroyed, she had been turned inside out: and yet she was living, still, convulsed with sobs of dismay and incredulity and gratitude.

Emil said nothing. He eased himself from her and lay for a while, holding her as she wept and murmured to him, *Love, love, I love.* . . . He held her loosely, one arm beneath her shoulders. Until it became numb. Until the position became distinctly uncomfortable. Then he eased surreptitiously away. She would have called out for him but she was too sleepy, too exhausted. Why was he abandoning her. . . . Why was it so cold. . . .

A long time later she heard, or believed she heard, someone talking. Muttering. She tried to rouse herself but her head ached. There was a person drawing near, there were footsteps, silent, she must have been lying on the floor, on the carpet, but where?—why? Someone laid a blanket atop her, tucking it under her chin.

"Sleep it off, love," came a small cool remote voice.

Afterward, Claire was intensely ashamed of her behavior: that ugly grasping maniacal passion. Her body had gone mad, that was all. And the spell of weeping. . . . She had wept and wept like a giant child though she had sensed, even at the time, in her half-conscious drunken state, her young husband's secret contempt.

She would have liked to vow to him—I will never be that way again. I will never submit the two of us to such an experience again.

She would have liked to beg him—Please forget! *Please forget!*

He hid himself from her, daydreaming. A book in his lap. A notebook opened on the table before him, his pen turning idly between his fingers. And sometimes he sat at the piano, depressing the notes so slowly that they hardly sounded.

There was sheet music in the piano bench—why didn't he play something? Her son Ted had taken lessons at one time, many years ago.

"I can't play with anyone else listening, I'd be too self-conscious," he said.

"But I *won't* listen. I'll be upstairs on the telephone."

He shrugged his shoulders indifferently. In recent weeks his face had become drained of all expression, he no longer clowned and carried on, he never teased her. When he raised his glasses to rub his eyes Claire saw that he looked drawn and tired, much older than his years. There were white crinkles about his eyes like tiny lines etched in the skin.

"You're bored" Claire said recklessly.

"Of course not," he said at once.

He adjusted his glasses and stared at her, blinking. His cheeks colored faintly as if he had been caught out in a lie.

"Of course you *are*," she said. "And it's quite natural. There isn't enough for you to do here. Wouldn't you like to continue with you theatrical work? There's an experimental theater in the city, I was reading about it in last Sunday's paper, it sounds exactly like something you would . . . But why are you staring at me like that? You *were* interested in the theater when I met you."

"Was I?"

"Well—weren' t you?"

"I never liked working with other people. In such close quarters. Subordinating myself to others' ideas. . . . You wouldn't understand," he said, yawning.

"Then what would you like to do?"

"Nothing."

"What?"

"I do what I am doing."

"Yes, but what *are* you doing?"

His pale lips stretched into a wide rapid humorless smile.

"You're too solicitous of me, love," he said softly. "I'm quite all right as I am. I'm perfectly happy. Idyllically happy. . . . I'm waiting."

"Waiting for what?" Claire asked sharply.

He shrugged his shoulders again. Even in his handsome new clothes he looked scrawny and unkempt.

"Would you like to take piano lessons again?—with a good pianist? You could audition at the conservatory."

"Too late. Too old," he said, drawling. He stretched his fingers at her. "Stiff joints."

As the months passed Emil rarely slept with Claire for an entire night: he slipped quietly away as soon as she slept, or as soon as he believed she slept. Once, startled out of a half-sleep, she asked him where he was going and he mumbled guiltily that he couldn't sleep right now—he was too rest-less. But why can't you sleep? she asked, pulling at his wrist, smiling. Come back to bed, I'll hold you, you'll be asleep in ten minutes.

He hesitated. Then said, "I'm afraid—well—your snoring keeps m awake."

"My snoring!" Claire said, deeply hurt. "But I haven't been asleep. . . . I'm sure I haven't been asleep. . . ."

He shrugged his shoulders and did not contradict her. But he did not return to bed.

Later that night Claire *did* wake herself with a hoarse loud snort. She woke, startled, to find her throat parched and painfully dry. She was grateful, then, that Emil wasn't with her.

He got into the habit of wandering about the house downstairs, late at night. She could not hear his footsteps, exactly—he was barefoot, and of course he moved lightly—but she could feel a subtle, almost imperceptible vibration in the house. He sprawled on the couch in her former husband's study and in the morning she saw the piles of books he had pulled off the shelf and had presumably leafed through. Hawthorne's *Tales, The Iliad, Great Philosophical Ideas of the Western World,* Flaubert's *Bouvard and Pécuchet:* books her husband had acquired over the years, had never read, and hadn't bothered to take along with him. Emil wrote in his notebook, tore the pages out impatiently, discarded them. But when Claire uncrumpled them she saw that he had written only nonsense scrawls, or had covered a page with doodles of misshapen people and animals. In one, a woman with gigantic breasts and a ribald leering smile strode forward, a half-dozen heads hanging from her right fist, held by their hair. In another a man had turned into a phallus—or a phallus had turned into a man—and stared upward with a melancholy expression.

Emil began to sit at the piano for hours, reading music, touching the keys listlessly. Occasionally he struck loud angry chords and the sound was astonishing: though Claire might be far away upstairs the sudden noise would alarm her, her heart would lurch in her chest. Sometimes he played rushed, uneven arpeggios, cursing when he hit a wrong note.

He became obsessed with Chopin, and bought all of Chopin's music. The preludes, the nocturnes, the mazurkas . . . even the polonaises. . . . This is the music in which death speaks secretly, Emil said, but you never know *quite* where. He leafed through the études, he tried to play, attacking the keyboard fiercely, then letting his hands fall on his knees. He couldn't play, he said petulantly, with someone always listening.

Claire returned from shopping late one afternoon to find Emil at the piano, exactly as he had been when she had left hours before. His face was pinched, his mouth puckered. Before him was a Chopin nocturne. In a flat but amused voice he told Claire that he had been trying to play the concluding cadenza, a single cadenza, for an hour and a half. Over and over he played. Each time he made a mistake he forced himself to begin again. It was discipline, it was punishment. He *would not stop* until he played the cadenza perfectly, as Chopin himself must have played it.

"Attention, love!" he said briskly. He flexed his fingers and wriggled them like a clown.

Claire opened her mouth to protest but he cut her short. And began the cadenza again, an octave above high C: his fingers moving so rapidly, so surely, that Claire stared in astonishment. The notes were struck softly, softly, and then gradually harder, building to a delicate crescendo and then almost immediately diminishing. Though Emil's head was tilted back and his eyes were half-closed the tendons in his throat were rigid and Claire could nearly feel his impatience, his terrible rage. She stood waiting helplessly. There was nothing to do but stare at those blurred fingers. He *was* an accomplished pianist, evidently. . . . Then he began a rapid, complex run down the keyboard, and still his fingers moved with an incredible rapid grace, an almost inhuman grace, and Claire held her breath, her own nails dug into her palms, and then—and then of course he struck a wrong note—

He did not scream, he did not bring his fist down on the keyboard. He merely sat there grinning. His breathing was quick and shallow, she could see his thin chest rising and falling, and very nearly feel his murderous heart.

Swaying, she brought her hand to her forehead.

"Oh please don't, please don't . . ." she whispered.

"Don't *what,* dear Claire?" Emil asked sharply.

"Don't, don't . . ."

He regarded her with silent contempt, and then laughed shrilly, like a child on the verge of hysteria.

"Don't *what?* Continue to exist?"

He glided, he slid, he plunged into dark moods. Would not sleep, would not eat. Would not leave the house. She came upon him slouched in his underclothes on her husband's old leather couch, staring out the window. How could he lie there so motionless, what was he brooding about, where was his mind . . . ? If she spoke his name he often did not respond at once. If she touched his shoulder he shivered; or, rather, his flesh shivered. Slowly, reluctantly, his spirit eased back into his body and he looked up at her, his eyes narrowed, the white lines edging them pinched and severe.

"Emil? Is something wrong? What are you thinking about?"

"What am I thinking about? . . . Nothing."

She was in danger of bursting into tears. But instead she laughed, a harsh mirthless laugh. And then, flushing deeply, went silent. "But I love you," she said in reproach.

He smiled faintly, quizzically. Love? She loved him? But what was love, where precisely was it? What did it mean?

"Well. I love you too," he said finally.

The moods lightened. He consented to be bathed by her, and to allow her to shampoo his hair. She was gentle, loving, sometimes playful. She stuck her soapy fingers in his ears and wiggled them. She tickled the crisp pale hair beneath his arms. Without his glasses his green-gray eyes were small and close-set and their gaze seemed comfortably blurred.

Now his spirits rose and he was Emil again, the old Emil. But then they sank. Hour by hour, quite perceptibly, they sank. How much can you believe in, Emil said, yawning, indicating with a dismissive wave of his arms the house, the grounds, the sky. How seriously can you take all this? Even when you own it.

Don't, Claire whispered.

She had always thought of depression as a simple pathological state, the consequence of self-indulgence and sluggishness; neither she nor her husband—her former husband—could tolerate it in others. Now, holding and rocking in her arms her stricken young lover, she wondered if it was in some way a sensitive and even intelligent response to certain . . . to certain implacable truths.

Yet she loved him, and she would nurse him back. And so it came about that his spirits *did* rise. . . . He had become interested in real estate, in property investment, and she gave him brochures to read, and articles torn out of *Fortune* and *Business Week*; she loved to answer his questions, which were often naïve, but sometimes surprisingly astute. Tax depreciation. . . . Insurance. . . . Tenants' rights. . . . Perhaps they should buy property in the Adirondacks, near Lake Placid? A summer home? A small hotel? A block of shops? A restaurant? Or a small apartment building here in the city, where Emil could oversee the manager at close quarters . . .

One night when he was especially euphoric he pulled her gently into their bed, and began to make love to her. (In recent months they had stopped making love. For some reason they had stopped. Neither mentioned it, of course, and Claire herself did not really think about it: if she began to think about it her mind simply went blank.) But then he paused. He drew away from her, half-sobbing.

"Emil . . . ?"

"I can't."

"Emil, please. It doesn't matter."

He lay very still. He rubbed the back of his forearm against his eyes roughly. "I can't, can't, *can't*," he whispered.

"It isn't important," Claire said gently.

"Isn't it!"

She could not tell—was his tone sarcastic, was it utterly serious—but when she tried to stroke his face he turned aside and swung his feet over the edge of the bed.

"Emil—"

She grasped his arm but he twisted violently away. "Don't touch!" he said.

He rose naked from the bed and ran from the room. She heard his footsteps on the stairs. . . . For a long time she lay immobile, deeply hurt. She had never been so hurt in her life. We aren't really married, she thought. He isn't really my husband.

She woke before dawn, alone. The bedclothes smelled of sweat and were badly rumpled. When she went downstairs she found him asleep on one of the sofas in the living room, still naked, breathing hoarsely through his mouth. He slept with the single-minded intensity of a small child, his hands curved toward his chest, his chin damp with saliva. So deeply was he plunged into sleep that he fairly quivered with the experience. How profound, how very profound, was the element into which he had fallen. . . . She stood above him, noting his trembling eyelids, the pallor of his hollow, hairless chest, the small pale shrunken penis in the sparse bush of pubic hair. Emil. Her lover Emil. Her husband. He appeared to be dreaming. Certainly he was dreaming. His eyeballs jerked behind his eyelids, his fingers and toes twitched. She gazed upon him calmly. She was not at all jealous. He was dreaming, and she was not jealous: perhaps her shadow fell upon his sleep and it was she of whom he dreamed.

Yet it was unfair, it was unjust, that the man she loved so deeply could slip away from her, and plunge into an element that contained him utterly and set her apart from him. What are the secrets of sleep, who can account for the isolation, the selfishness of that solitude. . . . Odd, she had never cared about her former husband's interior life. She had never thought about it at all. In fact she had often been relieved when in bed he turned from her, overtaken by drowsiness, relinquishing her to her own solitude, her own small universe of dreams. But Emil was different, she would have liked very much to know what he was experiencing, whether indeed she was queen of his sleep or whether there, in that kingdom, he did not know her at all.

She touched his shoulder. But he did not awake: he moaned softly, and tried to burrow into the cushions. His long thin bluish-white feet kicked feebly. So she relented, and went upstairs, and came back with an afghan and a pillow to slip beneath his head. Again the sight of him mesmerized her. He slept so hard, so very hard, and he *was* her husband. It crossed her mind that she could smother him, with the pillow. If she chose. She was capable of a single great act of strength and he, surprised, bereft in that other world, would have been powerless to withstand her. . . . But of course she merely slipped the pillow beneath his head, and laid the afghan carefully on top of him so that he would not catch cold. His nakedness was so frail, so vulnerable, except for the premature lines etched rather deeply into his throat, and those small white lines in his face, it was a boy's nakedness, striking in its blunt innocence.

Not long afterward she telephoned her former husband at his office. His voice rose cautiously at first but when he saw that she wanted only to talk, and to talk about casual things—mutual friends, property they had once owned together, finances, city politics—he was cordial, and seemed quite pleased to hear from her. Claire knew that he had received a certain nasty letter from their son because a carbon copy of the letter had been sent to her, in the same envelope with a very nasty letter to *her*. She supposed that her husband had received a carbon copy of her letter; and since both letters questioned their respective characters, what poor furious Ted called their "moral degeneracy," Claire saw no reason to mention them, nor did her husband.

And how is—? her husband asked.

Lovely. Just lovely, Claire said. And you—?

Lovely, he said.

They were silent for a long moment. Then Claire's former husband told her of a new restaurant downtown that *the two of you* might check out sometime: it was overpriced, of course, but charming, with an impressive wine list.

We'll do that, Claire said, delighted.

*   *   *

She had wanted to ask him . . . she had wanted to ask . . .

Well, what *is* marriage and how does one know when one is married? What *is* love, precisley? The questions were naïve and embarrassing, and yet they must be asked. Though Claire herself hadn't the courage.

She *hadn't* the courage, though she was over fifty years old and had lived, had lived, had lived forever.

Then the weather changed, and she and Emil flew to San Francisco for a marvelous two-week vacation—a second honeymoon, of a sort—and there acquired several fascinating jade figures, and looked up old friends of Claire's who were delighted to see them, not at all disapproving of the marriage as Claire had halfway feared. ("But you look radiant, Claire!" they said. "And Emil is so charming—and so deep, so obviously deep. You make a very attractive couple.") And when they returned, the house painters had finished with both the downstairs and upstairs rooms and everything looked lovely, clean and white and blank and new and lovely, and it would be a challenge, they both said, to acquire the right kind of art for the walls. . . . Claire spent much of her time shopping, and at her volunteer organizations; Emil joined an avant-garde theater group in the city. Sometimes they met for a drink downtown, at the Fairway, but often they didn't see each other until dinner, which was eaten late—never before eight o'clock. And there were times, of course, when Emil had rehearsals and wasn't back until one or two in the morning, and Claire, tired from her own activities, did not wait up for him.

It was a new season. A new autumn. Claire was elected first vice-president of the Friends of the Symphony. Emil's theater was to present a play by Lorca, the first of November. When his friends brought him home, when Claire came downstairs to join them for a drink, she saw the surprised, half-reluctant admiration in their faces: for of course they all gossiped about her, they speculated freely about Emil's "older" wife. But she had never looked more regal, more beautiful. Her skin bloomed darkly, her hair was now tinted a rich lustrous brown-black, fashioned to rise from her head in a winglike manner, exposing the prominent widow's peak She wore unusual clothes: black trousers, a coarse-knit white sweater; many-layered muslin skirts in the latest style; simple wrap-around housedresses from Saks. She said little, and smiled little. Emil came at once to stand beside her. He was obviously very proud of her. When he introduced her to his friends she shook hands like a man, and fixed her severe dark gaze upon them one by one, and did not allow herself to be too easily won over. For she knew, she knew very well, that young people like these did not value easy conquests.

Sometimes, in the morning, Emil would stroll casually into her dressing room, toweling his hair, or wiping his glasses with a tissue, and he would say, very casually, that he had liked the outfit she'd worn the night before—was it new?—he didn't remember having seen it before. Or he would say with a droll twist of his mouth that one of his friends had fallen in love with her—had begged to be invited back sometime, maybe to dinner—what did Claire think? Yes? No? Occasionally he apologized for their having stayed so late, and having made so much noise. But Claire prudently did not comment. She would *not* comment.

The important thing was—he was busy, he was absorbed in his new life, he was happy. When he forbade her to see the play she was disappointed but did not persist. Your presence in the audience would make me self-conscious, he said. He forbade her also to read any reviews of the opening. She promised that she would not, but sought them out nonetheless in a nearby library: only one review, hardly more than a paragraph, mildly enthusiastic, complimenting the cast on their energy and zeal, and the set designer for his imagination. The names of several actors were mentioned but Emil's was not among them.

After the play's two-week run came to an end Emil often stayed out late, and quite frequently his friends brought him home very early in the morning. Claire came to detest a short burly-chested youth with red curly hair and a thick red beard, whose laughter was always dissolving into coughing fits. He was blatant, he knew himself good-looking, and very young—much younger than Emil. And another creature: tall and thin and delicate-boned as Emil, with a whispery, rather mocking voice, and a bad limp. And there were girls, women, interchangeable, always uncomfortably intense in Claire's presence: to hear them talk they cared about nothing except their "careers," their "work." Claire refrained from questioning them about their plans, their exact plans, for the future. Nor did she comment dryly that so much partying, so much alcohol and marijuana and exhaustion, would hardly help.

But Emil was happy with them, or at any rate diverted from his spells of melancholy. She was not going to judge him, she had come to love him too much, to exalt in him . . . in his mere being, his existence, as one might exalt in the fact of a work of art, or a superbly proportioned animal, or a comely child. She hardly thought of him as her husband. Husband—what did that mean? Its meaning was parochial, claustrophobic. He's like a child of my own, a second son—yet far more interesting than any child of my own, she thought with a curious satisfaction.

And anyway one no longer wanted a *husband,* in the old sense. All that was dead, finished.

In mid-December Emil announced his birthday. It was that day, that very day. A small group of his closest friends, his favorite people, were coming that evening to help him celebrate, and he hoped Claire would not mind. They had been somewhat out of touch that week because of their conflicting schedules: for the first time in months Claire had had to attend a dinner, a fund-raising dinner for a local congressional candidate, and she hadn't returned home until well after midnight, and Emil mentioned the fact once or twice, always with a somewhat reproachful air. So they had been out of communication. It was not *his* fault.

"Your birthday . . . ?" Claire said, peering at him over her reading glasses.

"My thirty-fifth. What's wrong? Why stare at me like that? It's rude, it's eccentric. . . . Don't I deserve an occasional birthday, like the rest of you?"

"Your thirty-fifth . . . ?"

"Some of us age quickly," he said with a cheerful smile.

Somehow Claire had known beforehand that the party would be disastrous, and yet she did not forbid it; she felt too weak, too absurdly wounded, to protest. And then Emil did not quarrel fairly: he launched into one of his theatrical tantrums, or delivered a silly insulting speech at the top of his lungs, or threw things—pillows, vases, articles of clothing—onto the floor; or he went utterly cold, utterly silent, and regarded her with a pristine contempt she found terrifying.

Her heart ached, at such times. It was not farfetched to say that her very heart ached in her chest, between her tight constraining ribs. The real, the organic, the pounding heart and not a mere word, not a metaphor. . . . She grew short of breath, her body flushed with an obscure unspeakable shame.

She would stay away from the party. Would go to bed early. No: she would hurry out to the hairdresser's, and perhaps buy herself a new dress, something dramatic, stark, striking. So that he would gaze upon her with love and pride. But no. Perhaps it would be a better strategy to stay away from the party, and deny him the pleasure of seeing her. . . . Where is Claire, his friends would inquire, why is she keeping herself from us? Is she angry? Is she angry with you?

Even when the first guests began to arrive she could not make up her mind. She regarded herself in the mirror critically. She *was* looking rather tired, and there hadn't been a slot for her at the hairdresser's and the shortness of breath stayed with her, vexing as an insect buzzing close to her face, "Come on, come on, get a move on, horsey," Emil said gaily, tossing gowns from her closet onto the bed, selecting a pair of highheeled slippers, but she could not respond to his drollery and in the end sent him away. He made her a double Cuban Manhattan, one of their favorite drinks last summer, and brought it to her as a peace offering. She accepted it but decided against going downstairs. She *would* keep herself away, to punish him.

The party was extraordinarily noisy, and lasted until nearly four in the morning. Claire slept, and woke, and slept again; and still the sounds of gaiety continued.

And then it was silent, and Emil was pawing at her. He half-fell onto the bed, giggling. Before she could push him away he had torn her nightgown and turned her over roughly onto her stomach.

She smell alcohol on his breath but he did not seem to be
drunk: he was too euphoric, too manic. She shouted for him
to stop—what on earth was he doing to her—his lean hard
thighs gripping her hips, his fingers clenched in her hair. His
words were incoherent, interrupted by giggles and brief spasms
of coughing. "You like it! You know you like it! Hey, lady, you
know you like it! Lovely big soft marvelous thing! A little whale—
one of those little ones! They're so lovely! Oh, I love them! One
of those—what-do-you-call-them—walruses—a female walrus
on the beach! Oh, a cow! A walrus-cow! You know you love it,
don't you!"

She forced him off—she *was* stronger than he when it was
necessary—and struck him in the face. At once he shrank back.
He half-fell out of bed. Holding his mouth in both hands he
began to whimper.

"You hurt me. Oh, Claire, you *hurt* me. My lip is cut on the
inside, I can taste the . . ."

She pushed at him again and shouted at him to leave her alone,
to get out of the room. But still he crouched there, naked, his
chest hollow, his shoulders badly hunched. She saw two absurd
tears running down his cheeks.

"Don't be ridiculous. Go and rinse your mouth, you aren't
hurt, you're drunk and disgusting, you've been taking drugs,
haven't you, though you know I've forbidden it in this house!
You and your disgusting friends! Those preening exhibitionistic
boys, those ugly slutty little girls, drinking my liquor and injur-
ing my furniture and fouling my lovely house—"

"You don't love me," Emil whimpered. "You forgot my
birthday."

"Coming up here half-crazy—saying those unforgivable things—You *aren't* hurt, go and rinse the blood away! Are you too drunk to move?"

"I was born thirty-five years ago and if you loved me you would celebrate that fact," Emil said. "I *was* born thirty-five years ago. . . . Just like anyone else. . . . If you doubt me I have papers, I can prove it. . . . I grew up in a real place, we were all perfectly normal Americans, I have snapshots, I have documents, I want only to be cherished, a real wife is supposed to love her husband more than life itself, I *was* born in the Midwest just like anyone else. . . . In Topeka, Kansas. It's still there, you can look it up! Look it up on the map! Oh, Claire, I hate the taste of blood, it *frightens* me so . . ."

"I never want those hideous people in this house again, do you understand?"

"Oh, Claire, please—"

"Do you understand? Do you?"

"Yes, Claire, but please don't be angry, don't strike me again—"

She moved to take hold of him, the situation after all was more ludicrous, more silly, than serious, she would have to be the one to make the first gesture of reconciliation; but he misinterpreted her action and scrambled from the bed, as if deeply alarmed.

He backed away, still holding his mouth. Then grabbed at something to hide his nakedness—her ivory negligee, it was, lying where she had thrown it on a chair. "Don't—don't hurt me—don't be angry! I'll sleep somewhere else! I don't mind! I'm used to it! I don't mind!"

She could not determine if he was serious, or clowning—he was such a superb mimic, after all—but she made a gesture of dismissal and lay back, exhausted, in bed. Let him go, let him go, he was partly out of his mind, perhaps he was hallucinating, perhaps he saw someone else where she lay, some massive ugly creature that might actually hurt him.

He retreated. She tried to smooth down the covers, tried to slip back into sleep. But it was impossible of course. She kept thinking of him turning her so violently over, and riding her hips, her buttocks, his wild fists in her hair. How *dare* he approach her like that. . . . And what had he called her? A cow? A walrus-cow?

It struck her as amusing. She laughed, and then began to sob.

She wiped her face on the pillow. Well, it did no good to cry, she had not even bothered to cry that other time. . . . Something to do with a telephone conversation. A man locked in a room, on the telephone. Or had he been talking to himself. His words were inaudible she had only been able to register the tone of his voice, they had put the oxygen mask on, in those days no one attempted natural childbirth, something astonishing was forcing itself out between her legs but it seemed to have gotten up into her chest, her throat, as well, and into her brain, so that she was being split in two. . . . No, that was another time. That was not this time.

What time was it?—ah, almost five o'clock!

A very dark rainy December morning.

She knew she must go to him, to her wounded young lover, but at first the effort was too much, She sat up, she moved her swollen legs beneath the covers, she pressed her hand against her chest to still her heart. Carefully. Carefully.

He would catch cold, downstairs. Without a blanket. Alone. Without her.

She would take something to cover him. . . . But halfway to the door of her room she forgot, and it would be a great deal of trouble to blunder to the linen closet in the dark, she couldn't find the light switch, the best thing to do would be to bring him back upstairs to her warm bed, if they both moved slowly enough the trip back up the stairs would not defeat them, perhaps they could lean on each other, he would forgive her for her bad temper, he would sob into her shoulder. . . .

She found him in her husband's study, on the leather couch, sitting slumped in the dark. By the window. Huddled close to the window though it must have been rather chilly there. She approached him slowly, not wanting to frighten him. He was hunched in her white robe, he had managed to thrust both arms through it though of course he hadn't taken the time to tie the sash. . . . She hoped he had not ripped the material, it was so delicate, edged with genuine lace, so very costly, so very becoming against her pale skin and dark eyes and hair. . . .

"Emil?"

For a moment it looked as if someone were outside the window, looking in. But of course it was only Emil's glimmering reflection.

"You *are* awake, aren't you? Emil? . . . Why are you behaving like this, why are you doing this to me?"

She approached him. She was barefoot herself, and shivering. Her discomfort translated itself into anger but she could not remember why she was angry, what logic there was to it, what justice. Though she knew there *was* justice.

He sat immobile, the negligee open to show his chest, his small protruding stomach, the insulting tangle of hair between his legs, his legs themselves, covered with a very pale down.

Slack and indifferent and arrogant. Almost imperceptibly his head turned toward her. She thought, Without his glasses he can't even see me. . . .

"Why did you marry me if you don't love me, if you're going to behave like this?" she said.

Her voice was surprisingly harsh.

He looked toward her, evidently he saw her, but did not answer at first. Then he said, his lips barely moving, "You know."

She stood near him, but did not come close enough to touch him.

She hoped he would not hear her painful rasping breath.

"Why did you marry me, if you don't love me? Don't you love me?" She had not meant to beg—but there it was, in her voice.

A faint light from outside touched his face, which was a jester's face, narrow and shadowed and grave and unsmiling.

"Why do you treat me like this?" she asked.

"You know," he said in a neutral voice.

"But—I *don't*—"

"You know who I am," he said.

She dared come no nearer. Yet she could not turn away, she could not retreat. His hollow inflectionless voice was not one she had heard before but then he was so good at mimicry, at playacting. . . .

"I don't know," she said faintly.

"Yes, you do. You know."

They stared at each other for several minutes in silence. Then Emil rose unsteadily to his feet, the long ivory-pale gown falling gracefully below his knees; with a dignity that might have been ludicrous at another time he tied the sash, brushed his hair back from his face with a single rough gesture. Then came to her. He was very tall; because she was barefoot she had to look sharply up at him, it was kind of him to take her hand, and to hold it so firmly. The quarrel was over, why had they ever quarreled? She could not remember. She loved him so much. . . .

He led her into the living room, where a few lights were burning after all. Evidently the party was still in session . . . ? A number of guests remained. Odd, she had not noticed them, though they were making only a minimal attempt to be quiet.

"But Emil—" she protested.

"Hush," he said.

"But I thought we were alone—Can't we be alone—"

He led her into the room, and raised her hand to his lips in a ceremonial gesture. Everyone turned to them. Conversations were interrupted, there was an immediate and rather flattering silence. Claire, embarrassed at the eyes that were fixed upon her, half-saw that the room was larger than she remembered, and that more guests had crowded into it than she would have thought possible. In the darkness at the periphery of the room uncertain shapes moved, men or women Claire could not tell, and one figure with a pronounced limp stepped forward, and then paused, as if abashed by the sudden gravity of the situation.

"Queen of the Night," Emil said, kissing her hand again, and this time making a clownish lustful sucking noise with his lips, "I want you to meet my friends."

THE REVENGE OF THE FOOT, 1970

Is the foot male or female? they were asking. One of them had smuggled a human foot out of the medical school dissection lab and they were tossing it about in the kitchen amid rowdy male laughter and incredulous female squeals. "Look sharp, Yank! You bugger, look sharp!" The ox-faced red-haired Prewitt from North Bay tossed the foot, a frosty-luminous blur, an object at which you could not not look, at Wingate, or Wheelhell, whatever his name, the draft-defector from Minneapolis, who dumbly fumbled it, cursed and snatched it up from the linoleum floor where it had fallen heavy and solid as a foot made of concrete—the foot was frozen, they'd been keeping it in the freezer of the squat little Pullman refrigerator in the corner—and in turn tossed it at another of his suite-mates. And so an impromptu game of touch football started, the big, beefy boys stampeding and crashing through the rooms, and Elinor who had been brought uninvited to this party celebrating the end of final exams at the medical school, Elinor who knew not a single one of the five or six medical students who lived in this pigsty fifth-floor flat on Halifax Street, blinked in amazement and may even have laughed. A foot? A human *foot*? She had not expected such a diversion on this desperate Saturday night. She was holding a lukewarm Molson's in her hand which she did not recall having been given nor did she recall having known where her friends, casual acquaintances from the Arts College graduate school, in truth virtual strangers to her, were taking her, gathered up like a squirmy, willing fish in a wide net. Every weekend there were parties, often midweek there were parties, celebrating the completion of something or a farewell or an arrival or a birthday or a loss so terrible it could not be endured without beer and deafening rock music and the close, sweaty companionship of others, it was an era in which you began in a place known to you and progressed joltingly through the night, on foot or in cars driven by strangers, to places not known to you; wild improbable places that afterward, years afterward, you would remember with the eerie clarity of a waking dream as if these places had been permanent after all in a way that their inhabitants, including you, were not.

Elinor, unlike the other female guests at the party, several of whom had gone ghastly white at the sight of the flying foot, stared fascinated as the burly beer-flushed boys (you would have to call them *boys,* despite their size, not *men*) stumbled, careened, collided and crashed about the living room tossing the foot to one another amid shouts of "You sod!" and "Bugger!" A tubular floor lamp was violently overturned, empty beer bottles clattered rolling across the carpet which was so filthy it appeared, to the eye's cursory glance, to be an earthen floor. The air was a bluish haze of cigarette smoke and there was a trenchant odor of spilled beer and stopped-up drains and food (pizza crusts, the remains of Chinese take-out, Kentucky Fried Chicken bones and gristle) and urine. It was as if, celebrating the end of exams, the medical students were determined to wreck their living quarters. They were healthy, gregarious, not only Prewitt but the others muscular and randy as young oxen—their blunt names Nailles, Steadman, McMaster, Schnorr, Wingate or Wheelhell. "Pass!" they screamed at one another. "Score!" The foot, flying, looked too small to be significant and it was wrongly, awkwardly shaped.

Elinor, from a doorway, blinked through the haze of cigarette smoke and the frantic tilting lights thinking if she'd been in love with one of these prize masculine specimens she would be eager and hopeful and vulnerable to hurt, she would be obsessed with her appearance, my God how she would smile and smile, how she would *try*. The effort of making another love you in proportion to your love for him.

Yes it was hell. As much as, in these secular times, one might guess of hell.

But Elinor was in love with no one in this pigsty-festive place. If there was a drunken happiness here, a frenzy of animal spirits and sexual innuendo, she, a stranger, knew nothing of it and would know nothing for that was the point of having come here tonight. Elinor was in love with someone else.

Recovering from love, with someone else. Yes?

The other female guests, several of whom were surely in love with Prewitt, Nailles, Steadman, McMaster, Schnorr, Wingate or Wheelhell had recovered sufficiently from their shock at the sight of the foot to be crying now with flirty reproach, "Oh, how can you!" and "Aren't you awful!" and "What kind of doctors are you going to be?" and "What if that foot belonged to somebody you loved?"—this last shrill question made the boys laugh so hard tears ran hotly down their flushed cheeks and Prewitt with his coarse cherubic face took up the theme in a grieving falsetto, "Oh! what if this foot is somebody you love, you insensitive sods?" He waved the foot above his head as if he were about to fling it out boomerang-style. Gales of helpless laughter swept before him. "What if this frigging foot is *somebody you love?*"

Soon the game, which required much physical exertion, bored the boys, the thawing foot was tossed into the kitchen sink and seemingly forgotten except for Elinor who slipped into the kitchen to observe it while out of amplified speakers in the living room Mick Jagger was mock-crooning *time is on my side.* The Stones' percussion was so loud, so vibrating as to be, to Elinor, inaudible. She was drunk enough to think it likely that, if you're encased in deafening noise, you are also invisible. With a trembling forefinger shyly reaching out to touch the foot—of course, it was clammy-cold.

This was spring 1970, the Americans were still fighting their bloody war in Vietnam. Cast the blame there?

Was the foot male or female? Elinor thought it crucial to know yet could not determine from examining it. Probably female for it was of only moderate size looking so wan and battered-humble there amid bottle caps and Styrofoam food containers in the greasy sink. An adult foot, in any case. Long, narrow, bony and waxy-white. Where it had been skillfully sawed off from its ankle there was exposed white bone and cartilage and a frosty glittering like mica. Though the foot was longer than her own (which took a size seven shoe) by as much as two inches it did not appear to be much wider. Each of the big toes curved strangely inward and was disproportionately large in relation to the other toes; the nails of the big toes were thick as horn and yellowish while those of the other toes were small, thin, a transparent bluish color. Where veins and arteries had been there were now flattened wormlike striations of the hue of bruises, for of course all blood, thus the pressure of blood, had drained out of the foot.

Whose foot had it been, and when had she died, and where, and how, and why, now, out of all places in the universe, was the foot *here*. And why, what could it mean, what coincidence, what design, on this gusty spring night cold as winter, was Elinor *here*.

She would learn a few days later that this notorious party had lasted through the night and that more and more guests, invited and uninvited, had continued to arrive, pounding up the flights of stairs eager to celebrate, some bringing six-packs of beer, ale, some bringing dope, drinking and smoking and passing out and late Sunday morning rousing themselves to continue the celebration with a fresh influx of guests hauling a case of wine from somebody's family vineyard in Ontario but by then Elinor was long vanished, slipped away unnoticed shortly after midnight.

Descending the dimlit stairs, heart pounding with risk, daring, rectitude. She had stolen the foot out of the sink, by stealth wrapping it in double folds of aluminum foil still warm and smelling of the Kentucky Fried Chicken it had covered, with obsessive neatness then she'd wrapped the object in some pages of the *Globe and Mail* and slipped it into her shoulder bag, and was gone without saying goodbye even to the bushy-bearded young man from her Old English seminar who had brought her here.

Outside in the deserted street a bone-freezing drizzle blew upward in her face but Elinor told herself sternly that climate is a state of mind.

She told herself, I am immune from harm, now. Her foot is my talisman.

And she was instantly sober—that was the first good thing. The drunken vertigo was left behind in the medical students' flat with the smells, the cigarette smoke, the *boys*.

She began walking east on Halifax without hesitation. She did not know that she would walk to his house until she began, and once started in that direction she could not turn back. Her own apartment which she shared with two other girls was in the opposite direction but she was not thinking of that now. However many miles to her lover's house on Sullivan Street she would walk them, would not have taken a taxi even if she could afford a taxi, Elinor was the kind of person, rural-reared, frugal, who resisted even taking a bus if her destination was within reasonable walking distance and to such persons most destinations are within reasonable walking distance in the city. She would make her way alert and vigilant at this late, dangerous Saturday hour and in this scruffy "mixed" neighborhood south of the university hospital and the discipline would clear her thoughts. *I am immune, who can hurt me?*—walking quickly avoiding both curbs and doorways, darting like a furtive wild creature against the bright-lit trafficked intersections of Dominion and Simcoe, of course she was safe. The foot wrapped in aluminum foil and newspaper in her bag, the foot entrusted to her out of all the universe. For there was no one else.

If Elinor's family knew where Elinor was alone at this rowdy hour, in this city of which they disapproved, what desperation coursing through her veins, yes but they did not know and could not have guessed for Elinor was, like all the girls of her generation whom she'd known in college and now graduate school, determined to shield her family from hurtful knowledge of her personal life. A daughterly obligation. A task that brought anxiety but also a sense of vindication, high worth. Elinor was from a farming community west of Simcoe, Ontario, twenty-two years old completing her first year of graduate school at the University of Toronto in preparation for a teaching career in English literature even as her life was crumbling from within like an aged stone wall in an upheaval of the earth—except, and this was the crucial thing, this the weight in her bag thumping rhythmically against her thigh asserted as she made her way to 71 Sullivan Street, it was not crumbling so long as she could hold it together. And she was not pregnant.

Thinking, From now on I am immune.

How do I know?—I know.

It was 12:48 A.M. when Elinor turned up Sullivan Street. Until this time she'd been invisible but now nearing her lover's house, which was a modestly restored brownstone in a row of part-derelict part-restored brownstones of the 1920s, she felt herself, like a materializing Polaroid image, becoming visible. A petite, slender young woman with olive-sallow skin, round wire-rimmed glasses and a defiant schoolgirl look, her hair a pale straight blond spilling shimmering over the shoulders of her khaki jacket. So plain, she believed, as to appear in the eyes of willful perverse men like her lover, beautiful. She saw herself through others' eyes exclusively and through her lover's critical eyes obsessively, for what other vision of Elinor mattered?—none, really. Elinor knew herself thoroughly, she believed, and she was proud of her intelligence and her acuity and her accomplishments thus far though they were entirely academic accomplishments, she was secretly rather vain: yet no other vision except her lover's mattered to her, really. If he ceased loving her she would die because she would not wish to live, so simple was it.

Which was why, approaching 71 Sullivan Street, seeing the upstairs bedroom window lit, the downstairs darkened, she began to be frightened. He had said his wife was away for the weekend—frequently, these past several months, his wife was often "away"—but Elinor had not spoken with him for a day and a half and perhaps the wife had returned unexpected? Perhaps her lover had summoned his wife back?

You did not know. You knew, you guessed, but you did not know, really. And better not to know.

Nonetheless Elinor could not turn back. Clutching the bag, her eyes stark in her pale face, daring to ring the doorbell *as if she had the right*. Panting as if she'd run the many blocks from Halifax to this spot composing her terrified features into a smile, for you must always smile, you must *try*. Not thinking, Why am I here, what am I doing to myself, and to this man? Yet she could not turn back, this was the sole certainty.

Elinor heard footsteps on the stairs inside. She knew those interior stairs, she'd ascended them many times. And now a light came on illuminating from within the blind of the front window, and another light above the door, and cautiously at first the man who was her lover unlocked the door, unbolted and opened it and the shock of seeing her showed in his face yet in the next instant of course he was smiling, gripping her shoulders, passionate, half-angry, "Elinor, thank God!—where have you been, I've been calling and calling you—" and he pulled her inside and firmly the door was locked and bolted again behind her and they were holding each other, and kissing eager and blind as always at such moments, and Elinor felt her antagonism against this man melt away as if it had never been, if indeed it had been antagonism and not instead apprehension and wonder and vertigo for *after all he did love her, what further proof*? It was that simple.

The wife must be gone away, then. He'd been about to go to bed, upstairs watching television, sipping red wine. Yes and lonely for her, and a little hurt, and angry, at Elinor's behavior.

Yes but I can't help myself, I am in love, no don't blame me, I am innocent, look into my eyes. As I look into yours.

The wife absent, and Elinor would not think of her, would refuse.

Nor even to inquire, hesitantly, are they separated?––for the marriage, according to oblique remarks made by Elinor's lover, and by stray rumors that had come to Elinor's attention, was not a happy one.

Elinor had known the man who was her lover, who had been, her first semester in graduate school, her linguistics professor, since the previous September and they had been intimate for all but five weeks of that period of time and Elinor believed she had come to know the man thoroughly and at the same time she believed she did not know him, of course she did not know him, nor could she trust him. Nor he, her. Yet when they were alone together, clutching at each other, and kissing—how easy, how unambiguous, like the sun shining out of an empty blue sky.

How do I know?—I know.

The shabby book bag Elinor toted everywhere with her—her lover took no more notice of it than he ever did as, half-sobbing in his embrace, she lowered it to the floor.

They would make love of course. He was not angry with her for frightening him with her willful refusal to see him these past several days and she was not angry with him for whatever reason, she could not now in fact remember, she'd believed herself to be

angry with him and had so wanted to die. But not now. They
were trembling, shivering with the need to make love. To be
naked together, upstairs in his bed, which was a bed he shared
with another woman as he shared years of intimacy with this
other woman but of that you don't think, you refuse to think.
For why otherwise had Elinor S. come to 71 Sullivan Street at
this hour of a Sunday morning, what other purpose?

The wife *was* gone—obviously.

It was an era in which wives were the enemy. You were the
predator prowling for love yet you were also the prey. You pursued the man, and then you waited.

Elinor would use the downstairs bathroom as often she had
in the past while her lover hurried upstairs. (For what purpose?
To use a bathroom there? To hastily tidy up the bedroom? The
first time he had brought Elinor here, the two of them reeling
with desire, breathless and excited as if they were walking a high
tightrope, Elinor had happened to notice through the bedroom
doorway a disheveled bed and clothes including a woman's blouse
lying across a bureau but when she'd returned a few minutes later
the room had been chastely tidied up. All signs of the absent
wife missing.) So Elinor went to use the bathroom noting that
her face was drained of blood, the eyes sallow and triumphant.
Her hands, her ridiculous hands, were shaking badly. She used
the toilet urinating with difficulty and afterward wiped herself,
daring to glance squinting at the crotch of her panties. Which
portion of a female's clothing could betray so much?

For eleven days the previous month Elinor had tortured herself
with the unthinkable *Am I pregnant?* but the terror had proved
false. Rather, the terror had been real enough, but its cause
false. For at last, grudgingly, achingly, she'd begun to bleed. The

profound weeping relief and the gut-sick sensation. *Is this happiness, now? am I saved, now?* she'd been too ashamed to share with the man who had—who had *not*—impregnated her. For what after all could Elinor have said that would not strike the masculine ear as crude, sad, embarrassing, ridiculous?

That was the horror, Elinor suddenly realized: the foot tossed about by the medical students, the thawing-meat foot, was ridiculous.

On her way from the bathroom Elinor slipped into the darkened kitchen. She'd been in this kitchen only once or twice, to make coffee and to hunt up food, they'd both been ravenous once, several hours of lovemaking. Quietly she opened the freezer door of the refrigerator and saw to her relief that there was space enough: her lover's wife was a conscientious homemaker however unhappy or neurotic or otherwise disappointing as a wife, she had not let frost accumulate in the freezer nor were frozen items haphazardly stored. Blue plastic ice cube trays in a row on the top shelf; two-thirds of a loaf of bread from the Whole Earth Co-Op, to which Elinor also belonged; a quart of marshmallow-chocolate ice cream; a package of Bird's Eye frozen halibut and a package of chicken breasts. Elinor removed the foot from her bag, calmly unwrapped the newspaper pages and discarded them in a wastebasket beneath the sink, then pushed the aluminum-wrapped foot into the freezer snugly between the loaf of bread and the halibut, a dull-glimmering object no larger than the loaf of bread and inconspicuous there in the freezer where her lover's wife would discover it within a week.

When she hurried to her lover he was on the stairs waiting for her. He'd removed his shirt and his chest, leanly muscular beneath matted frizzy graying-brown hairs, gleamed with perspiration. Elinor lifted her arms to him. His eyes shone with greedy love for her or what in those years Elinor believed to be love. Breathless she embraced him, her cheeks were damp with tears as he drew her swiftly upstairs and into the bedroom she'd memorized without knowing she had done so, one of those places, those settings, stark and vividly lit, that would outlive their inhabitants. "Why are you trembling so, Elinor?" he whispered. "You know I would never hurt you, darling. You know I love you, don't you?" Elinor pressed herself into the man's arms, his body was warm and enveloping and protecting and she held him as if for very life, "I know, I know," she whispered, tears blinding her vision so the bedside lamp seemed to melt, blur, and expand like flame, "—oh God, I know."

THE DOLL

Many years ago a little girl was given, for her fourth birthday, an antique dolls' house of unusual beauty and complexity, and size: for it seemed large enough, almost, for a child to crawl into.

The dolls' house was said to have been built nearly one hundred years before, by a distant relative of the little girl's mother. It had come down through the family and was still in excellent condition: with a steep gabled roof, many tall, narrow windows fitted with real glass, dark green shutters that closed over, three fireplaces made of stone, mock lightning rods, mock shingle-board siding (white), a veranda that nearly circled the house, stained glass at the front door and at the first floor landing, and even a cupola whose tiny roof lifted miraculously away. In the master bedroom there was a canopied bed with white organdy flounces and ruffles; there were tiny window boxes beneath most of the windows; the furniture—all of it Victorian, of course—was uniformly exquisite, having been made with the most fastidious care and affection. The lampshades were adorned with tiny gold fringes, there was a marvelous old tub with claw feet, and nearly every room had a chandelier. When she first saw the dolls' house on the morning of her fourth birthday the little girl was so astonished she could not speak: for the present was unexpected, and uncannily "real." It was to be the great present, and the great memory, of her childhood.

Florence had several dolls which were too large to fit into the house, since they were average-size dolls, but she brought them close to the house, facing its open side, and played with them there. She fussed over them, and whispered to them, and scolded them, and invented little conversations between them. One day, out of nowhere, came the name *Bartholomew*—the name of the family who owned the dolls' house. Where did you get that name from, her parents asked, and Florence replied that those were the people who lived in the house. Yes, but where did the name come from? they asked.

The child, puzzled and a little irritated, pointed mutely at the dolls.

One was a girl-doll with shiny blond ringlets and blue eyes that were thickly lashed, and almost too round; another was a red-haired freckled boy in denim coveralls and a plaid shirt. It was obvious that they were sister and brother. Another was a woman-doll, perhaps a mother, who had bright red lips and who wore a hat cleverly made of soft gray-and-white feathers. There was even a baby-doll, made of the softest rubber, hairless and expressionless, and oversized in relationship to the other dolls; and a spaniel, about nine inches in length, with big brown eyes and a quizzical upturned tail. Sometimes one doll was Florence's favorite, sometimes another. There were days when she preferred the blond girl, whose eyes rolled in her head, and whose complexion was a lovely pale peach. There were days when the mischievous red-haired boy was obviously her favorite. Sometimes she banished all the human dolls and played with the spaniel, who was small enough to fit into most of the rooms of the dolls' house.

Occasionally Florence undressed the human dolls, and washed them with a tiny sponge. How strange they were, without their clothes . . . ! Their bodies were poreless and smooth and blank, there was nothing secret or nasty about them, no crevices for dirt to hide in, no trouble at all. Their faces were unperturbable, as always. Calm wise fearless staring eyes that no harsh words or slaps could disturb. But Florence loved her dolls very much, and rarely felt the need to punish them.

Her treasure was, of course, the dolls' house with its steep Victorian roof and its gingerbread trim and its many windows and that marvelous veranda, upon which little wooden rocking chairs, each equipped with its own tiny cushion, were set. Visitors—friends of her parents or little girls her own age—were always astonished when they first saw it. They said: Oh, isn't it beautiful! They said: Why, it's almost the size of a real house, isn't it?—though of course it wasn't, it was only a dolls' house, a little less than thirty-six inches high.

Nearly four decades later while driving along East Fainlight Avenue to Lancaster, Pennsylvania, a city she had never before visited, and about which she knew nothing, Florence Parr was astonished to see, set back from the avenue, at the top of a stately elm-shaded knoll, her old dolls' house—that is, the replica of it. The house. The house itself.

She was so astonished that for the passage of some seconds she could not think what to do. Her most immediate reaction was to brake her car—for she was a careful, even fastidious driver;

at the first sign of confusion or difficulty she always brought her car to a stop.

A broad handsome elm- and plane tree-lined avenue, in a charming city, altogether new to her. Late April: a fragrant, even rather giddy spring, after a bitter and protracted winter. The very air trembled, rich with warmth and color. The estates in this part of the city were as impressive, as stately, as any she had ever seen: the houses were really mansions, boasting of wealth, their sloping, elegant lawns protected from the street by brick walls, or wrought-iron fences, or thick evergreen hedges. Everywhere there were azaleas, that most gorgeous of spring flowers—scarlet and white and yellow and flamey-orange, almost blindingly beautiful. There were newly cultivated beds of tulips, primarily red; and exquisite apple blossoms, and cherry blossoms, and flowering trees Florence recognized but could not identify by name. *Her* house was surrounded by an old-fashioned wrought-iron fence, and in its enormous front yard were red and yellow tulips that had pushed their way through patches of weedy grass.

She found herself on the sidewalk, at the front gate. Like the unwieldy gate that was designed to close over the driveway, this gate was not only open but its bottom spikes had dug into the ground; it had not been closed for some time and could probably not be dislodged. Someone had put up a hand-lettered sign in black, not long ago: 1377 EAST FAINLIGHT. But no name, no family name. Florence stood staring up at the house, her heart beating rapidly. She could not quite believe what she was seeing. Yes, there it was, of course—yet it *could* not be, not in such detail.

The antique dolls' house. *Hers.* After so many years. There was the steep gabled roof, in what appeared to be slate; the old lightning rods; the absurd little cupola that was so charming;

the veranda; the white shingleboard siding (which was rather weathered and gray in the bright spring sunshine); most of all, most striking, the eight tall, narrow windows, four to each floor, with their dark shutters. Florence could not determine if the shutters were painted a very dark green, or black. What color had they been on the dolls' house . . . She saw that the gingerbread trim was badly rotted.

The first wave of excitement, almost of vertigo, that had over-taken her in the car had passed; but she felt, still, an unpleasant sense of urgency. Her old dolls' house. Here on East Fainlight Avenue in Lancaster, Pennsylvania. Glimpsed so suddenly, on this warm spring morning. And what did it mean . . . ? Obviously there was an explanation. Her distant uncle, who had built the house for his daughter, had simply copied this house, or another just like it; no doubt there were many houses like this one. Florence knew little about Victorian architecture but she supposed that there were many duplications, even in large, costly houses. Unlike contemporary architects, the architects of that era must have been extremely limited, forced to use again and again certain basic structures, and certain basic ornamentation—the cupolas, the gables, the complicated trim. What struck her as so odd, so mysterious, was really nothing but a coincidence. It would make an interesting story, an amusing anecdote, when she returned home, though perhaps it was not even worth mention-ing. Her parents might have been intrigued but they were both dead. And she was always careful about dwelling upon herself, her private life, since she halfway imagined that her friends and acquaintances and colleagues would interpret nearly anything she said of a personal nature according to their vision of her as a public person, and she wanted to avoid that.

There was a movement at one of the upstairs windows that caught her eye. It was then transmitted, fluidly, miraculously, to the other windows, flowing from right to left. . . . But no, it was only the reflection of clouds being blown across the sky, up behind her head.

She stood motionless. It was unlike her, it was quite uncharacteristic of her, yet there she stood. She did not want to walk up to the veranda steps, she did not want to ring the doorbell, such a gesture would be ridiculous, and anyway there was no time: she really should be driving on. They would be expecting her soon. Yet she could not turn away. Because it *was* the house. Incredibly, it was her old dolls' house. (Which she had given away, of course, thirty—thirty-five?—years ago. And had rarely thought about since.) It was ridiculous to stand here, so astonished, so slow-witted, so perversely vulnerable . . . yet what other attitude was appropriate, what other attitude would not violate the queer sense of the sacred, the otherworldly, that the house had evoked?

She would ring the doorbell. And why not? She was a tall, rather wide-shouldered, confident woman, tastefully dressed in a cream-colored spring suit; she was rarely in the habit of apologizing for herself, or feeling embarrassment. Many years ago, perhaps, as a girl, a shy, silly, self-conscious girl: but no longer. Her wavy graying hair had been brushed back smartly from her wide, strong forehead. She wore no makeup, had stopped bothering with it years ago, and with her naturally high-colored, smooth complexion, she was a handsome woman, especially attractive when she smiled and her dark staring eyes relaxed. She *would* ring the doorbell, and see who came to the door, and say whatever flew into her head. She was looking for a family who lived in the neighborhood, she was canvassing for a school mill-age vote, she was inquiring whether they had any old clothes, old furniture, for . . .

Halfway up the walk she remembered that she had left the keys in the ignition of her car, and the motor running. And her purse on the seat.

She found herself walking unusually slowly. It was unlike her, and the disorienting sense of being unreal, of having stepped into another world, was totally new. A dog began barking some-where near: the sound seemed to pierce her in the chest and bowels. An attack of panic. An involuntary fluttering of the eyelids. . . . But it was nonsense of course. She would ring the bell, someone would open the door, perhaps a servant, per-haps an elderly woman, they would have a brief conversation, Florence would glance behind her into the foyer to see if the circular staircase looked the same, if the old brass chandelier was still there, if the "marble" floor remained. Do you know the Parr family, Florence would ask, we've lived in Cummington, Massachusetts, for generations, I think it's quite possible that someone from my family visited you in this house, of course it was a very long time ago. I'm sorry to disturb you but I was driving by and I saw your striking house and I couldn't resist stopping for a moment out of curiosity. . . .

There were the panes of stained glass on either side of the oak door! But so large, so boldly colored. In the dolls' house they were hardly visible, just chips of colored glass. But here they were each about a foot square, starkly beautiful: reds, greens, blues. Exactly like the stained glass of a church.

I'm sorry to disturb you, Florence whispered, but I was driv-ing by and . . .

I'm sorry to disturb you but I am looking for a family named Bartholomew, I have reason to think that they live in this neighborhood. . . .

But as she was about to step onto the veranda the sensation of panic deepened. Her breath came shallow and rushed, her thoughts flew wildly in all directions, she was simply terrified and could not move. The dog's barking had become hysterical.

When Florence was angry or distressed or worried she had a habit of murmuring her name to herself, Florence Parr, Florence Parr, it was soothing, it was mollifying, Florence Parr, it was often vaguely reproachful, for after all she *was* Florence Parr and that carried with it responsibility as well as authority. She named herself, identified herself. It was usually enough to bring her undisciplined thoughts under control. But she had not experienced an attack of panic for many years. All the strength of her body seemed to have fled, drained away; it terrified her to think that she might faint here. What a fool she would make of herself. . . .

As a young university instructor she had nearly succumbed to panic one day, midway through a lecture on the metaphysical poets. Oddly, the attack had come not at the beginning of the semester but well into the second month, when she had come to believe herself a thoroughly competent teacher. The most extraordinary sensation of fear, unfathomable and groundless fear, which she had never been able to comprehend afterward. . . . One moment she had been speaking of Donne's famous image in "The Relic"—a bracelet of "bright hair about the bone"—and the next moment she was so panicked she could hardly catch her breath. She wanted to run out of the classroom, wanted to run out of the building. It was as if a demon had appeared to her. It breathed into her face, shoved her about, tried to pull her under. She would suffocate: she would be destroyed. The sensation was possibly the most unpleasant she had ever experienced in her life though it carried with it no pain and no specific images. Why she was so frightened she could not grasp. Why she wanted nothing more than to run out of the classroom, to escape her students' curious eyes, she was never to understand.

But she did not flee. She forced herself to remain at the podium. Though her voice faltered she did not stop; she continued with the lecture, speaking into a blinding haze. Surely her students must have noticed her trembling . . . ? But she was stubborn, she was really quite tenacious for a young woman of twenty-four, and by forcing herself to imitate herself, to imitate her normal tone and mannerisms, she was able to overcome the attack. As it lifted, gradually, and her eyesight strengthened, her heartbeat slowed, she seemed to know that the attack would never come again in a classroom. And this turned out to be correct.

But now she could not overcome her anxiety. She hadn't a podium to grasp, she hadn't lecture notes to follow, there was no one to imitate, she was in a position to make a terrible fool of herself. And surely someone was watching from the house. . . . It struck her that she had no reason, no excuse, for being here. What on earth could she say if she rang the doorbell? How would she explain herself to a skeptical stranger? I simply must see the inside of your house, she would whisper. I've been led up this walk by a force I can't explain, please excuse me, please humor me, I'm not well, I'm not myself this morning, I only want to see the inside of your house to see if it *is* the house I remember. . . . I had a house like yours. It was yours. But no one lived in my house except dolls; a family of dolls. I loved them but I always sensed that they were blocking the way, standing between me and something else. . . .

The barking dog was answered by another, a neighbor's dog. Florence retreated. Then turned and hurried back to her car, where the keys were indeed in the ignition, and her smart leather purse lay on the seat where she had so imprudently left it.

So she fled the dolls' house, her poor heart thudding. What a fool you are, Florence Parr, she thought brutally, a deep hot blush rising into her face.

The rest of the day—the late afternoon reception, the dinner itself, the after-dinner gathering—passed easily, even routinely, but did not seem to her very real; it was not very convincing. That she was Florence Parr, the president of Champlain College, that she was to be a featured speaker at this conference of administrators of small private liberal arts colleges: it struck her for some reason as an imposture, a counterfeit. The vision of the dolls' house kept rising in her mind's eye. How odd, how very odd the experience had been, yet there was no one to whom she might speak about it, even to minimize it, to transform it into an amusing anecdote. . . . The others did not notice her discomfort. In fact they claimed that she was looking well, they were delighted to see her and to shake her hand. Many were old acquaintances, men and women, but primarily men, with whom she had worked in the past at one college or another; a number were strangers, younger administrators who had heard of her heroic effort at Champlain College, and who wanted to be introduced to her. At the noisy cocktail hour, at dinner, Florence heard her somewhat distracted voice speaking of the usual matters: declining enrollments, building fund campaigns, alumni support, endowments, investments, state and federal aid. Her remarks were met with the same respectful attention as always, as though there were nothing wrong with her.

For dinner she changed into a linen dress of pale blue and dark blue stripes which emphasized her tall, graceful figure, and drew the eye away from her wide shoulders and her stolid thighs; she wore her new shoes with the fashionable three-inch heel, though she detested them. Her haircut was becoming, she had manicured and even polished her nails the evening before, and she supposed she looked attractive enough, especially in this context of middle-aged and older people. But her mind kept drifting away from the others, from the handsome though rather dark colonial dining room, even from the spirited, witty after-dinner speech of a popular administrator and writer, a retired president of Williams College, and formerly—a very long time ago, now—a colleague of Florence's at Swarthmore. She smiled with the others, and laughed with the others, but she could not attend to the courtly, white-haired gentleman's astringent witticisms; her mind kept drifting back to the dolls' house, out there on East Fainlight Avenue. It was well for her that she hadn't rung the doorbell, for what if someone who was attending the conference had answered the door; it was, after all, being hosted by Lancaster College. What an utter fool she would have made of herself. . . .

She went to her room in the fieldstone alumni house shortly after ten, though there were people who clearly wished to talk with her, and she knew a night of insomnia awaited. Once in the room with its antique furniture and its self-consciously quaint wallpaper she regretted having left the ebullient atmosphere downstairs.

Though small private colleges were in trouble these days, and though most of the administrators at the conference were having serious difficulties with finances, and faculty morale, there was nevertheless a spirit of camaraderie, of heartiness. Of course it was the natural consequence of people in a social gathering. One simply cannot resist, in such a context, the droll remark, the grateful laugh, the sense of cheerful complicity in even an unfortunate fate. How puzzling the human personality is, Florence thought, preparing for bed, moving uncharacteristically slowly, when with others there is a public self, alone there is a private self, and yet both are real. . . . Both are experienced as real. . . .

She lay sleepless in the unfamiliar bed. There were noises in the distance; she turned on the air conditioner, the fan only, to drown them out. Still she could not sleep. The house on East Fainlight Avenue, the dolls' house of her childhood, she lay with her eyes open, thinking of absurd, disjointed things, wondering now why she had *not* pushed her way through that trivial bout of anxiety to the veranda steps, and to the door, after all she was Florence Parr, she had only to imagine people watching her—the faculty senate, students, her fellow administrators—to know how she should behave, with what alacrity and confidence. It was only when she forgot who she was, and imagined herself utterly alone, that she was crippled by uncertainty and susceptible to fear.

The luminous dials of her watch told her it was only 10:35. Not too late, really, to dress and return to the house and ring the doorbell. Of course she would only ring it if the downstairs was lighted, if someone was clearly up. . . . Perhaps an elderly gentleman lived there, alone, someone who had known her grandfather, someone who had visited the Parrs in Cummington. For there *must* be a connection. It was very well to speak of coincidences, but she knew, she knew with a deep, unshakable conviction, that there was a connection between the dolls' house and the house here in town, and a connection between her childhood and the present house. . . . When she explained herself to whoever opened the door, however, she would have to be casual, conversational. Years of administration had taught her diplomacy; one must nor appear to be *too* serious. Gravity in leaders is disconcerting, what is demanded is the light, confident touch, the air of private and even secret knowledge. People do not want equality with their leaders: they want, they desperately need, them to be superior. The superiority must be tacitly communicated, however, or it becomes offensive. . . .

Suddenly she was frightened: it seemed to her quire possible that the panic attack might come upon her the next morning, when she gave her address ("The Future of the Humanities in American Education"). She was scheduled to speak at 9:30, she would be the first speaker of the day, and the first real speaker of the conference. And it was quite possible that that disconcerting weakness would return, that sense of utter, almost infantile helplessness. . . .

She sat up, turned on the light, and looked over her notes. They were handwritten, not typed, she had told her secretary not to bother typing them, the address was one she'd given before in different forms, her approach was to be conversational rather than formal though of course she would quote the necessary statistics. . . . But it had been a mistake, perhaps, not to have the notes typed. There were times when she couldn't decipher her own handwriting.

A drink might help. But she couldn't very well go over to the Lancaster Inn, where the conference was to be held, and where there was a bar; and of course she hadn't anything with her in the room. As a rule she rarely drank. She never drank alone. . . . However, if a drink would help her sleep: would calm her wild racing thoughts.

The dolls' house had been a present for her birthday. Many years ago. She could not recall how many. And there were her dolls, her little family of dolls, which she had not thought of for a lifetime. She felt a pang of loss, of tenderness. . . .

Florence Parr who suffered quite frequently from insomnia. But of course no one knew.

Florence Parr who had had a lump in her right breast removed, a cyst really, harmless, absolutely harmless, shortly after her thirty-eighth birthday. But none of her friends at Champlain knew. Not even her secretary knew. And the ugly little thing turned out to be benign: absolutely harmless. So it was well that no one knew.

Florence Parr of whom it was said that she was distant, even guarded, at times. You can't get close to her, someone claimed. And yet it was often said of her that she was wonderfully warm and open and frank and totally without guile. A popular president. Yet she had the support of her faculty. There might be individual jealousies here and there, particularly among the vice presidents and deans, but in general she had everyone's support and she knew it and was grateful for it and intended to keep it.

It was only that her mind worked, late into the night. Raced. Would not stay still.

Should she surrender to her impulse, and get dressed quickly and return to the house? It would take no more than ten minutes. And quite likely the downstairs lights would *not* be on, the inhabitants would be asleep, she could see from the street that the visit was totally out of the question, she would simply drive on past. And be saved from her audacity.

If I do this, the consequence will be . . .

If I fail to do this . . .

She was not, of course, an impulsive person. Nor did she admire impulsive "spontaneous" people: she thought them immature, and frequently exhibitionistic. It was often the case that they were very much aware of their own spontaneity. . . .

She would defend herself against the charge of being calculating. Of being overly cautious. Her nature was simply a very pragmatic one. She took up tasks with extreme interest, and absorbed herself deeply in them, one after another, month after month and year after year, and other considerations simply had to be shunted to the side. For instance, she had never married. The surprise would have been not that Florence Parr had married, but that she had had time to cultivate a relationship that would end in marriage. I am not opposed to marriage for myself, she once said, with unintentional naiveté, but it would take so much time to become acquainted with a man, to go out with him, and talk. . . . At Champlain where everyone liked her, and shared anecdotes about her, it was said that she'd been even as a younger woman so oblivious to men, even to attentive men, that she had failed to recognize a few years later a young linguist whose carrel at the Widener Library had been next to hers, though the young man claimed to have said hello to her every day, and to have asked her out for coffee occasionally. (She had always refused, she'd been far too busy.) When he turned up at Champlain, married, the author of a well-received book on linguistic theory, an associate professor in the Humanities division, Florence had not only been unable to recognize him but could not remember him at all, though he remembered her vividly, and even amused the gathering by recounting to Florence the various outfits she had worn that winter, even the colors of her knitted socks. She had been deeply embarrassed, of course, and yet flattered, and amused. It was proof, after all, that Florence Parr was always at all times Florence Parr.

Afterward she was somewhat saddened, for the anecdote meant, did it not, that she really *had* no interest in men. She was not a spinster because no one had chosen her, not even because she had been too fastidious in her own choosing, but simply because she had no interest in men, she did not even "see" them when they presented themselves before her. It was sad, it was irrefutable. She was an ascetic not through an act of will but through temperament.

It was at this point that she pushed aside the notes for her talk, her heart beating wildly as a girl's. She had no choice, she *must* satisfy her curiosity about the house, if she wanted to sleep, if she wanted to remain sane.

As the present of the dolls' house was the great event of her childhood, so the visit to the house on Ease Fainlight Avenue was to be the great event of her adulthood: though Florence Parr was never to allow herself to think of it, afterward.

It was a mild, quiet night, fragrant with blossoms, not at all intimidating. Florence drove to the avenue, to the house, and was consoled by the numerous lights burning in the neighborhood: of course it wasn't late, of course there was nothing extraordinary about what she was going to do.

Lights were on downstairs. Whoever lived there was up, in the living room. Waiting for her.

Remarkable, her calmness. After so many foolish hours of indecision.

She ascended the veranda steps, which gave slightly beneath her weight. Rang the doorbell. After a minute or so an outside light went on: she felt exposed: began to smile nervously. One smiled, one soon learned how. There was no retreating.

She saw the old wicker furniture on the porch. Two rocking chairs, a settee. Once painted white but now badly weathered. No cushions.

A dog began barking angrily.

Florence Parr, Florence Parr. She knew who she was, but there was no need to tell *him*. Whoever it was, peering out at her through the dark stained glass, an elderly man, someone's left-behind grandfather. Still, owning this house in this part of town meant money and position: you might sneer at such things but they do have significance. Even to pay the property taxes, the school taxes. . . .

The door opened and a man stood staring out at her, half smiling, quizzical. He was not the man she expected, he was not elderly, but of indeterminate age, perhaps younger than she. "Yes? Hello? What can I do for . . . ?" he said.

She heard her voice, full-throated and calm. The rehearsed question. Questions. An air of apology beneath which her confidence held firm. ". . . driving in the neighborhood earlier today, staying with friends. . . . Simply curious about an old connection between our families. . . . Or at any rate between my family and the people who built this. . . ."

Clearly he was startled by her presence, and did not quite grasp her questions. She spoke too rapidly, she would have to repeat herself.

He invited her in. Which was courteous. A courtesy that struck her as unconscious, automatic. He was very well mannered. Puzzled but not suspicious. Not unfriendly. Too young for this house, perhaps—for so old and shabbily elegant a house. Her presence on his doorstep, her bold questions, the bright strained smile that stretched her lips must have baffled him but he did not think her *odd*: he respected her, was not judging her. A kindly, simple person. Which was of course a relief. He might even be a little simple-minded. Slow-thinking. He certainly had nothing to do with . . . with whatever she was involved in, in this part of the world. He would tell no one about her.

". . . a stranger to the city? . . . staying with friends?"

"I only want to ask: does the name Parr mean anything to you?"

A dog was barking, now frantically. But kept its distance.

Florence was being shown into the living room, evidently the only lighted room downstairs. She noted the old staircase, graceful as always. But they had done something awkward with the wainscoting, painted it a queer slate blue. And the floor was no longer of marble but a poor imitation, some sort of linoleum tile. . . .

"The chandelier," she said suddenly.

The man turned to her, smiling his amiable quizzical worn smile.

"Yes . . . ?"

"It's very attractive," she said. "It must be an antique."

In the comfortable orangish light of the living room she saw that he had sandy red hair, thinning at the crown. But boyishly frizzy at the sides. He might have been in his late thirties but his face was prematurely lined and he stood with one shoulder

slightly higher than the other, as if he were very tired. She began
to apologize again for disturbing him. For taking up his time
with her impulsive, probably futile curiosity.

"Not at all," he said. "I usually don't go to bed until well past
midnight."

Florence found herself sitting at one end of an overstuffed sofa.
Her smile was strained but as wide as ever, her face had begun
to grow very warm. Perhaps he would not notice her blushing.

". . . insomnia?"

"Yes. Sometimes."

"I too . . . sometimes."

He was wearing a green-and-blue plaid shirt, with thin red
stripes. A flannel shirt. The sleeves rolled up to his elbows. And
what looked like work-trousers. Denim. A gardener's outfit perhaps. Her mind cast about desperately for something to say and
she heard herself asking about his garden, his lawn. So many
lovely tulips. Most of them red. And there were plane trees, and
several elms. . . .

He faced her, leaning forward with his elbows on his knees.
A faintly sunburned face. A redhead's complexion, somewhat
freckled.

The chair he sat in did not look familiar. It was an ugly brown,
imitation brushed velvet. Florence wondered who had bought
it: silly young wife perhaps.

". . . Parr family?"

"From Lancaster?"

"Oh no. From Cummington, Massachusetts. We've lived there
for many generations."

He appeared to be considering the name, frowning at the
carpet. ". . . *does* sound familiar . . ."

"Oh, does it? I had hoped . . ."

The dog approached them, no longer barking. Its tail wagged and thumped against the side of the sofa, the leg of an old-fashioned table, nearly upsetting a lamp. The man snapped his fingers at the dog and it came no further, it quivered, and made a half growling, half sighing noise, and lay with its snout on its paws and its skinny tail outstretched, a few feet from Florence. She wanted to placate it, to make friends. But it was such an ugly creature—partly hairless, with scruffy white whiskers, a naked sagging belly.

"If the dog bothers you . . ."

"Oh no, no. Not at all."

"He only means to be friendly."

"I can see that," Florence said, laughing girlishly. ". . . He's very handsome."

"Hear that?" the man said, snapping his fingers again. "The lady says you're very handsome! Can't you at least stop drooling, don't you have any manners at all?"

"I haven't any pets of my own. But I like animals."

She was beginning to feel quite comfortable. The living room was not exactly what she had expected but it was not *too* bad. There was the rather low, overstuffed sofa in which she sat, the cushions made of a silvery-white, silvery-gray material, with a feathery sheen, plump, immense, like bellies or breasts, a monstrous old piece of furniture yet nothing one would want to sell: for certainly it had come down in the family, it must date from the turn of the century. There was the Victorian table with its coy ornate legs, and its tasseled cloth, and its extraordinary oversized lamp: the sort of thing Florence would smile at in an antique shop, but which looked fairly reasonable here. In fact she should comment on it, since she was staring at it so openly.

". . . antique? European?"

"I think so, yes," the man said.

"Is it meant to be fruit, or a tree, or . . ."

Bulbous and flesh-colored, peach-colored. With a tarnished brass stand. A dust-dimmed golden lampshade with embroidered blue trim that must have been very pretty at one time.

They talked of antiques. Of old houses. Families.

A queer odor defined itself. It was not unpleasant, exactly.

"Would you like something to drink?"

"Why yes I—"

"Excuse me just a moment."

Alone she wondered if she might prowl about the room. But it was long and narrow and poorly lighted at one end: in fact, one end dissolved into darkness. A faint suggestion of furniture there, an old spinet piano, a jumble of chairs, a bay window that must look out onto the garden. She wanted very much to examine a portrait above the mantel of the fireplace but perhaps the dog would bark, or grow excited, if she moved.

It had crept closer to her feet, shuddering with pleasure.

The redheaded man, slightly stooped, brought a glass of something dark to her. In one hand was his own drink, in the other hand hers.

"Taste it. Tell me what you think."

"It seems rather strong. . . ."

Chocolate. Black and bitter. And thick.

"It should really be served hot," the man said.

"Is there a liqueur of some kind in it?"

"Is it too strong for you?"

"Oh no. No. Not at all."

Florence had never tasted anything more bitter. She nearly gagged.

But a moment later it was all right: she forced herself to take a second swallow, and a third. And the prickling painful sensation in her mouth faded.

The redheaded man did not return to his chair, but stood before her, smiling. In the other room he had done something hurried with his hair: had tried to brush it back with his hands, perhaps. A slight film of perspiration shone on his high forehead.

"Do you live alone here?"

"The house does seem rather large, doesn't it?—for a person to live in it alone."

"Of course you have your dog . . ."

"Do *you* live alone now?"

Florence set the glass of chocolate down. Suddenly she remembered what it reminded her of: a business associate of her father's, many years ago, had brought a box of chocolates back from a trip to Russia. The little girl had popped one into her mouth and had been dismayed by their unexpectedly bitter taste.

She had spat the mess out into her hand. While everyone stared.

As if he could read her thoughts the redheaded man twitched, moving his jaw and his right shoulder jerkily. But he continued smiling as before and Florence did not indicate that she was disturbed. In fact she spoke warmly of the living room's furnishings, and repeated her admiration for handsome old houses like this one. The man nodded, as if waiting for her to say more.

". . . a family named Bartholomew? Of course it was many years ago."

"Bartholomew? Did they live in this neighborhood?"

"Why yes I think so. That's the real reason I stopped in. I once knew a little girl who—"

"Bartholomew, Bartholomew," the man said slowly, frowning. His face puckered. One corner of his mouth twitched with the effort of his concentration: and again his right shoulder jerked. Florence was afraid he would spill his chocolate drink.

Evidently he had a nervous ailment of some kind. But she could not inquire.

He murmured the name *Bartholomew* to himself, his expression grave, even querulous. Florence wished she had not asked the question because it was a lie, after all. She rarely told lies. Yet it had slipped from her, it had glided smoothly out of her mouth.

She smiled guiltily, ducking her head. She took another swallow of the chocolate drink.

Without her having noticed, the dog had inched forward. His great head now rested on her feet. His wet brown eyes peered up at her, oddly affectionate. A baby's eyes. It was true that he was drooling, in fact he was drooling on her ankles, but of course he could not help it. . . . Then she noted that he had wet on the carpet. Only a few feet away. A dark stain, a small puddle.

Yet she could not shrink away in revulsion. After all, she was a guest and it was not time for her to leave.

". . . Bartholomew. You say they lived in this neighborhood?"

"Oh yes."

"But when?"

"Why I really don't . . . I was only a child at the . . ."

"But when was this?"

He was staring oddly at her, almost rudely. The twitch at the corner of his mouth had gotten worse. He moved to set his glass down and the movement was jerky, puppet-like. Yet he stared at her all the while. Florence knew people often felt uneasy because of her dark over-large staring eyes: but she could not help it. She did not *feel* the impetuosity, the reproach, her expression suggested. So she tried to soften it by smiling. But sometimes the smile failed, it did not deceive anyone at all.

Now that her host had stopped smiling she could see that he was really quite mocking. His tangled sandy eyebrows lifted ironically.

"You said you were a stranger to this city, and now you're saying you've been here. . . ."

"But it was so long ago, I was only a . . ."

He drew himself up to his full height. He was not a tall man, nor was he solidly built. In fact his waist was slender, for a man's—and he wore odd trousers, or jeans, tight-fitting across his thighs and without zipper or snaps, crotchless. They fit him tightly in the crotch, which was smooth, seamless. His legs were rather short for his torso and arms.

He began smiling at Florence. A sly accusing smile. His head jerked mechanically, indicating something on the floor. He was trying to point with his chin and the gesture was clumsy.

"You did something nasty on the floor there. On the carpet."

Florence gasped. At once she drew herself away from the dog, at once she began to deny it. "I didn't—It wasn't—"

"Right on the carpet there. For everyone to see. To smell."

"I certainly did not," Florence said, blushing angrily. "You know very well it was the—"

"Somebody's going to have to clean it up and it isn't going to be *me*," the man said, grinning.

But his eyes were still angry.

He did not like her at all: she saw that. The visit was a mistake, but how could she leave, how could she escape, the dog had crawled up to her again and was nuzzling and drooling against her ankles, and the redheaded man who had seemed so friendly was now leaning over her, his hands on his slim hips, grinning rudely.

As if to frighten her, as one might frighten an animal or a child, he clapped his hands smartly together. Florence blinked at the sudden sound. And then he leaned forward and clapped his hands together again, right before her face. She cried out for him to leave her alone, her eyes smarted with tears, she was leaning back against the cushions, her head back as far as it would go, and then he clapped his hands once again, hard, bringing them against her burning cheeks, slapping both her cheeks at once, and a sharp thin white-hot sensation ran through her body, from her face and throat to her belly, to the pit of her belly, and from the pit of her belly up into her chest, into her mouth, and even down into her stiffened legs. She screamed for the redheaded man to stop, and twisted convulsively on the sofa to escape him.

"Liar! Bad girl! Dirty girl!" someone shouted.

She wore her new reading glasses, with their attractive plastic frames. And a spring suit, smartly styled, with a silk blouse in a floral pattern. And the tight but fashionable shoes.

Her audience, respectful and attentive, could not see her trembling hands behind the podium, or her slightly quivering knees. They would have been astonished to learn that she hadn't been able to eat breakfast that morning—that she felt depressed and exhausted though she had managed to fall asleep the night before, probably around two, and had evidently slept her usual dreamless sleep.

She cleared her throat several times in succession, a habit she detested in others.

But gradually her strength flowed back into her. The morning was so sunny, so innocent. These people were, after all, her colleagues and friends: they certainly wished her well, and even appeared to be genuinely interested in what she had to say about the future of the humanities. Perhaps Dr. Parr knew something they did not, perhaps she would share her professional secrets with them. . . .

As the minutes passed Florence could hear her voice grow richer and firmer, easing into its accustomed rhythms. She began to relax. She began to breathe more regularly. She was moving into familiar channels, making points she had made countless times before, at similar meetings, with her deans and faculty chairmen at Champlain, with other educators. A number of people applauded heartily when she spoke of the danger of small private colleges competing unwisely with one another; and again when she made a point, an emphatic point, about the need for the small private school in an era of multiversities. Surely these were remarks anyone might have made, there was really nothing original about them, yet her audience seemed extremely pleased to hear them from her. They *did* admire Florence Parr—that was clear.

She removed her reading glasses. Smiled, spoke without needing to glance at her notes. This part of her speech—an amusing summary of the consequences of certain experimental programs at Champlain, initiated since she'd become president—was more specific, more interesting, and of course she knew it by heart.

The previous night had been one of her difficult nights. At least initially. Her mind racing in that way she couldn't control, those flame-like pangs of fear, insomnia. And no help for it. And no way out. She'd fallen asleep while reading through her notes and awakened suddenly, her heart beating erratically, body drenched in perspiration—and there she was, lying twisted back against the headboard, neck stiff and aching and her left leg numb beneath her. She'd been dreaming she'd given in and driven out to see the dolls' house; but of course she had not, she'd been in her hotel room all the time. *She'd never left her hotel room.*

She'd never left her hotel room but she'd fallen asleep and dreamt she had but she refused to summon back her dream, not that dream nor any others; in fact she rather doubted she did dream, she never remembered afterward. Florence Parr was one of those people who, as soon as they awake, are *awake.* And eager to begin the day.

At the conclusion of Florence's speech everyone applauded enthusiastically. She'd given speeches like this many times before and it had been ridiculous of her to worry.

Congratulations, handshakes. Coffee was being served.

Florence was flushed with relief and pleasure, crowded about by well-wishers. This was her world, these people her colleagues, they knew her, admired her. Why does one worry about anything! Florence thought, smiling into these friendly faces, shaking more hands. These were all good people, serious professional people, and she liked them very much.

At a distance a faint fading jeering cry *Liar! Dirty girl!* but Florence was listening to the really quite astute remarks of a

youngish man who was a new dean of arts at Vassar. How good
the hot, fresh coffee was. And a thinly layered apricot brioche
she'd taken from a proffered silver tray.

The insult and discomfort of the night were fading; the vision
of the dolls' house was fading, dying. She refused to summon
it back. She would not give it another thought. Friends—
acquaintances—well-wishers were gathering around her, she
knew her skin was glowing like a girl's, her eyes were bright
and clear and hopeful; at such times, buoyed by the presence of
others as by waves of applause, you forget your age, your loneliness—the very perimeters of your soul.

Day is the only reality: She'd always known.

Though the conference was a success, and colleagues at home
heard that Florence's contribution had been particularly well
received, Florence began to forget it within a few weeks. So many
conferences!—so many warmly applauded speeches! Florence
was a professional woman who, by nature more than design,
pleased both women and men; she did not stir up controversy,
she "stimulated discussion." Now she was busily preparing for
her first major conference, to be held in London in September:
"The Role of the Humanities in the 21st Century." Yes, she was
apprehensive, she told friends—"But it's a true challenge."

When a check arrived in the mail for five hundred dollars, an
honorarium for her speech in Lancaster, Pennsylvania, Florence
was puzzled at first—not recalling the speech, nor the circumstances. How odd! She'd never been there, had she? Then, to a
degree, as if summoning forth a dream, she remembered: the
beautiful Pennsylvania landscape, ablaze with spring flowers;

a small crowd of well-wishers gathered around to shake her hand. Why, Florence wondered, had she ever worried about her speech?—her public self? Like an exquisitely precise clockwork mechanism, a living mannequin, she would always do well: you'll applaud too, when you hear her.

LITTLE WIFE

I

Damn his soul to hell, Judd was the first to notice the girl across the street from the café though he was too sleepy to know that he was watching her especially or even, at first, that she was a girl. She might have been a boy his age or a few years older. Hanging out, alone, by the bus station; not by the lighted drive where buses pulled up every half hour or so but by the entrance to the darkened garage where the buses were parked overnight and serviced during the day. She must have arrived on the eight-thirty bus because after it pulled away Judd noticed her standing there, waiting by the curb, a purse or duffel bag slung across her shoulder. At first she seemed to be looking across the street at the café. Then it appeared she was waiting for somebody. If Judd had given it much thought he would have supposed she was waiting for a car to drive up, it would slow, stop, the headlights on, he'd see her open the door on the passenger's side and get in, the driver would be her father, maybe, or an older brother, they'd drive away and be home in a few minutes. It was a time of day when people were going home.

Then he noticed that she was panhandling, or trying to. Standing back in the shadows until somebody came walking by. But she didn't know how to go about it. She was slow and clumsy and maybe frightened. When she saw somebody she would advance with her hand held out and the man would just quicken his pace and hurry past without looking at her. She made it too easy for them to get away, Judd thought. Once he had panhandled himself for a day or two, in a town upriver, after his mother had kicked him out and before he'd gone back to live with his father. He wasn't any fool, was Judd, shrewd like a fox or a monkey his mother used to say—it was the kind of remark you couldn't always figure out, did it mean good? bad? or was it just funny?—bur he had known enough to study the older panhandlers and see how they went about their business. First of all you need to place yourself on a busy corner, by an intersection if you can with a traffic light so that people can't rush by, you need to get them to look you direct in the eyes, if you got them direct in the eyes you had them, usually. At that time Judd hadn't looked much more than ten years old. Small-boned, runty, with grayish skin, damp squinting eyes, his nose running and his face dirty. It had been winter, after Christmas, and he hadn't any hat or gloves. Or boots: he was wearing sneakers. If he managed to get people to look at him, men or women, it didn't seem to matter which, then they'd give him something most of the time, a dime or two or a quarter or a half-dollar dropped into his hand, rarely anything larger, the sons of bitches. The main feeling was them wanting to get away, and giving Judd a coin or two was payment for getting away but he hadn't cared, he'd made almost twenty dollars in those two days, which was the most money he had ever held in his hand at one time. Later almost half the money was stolen away from him but that wasn't the point, that was another story.

Twenty minutes. Half an hour. Now it was past nine-thirty and dark, and the girl was still across the street by the Greyhound station. Judd was a little nervous waiting for something to happen. A car to drive up after all and take her away. Maybe a police patrol car. As near as he could see she'd approached only five or six people in all this time and only one of them had given her something. The others carefully avoided her. When a bus pulled up to let passengers off she stood back in the shadows waiting, the duffel bag at her feet. Judd leaned against the window and stared out, he hadn't anything better to do. It was early, not even ten o'clock yet, his father and his father's friends Vern and Al and Ryan were drinking beer and had a long way to go, Judd would be lucky if he got to bed by one. In any case they weren't going home—it wasn't clear these days where "home" was—they were staying with Vern Decker out in the country, Decker's parents' old place, most of the acreage sold off and only the farmhouse and a few outbuildings left. Judd's eyes ached with the need to sleep and his stomach ached from the cheeseburger he'd eaten so fast. The French fries and sugary cole slaw. Lukewarm Pepsi-Cola. He could feel something moving low in his bowels like a snake uncoiling and pressing forward with its hard blunt head. He hoped to Christ he wouldn't get sick suddenly and need to use the lavatory, his father would be annoyed, or make one of his embarrassing jokes.

Judd's father called himself Judd Senior sometimes, at other times he called himself just Kovacs, which was his last name. He was a flush-faced good-looking man, hair receding from his forehead but he wore a mustache, full, drooping, coppery-brown;

unlike the other men he sometimes wore a necktie when they went into town, or a string tie that gave him a western look. He was forty-three years old and he told the joke on himself that he had never expected to live past thirty let alone forty: but here he was, and what the hell. He and Judd were staying temporarily at Vern's until he got them on their feet again. He'd had a string of bad breaks going back for years, the final blow was his car giving out, a '78 Plymouth, and all the decent-paying work he could get right now was part-time construction work on a crew with Vern Decker and Charley Ryan. He liked to tell people that Judd Junior was the primary thing in his life. Judd Junior was his main reason for living. Otherwise what was the point? The boy's mother had left them and betrayed them both. But now it was his responsibility to make things right again. And it wasn't easy, in fact it was fucking hard, a steady uphill climb.

Just for fun Judd took up his father's glass and swallowed a big mouthful of beer, almost gagging to get it down. His father was telling a story and laughing hard; he scarcely noticed. Most of the evening the men had been talking about people Judd didn't know, things he wasn't interested in, he was bored, sleepy, slightly sick, he couldn't even watch television because the bartender wouldn't let him sit at the bar. Once in a while Vern Decker would wink at him and say, "How's it going?" but the other men ignored him and in any case Vern didn't mean anything by it. Judd heard himself say suddenly that there was somebody right across the street, a girl, it looked like, did they see her? She'd been out there a long time, acting strange. Why he brought this information up out of nowhere he didn't know. So the men craned their necks around and looked. It surprised Judd that they were so immediately interested. Was she a hooker? Not dressed like that. Was she a kid? Panhandling? A runaway? The girl had come out to stand by the curb beneath a streetlamp, hands on her hips, hair blowsy and shaggy, one foot lightly tapping. Ryan said she looked good to him. Vern said she might be kind of young. Judd's father said she must be waiting for somebody and Judd couldn't resist saying no she wasn't: she'd been out there an hour just standing around, acting strange. He'd been watching her, he said. She didn't know what the hell she was doing.

So Judd's father heaved himself up out of the booth and smoothed down his hair and said, "Okay fellas, I'll check her out."

Judd watched in disbelief as his father left the café and crossed the street with brisk purposeful strides and came right up to the girl and began talking to her. He hadn't meant for anything like this to happen! He wondered if his old man was drunker than he appeared. It puzzled him too that Decker and Al and Ryan were so interested in what was happening across the street, craning their necks, watching, speculating: would she come back with him . . . ? They laughed and thumped the table in triumph when it appeared she would. Judd's father was carrying her duffel bag slung over his shoulder.

At first the girl refused to tell them her name. "That's for me to know and you to find out," she said in a nasal singsong voice, as if she were already slightly drunk. And where was she from? "That's for me to know and you to find out." She squeezed into the booth between Judd Junior and Judd Senior, taking up a good deal of room for her size, giving off a stink, Judd thought, of nervousness and excitement. She might have been eighteen years old—she was older, close up, than she'd seemed. Judd didn't think she was pretty at all. He thought in fact she was ugly. Her skin was flushed and coarse, her eyes close-set, damp, gray, something mean and smirking about her mouth, which was damp too, and fleshy. She had a broad face and prominent cheekbones but her nose was small and looked pushed in: Judd could see tiny blackheads in the flesh. Why was she so wriggly and excited, Judd wondered. She'd taken up the men's banter as if they were all old friends. She was hungry, she admitted, but she didn't care what they ordered for her. God she *was* hungry, she said, laughing, squirming. Al pushed a plate of cold French fries in her direction and she began eating them with her fingers, almost daintily at first. She drank thirstily from Judd's father's beer glass. Then the waitress came over and they ordered for her—beer, a hot roast beef sandwich with gravy, French fries, cole slaw, the works. She hadn't eaten, she admitted, in a while. She'd been on a bus.

Eventually it came out that her name was Agnes.

"Agnes—that's a pretty name," Judd's father said. "That's an unusual name."

"Oh hell it's *not*," Agnes said, making a swipe at him with the flat of her hand, as if he'd said something too intimate. When the roast beef sandwich came she ate quickly, leaning toward the plate, though she kept up a steady flirty conversation with the men, interrupted by explosions of laughter. She'd taken off her jacket because it was hot in the booth, everybody jammed together, and Judd smelled her underarms, her unwashed hair. The hair was a fair brown shade streaked with blond but badly matted as if she hadn't combed it in days. She was wearing a black V-neck sweater in a thin synthetic fabric that fitted her tight across the breasts and shoulders and showed the lumpy outline of her brassiere. Her blue jeans were tight too, and faded almost colorless. She loved the men's attention, them staring at her, asking questions, teasing, but she wouldn't tell them her last name or where she was headed. "That's for me to know and you to find out," she said, wiping her mouth with a paper napkin.

She'd only glanced at Judd when she slid into the booth and never bothered with him afterward.

He couldn't see that she was pretty, he wondered why his father seemed so interested in her. She wasn't nearly so pretty as his mother. She had a pimply forehead, a rough-looking skin, there was something piggish about her, and jumpy, and hot. She gave off heat, you could smell it. The men told her there was a party she was invited to out in the country and she kept saying in her singsong reedy voice, "The hell you say," giving a swipe of her hand, giggling and squirming in her seat. Under the table she kicked Judd a half-dozen times without seeming to notice. Her cheeks were flushed, her eyes so happy Judd didn't like to see. Was she crazy? he wondered. Or simpleminded? Retarded? She kept saying, "The hell you say," and blushing deeper. She told them she had business of her own in town, a place she was expected at, she surely wasn't going to any party out in the country she hadn't heard about till five minutes ago. Judd's father leaned toward her smiling and his mustache glistened with moisture. His eyes were a little sleepy-lidded, his smile slightly crooked. He called her Agnes. Agnes this, Agnes that. He belched and excused himself in a comical way. He asked her did she believe in the division of labor and the division of property; the revolt of class slaves; the rise of the people. Did she know she was of the people, he asked, good solid country people, the salt of the earth. Was she Protestant? he asked. She laughed wildly and told him he was crazy. Then she said she'd been baptized Methodist but had fallen away in recent years. "That means you're Protestant," Judd's father said, "and you're among friends."

They were discussing whether Agnes should ride out to Decker's with Al or Ryan, or with Decker in his car. Al and Ryan had their motorcycles parked outside. Agnes squirmed with pleasure. Though she seemed insulted too. "Ride on some goddamn old dangerous motorcycle?" she said, rolling her eyes, appealing suddenly to Judd. "I'm riding in a car like any normal person."

So it seemed to be decided, Judd hadn't noticed just when. He felt sick and sleepy and worried, he hated the way the men stared at Agnes and he hated how slow and stupid she was, how hopeful her gray eyes shone, he told himself he wasn't going to care, he wasn't going to give the slightest damn, whatever happened to her.

When Judd's mother left them for the first time they were living in a trailer park in Port Huron. She'd promised him she would be coming back to get him if she could, she'd telephone, she said, every night, bur weeks went by, a month, and Judd's father said she'd lied to them both but it didn't surprise him. When the telephone rang Judd's father shut the door so that Judd couldn't overhear.

He got in trouble at school for fighting, worse yet, for "issuing death threats" as the parents of one of his classmates called it. He said he'd stick a blade in some kid's guts and the little fucker pretended to take him seriously. And there was Judd trying to keep from laughing in their faces. And there was Judd staring at himself in a water-specked mirror in the boys' lavatory, that fox-faced runty kid, red-eyed, a sore on his upper lip, a silly grin. Is that me? Who the hell is that? But he didn't really care, he knew how things would keep on without him, drift on their own way.

His father made arrangements in secret and one day they drove south to Bethany Falls, where his mother seemed to be waiting. She acted almost as if she hadn't been gone for half a year so Judd fell in with the pretense. They lived in another trailer park not very different from the one in Port Huron except now he had to take a bus to school and the ride was forty-five minutes, he was in fifth grade, he had the idea he'd been in fifth grade at this school before, a long time ago in another lifetime maybe: his mother believed, she said, in former lifetimes, it was this lifetime, she said, laughing, she was having trouble with.

At this time Judd's father was a security guard for a local service that hired out guards to watch over warehouses, car lots, fresh produce markets, and the like, he even had a khaki-colored uniform and a cap, *Hercules Protection Services Inc.* stitched on his jacket. But he quit after a few months when he couldn't get licensed to carry a pistol. His pride was injured but mainly it was practical: he didn't want to be unarmed if a dangerous situation arose. "A man has only one life," he said. He was on unemployment for six weeks, which made living in the little trailer difficult, then he got another job in the machine shop of a nonunionized factory that manufactured small parts for General Motors. When automobile sales were stable the men had work, when sales dipped they were laid off, it was a rhythm no one could predict in advance and it left the men apprehensive and suspicious. Afternoons when Judd got off the school bus he would sit on the edge of a deep clay drainage ditch near the trailer waiting until he thought it might be all right for him to go home. He had memorized the wildflowers and thistles in the

ditch, the old rotted tires, broken bottles, parts of furniture, toys.
If his father was home he would have been drinking beer all day.
If only his mother was home the situation might go either way:
it might be unpleasant, it might be all right. There were times
when his mother acted as if she were surprised to see him, as if
he were coming home at the wrong time, meaning to frighten
her. Then he'd have to endure being hugged, hard. Trying not to
smell her breath. *Mus-ca-tel*, he thought. *Mus-ca-tel*. He'd tasted
it himself more than once, it was sweet, syrupy, very different
from the beer and ale his father drank.

Judd's mother's name was Irene (pronounced "Irene-y"). She
was a bright-faced pretty woman with faint lines between her eyes
from frowning. She had cloudy frizzy dark hair like Judd's and
long thin arms, the wrists especially chin, all bones. A flash of
teeth and gums when she laughed. Even if she hadn't felt strong
enough to get dressed that day she liked to fix Judd a peanut
butter and jelly sandwich after school and watch him eat. It
seemed to make her happy. Sometimes Judd could smell vomit
in the tiny bathroom though she had been careful to flush it all
away. He cranked open the window slats to let the odor our so
that his father wouldn't know when he came home.

When Judd's mother came out looking for him, the wind
blowing her hair, her lipsticked mouth bright in her face, Judd's
friends said it was hard to believe she was anybody's mother.
She didn't look like a mother, they said. "No," said Judd, embarrassed, nor knowing what he meant. "She isn't." She told
him she suffered premonitions of disaster, seeing him lying
on the ground with a bleeding head, lying on the edge of
the highway, at the bottom of the drainage ditch. She'd come
calling for him, frightened, excited, rousing up half the trailer

park. To spite her he hid from her back in the woods. He told himself he hated her.

After she went away for the second time he knew he had been hating her beforehand to save himself grief.

Judd's father couldn't believe that his wife had filed for divorce this time—"filed for divorce"—it sounded like something in the newspaper. The first thing he did was get drunk, the second was to quit his job. He got drunk three nights in a row and when he came home stumbling and talking to himself, Judd pressed his forearms over his ears so that he wouldn't hear. Some nights Judd's father was so lonely he slept with him, lying atop the covers, only partly undressed, snoring and making weeping noises in his sleep. When he caught Judd dialing one of the telephone numbers Judd's mother had left behind he snatched the receiver out of Judd's hand and slapped him hard. It wasn't a time for disloyalty between father and son, he said. His eyes shone with tears that wouldn't spill and his voice trembled as Judd had never heard it before.

Judd's father had known about the muscatel, the secret drinking. It was hardly a secret when half the trailer park knew. They quarreled mainly because she lied to him, she couldn't be trusted. If he gave her money he couldn't trust her to spend it on groceries. People who drink by themselves are sick, he told Judd, you have to learn to pity them but not be taken in by their lies. On weekends he himself might drink two cases of ale—one case on Saturday, one on Sunday—but he never showed the slightest effect and he could get up on time for work Monday morning. All his friends were like him, they could hold their alcohol, only very rarely did they get drunk and that was for special occasions.

It's the difference, Judd's father told him, between alcoholic susceptibility and alcoholic immunity.

When Judd's mother left she packed her things carefully, took her time, she was nervous but she knew Judd's father wouldn't be home till past six o'clock and it was still early afternoon. She gave Judd three addresses because she didn't know exactly where she was going. And some telephone numbers too. When she got settled, she said, she'd be sending for him to come live with her. "Are you going to get married again?" Judd asked. He wasn't angry, in fact his voice came out bored. His mother didn't seem to hear the question though finally she said, "No, I wouldn't do that. No. Never again."

Weeks went by, months, Judd's father never spoke of her though Judd heard him on the telephone sometimes, speaking in a slow sarcastic voice or asking questions, short, laughing, angry, sarcastic, "Oh yes, *when*—?" "What—?" "Who—?" "*What* did you say?—didn't catch that." When he had to meet with her lawyer, or with his own, he came back subdued and tired-looking but Judd knew enough to keep out of his way; these were the most dangerous times. He was having credit card trouble too. And trouble with the Plymouth. "What is imminent is a complete change in our lives," he said frequently, smiling at Judd, his fingers picking at his mustache. "But I have to think how to maneuver." When he applied for his old job back at the factory and they turned him down he conceded it was for the best. He was finished with Bethany Falls and with the trailer living, he said. From now on it would be just the two of them, Judd Junior and Judd Senior.

The night they brought Agnes out to the farm Judd slept in the hay barn where he sometimes slept in the summer or when things were noisy at the house. He knew they'd be partying a long time—they were going to telephone some other friends, they'd bought several cases of beer—and he didn't want to be in anybody's way. There was a mattress for him in one of the upstairs rooms of the house but he preferred the barn, he had a craving for certain smells, subtle mysterious smells, dust, old half-rotted hay, old cow manure, it made colors sift through his mind, goldenrod, sunshine, in the hayloft he had made a place for himself with a horse blanket, a pillow, he liked the smell of the old horse blanket too, and the leathery smell of the straps, it was a secret place of his where he could hide away during the day too if he had reasons for hiding. He didn't listen to noises from the house. Laughter, loud voices. He'd heard them before. If Agnes was lucky there would be a few women at the party for a while, girlfriends of the other men, if she wasn't lucky there wouldn't be any other women at all, but in any case the other women would be going home when the party was over and Agnes wasn't going anywhere at all.

But he wasn't going to think about her.

He wasn't going to think about his father, either. Or his mother and his mother's fiancé.

There was a promise to himself that in the barn he didn't have to think any of his regular thoughts. He might be off on his own, a thousand miles away, in the morning he wouldn't see Vern Decker's house or any landscape he knew. He could lie awake watching moonlight through cracks in the rough planks of the walls and thinking about nothing at all except how happy he was to be alone, how there were accidents in life (his father selling the trailer, his father meeting up with Vern, this barn behind Vern's house, and so forth) as wispy and delicate as a cobweb you could break without meaning to but you could avoid breaking too if you were careful. He never knew when he fell asleep, except his thinking seemed to blur at the edges. Ideas of things changed to pictures but the pictures came sideways, at a slant. Sometimes they were pictures of people he knew but most of the time they were strangers. Then he'd be asleep, he'd be gone, and in the morning he always woke early because of roosters crowing on a farm close by. He'd wake up stiff and dry-mouthed from breathing in the hay dust for so many hours but it was a good feeling to be awake so early, before any of the others, sometimes two or three hours before he could go in for breakfast. The point was, he could do anything he wanted: sneak out to the highway and hitch a ride north or south, flag down a Greyhound bus and see how far a dollar or two could take him. That was a promise he had made himself too, something that was waiting, but he didn't want to leave his father exactly, he didn't want to cause his father grief. He knew his father loved him because there wasn't anything else to love.

Little wife they started calling her after the first week or so, it was Judd's father's expression, teasing, mock serious, he'd sing a few loud lines of an old Johnny Cash song and mix in *Little wife, sweet little wife*, clowning around in the kitchen trying to get Agnes to dance with him. But if she fell in with him, raising her arms, smiling, a slow uncertain open-mouthed grin that showed her crooked front teeth, he'd back off and leave her standing there.

Judd didn't feel sorry for her because, near as he could tell, she wasn't ever surprised, or disappointed, or thrown off stride for long. She'd known to fit herself in with the rhythm of the household from the first.

Little wife, little wife. She'd bang around the house, upstairs and down, even in the cellar, as if she owned it. Humming the tune to Judd's father's drawling song.

Right away she lorded if over Judd. He saw that coming. He was only a kid, he was only twelve, but he'd have to help her out with things, washing up after meals especially, keeping the house picked up, and she didn't want him in her way or gaping at her. As if Judd would gape at her! She was nervous and giggly with so many men prizing her—not just Judd's father (who seemed to be her favorite) and Vern Decker but whoever else dropped by—and soon got bossy enough to nag Vern into getting the TV repaired. It had been on the fritz for months and nobody tried to watch it any more but Agnes insisted, Agnes put her foot down, as she said, and in twelve days it was working good as new and if she was left alone in the big old damn house—as she called it—at least she wasn't *lonely*. She kept the sound up loud whether she was in the room with the TV or not. Judd knew too that she talked back to the TV voices or was she maybe just talking to herself? rehearsing things she might say to all the men who were so crazy about her?

Much of the time she wore jeans but she took care to add a bright-colored blouse or sweater; she favored a shiny patent leather belt that cinched her waist in so tight Judd wondered how she could breathe. When her hair was washed it was fluffed and curly, she wore lipstick even during the day, sprayed herself with the strong lilac perfume Charley Ryan bought her at the Woolworth's in town. *Little wife, little wife.* She chattered when nobody was much listening but she didn't seem to mind. They'd given her her own room at the back of the house—a real bed with a mattress. Near as Judd cared to figure the men shared her, there was nothing secret or furtive about it after the first few days when Judd's father avoided looking directly at him or talking with him much, it was just the way things were going to be, Judd wasn't even sure how he felt or that he was called upon to feel anything. What business was it of his? What did he care? Agnes was quick to guess the moods the men were in—they could swing from being happy one minute to being angry the next—she was sensitive, Judd thought, even if she wasn't very bright—so it was mainly with Judd that she complained or tossed things around in the kitchen or shut doors hard. Sometimes it seemed she wanted him on her side, that they were both kids together, brother and sister maybe, other times she ordered him around, asked him what the hell he was gaping at, who he thought *he* was. Once she slitted her eyes at him as if she were practicing slitting them at somebody else. She said in a low breathy voice, "I got as much right to be here as you. You don't own the place either, you and your hotshit daddy."

Sometimes it was Agnes and Judd's father, sometimes it was Agnes and Vern whispering in corners, exchanging secret looks, then again it might be Agnes and Al for a few days, or, after a wild ride on Charley Ryan's motorcycle one Sunday in early September, Agnes and Charley for a few days. He had finally managed to get Agnes drunk enough to climb behind him on the sheepskin-covered seat of the big black bike and clasp her arms around his waist and off they went, gone for much of the night. And when they returned nobody much noticed—Judd's father, for instance, was paired off with a woman of his own and anything that Agnes and fat-faced Charley Ryan did together wasn't significant.

Still, it gave Agnes a special nervous bloom for a while. Charley Ryan coming around, taking her to town on his cycle. Treating her good. It proved Agnes could get a man for herself, exclusively for herself, any time she wanted.

But she was jealous of women who came to parties at Vern's house. She accused them of looking down on her, not talking to her, laughing at her behind her back. She hated them, she said. Who did they think they were?—cunts like anybody else. So she'd sulk and hide away in her room with a bottle. And maybe none of the men would give a damn, or maybe one of them would kick the door open and haul her out. "Here's Agnes. Here's our pal!" The mood of the party might be teasing and good-natured or it might not be so good-natured and the teasing got a little rough. Agnes shouted that she had her dignity and she intended to leave the next morning. She had business of her own, she said, and nobody had better try to stop her. Agnes with her hair in her eyes, her bright lipstick smeared, cords standing out in her neck. Then she'd start crying and Judd's father would be the one to calm her, patting her back, hugging her and winking at his buddies over her head. She was crazy about Judd Senior, that was obvious. "You know you're free to leave us any time you want, honey," he said, puckering his lips. "Don't you mind you'd be breaking all our hearts."

So she'd cry for half an hour more, then forgive them.

And in the morning Judd might catch a glimpse of her staggering into the bathroom at the rear of the house, just off the kitchen. He was never watching for her but it seemed he was always seeing her and then it was too late to look away. Agnes wearing that old lemon-colored "silk" shirt of his father's, a pair of white underpants or no underpants at all, the movement of her legs pale and fishlike in the shadows, all her movements vague, dim, swimming, as if she went where she went by instinct, her eyes closed. She didn't always close the bathroom door tight. He'd hear her inside, using the toilet. Or being sick—gagging and retching. Or crying. She did a good deal of crying now. And singing to herself on good mornings. Singing while she ran the faucet or the shower. Judd didn't know which of her noises he hated the most, he wasn't even sure he could distinguish between them.

For a while there was a joke in the household about Agnes having to use the john so much. Peeing every half hour, it seemed. Agnes said angrily that she couldn't help it. They teased her, they'd let it drop for a while then bring it up again, watching her get red, her eyes fill with tears. She didn't know what was wrong, she said, she just *had* to. And it burned, she said, every time she went. "Maybe I better go to a doctor," she said one day, but in such a vague flat voice it seemed she knew nobody was listening.

Agnes was in love with Judd's father so naturally she had questions to ask about Judd's mother but Judd knew enough not to get roped into answering them. What did Judd's mother look like; was she pretty; was she smart; did Judd favor her, or him? Judd just shrugged his shoulders and mumbled that he didn't know.

And it was true, he didn't. Or if it wasn't true it should have been.

She believed in reincarnation too, sort of. "Re-in-car-nation"— carefully pronounced. Souls dying in one place and being born somewhere else, ancient lives like in Egypt some people could remember and describe perfectly . . . like on TV one night there was a whole hour program devoted to the subject, wasn't there? And they wouldn't just lie about something so important.

She got in a funny quarrel with Judd Senior over what Judd Senior called the logistics of reincarnation. For instance, there are a hell of a lot more people living today than in the year 1000 B.C., right?—so where do the extra ones come from?

But Agnes didn't understand. "Extra ones . . . ?"

Judd Senior tried to explain but she couldn't follow. She was sitting at the kitchen table frowning and squinting. Her skin gave off a fruity warmth, her gray eyes, narrowed, looked shrewd and almost intelligent. Finally she said in a voice quavering with triumph, a slow gloating awakening to triumph, "Okay but *where did the first ones come from, of all?*" Judd's father just waved her away as if she were too stupid to deal with but Agnes thumped the table with both fists, hot and flushed, noisy as a child. "Okay Mr. Hotshot where did the first ones come from? Huh? You don't know, do you! *You don't know any goddam fucking more than I do!*"

She kept herself so secret about certain things, where she was from, for instance, who her people were, they couldn't help wondering, Judd Senior especially. He'd ask sly questions like was she the runaway wife of some crazy old millionaire? or the runaway mother of a half-dozen squawling brats? or an escapee from the women's detention up in Fredericktown . . . ? Which would get poor Agnes going, red-faced and laughing, or angry, or confused, giving Judd Senior a shove in the chest (though she learned to be careful since Judd Senior never allowed any female to poke him without he poked her right back). Eventually it came out that she was from a farm, or what was left of a farm, about fifty miles north of town. She couldn't get along with her family, she said. She'd had enough of them, she didn't want to talk about it.

Judd Senior kept asking, though. As Judd Junior knew, he didn't like secrets because secrets meant somebody was deceiving him. It was a kind of cheating too, Judd Senior explained, almost like you were being denied something that belonged to you. So he kept poking, asking his sly funny teasing questions, and one night in October Agnes got drunk and started telling them about her mother and her married sister who lived at home with her husband and kids, how they got in her way and tried to boss her around, ever since she'd dropped out of high school they were after her, it was Agnes this, Agnes that, if she had a boyfriend they raised hell because it wasn't the right kind of boyfriend and if she didn't have a boyfriend they talked about nobody wanting to marry her, and then her father got sick, he'd had to give up farming a long time ago because he couldn't make a living at it, then he worked where he could get work then he got sick, some kind of kidney disease they said wasn't cancer exactly but it sure as hell sounded like cancer to Agnes, then he died but it took him almost a year to die, he was a real nice man Agnes said, starting to cry, it was just how things happened to him that made him act the way he did, she could see that, she could understand that, but by the time he died everybody was afraid of him and hated him, Agnes thought she sort of hated him too, then after he died they were all still mad about something, she just couldn't take that kind of shit any longer, she had to get out and she wasn't ever going back. Now she was

crying, sobbing, rocking back and forth on the sofa. The men
were embarrassed and bored and it fell to Judd's father to pat
her on the shoulder and tell her okay, that was enough, but she
couldn't seem to stop, now that she got started she couldn't seem
to stop, wanted to sit there crying and talking about her father,
her married sister she hated, her grandmother who always had
to know her business, saying she loved her, but the men drifted
into another room and Judd wasn't going to get stuck with her
so he turned the TV sound up loud so that, maybe, the TV
would distract her, or make her feel better.

It was the next night that one of the men—Vern, or was it
Charley Ryan—slapped her and bloodied her nose.

And nobody told him to stop.

And Judd Senior said she deserved it, talking so much, acting
so smart-ass around the place as if she owned it.

And Agnes looked at the men and understood it was important not to cry right then, not to say anything, just to turn and
go to the bathroom and fix up her face; and stay out of their
way for the rest of the night.

II

The previous year, when Judd went to stay with his mother, the
plan was that he could stay with her—with them—as long as he
wanted. If things worked out. If they all got along. But Judd's
father wasn't to know that that was the plan, exactly. He could
be told later. So far as he knew Judd was going to stay with
his mother a few weeks and that was all. Over the telephone,
however, Judd's mother had said excitedly that she wanted him

with her as long as he wanted to be with her, she missed him so, thought about him every hour, her precious baby, sweet foxy little Judd, she didn't want a new baby, she said, she wanted *him*, then she was crying, short breathless sobs that sounded almost like laughing, and Judd held the receiver away from his ear, his eyes shut tight: if one person gave in to crying the other had better not. That was some wisdom of Judd Senior's he'd overheard.

Judd's mother had left Bethany Falls in February and it wasn't until late November that Judd went to stay with her in a small-sized city named Cicero in the southernmost tip of the state. By then she was divorced from Judd's father and beginning a new life. She'd had a hard time, she said, but she wouldn't dwell upon it, now she was engaged to a man, a gentleman actually, named Flagler, whom Judd was to call Mr. Flagler: he was an insurance and real estate salesman, a very nice man, but sensitive, she warned, and ambivalent—"ambivalent" was his word—about the future. Judd didn't understand, what did ambivalent mean? His mother said vaguely that he could look it up in the dictionary. She hadn't actually looked it up herself but she believed she knew what it meant. The main thing was, she added, that small children made Mr. Flagler nervous because they reminded him of when his own were small.

Judd would have supposed that "small" meant children of two or three or four, nor eleven, but he couldn't altogether be certain. It might apply to him as a warning.

He took the Greyhound bus to Cicero by himself, a five-hour ride. His father hardly spoke to him for days beforehand, then, seeing him off, he hugged him hard and said in a voice heavy with sarcasm, "Say hello to your mother's *boyfriend* for me, don't forget. Give your mother's *boyfriend* her husband's *congratulations and good wishes,*" but he was smiling too, one of his big broad mustache-curling smiles, so Judd smiled back and climbed onto the bus. He wasn't ever coming back again, that was *his* secret.

But the visit to Cicero didn't work out. Judd understood even before meeting his mother's fiancé that it was a mistake. They were living together in a large apartment complex called Cicero Acres that consisted of a number of two-story stucco buildings facing a central courtyard that held a swimming pool covered with a rotted tarpaulin. There were north, east, south, and west wings, and units ranging from "A" to "K." The sidewalks were gritty with ice and when Judd arrived in the late morning a crew of garbagemen, all black, was unloading garbage cans. They made so much noise crashing the cans against the dump truck, tossing them onto the ground, their shouts to one another were so loud and spirited, by the time Judd found his mother's apartment, number 11 in East Wing Unit "G," he had to ring the bell and knock for almost ten minutes because his mother was afraid to answer the door. She came to peek through the closed venetian blinds, finally, and let him in, hugging him in relief, kissing him wildly. She was terrified, she said, of those garbagemen— Wednesdays and Saturdays were their days—she was sorry she hadn't run to let him in right away. Even so, Judd could feel her trembling. She looked thinner than he remembered, the delicate bones on the backs of her hands stood out, and her hair was short, tightly curled, a lighter shade than he remembered. Her breath smelled just faintly sweet. Unpacking his bag she started to tell him about something that had happened a few weeks ago to a woman in a neighboring building, a woman living alone, her assailant was described only as a "black youth" and

he hadn't yet been apprehended; then she thought better of it
and changed the subject. He must be starving, she said brightly.
All those hours on the bus.

Judd stayed with his mother for a little more than two weeks
though he understood in the first day or two that he wasn't
wanted: not really.

There was some pretense in the beginning that Flagler wasn't
actually living in the apartment, just dropping by to meet Judd
and to stay for dinner, watching TV in the evening with Judd
and Judd's mother. He took them to see *Ghostbusters*, which
had been playing at the Cicero mall for six months, then to a
Howard Johnson's afterward; he even took Judd to a roller rink
one Saturday afternoon and sat alone, smoking, his big body soft
and relaxed-looking back in the shadows, his expression amiable, vague. Judd's mother had stayed back in the apartment so
that Judd and Mr. Flagler could become better acquainted but
when they were alone together they had nothing much to say.
Judd considered giving the man his father's message, imitating
the drawl and angry dip of his father's voice, but he hadn't that
kind of nerve, in any case he didn't hate Flagler that much. Actually he didn't hate him at all. Flagler had a small dark mustache
one quarter the size of Judd's father's, he had a puffy suety face,
small sad evasive eyes, a weak mouth. Even when he smiled he
looked aggrieved. His voice was surprisingly high for a man of
his size and his words frequently trailed off into an embarrassed
silence as if he'd lost the thread of what he was trying to say and
it hardly seemed important enough to retrieve.

Still, Judd could hear his mother and Flagler talking alone together, their voices urgent and hurried. They weren't quarreling—
he knew what quarrels sounded like—in fact Flagler never raised

his voice all the time Judd stayed with them—but he knew they were talking about him. Flagler was being reasonable, Flagler was asking how long Judd meant to stay, what about Judd's father, etc., and probably Judd's mother was doing her best to answer, telling the truth as she saw it, or some kind of truth at least. Judd wasn't anxious or even especially curious about what they were saying because it wouldn't be a surprise to him. Most things, he thought, weren't going to be surprises to him any longer.

It was almost a year later that Judd started taking a school bus to a consolidated county school a few miles from Decker's house. He hadn't wanted to go back to school, any school, and his father hadn't wanted him to—Judd Senior was down on public education, conformist American brainwashing as he called it—but a county agent had come out to Decker's asking questions about Judd. How old was he, where had he been born, who were his parents, etc. Now that Judd's father paid some of Decker's monthly mortgage he was a bona fide resident of Fayette County and his school-age children if he had any were not only eligible to attend Fayette County public schools but obliged under federal law to do so.

By this time the men were getting fairly brutal with Agnes so Judd was grateful for school. He stayed away from the house as long as he could and when he was home he kept to himself, working on his homework or reading. He'd stopped asking when they were going to leave Decker's house because the question seemed to upset his father, and he knew better than to ask what was wrong, what was happening with Agnes: why the men didn't seem to like her any more. Stupid cunt, they called her. It was a joky kind of thing most of the time. Stupid cow. Fatass. Fuck-face. But sometimes they hit her, pushed her around, knocked her against the wall, for the hell of it, maybe, or because she provoked them. She started crying or screamed at them and that made things worse. Even when nothing had happened for a day or two Judd could feel the charged atmosphere, an undercurrent of excitement in the house like the air before a thunderstorm.

He didn't know if he felt sorry for Agnes or if he was frightened for himself. He asked his father about it just once, when they were alone together, and his father stared at him and said, "Who wants to know?"

Poor dumb Agnes, poor little wife, that cunt with the pouting face, the swollen lip. Sometimes one or both of her eyes might be blackened, her nostrils encrusted with blood. They apologized afterward, the next day they'd all have hangovers and be sorry. The problem was that she provoked them. The kinds of meals she tried to get away with, the smart-ass things she said under her breath. She tried to play the men against one another and they didn't like that. She complained a lot and they didn't like that. Then she'd have a few beers too many and lose control and threaten to call the police and that would start it all again. A few days of peace and calm then another heavy session, Agnes screaming and slapping and scratching and kicking, and that meant real trouble: that meant one of the men might have to be held back by the others, and it always caused bad feelings among them afterward.

"The most devious thing about a woman," Judd's father told him, "is the trick of turning a man against his buddies. You watch for that, you hear?"

Agnes threatened to call the police so they told her to call the police. She threatened to leave so they told her to leave. But when Judd came home from school the next day nothing had changed, Agnes was still there, watching TV or messing around in the kitchen. Sometimes she seemed to want to talk, she asked him questions about school, if he was making friends, if he missed his mother, what his mother's new boyfriend was like, and Judd felt almost dizzy with wanting to get away; sometimes she'd give him a look of hatred and say nothing. A few days later there might be a party and he'd see her drunk and giggly, sprawled on somebody's lap—his father's, Vern Decker's, a stranger's—as if nothing had happened.

Maybe nothing had happened, Judd thought. If Agnes didn't think it had.

You guys gonna kill her? Judd wanted to ask.

If he knew to ask the question in just the right way, grinning with half his mouth like Judd Senior, screwing up one of his eyes like crazy Al—if he knew how to get the words out right—then he'd swallow hard and ask. *You guys gonna kill her? Okay but why? Don't you like her any more?*

But he didn't know how. His throat closed up at the thought of asking, his lips were numb. And it wasn't any of his business, was it. He was just a kid, not even thirteen years old. Enrolled, in the seventh grade at the Fayette County Consolidated School up the road.

One morning when the house was empty except for Agnes and Judd he peeked into her bedroom on his way out to catch the school bus. It was after eight o'clock but she was still asleep, she slept long and heavy and hard like a sick person. Lying on her back at a twisted angle across the bed, her head turned to the side, mouth open, a wet rasping gurgling snore. Her hair was stringy and greasy, her eyelids puffy. The blanket was pulled down to expose one of her breasts. Judd saw that she was thinner, her chest bones prominent, the skin pale and pimply except where it was discolored by bruises. Her nipple was raw-looking, rosy brown. The breast looked slack and queer just by itself. Was she sleeping? Judd wondered, uneasy, standing in the doorway. Or was she just pretending?

Judd's father said Agnes was always "putting on an act": even her shrieks and crying jags. His father said with a wave of his hand, Poor dumb cunt Agnes, don't pay no heed to *her*, she doesn't know her ass from her elbow.

She'd thought she was pregnant for a week or two but it was a false alarm.

She'd thought she had some secret thing going with one of Vern's pals from work, him and her talking on the telephone when nobody was around, making plans, plotting behind Vern's and Judd Senior's backs, but it all fizzled out: the guy wasn't that much of an asshole to fall for a pig like *her*.

Judd stood in the doorway, staring. He knew he should leave but he simply stood there. It was a surprise to him that Agnes's room was so small—about the size of the room they'd given him, upstairs. A stink of old unwashed bedclothes, lilac perfume, beer. The men's sweat and Agnes's own sweetish-stale smell. There was an odor too of menstrual blood, rank, rich, dark-smelling, Judd knew the mattress was stained because he'd overheard one of the men complaining and Agnes shooting back that it wasn't for Christ's sake *her* fault, as if it would be *her* fault, doing stuff like that when she only wanted to be left alone. . . . The blind on the window hung torn and crooked, yanked off its roll. Judd had the idea that somebody might come to look in, he'd see both Agnes and Judd, both of them at the same time. He felt his groin tighten with danger. If she opened her eyes, if she saw him, what then. Her cherry-red lipstick was nearly worn off but her mouth looked fleshy and damp. Her breathing was labored and irregular as if, each time, she had to think how to breathe; how to suck in air. Last night the men had been playing poker in the kitchen. Seven or eight men, Agnes hanging over their shoulders, caught up in the tension. Four clubs! Five spades! Queen! King! Ace of hearts! They told her she didn't know shit about poker but she insisted she had a lucky streak sometimes in any card game she tried especially gin rummy, why didn't they play a few hands of gin rummy and she'd show them, but the men weren't interested in gin rummy. Go watch TV, Agnes. Go stick your head in the toilet.

Why do you want to hurt me, says poor little wife, poor dumb cunt Agnes. Why do you want to hurt me don't you love me Jesus look how I love *you*. Swigging ale like one of the men, lifting the bottle to her mouth. Blue jeans with a fly front open at the waist, tight red sweater, sleeveless, though the goddam house is freezing: none of the windows fits right. Is Judd spying? Is Judd listening? He's doing his math homework upstairs and doesn't give a damn about what goes on downstairs. For instance if Agnes loses her temper and starts throwing plates and silverware on the floor, screaming she's going to call the sheriff she's going to call her fucking brother-in-law to come get her, she's had enough of their shit.

But hey why do you want to hurt me? You know how I love
you.

Love ya. Love ya.

Judd stood in the doorway, his own breathing queer and irregular. He hadn't slept many hours the night before and now
he felt asleep on his feet. Once, a long time ago when Agnes had
just moved in with them, he had opened the bathroom door by
mistake and almost walked in on her and his father. They were
both naked, fooling around, running water in the tub, hot and
noisy and splashing, the air thick with steam. Judd's father had
turned with an angry laugh—"Hey! Get the hell out!"—and
Agnes had given a high foolish shriek, eyes wide, hiding her
breasts with a towel. In disgust Judd had slammed the door on
them and run away and hid in the barn and he hadn't thought
of it since then, not that he knew. But he was still disgusted.

The sky was lightening, there were birds in the eaves, the
crowing of roosters in the distance. Pale sunlight slanted through
the cracked shade. It was a time of day he liked when he was
outside and away from the house. He heard Agnes grating her
teeth faintly, sighing in her sleep. One of her fists clenched. Her
puffy eyelids twitching. The nipple on her breast looked like a
tiny bud that had been injured and would never open.

He waited for her to wake and see him, he waited for the
next thing to happen that would happen. But she didn't wake,
she looked dopey, drugged. And he remembered the school bus
suddenly. And he wondered if he had already missed it.

He had missed the school bus, yes, but it couldn't be helped.

He tossed his books down by Decker's mailbox and ran along
the road for a while. No reason, just to run. His breath steamed,

his heart was pounding. Nothing came by accident really. Nothing came by accident really: he believed that. But he wasn't going back to the house. He ran along the road, he followed a farmer's lane back into a field, running slow, trotting, his lungs beginning to ache in a way he liked, his eyes stinging from the cold. He had the whole morning, nobody knew where he was. He had the whole day. Through a stand of scrubby trees he could see a sheet of water, a frozen pond, then he saw a field of flowers, golden yellow, but how could there be flowers in the winter?—and when he got there he saw it was the remains of a soybean crop. The flowers were just leaves, dried and yellowed, dried to different shades of yellow and brown. But the field was pretty in the sun. The leaves were almost flowers. He picked one of the twisty little beans that hadn't been harvested and squeezed it between his fingernails, how hard, tiny beans inside like pebbles. He stood in the sun catching his breath, getting warm. Then he was almost too warm inside his clothes. He'd decided something without knowing what it was. He didn't have to think of it, it was done.

But he didn't go back to the house, he had the whole day. Farther along the lane he found a pile of debris neatly raked together, mainly tree limbs, broken branches, leaves, but a pane of glass too, cracked glass, about the size of a window. How could a windowpane get so far out here, Judd wondered. Who brought it out here, and why, and where was it from, where had it originally been used as a window? Judd stood staring for a long time. He might have been half asleep on his feet, he seemed to see the sun flashing hot on his hair, the back of his head. He was waiting for some notion to come to him, one of those quick flashing dreams that come just before sleep. But there was nothing. Just the broken glass, the way the soybean leaves had looked like flowers, like goldenrod, the way he was sweating inside his clothes and his lungs still slightly aching from the cold air. He was reaching but nothing came and it was all right, it didn't matter, it was done. It was decided and done.

Is Agnes sick? Judd asked.

She isn't *sick*, they said.

Her jaw was swollen, both her eyes blackened, one morning she was coughing up blood, too weak to get out of bed. She whined that her jaw was broken—she was scared—she couldn't hardly move her mouth—couldn't eat anything solid. Judd's father went in to sit on the edge of the bed and calm her down, smoking one cigarette after another, he was nervous and bored, getting fed up with the task. Hell sweetheart you'll be fine, he said, didn't nobody mean to hurt you and you know it but see it don't happen again. She whined would he call a doctor and he said sure. But a day went by, and another day, and Agnes didn't get out of bed, then it was a week and by that time she seemed to have forgotten. She'd stopped complaining and she'd stopped calling out for Judd Junior to come help, she began to sleep most of the time. Her skin tinged yellow, mucus in the corners of her eyes. The room stank of sweat and dried urine. She couldn't get out of bed to use the bathroom and nobody was around to help, it was just something she'd have to get over, they said, like the flu.

Judd asked his father who had beaten Agnes so bad this time, had he wanted to kill her, and Judd's father said vaguely that he didn't know exactly, he hadn't been in the house right then. "But shouldn't we get some help? Like a doctor?" Judd said. "She doesn't need help," Judd's father said. "Hell she's getting better on her own—it's just her attitude."

A while later he leaned into Judd's room, a can of beer in his hand, and said, "Look kid none of this is your worry, okay? Just concentrate on your schoolwork like you been doing." He smiled at Judd with the lower part of his mouth. The corners of his eyes puckered. "Keep your nose to yourself, you know?—we'll probably be moving out in a while, as soon as thing's get settled—I tell you I'm getting a new car the first of February?—so things are okay, hon, they're really *okay*."

Judd raised his eyes to his father's face. The room was so small, the mattress so close to the door, he could have reached out to touch his father's leg with his toes. He swallowed hard and didn't know what to say.

"How's it sound, kid? Nineteen-eighty Mercury owned by only one other person," Judd's father said. He was still smiling, stroking his mustache. "And we'll be moving out of here sometime soon, I promise you that."

Judd said faintly that it sounded great.

Past New Year's, and Agnes had been sick for almost two weeks, and they wouldn't let Judd go see her, but one day Vern explained to him what had happened, more or less.

It seems that this buddy of theirs, this guy, had come out from town to see her. Actually they'd already met—Agnes knew who he was—but she wouldn't cooperate. She was drunk and in a real bitch of a mood and she tried to give them a lot of shit, calling the sheriff, calling her brother-in-law, the same old shit, and next thing they knew she was running out the driveway barefoot in the snow, wanted to flag down a car or something, and they had to wrestle her down and carry her back to the house, it took three or four of them, Jesus she was strong, scratching and kicking and biting like a maniac, she *was* a maniac in fact, and that was how the trouble started.

Give a bitch like that a knife, Vern said, shaking his head, grinning, and she'd cut all their throats.

Judd wasn't going to peek into the room, he didn't want to see her. Through the door he could hear the TV voices—somebody had carried the set in so that she could watch all she wanted, they'd turned it on and left the volume high, but Judd didn't know if Agnes could watch TV any more, he'd heard the men joking that she had all she wanted now she sure as hell didn't need them.

The house was freezing, the house stank of food left lying around, dishes in the sink, underwear, towels, the bathroom that nobody ever cleaned now that Agnes was sick. Sinks scummy with dirt, dust balls on the floor. She was dying, Judd could smell her dying, it was the strongest smell of all. "How come the doctor never came?" Judd asked Vern and Vern shrugged his shoulders and never bothered to answer. He didn't ask his father because he was afraid of his father now.

So one morning he hid in the barn until the school bus passed, then hiked three or four miles out to the highway, to a Sunoco station where he knew there was an outdoor telephone booth. It was freezing cold and his breath steamed and his lungs ached from walking fast in a way that might almost scare him but he hadn't time to be scared. He could have made the call from the house—nobody was home—nobody except

Agnes—but he didn't want to take the chance of any of them coming back.

He had two dimes ready in his jacket pocket. He had memorized the number of the county sheriff's office. He knew most of what he would tell them, the exact words even: a girl who was sick, a girl who was dying, a girl kept locked up by some men, then he'd give them Vern Decker's name and the location of the house, he'd repeat the information but he wouldn't give his name and he wouldn't say where he was calling from. Then he'd hang up. Quick and easy, like that. Like that, and it would be done.

It would be done and what happened next would happen without him.

He was shivering and sweating too, damp inside his clothes; his breath came fast and shallow as if he'd been running. This is it, he thought. Okay, you little fucker, this is it. He could hear his voice saying the sheriff's telephone number, it wasn't a number he was likely to forget by now and if he did forget it he could dial information. He knew exactly what he would say when the call went through but he didn't yet know what he would do in the half minute and minute and hour following the call, after he'd hung up. That was the hard part he hadn't memorized. It was the part he would have to get through on his own. After he gave the information, repeated his slow careful words, hung up. He could picture himself slipping the receiver quickly back into its cradle like somebody in a movie worried that the telephone call could be traced if he was too slow. He could see that, and he could see the traffic out on the highway, cars, a truck, a bus, more cars, a big truck hauling cattle, the gritty snow humped against the road divider, the sun at its sharp morning angle in

the sky, he could see the pavement cold and glistening stretching off in both directions but he couldn't see himself walking at
the edge of the road, he couldn't see which side he would take,
he'd have to wait for some notion to come to him when it was
time, some strong nudge, which side of the road, which direction he'd take, whether he would be pulled one way or another,
he'd have to wait.

YARROW

He was afraid to borrow the money from a bank.

It was a Saturday morning in early April, still winter, soft wet snow falling, clumps the size of blossoms.

A messy season, flu season, dirt-raddled snow drifted against the edges of things, mud thawing on the roads. A cavernous-clouded sky and blinding sunshine, and it was the longest drive he'd made in his truck in memory, three miles to his cousin Tyrone Clayton's house.

Tyrone saw it in his face. Asked him inside, asked him did he want an ale? Irene and the children were in town shopping.

The radio was turned up loud: Fats Domino singing "Blueberry Hill."

Mud on Jody's boots so he said he wouldn't come all the way into the house, he'd talk from the doorway. Didn't want to track up Irene's clean floor.

He could only stay a minute, he said. He had a favor to ask.

"Sure," Tyrone said. Laying his cigarette carefully in an ashtray.

"I need to borrow some money."

"How much?"

"Five hundred dollars."

Jody spoke in a low quick voice just loud enough for Tyrone to hear. Then exhaled as if he'd been holding his breath in for a long time.

Tyone said, keeping his voice level and easy, "Guess I can manage that."

"I'll pay you back as soon as I can," Jody said. "By June at the latest."

"No hurry," Tyrone said.

Then they were silent. Breathing hard. Excited, deeply embarrassed. Tyrone knew that Jody needed more than $500—much more than $500—but the way things were right now he couldn't afford to lend him more. He just couldn't afford it, and even $500 was going to be hard. He knew that Jody knew all this but Jody had had to come to him anyway, knowing it, asking the favor knowing that Tyrone would say yes but knowing that Tyrone could barely afford it either. Because Jody was desperate, and if Tyrone hadn't quite wanted to understand that until this minute he had to understand it now.

His cousin's young aggrieved handsome face inside a sallow face blurred and pocked by fatigue. Three days' growth of whiskers on his chin and he wouldn't meet Tyrone's eyes, he was that ashamed.

Tyrone said he could get to the bank Monday noon, would that be soon enough?

Jody said as if he hadn't been listening that he wanted to pay the going rate of interest on the loan. "Ask them at the bank, will you? And we'll work it out."

"Hell, no," Tyrone said, laughing, surprised, "I don't want any interest."

"Just find out," Jody said, an edge to his voice, "and we'll work it out."

Tyrone asked how was Brenda these days, he'd heard from Irene she was getting better? But his voice came out weak and faltering.

Jody said she *was* getting better, she rested a lot during the day, the stitches from the surgery had come out, but she still had a lot of pain and the doctor warned them about rushing things so she had to take it slow.

He did the grocery shopping, for instance. All the shopping. Not that he minded—he didn't, he was damned glad Brenda was alive—but it took time and he only had Saturdays really.

Then this afternoon if the snow didn't get worse he was hoping to put in a shift at the quarry, three or four hours. Shoveling, mainly, some cleanup.

He was speaking faster, with more feeling. A raw baffled voice new to him, and his eyes puffy and red-rimmed as if he'd been rubbing at them.

All this while Jody's truck was idling in the driveway, spewing out clouds of exhaust. He'd left the key in the ignition, which Tyrone thought was a strange thing to do, almost rude.

Snowflakes were falling thicker now, blown in delicate skeins by the wind. Twisting and turning and looping like narrowing your eyes to shift your vision out of focus so that it's your own nerve endings you see out there.

Wet air, colder than the temperature suggested. Flu season, and everybody was passing it around to everybody else.

Something more needed to be said before Jody left, but Tyrone couldn't think what it was.

He stood in the doorway watching Jody maneuver the truck out onto the road. It was a heavy-duty dump truck, Jody's own truck, a '49 Ford he'd have to be replacing soon. Tyrone was thinking they should have shaken hands or something, but it wasn't a gesture that came naturally or easily to them. He couldn't remember when he had last shaken hands with somebody as close to him as Jody, and this morning wasn't the time to start.

He watched Jody drive away. He hadn't gotten around to shaving yet that morning himself and he stood vague and dazed, rubbing his stubbled jaw, thinking how much it had cost Jody McIllvanney to ask for that $500, and how much it would cost him.

For the past year or more Jody's wife, Brenda, had been sick. Twenty-eight years old, thin, nervous, red-haired, pretty, she'd had four children now ranging in age from Dawn, who was thirteen years old and said to be troublesome, to the baby boy, who was only eighteen months. In between were two more boys, ten years and six years. Brenda had never quite recovered from the last pregnancy, came down with a bladder infection, had to have an operation just after Christmas—at a city hospital forty miles away, which meant people in Yarrow had to drive eighty miles round-trip to see her. Which meant, too, more medical bills the McIllvanneys couldn't afford.

The day before she was scheduled to enter the hospital, Brenda spoke with Irene Clayton on the phone and said she was frightened she was going to die.

"Don't talk that way," Irene said sharply.

Brenda was crying as if her heart was broken, and Irene was afraid she too would start to cry.

"I just don't think Jody could manage without me," Brenda was saying. "Him and the children—and all the bills we owe—I just don't think he could keep going."

"You know better than to talk that way," Irene said. "That's a terrible thing to say." She listened to Brenda crying and felt helpless and frightened herself. She said, "You hadn't better let Jody hear you going on like that."

The McIllvanneys lived in Brenda's parents' old farmhouse, which wasn't by choice but all they could afford. Some years ago Jody had started building his own house at the edge of town but he ran out of money shortly after the basement was finished— Jody was a trucker, self-employed; his work tended to be local, seasonal, not very reliable—and for more than a year the family lived in the basement, below ground. (The roof was tarpapered over and there were windows but still the big single room was damp, chilly, depressing; the children were always coming down with colds. Dawn called it a damn dumb place to live, no wonder the kids on the school bus laughed at them all. Living like rats in a hole!) After Brenda's mother died they moved into the old farmhouse, which was free and clear, no mortgage, except it had been built in the 1880s and was termite-ridden and needed repairs constantly. Rotting shingles, leaky roof, earthen cellar that flooded when it rained: you name it. Bad as the *Titanic*, Jody said. He wished the damn thing *would* sink.

When Brenda got pregnant for the fourth time Jody began working part-time at the limestone quarry in Yarrow Falls: hard filthy backbreaking work he hated, but it paid better than anything else he could find. Jody handled a shovel, he climbed ladders, he operated drills and tractors and wire saws; when it rained he stood in the pit, water to his knees, coughing up phlegm, his feet aching as if they were on fire. Just temporary work he hoped wouldn't kill him.

Worse yet, he told Tyrone, he might develop a taste for the quarry. Like most of the quarriers. The limestone, the open fresh air, the weird machines that were so noisy and dangerous—it was work not just anybody could do. You had to have a strong back and the guts for it, and anything like that, it tended to get under your skin if you weren't careful. It brought some pride with it after all.

The Clayton children, Janice and Bobby, were fond of their Uncle Jody, as they were taught to call him—Janice knew he was really a cousin of theirs, just as he was a cousin of their father's—except when he was in one of his bad moods. Then he wouldn't really look at them, he'd just mutter hello without smiling. He had a worse temper than their father, and he was a bigger man than their father: muscled arms and shoulders that looked as if they were pumped up and that the flesh would hurt, ropy veins, and skin stretched tight. But he could be funny, loud-laughing as a kid, with a broad side-slanting grin and a way of teasing that left you breathless and excited as if you'd been tickled with quick hard fingers. Their own father was lean and hard and soft-spoken, an inch or two shorter than his cousin. He worked at the Allis Chalmers plant in town and never had anything interesting to say about it—just that it was *work*, and it *paid*—while Jody had all sorts of tales, some believable and some not, about driving his truck. "Never a dull minute with Jody around!" Irene always said. Tyrone said that was true, but "You know how he exaggerates."

One summer when Janice was a small child her Uncle Jody came over to the house with a half-dozen guinea chicks in a cardboard box, a present for them, and Janice had loved the chicks, tiny enough to stand in the palm of her hand; they didn't weigh anything! No feathers like the adults, just fuzzy blond down, stubby wings, and legs disproportionately long for their bodies. They were fearless, unlike the adults that were so suspicious and nerved up all the time.

"They're pretty birds," Jody said. "I like seeing them around the place—you get kind of used to them."

The Claytons tried to raise the guinea fowl according to Jody's instructions but they died off one by one and in the end even Janice lost her enthusiasm for them. She'd given them special names—Freckles, Peewee, Queenie, Bathsheba—but they disappointed her because all they wanted to do was eat.

They only liked her, she said, because she fed them.

After Jody borrowed the $500 from Tyrone he didn't drop by the house for a long time. And Tyrone didn't seek him out, feeling embarrassed and uncomfortable: he didn't want Jody to think he was waiting to be paid back or even that he was thinking about the money.

(Was he thinking about it? Only occasionally, when it hit him like a blow to the gut.)

Irene didn't hear from Brenda very often either, which was strange, she said, and sad, and she hoped the money wouldn't come between them because Brenda was so sweet and such a good friend and needed somebody to talk to what with Jody and Jody's moods—and that Dawn was a handful too, judging from what Janice said. (Dawn was a year older than Janice but in her class at school.) Irene said, "Why don't we invite them over here for a supper or something? We haven't done that in a long time." But Tyrone thought the McIllvanneys might misunderstand. "He'll think I'm worried about that money," Tyrone said.

It wasn't until midsummer that Jody made what he called the first payment on the loan, $175 he gave Tyrone in an envelope, and Tyrone was relieved, and embarrassed, and tried to tell him why not keep it for a while since probably he needed it—didn't he need it?—and there wasn't any hurry anyway. But Jody insisted. Jody said it was the least he could do.

Then word got back to Tyrone that Jody had borrowed money from a mutual friend of theirs at about the time he'd borrowed the $500 from Tyrone *and he had paid all of it back*: $350, and he'd paid it all back in a lump sum, and Tyrone was damned mad to hear about it. Irene tried to tell him it didn't mean anything, only that Jody knew Tyrone better, was closer to Tyrone, like a brother; also, if he'd only borrowed $350 from the other man it was easier to pay it all back and close out the debt. Sure, said Tyrone. That makes me the chump.

But he didn't mean it and when, a few days or a week later, Irene brought the subject up again, wondering when Jody was going to pay the rest of the money, he cut her off short, saying it was his money, not hers, and it was between him and Jody and hadn't anything to do with her, did she understand that?

Janice didn't want to tell her mother, but when they went back to school in the fall Dawn McIllvanney began to behave mean to her. And Dawn could be really mean when she wanted to be.

She was a chunky thick-set girl, swarthy skin like her father's, sly eyes, a habit of grinning so it went through you like a sliver of glass; not a bit of friendliness in it. Called Janice "*Jan-y*" in a sliding whine and shoved her on the school bus or when they were waiting in the cafeteria line. "Oh, excuse me, *Jan-y!*" she'd say, making anyone who was listening laugh. Dawn was the center of a circle of four or five girls who were rough and pushy and loud, belligerent as boys; she got poor grades in school not because she was stupid—though she might have been a little slow—but because she made a show of not trying, not handing in homework, wising off in class and angering her teachers. Janice thought it was unfair that Dawn McIllvanney had such a pretty red-haired mother while she had a mother who was like anybody's mother—plain and pleasant and boring. She'd always thought, before the trouble started, that Brenda McIllvanney would rather have had *her* for a daughter than Dawn.

Janice soon understood that Dawn hated her and she'd better keep her distance from her, but it happened that in gym class she couldn't and that was where Dawn got her revenge: threw a basketball right into Janice's face one time, broke Janice's pink plastic glasses, claimed afterward it was an accident: "*Jan-y*" got in her way. Another time, when the girls were doing gymnastics, Dawn stuck her big sneakered foot out in front of Janice as Janice—who was wiry and quick, one of the best gymnasts in the class—did a series of cartwheels the full length of the mat, and naturally Janice fell, fell sideways, fell hard, seeing as she fell her cousin's face pinched with hatred, the rat-glittering little eyes. Pain shot like a knife, like many knives, through Janice's body, and for a long time she couldn't move—just lay there sobbing, hearing Dawn McIllvanney's mock-incredulous voice as the gym instructor reprimanded her. *Hey, I didn't do anything, what the hell are you saying? Look, it was her, she's the one, it was her own damn fault, the little crybaby!*

Janice never told her mother about the incident. She tried not to think that Dawn, who was her cousin after all, had wanted to hurt her really—break her neck or her backbone, cripple her for life. She tried not to think that.

One warm autumn day Irene Clayton met Brenda McIllvanney in the A&P in town—Brenda, whom she hadn't seen in month—Brenda, who was thin, almost gaunt, but wearing a flowery print dress—red lipsticked lips and hard red nails and a steely look that went through Irene like a razor. And Irene just stood there staring as if the earth had opened at her feet.

In her parked car in the lot Irene leaned her forehead against the steering wheel and began to cry. She made baffled sobbing sounds that astonished and deeply embarrassed the children; Janice and Bobby had never seen their mother cry in such a public place, and for so little reason they could understand. She usually wept in a rage at them!

Bobby threw himself against the back seat, pressing his hands over his ears. Janice, in the passenger's seat, looked out the window and said, "Momma, you're making a fool of yourself," in the coldest voice possible.

Tyrone wasn't accustomed to thinking about such things, poking into his own motives or other people's. But he'd known, he said. As soon as he'd handed Jody the money, that was it.

Irene said she didn't believe it.

She knew Brenda, and she knew Jody, and she didn't believe it.

Jody had thanked him but he hadn't wanted to look at him, Tyrone said. Took the money 'cause he couldn't not take it but that was that.

"I don't believe it, *really*," Irene said, wiping at her eyes.

Tyrone said nothing, lighting up a cigarette, shaking out the match. His movements were jerky and angry these days, these many days. Often it looked as if he was quarreling with someone under his breath. Irene said, "I don't believe it, *really*."

Jody sold his truck, gave up trucking for good, worked full-time now at the limestone quarry, still in debt, and that old house of theirs looked worse than ever—chickens and guinea fowl picking in the grassless front yard amid tossed-out trash, Brenda's peony beds overgrown with weeds as if no woman lived in the house at all—but still, somehow, Jody managed to buy a '53 Chevrolet up in Yarrow Falls, and he and Brenda were going out places together again, roadhouses and taverns miles away where no one knew them. Sometimes they were alone and sometimes they were with another couple. Their old friends rarely saw them now.

Tyrone was always hearing from relatives that the McIllvan-neys couldn't seem to climb out of their bad luck, though Jody was working ten, twelve hours a day at the quarry et cetera, poor Brenda had some kind of thyroid condition now and had to take medicine so expensive you couldn't believe it et cetera, and Tyrone listened ironically to all this and said, "O.K., but what about me? *What about me?*" And there never seemed to be any answer to that.

If Tyrone ran into Jody in town it was sheerly by accident. And damned clumsy and embarrassing: Jody pretended he didn't see Tyrone, turned nonchalantly away, whistling, hands in his pockets: turned a corner and walked fast and disappeared.

Asshole. As if Tyrone didn't see *him*.

Tyrone complained freely of his cousin to anyone who would listen: old friends, mutual acquaintances, strangers. He was baffled and bitter and hurt and furious, wondering aloud when he'd get his money back. And would he get it *with interest* as Jody had promised.

When he'd been drinking a bit, Tyrone said that nobody had ever thought Jody McIllvanney would turn out the way he had, a man whose word wasn't worth shit—not much better than a common crook—a man who couldn't even support his wife and children. "Anybody that bad off, he might as well hang himself," Tyrone would say. "Stick a shotgun barrel into his mouth and pull the trigger."

He had to stop thinking about Jody all the time, Irene said. She was getting scared he'd make himself sick.

She'd lain awake too many nights herself thinking about the McIllvanneys—Brenda in particular—and she wasn't going to think about them any longer. "It isn't healthy," she said, pleaded. "Ty? It eats away at your heart."

But Tyrone ignored her; he was calculating (sitting at the kitchen table, a sheet of paper before him, pencil in hand, bottle of Molson's Ale at his elbow) how much Jody was probably earning a week up at the Fall now that he'd been promoted from shoveler to drill runner. It made him sick to think that—subtracting union dues, Social Security, and the rest—Jody was probably making a few more dollars a week than he made at Allis Chalmers. And if Jody could get an extra shift time-and-a-half on Saturdays he'd be making a damn sight more.

When Tyrone stood he felt dizzy and panicky, as if the floor was tilting beneath his feet.

Most people in Yarrow were on Tyrone's side, but he sensed there were some on Jody's side and lately he'd begun to hear that Jody was saying things about *him*, bad-mouthing him so you'd almost think it was Tyrone Clayton who owed Jody McIllvanney money and not the other way around. Hadn't Jody helped him put asbestos siding on his house when he and Irene had first moved in? (Yes, but he, Tyrone, had helped Jody with that would-be house of his, helping to put in the concrete, lay the beams for the basement ceiling, tarpaper the goddamned roof in the middle of the summer.) Tyrone went out drinking to the places he'd always gone and there were the men he'd been seeing for years, men he'd gone to school with, but Jody wasn't there; there was a queer sort of authority in Jody's absence, as if, the more *he* said, the more his listeners were inclined to believe *Jody*. "I know things are still bad for Jody and Brenda," he'd say, speaking passionately, conscious of the significance of his words—which might be repeated after all to Jody—"and I don't even want the fucking money back, but I do want respect. I do want respect from that son of a bitch."

(Though in fact he did want the money back: every penny of it. And he tended to think Jody still owed him $500, the original sum, plus interest, no matter he'd insisted at the time of the loan that he didn't want "interest" from any blood relation.)

There were nights he came home drunk; other nights he was so agitated he couldn't sit still to eat his supper because he'd heard something at work that day reported back to him, and Irene tried to comfort him, Irene said he was frightening the children, Irene said in a pleading voice, Why not try to forget?—forgive? like in the Bible; wasn't that real wisdom?—and just not lend anybody any money ever again in his life. "What the hell was I supposed to do?" Tyrone would say, turning on her furiously. "Tell my own cousin I grew up with that I wouldn't help him out? Tell him to get out of that doorway there?" Irene backed off, saying, "Ty, I don't know what you were supposed to do, but it turned out a mistake, didn't it?" And Tyrone said, his face contorted with rage and his voice shaking, "It wasn't a mistake at the time, you stupid bitch. *It wasn't a mistake at the time.*"

One night that fall the telephone rang at 9 P.M. and Irene answered and it was Jody McIllvanney, whose voice she hadn't heard in a long time, drunk and belligerent and demanding to speak to Tyrone—who luckily wasn't home. So Jody told Irene to tell him he'd been hearing certain things that Tyrone was saying behind his back and he didn't like what he'd heard and if Tyrone had something to say to him why not come over to the house and tell it to his face, and if Tyrone was afraid to do that he'd better keep his mouth shut or *he'd* come over *there* and beat the shit out of Tyrone.

Jody was shouting, saying he'd pay back the goddamn money when he could, that was the best he could do; he hadn't asked to be born; that was the best he could do, goddamn it—and Irene, speechless, terrified, slammed down the receiver.

Afterward she said she'd never heard anyone anywhere sounding so crazy. Like he'd have killed her if he'd been able to get hold of her.

A chilly breezy November day but there was Jody McIllvanney in coveralls and a T-shirt, no jacket, bareheaded, striding along the sidewalk not looking where he was going: and Janice Clayton stared at him, shocked at how he'd changed—my God he was big now, what you'd call *fat!*—weighing maybe two hundred sixty pounds, barrel-chested, big jiggly stomach pressing against the fabric of his overalls, his face bloated too and his skin lumpy. It was said that stone quarriers ate and drank like hogs, got enormous, and there was Jody the shape of a human hog, even his hair long and shaggy, greasy, like a high school kid or a Hell's Angel. Janice stood frozen on the sidewalk, her schoolbooks pressed against her chest, hoping praying her Uncle Jody wouldn't glance up and see her or if he did he wouldn't recognize her though her heart kicked and she thought, *I don't hate him like I'm supposed to.*

But he looked up. He saw her. Saw how she was shrinking out toward the curb to avoid him and so he let her go, just mumbled a greeting she couldn't hear, and the moment was past, she was safe, she pushed her glasses up her nose and half ran up the street to escape. She remembered how he used to call out "How's it going?" to her and Bobby instead of saying hello—winking to show that it was a joke (what did any adult man care about how things were going for children) but serious in a way too. And she'd never known how to answer, nor had Bobby. "O.K.," they'd say, embarrassed, blushing, flattered. "All right, I guess."

(Janice had no anticipation, not the mildest of premonitions, that that would be the last time she'd see her Uncle Jody, but long afterward the sight of him would remain vivid in her memory, powerful, reproachful, and the November day too of gusty winds and the smell of snow in the air, a texture like grit. Waiting for the bus she was dreamy and melancholy, watching how the town's southside mills gave off smoke that rose into the air like mist. Powdery, almost iridescent, those subtle shifting colors

of the backs of pigeons—iridescent gray, blue, purple shading
into black.

The guinea fowl had long since died off but Janice had snapshots of her favorites, their names carefully recorded.)

Shortly after the New Year, Tyrone was driving to town when he
saw a man hitchhiking by the side of the road, and sure enough
it was Jody McIllvanney: Jody in his sheepskin jacket a wool cap
pulled low over his forehead, thumb uplifted. His face looked
closed in as a fist; he might have recognized Tyrone but gave no
sign just as Tyrone, speeding past, gave no sign of recognizing
him. It had all happened so swiftly Tyrone hadn't time to react. He
wondered if Jody's new car had broken down and he laughed aloud
harshly, thinking, Good. Serve him right. Serve them all right.

He watched his cousin's figure in the rearview mirror, diminishing with distance.

Then, for some reason he'd never be able to explain, he decided to turn his car around, drive back to Jody; maybe he'd
slow down and shout something out the window or maybe—
just maybe—he'd give the son of a bitch a ride if it looked like
that might be a good idea. But as he approached Jody it was
clear that Jody intended to stand his ground, didn't want any
favors from him: you could see from his arrogant stance that
he'd rather freeze his ass off than beg a ride from Tyrone; he'd
lowered his arm and stood there in the road, legs apart, waiting.
A big beefy glowering roan you could tell wanted a fight even
without knowing who he was.

Tyrone's heart swelled with fury and righteousness.

Tyrone hit the horn with the palm of his hand to scare the
son of a bitch off the road.

He was laughing, shouting, *Thief! Liar! Lying betraying bastard!*
What did he do then but call Jody's bluff, aim the car straight
at him, fifty miles an hour, and he'd lost control even before he
hit a patch of cobbled ridged ice and began to skid—hardly had
time before the impact to turn the wheel, pump desperately at
the brakes—and he saw his cousin's look of absolute disbelief,
not even fear or surprise, as the left fender slammed into him
and the chassis plowed into his body and threw it aside and out
of Tyrone's sight.

The steering wheel caught Tyrone in the chest. But he was all
right. He was coughing, choking, but he was all right, gripping
the wheel tight and pumping the brakes as the car leveled out
of its wild swerve and came to a bumpy rest in a ditch. Scrub
trees and tall grasses clawing at the windshield and Jesus, his
nose was bleeding and he couldn't see anything in the rearview
mirror but he knew Jody was dead; that sickening thud, that
enormous impact like a man-sized boulder flung against the car,
that's what it meant.

"Jesus."

Tyrone sat panting in his car, the motor racing, clouds of
exhaust lifting behind; he was terrified, his bladder contracted,
heart pumping like crazy, and it couldn't have happened, could
it, that quickly?—hairline cracks on his windshield and his nose
clogged with blood?—except he'd felt the body snapping beneath the car; it wasn't something you were likely to mistake as
anything but death.

He didn't have to drive back another time. Didn't have to see
the bright blood on the snow.

He pressed his forehead against the steering wheel. A terrible
hammering in his chest he'd have to wait out.

"Damn you, fuck you, *Jody*. . . ."

Tyrone busied himself maneuvering his car out of the ditch, rocking the chassis, concentrating on the effort, which involved his entire physical being; he was panting, grunting, whispering *C'mon baby c'mon for Christ's sweet sake*; then he was free and clear and back on the road and no one knew.

He'd begun to shiver convulsively. Though he was sweating too inside his clothes. And his bladder pinched in terror as he hadn't felt it in a long, long time.

But he was all right, wasn't he? And the car was operating.

He drove on, slowly at first, then panic hit him in a fresh wave and he began to drive faster, thinking he was going in the wrong direction but he had to get somewhere—where?—had to get help.

Police, ambulance. He'd go home and telephone.

There's a man dead on the road. Hitchhiker and he'd stepped in front of the car and it was over in an instant.

Blood dripping from his nose onto his fucking jacket and those hairline cracks in the windshield, like cracks in his own skull. He was crying, couldn't stop.

He'd tell Irene to make the call. Wouldn't tell her who it was he'd hit. Then he'd drive back to Jody, *Hey, you know I didn't mean it why the hell didn't you get out of the way I was just kidding around, then the ice, why the hell didn't you get out of the way goddamn you you did it on purpose didn't you—*

But maybe it would be better if he stopped at the first house, a neighbor's house.

Police, or the ambulance? Or both? There was an emergency number he'd never memorized the way you were supposed to. . . .

His mind was shifting out of focus, going blank in patches, empty and white-glaring as the snowy fields.

Those fields you could lose yourself in at this time of year. Staring and dreaming, stubbled with grass and grain and tracked over with animal prints, but you couldn't see that at a distance—everything clean and clear, dazzling blinding white. At a distance.

It was a secret no one knew: Jody McIllvanney was dead.

Bleeding his life out in a ditch. In the snow.

He hadn't survived the impact of the car, Tyrone knew that. No chance of it, plowing into a human being like that full in the chest and the gut; he'd felt the bones being crushed, the backbone snapped—*felt* it.

He'd seen bodies crumpled, Jesus, he'd seen more than his fair share. Kids his own age, Americans, Japs, in uniform, near naked, bleeding, broken bones, eyes rolled up into their skulls. But mostly he'd been lucky enough to come upon them after death had come and gone and only the body was left.

No witnesses.

No one on the road this time of day.

He had to get help, but help was a long way off.

His foot pressing down hard on the accelerator, then letting up when the tires began to spin—it was dangerous driving in the winter along these roads, dangerous driving any time the roads were likely to be slippery—now approaching a single-lane bridge crashing over the bridge the floorboards bouncing and kicking and the car trembling. Oh, sweet Jesus, help me.

Explaining to someone, a patrolman on the highway, how it wasn't his fault. The hitchhiker standing flat-footed in the road, not dodging out of the way even when the car began to skid.

He'd lost control of the car. But then he'd regained it.

No witnesses.

How could he be held to blame?

If Jody had paid in installments, for instance $25, even $10 every month or so. Paring back on the debt just to show his good faith. His gratitude.

He couldn't be held responsible. He'd kill himself if they came to arrest him.

Except: no witnesses.

Except: his car was damaged.

The fender crushed, the bumper, part of the hood—that's how they would know. Blood splashed on the grill.

That's how they would find him.

That's how they would arrest him.

He and Jody used to go deer hunting farther north; you sling the carcass over the fender unless it's too big, then you tie it to the roof of the car. Twine tied tight as you can tie it.

He'd known without having to look.

Asshole. Bleeding his life out back in a ditch.

But who would know? If he kept going.

If he drove on past his house—just kept driving as if it wasn't any house he knew, any connection to him—drive and drive up into the northern part of the state until something happened to stop him. Until his gas gave out.

HAUNTED

Haunted houses, forbidden houses. The old Medlock farm. The Erlich farm. The Minton farm on Elk Creek. NO TRESPASSING the signs said but we trespassed at will. NO TRESPASSING NO HUNTING NO FISHING UNDER PENALTY OF LAW but we did what we pleased because who was there to stop us?

Our parents warned us against exploring these abandoned properties: the old houses and barns were dangerous, they said. We could get hurt, they said. I asked my mother if the houses were haunted and she said, Of course not, there aren't such things as ghosts, you know that. She was irritated with me; she guessed how I pretended to believe things I didn't believe, things I'd grown out of years before. It was a habit of childhood— pretending I was younger, more childish, than in fact I was. Opening my eyes wide and looking puzzled, worried. Girls are prone to such trickery, it's a form of camouflage, when every other thought you think is a forbidden thought and with your eyes open staring sightless you can sink into dreams that leave your skin clammy and your heart pounding—dreams that don't seem to belong to you that must have come to you from some-where else from someone you don't know who knows *you*.

There weren't such things as ghosts, they told us. That was just superstition. But we could injure ourselves tramping around where we weren't wanted—the floorboards and the staircases in old houses were likely to be rotted, the roofs ready to collapse, we could cut ourselves on nails and broken glass, we could fall into uncovered wells—and you never knew who you might meet up with, in an old house or barn that's supposed to be empty. "You mean a bum?—like somebody hitch-hiking along the road?" I asked. "It could be a bum, or it could be somebody you know," Mother told me evasively. "A man, or a boy—somebody you know . . ." Her voice trailed off in embarrassment and I knew enough not to ask another question.

There were things you didn't talk about, back then. I never talked about them with my own children, there weren't the words to say them.

We listened to what our parents said, we nearly always agreed with what they said, but we went off on the sly and did what we wanted to do. When we were little girls; my neighbor Mary Lou Siskin and me. And when we were older, ten, eleven years old, tomboys, roughhouses our mothers called us. We liked to hike in the woods and along the creek for miles, we'd cut through farmers' fields, spy on their houses—on people we knew, kids we knew from school—most of all we liked to explore abandoned houses, boarded-up houses if we could break in, we'd scare ourselves thinking the houses might be haunted though really we knew they weren't haunted, there weren't such things as ghosts. Except—

I am writing in a dime-store notebook with lined pages and a speckled cover, a notebook of the sort we used in grade school.

Once upon a time as I used to tell my children when they were tucked safely into bed and drifting off to sleep. *Once upon a time* I'd begin, reading from a book because it was safest so: the several times I told them my own stories they were frightened by my voice and couldn't sleep and afterward I couldn't sleep either and my husband would ask what was wrong and I'd say, Nothing, hiding my face from him so he wouldn't see my look of contempt.

I write in pencil, so that I can erase easily, and I find that I am constantly erasing, wearing holes in the paper. Mrs. Harding, our fifth grade teacher, disciplined us for handing in messy notebooks: she was a heavy, toad-faced woman, her voice was deep and husky and gleeful when she said, "You, Melissa, what have you to say for yourself?" and I stood there mute, my knees trembling. My friend Mary Lou laughed behind her hand, wriggled in her seat she thought I was so funny. Tell the old witch to go to hell, she'd say, she'll respect you then, but of course no one would ever say such a thing to Mrs. Harding. Not even Mary Lou. "What have you to say for yourself, Melissa? Handing in a notebook with a ripped page?" My grade for the homework assignment was lowered from A to B, Mrs. Harding grunted with satisfaction as she made the mark, a big swooping B in red ink, creasing the page. "More is expected of you, Melissa, so you disappoint me more," Mrs. Harding always said. So many years ago and I remember those words more clearly than words I heard the other day.

One morning there was a pretty substitute teacher in Mrs. Harding's classroom. "Mrs. Harding is unwell, I'll be taking her place today," she said, and we saw the nervousness in her face, we guessed there was a secret she wouldn't tell and we waited and a few days later the principal himself came to tell us that Mrs. Harding would not be back, she had died of a stroke. He spoke carefully as if we were much younger children and might be upset and Mary Lou caught my eye and winked and I sat there at my desk feeling the strangest sensation, something flowing into the top of my head, honey-rich and warm making its way down my spine. *Our Father Who art in Heaven* I whispered in the prayer with the others my head bowed and my hands clasped tight together but my thoughts were somewhere else leaping wild and crazy somewhere else and I knew Mary Lou's were too.

On the school bus going home she whispered in my ear, "That was because of us, wasn't it!—what happened to that old bag Harding. But we won't tell anybody."

Once upon a time there were two sisters, and one was very pretty and one was very ugly. . . . Though Mary Lou Siskin wasn't my sister. And I wasn't ugly, really: just sallow-skinned, with a small pinched ferrety face. With dark almost lashless eyes that were set too close together and a nose that didn't look right. A look of yearning, and disappointment.

But Mary Lou was pretty, even rough and clumsy as she sometimes behaved. That long silky blond hair everybody remembered her for afterward, years afterward. . . . How, when she had to be identified, it was the long silky white-blond hair that was unmistakable. . . .

Sleepless nights but I love them. I write during the nighttime hours and sleep during the day; I am of an age when you don't require more than a few hours sleep. My husband has been dead for nearly a year and my children are scattered and busily absorbed in their own selfish lives like all children and there is no one to interrupt me no one to pry into my business no one in the neighborhood who dares come knocking at my door to see if I am all right. Sometimes out of a mirror floats an unexpected face, a strange face, lined, ravaged, with deep-socketed eyes always damp, always blinking in shock or dismay or simple bewilderment—but I adroitly look away. I have no need to stare.

It's true, all you have heard of the vanity of the old. Believing ourselves young, still, behind our aged faces—mere children, and so very innocent!

Once when I was a young bride and almost pretty my color up when I was happy and my eyes shining we drove out into the country for a Sunday's excursion and he wanted to make love I knew, he was shy and fumbling as I but he wanted to make love and I ran into a cornfield in my stockings and high heels, I was playing at being a woman I never could be, Mary Lou Siskin maybe, Mary Lou whom my husband never knew, but I got out of breath and frightened, it was the wind in the cornstalks, that dry rustling sound, that dry terrible rustling sound like whispering like voices you can't quite identify and he caught me and tried to hold me and I pushed him away sobbing and he said, What's wrong? My God what's wrong? as if he really loved me as if his life was focused on me and I knew I could never be equal to it, that love, that importance, I knew I was only Melissa the ugly one the one the boys wouldn't give a second glance, and one day he'd understand and know how he'd been cheated. I pushed him away, I said, Leave me alone! don't touch me! You disgust me! I said.

He backed off and I hid my face, sobbing.

But later on I got pregnant just the same. Only a few weeks later.

*   *   *

Always there were stories behind the abandoned houses and always the stories were sad. Because farmers went bankrupt and had to move away. Because somebody died and the farm couldn't be kept up and nobody wanted to buy it—like the Medlock farm across the creek. Mr. Medlock died aged seventy-nine and Mrs. Medlock refused to sell the farm and lived there alone until someone from the county health agency came to get her. Isn't it a shame, my parents said. The poor woman, they said. They told us never, never to poke around in the Medlocks' barns or house—the buildings were ready to cave in, they'd been in terrible repair even when the Medlocks were living there.

It was said that Mrs. Medlock had gone off her head after she'd found her husband dead in one of the barns, lying flat on his back his eyes open and bulging, his mouth open, tongue protruding, she'd gone to look for him and found him like that and she'd never gotten over it they said, never got over the shock. They had to commit her to the state hospital for her own good (they said) and the house and the barns were boarded up, everywhere tall grass and thistles grew wild, dandelions in the spring, tiger lilies in the summer, and when we drove by I stared and stared narrowing my eyes so I wouldn't see someone looking out one of the windows—a face there, pale and quick-—or a dark figure scrambling up the roof to hide behind the chimney—

Mary Lou and I wondered was the house haunted, was the barn haunted where the old man had died, we crept around to spy, we couldn't stay away, coming closer and closer each time until something scared us and we ran away back through the woods clutching and pushing at each other until one day finally we went right up to the house to the back door and peeked in one of the windows. Mary Lou led the way, Mary Lou said not to be afraid, nobody lived there any more and nobody would catch us, it didn't matter that the land was posted, the police didn't arrest kids our ages.

We explored the barns, we dragged the wooden cover off the well and dropped stones inside. We called the cats but they wouldn't come close enough to be petted. They were barn cats, skinny and diseased-looking, they'd said at the county bureau that Mrs. Medlock had let a dozen cats live in the house with her so that the house was filthy from their messes. When the cats wouldn't come we got mad and threw stones at them and they ran away hissing—nasty dirty things, Mary Lou said. Once we crawled up on the tar-paper roof over the Medlocks' kitchen, just for fun, Mary Lou wanted to climb up the big roof too to the very top but I got frightened and said, No. No please don't, no Mary Lou please, and I sounded so strange Mary Lou looked at me and didn't tease or mock as she usually did. The roof was so steep, I'd known she would hurt herself. I could see her losing her footing and slipping, falling, I could see her astonished face and her flying hair as she fell, knowing nothing could save her. You're no fun, Mary Lou said, giving me a hard little pinch. But she didn't go climbing up the big roof.

Later we ran through the barns screaming at the top of our lungs just for fun for the hell of it as Mary Lou said, we tossed things in a heap, broken-off pares of farm implements, leather things from the horses' gear, handfuls of straw. The farm animals had been gone for years but their smell was still strong. Dried horse and cow droppings that looked like mud. Mary Lou said, "You know what—I'd like to burn this place down." And she looked at me and I said, "Okay—go on and do it, burn it down." And Mary Lou said, "You think I wouldn't?—just give me a match." And I said, "You know I don't have any match." And a look passed between us. And I felt something flooding at the top of my head, my throat tickled as if I didn't know would I laugh or cry and I said, "You're crazy—" and Mary Lou said with a sneering little laugh, "*You're* crazy, dumbbell—I was just testing you."

By the time Mary Lou was twelve years old Mother had got to hate her, was always trying to turn me against her so I'd make friends with other girls. Mary Lou had a fresh mouth, she said. Mary Lou didn't respect her elders—not even her own parents. Mother guessed that Mary Lou laughed at her behind her back, said things about all of us. She was mean and snippy and a smart-ass, rough sometimes as her brothers. Why didn't I make other friends? Why did I always go running when she stood out in the yard and called me? The Siskins weren't a whole lot better than white trash, the way Mr. Siskin worked that land of his.

In town, in school, Mary Lou sometimes ignored me when other girls were around, girls who lived in town, whose fathers weren't farmers like ours. But when it was time to ride home on the bus she'd sit with me as if nothing was wrong and I'd help her with her homework if she needed help, I hated her sometimes but then I'd forgive her as soon as she smiled at me, she'd say, "Hey 'Lissa are you mad at me?" and I'd make a face and say no as if it was an insult, being asked. Mary Lou was my sister I sometimes pretended, I told myself a story about us being sisters and looking alike, and Mary Lou said sometimes she'd like to leave her family her god-damned family and come live with me. Then the next day or the next hour she'd get moody and be nasty to me and get me almost crying. All the Siskins had mean streaks, bad tempers, she'd tell people. As if she was proud.

Her hair was a light blond, almost white in the sunshine, and when I first knew her she had to wear it braided tight around her head—her grandmother braided it for her, and she hated it. Like Gretel or Snow White in one of those damn dumb picture books for children, Mary Lou said. When she was older she wore it down and let it grow long so that it fell almost to her hips. It was very beautiful—silky and shimmering. I dreamt of Mary Lou's hair sometimes but the dreams were confused and I couldn't remember when I woke up whether I was the one with the long blond silky hair, or someone else. It took me a while to get my thoughts clear lying there in bed and then I'd remember Mary Lou, who was my best friend.

She was ten months older than I was, and an inch or so taller, a bit heavier, not fat but fleshy, solid and fleshy, with hard little muscles in her upper arms like a boy. Her eyes were blue like washed glass, her eyebrows and lashes were almost white, she had a snubbed nose and Slavic cheekbones and a mouth that could be sweet or twisty and smirky depending upon her mood. But she didn't like her face because it was round—a moon-face she called it, staring at herself in the mirror though she knew damned well she was pretty—didn't older boys whistle at her, didn't the bus driver flirt with her?—calling her "Blondie" while he never called me anything at all.

Mother didn't like Mary Lou visiting with me when no one else was home in our house: she didn't trust her, she said. Thought she might steal something, or poke her nose into parts of the house where she wasn't welcome. That girl is a bad influence on you, she said. But it was all the same old crap I heard again and again so I didn't even listen. I'd have told her she was crazy except that would only make things worse.

Mary Lou said, "Don't you just hate them?—your mother, and mine? Sometimes I wish—"

I put my hands over my ears and didn't hear.

The Siskins lived two miles away from us farther back the road where it got narrower. Those days, it was unpaved, and never got plowed in the winter. I remember their barn with the yellow silo, I remember the muddy pond where the dairy cows came to drink, the muck they churned up in the spring. I remember Mary Lou saying she wished all the cows would die—they were always sick with something—so her father would give up and sell the farm and they could live in town in a nice house. I was hurt, her saying those things as if she'd forgotten about me and would leave me behind. Damn you to hell, I whispered under my breath.

I remember smoke rising from the Siskins' kitchen chimney, from their wood-burning stove, straight up into the winter sky like a breath you draw inside you deeper and deeper until you begin to feel faint.

Later on, that house was empty too. But boarded up only for a few months—the bank sold it at auction. (It turned out the bank owned most of the Siskin farm, even the dairy cows. So Mary Lou had been wrong about that all along and never knew.)

As I write I can hear the sound of glass breaking, I can feel glass underfoot. *Once upon a time there were two little princesses, two sisters, who did forbidden things.* That brittle terrible sensation under my shoes—slippery like water—"Anybody home? Hey—anybody home?" and there's an old calendar tacked to a kitchen wall, a faded picture of Jesus Christ in a long white gown stained with scarlet, thorns fitted to His bowed head. Mary Lou is going to scare me in another minute making me think that someone is in the house and the two of us will scream with laughter and run outside where it's safe. Wild frightened laughter and I never knew afterward what was funny or why we did these things. Smashing what remained of windows, wrenching at stairway railings to break them loose, running with our heads ducked so we wouldn't get cobwebs in our faces.

One of us found a dead bird, a starling, in what had been the parlor of the house. Turned it over with a foot—there's the open eye looking right up calm and matter-of-fact. *Melissa*, that eye tells me, silent and terrible, *I see you.*

That was the old Minton place, the stone house with the caved-in roof and the broken steps, like something in a picture book from long ago. From the road the house looked as if it might be big but when we explored it we were disappointed to see that it wasn't much bigger than my own house, just four narrow rooms downstairs, another four upstairs, an attic with a steep ceiling, the roof partly caved in. The barns had collapsed in upon themselves; only their stone foundations remained solid. The land had been sold off over the years to other farmers, nobody had lived in the house for a long time. The old Minton house, people called it. On Elk Creek where Mary Lou's body was eventually found.

In seventh grade Mary Lou had a boy friend she wasn't supposed to have and no one knew about it but me—an older boy who'd dropped out of school and worked as a farmhand. I thought he was a little slow—not in his speech which was fast enough, normal enough, but in his way of thinking. He was sixteen or seventeen years old. His name was Hans; he had crisp blond hair like the bristles of a brush, a coarse blemished face, derisive eyes. Mary Lou was crazy for him she said, aping the older girls in town who said they were "crazy for" certain boys or young men. Hans and Mary Lou kissed when they didn't think I was watching, in an old ruin of a cemetery behind the Minton house, on the creek bank, in the tall marsh grass by the end of the Siskins' driveway. Hans had a car borrowed from one of his brothers, a battered old Ford, the front bumper held up by wire, the running board scraping the ground. We'd be out walking on the road and Hans would come along tapping the horn and stop and Mary Lou would climb in but I'd hang back knowing they didn't want me and the hell with them: I preferred to be alone.

"You're just jealous of Hans and me," Mary Lou said, unforgivably, and I hadn't any reply. "Hans is sweet. Hans is nice. He isn't like people say," Mary Lou said in a quick bright false voice she'd picked up from one of the older, popular girls in town. "He's—" And she stared at me blinking and smiling not knowing what to say as if in fact she didn't know Hans at all. "He isn't *simple*," she said angrily, "—he just doesn't like to talk a whole lot."

When I try to remember Hans Meunzer after so many decades I can see only a muscular boy with short-trimmed blond hair and protuberant ears, blemished skin, the shadow of a mustache on his upper lip—he's looking at me, eyes narrowed, crinkled, as if he understands how I fear him, how I wish him dead and gone, and he'd hate me too if he took me that seriously. But he doesn't take me that seriously, his gaze just slides right through me as if nobody's standing where I stand.

There were stories about all the abandoned houses but the worst story was about the Minton house over on the Elk Creek Road about three miles from where we lived. For no reason anybody ever discovered Mr. Minton had beaten his wife to death and afterward killed himself with a .12-gauge shotgun. He hadn't even been drinking, people said. And his farm hadn't been doing at all badly, considering how others were doing.

Looking at the ruin from the outside, overgrown with trumpet vine and wild rose, it seemed hard to believe that anything like that had happened. Things in the world even those things built by man are so quiet left to themselves. . . .

The house had been deserted for years, as long as I could remember. Most of the land had been sold off but the heirs didn't want to deal with the house. They didn't want to sell it and they didn't want to raze it and they certainly didn't want to live in it so it stood empty. The property was pasted with NO TRESPASSING signs layered one atop another but nobody took them seriously. Vandals had broken into the house and caused damage, the McFarlane boys had tried to burn down the old hay barn one Hallowe'en night. The summer Mary Lou started seeing Hans she and I climbed in the house through a rear window— the boards guarding it had long since been yanked away—and walked through the rooms slow as sleepwalkers our arms around each other's waist our eyes staring waiting to see Mr. Minton's ghost as we turned each corner. The inside smelled of mouse droppings, mildew, rot, old sorrow. Strips of wallpaper torn from the walls, plasterboard exposed, old furniture overturned and smashed, old yellowed sheets of newspaper underfoot, and broken glass, everywhere broken glass. Through the ravaged windows sunlight spilled in tremulous quivering bands. The air was afloat, alive: dancing dust-atoms. "I'm afraid," Mary Lou whispered. She squeezed my waist and I felt my mouth go dry for hadn't I been hearing something upstairs, a low persistent murmuring like quarreling like one person trying to convince another going on and on and on but when I stood very still to listen the sound vanished and there were only the comforting summer sounds of birds, crickets, cicadas.

I knew how Mr. Minton had died: he'd placed the barrel of the shotgun beneath his chin and pulled the trigger with his big toe. They found him in the bedroom upstairs, most of his head blown off. They found his wife's body in the cistern in the cellar where he'd tried to hide her. "Do you think we should go upstairs?" Mary Lou asked, worried. Her fingers felt cold; but I could see tiny sweat beads on her forehead. Her mother had braided her hair in one thick clumsy braid, the way she wore it most of the summer, but the bands of hair were loosening. "No," I said, frightened. "I don't know." We hesitated at the bottom of the stairs—just stood there for a long time. "Maybe not," Mary Lou said. "Damn stairs'd fall in on us."

In the parlor there were bloodstains on the floor and on the wall—I could see them. Mary Lou said in derision, "They're just waterstains, dummy."

I could hear the voices overhead, or was it a single droning persistent voice. I waited for Mary Lou to hear it but she never did.

Now we were safe, now we were retreating, Mary Lou said as if repentant, "Yeah—this house *is* special."

We looked through the debris in the kitchen hoping to find
something of value but there wasn't anything—just smashed
chinaware, old battered pots and pans, more old yellowed newspaper. But through the window we saw a garter snake sunning
itself on a rusted water tank, stretched out to a length of two
feet. It was a lovely coppery color, the scales gleaming like perspiration on a man's arm; it seemed to be asleep. Neither one
of us screamed, or wanted to throw something—we just stood
there watching it for the longest time.

Mary Lou didn't have a boy friend any longer, Hans had stopped
coming around. We saw him driving the old Ford now and then
but he didn't seem to see us. Mr. Siskin had found out about
him and Mary Lou and he'd been upset—acting like a damn
crazy man Mary Lou said, asking her every kind of nasty question then interrupting her and not believing her anyway, then
he'd put her to terrible shame by going over to see Hans and
carrying on with him. "I hate them all," Mary Lou said, her face
darkening with blood. "I wish—"
    We rode our bicycles over to the Minton farm, or tramped
through the fields to get there. It was the place we liked best.
Sometimes we brought things to eat, cookies, bananas, candy
bars, sitting on the broken stone steps out front, as if we lived
in the house really, we were sisters who lived here having a
picnic lunch out front. There were bees, flies, mosquitoes, but
we brushed them away. We had to sit in the shade because the
sun was so fierce and direct, a whitish heat pouring down from
overhead.
    "Would you ever like to run away from home?" Mary Lou
said. "I don't know," I said uneasily. Mary Lou wiped at her

mouth and gave me a mean narrow look. " 'I don't know,' " she said in a falsetto voice, mimicking me. At an upstairs window someone was watching us—was it a man or was it a woman— someone stood there listening hard and I couldn't move feeling so slow and dreamy in the heat like a fly caught on a sticky petal that's going to fold in on itself and swallow him up. Mary Lou crumpled up some wax paper and threw it into the weeds. She was dreamy too, slow and yawning. She said, "Shit—they'd just find me. Then everything would be worse."

I was covered in a thin film of sweat but I'd begun to shiver. Goose bumps were raised on my arms. I could see us sitting on the stone steps the way we'd look from the second floor of the house, Mary Lou sprawled with her legs apart, her braided hair slung over her shoulder, me sitting with my arms hugging my knees my backbone tight and straight knowing I was being watched. Mary Lou said, lowering her voice, "Did you ever touch yourself in a certain place, Melissa?" "No," I said, pretending I didn't know what she meant. "Hans wanted to do that," Mary Lou said. She sounded disgusted. Then she started to giggle. "I wouldn't let him, then he wanted to do something else—started unbuttoning his pants—wanted me to touch *him*. And—"

I wanted to hush her, to clap my hand over her mouth. But she just went on and I never said a word until we both started giggling together and couldn't stop. Afterward I didn't remember most of it or why I'd been so excited my face burning and my eyes seared as if I'd been staring into the sun.

On the way home Mary Lou said, "Some things are so sad you can't say them." But I pretended not to hear.

*   *   *

A few days later I came back by myself. Through the ravaged cornfield: the stalks dried and broken, the tassels burnt, that rustling whispering sound of the wind I can hear now if I listen closely. My head was aching with excitement. I was telling myself a story that we'd made plans to run away and live in the Minton house. I was carrying a willow switch I'd found on the ground, fallen from a tree but still green and springy, slapping at things with it as if it was a whip. Talking to myself. Laughing aloud. Wondering was I being watched.

I climbed in the house through the back window and brushed my hands on my jeans. My hair was sticking to the back of my neck.

At the foot of the stairs I called up, "Who's here?" in a voice meant to show it was all play, I knew I was alone.

My heart was beating hard and quick, like a bird caught in the hand. It was lonely without Mary Lou so I walked heavy to let them know I was there and wasn't afraid. I started singing. I started whistling. Talking to myself and slapping at things with the willow switch. Laughing aloud, a little angry. Why was I angry, well I didn't know, someone was whispering telling me to come upstairs, to walk on the inside of the stairs so the steps wouldn't collapse.

The house was beautiful inside if you had the right eyes to see it. If you didn't mind the smell. Glass underfoot, broken plaster, stained wallpaper hanging in shreds. Tall narrow windows looking out onto wild weedy patches of green. I heard something in one of the rooms but when I looked I saw nothing much more than an easy chair lying on its side. Vandals had ripped stuffing out of it and tried to set it afire. The material was filthy but I could see that it had been pretty once—a floral design—tiny yellow flowers and green ivy. A woman used to sit in the chair, a big woman with sly staring eyes. Knitting in her lap but she wasn't knitting just staring out the window watching to see who might be coming to visit.

Upstairs the rooms were airless and so hot I felt my skin prickle like shivering. I wasn't afraid!—I slapped at the walls with my springy willow switch. In one of the rooms high in a corner wasps buzzed around a fat wasps' nest. In another room I looked out the window leaning out the window to breathe thinking this was my window, I'd come to live here. She was telling me I had better lie down and rest because I was in danger of heatstroke and I pretended not to know what heatstroke was but she knew I knew because hadn't a cousin of mine collapsed haying just last summer, they said his face had gone blotched and red and he'd begun breathing faster and faster not getting enough oxygen until he collapsed. I was looking out at the overgrown apple orchard, I could smell the rot, a sweet winey smell, the sky was hazy like something you can't get clear in your vision, pressing in close and warm. A half-mile away Elk Creek glittered through a screen of willow trees moving slow glittering with scales like winking.

Come away from that window, someone told me sternly.

But I took my time obeying.

In the biggest of the rooms was an old mattress pulled off rusty bedsprings and dumped on the floor. They'd torn some of the stuffing out of this too, there were scorch marks on it from cigarettes. The fabric was stained with something like rust and I didn't want to look at it but I had to. Once at Mary Lou's when I'd gone home with her after school there was a mattress lying out in the yard in the sun and Mary Lou told me in disgust that it was her youngest bother's mattress—he'd wet his bed again and the mattress had to be aired out. As if the stink would ever go away, Mary Lou said.

Something moved inside the mattress, a black-glittering thing, it was a cockroach but I wasn't allowed to jump back. Suppose you have to lie down on that mattress and sleep, I was told. Suppose you can't go home until you do. My eyelids were heavy, my head was pounding with blood. A mosquito buzzed around me but I was too tired to brush it away. Lie down on that mattress, Melissa, she told me. You know you must be punished.

I knelt down, not on the mattress, but on the floor beside it. The smells in the room were close and rank but I didn't mind, my head was nodding with sleep. Rivulets of sweat ran down my face and sides, under my arms, but I didn't mind. I saw my hand move out slowly like a stranger's hand to touch the mattress and a shiny black cockroach scuttled away in fright, and a second cockroach, and a third—but I couldn't jump up and scream.

Lie down on that mattress and take your punishment.

I looked over my shoulder and there was a woman standing in the doorway—a woman I'd never seen before.

She was staring at me. Her eyes were shiny and dark. She licked her lips and said in a jeering voice, "What are you doing here in this house, miss?"

I was terrified. I tried to answer but I couldn't speak.

"Have you come to see me?" the woman asked.

She was no age I could guess. Older than my mother but not old-seeming. She wore men's clothes and she was tall as any man, with wide shoulders, and long legs, and big sagging breasts like cows' udders loose inside her shirt not harnessed in a brassiere like other women's. Her thick wiry gray hair was cut short as a man's and stuck up in tufts that looked greasy. Her eyes were small, and black, and set back deep in their sockets; the flesh around them looked bruised. I had never seen anyone like her before—her thighs were enormous, big as my body. There was a ring of loose soft flesh at the waistband of her trousers but she wasn't fat.

"I asked you a question, miss. Why are you here?'"

I was so frightened I could feel my bladder contract. I stared at her, cowering by the mattress, and couldn't speak.

It seemed to please her that I was so frightened. She approached me, stooping a little to see through the doorway. She said, in a mock-kindly voice, "You've come to visit with me—is that it?"

"No," I said.

"No!" she said, laughing. "Why, of course you have."

"No. I don't know you."

She leaned over me, touched my forehead with her fingers. I shut my eyes waiting to be hurt but her touch was cool. She brushed my hair off my forehead where it was sticky with sweat. "I've seen you here before, you and that other one," she said. "What is her name? The blond one. The two of you, trespassing."

I couldn't move, my legs were paralyzed. Quick and darting and buzzing my thoughts bounded in every which direction but didn't take hold. "Melissa is *your* name, isn't it," the woman said. "And what is your sister's name?"

"She isn't my sister," I whispered.

"What is her name?"

"I don't know."

"You don't know!"

"—don't know," I said, cowering.

The woman drew back half sighing half grunting. She looked at me pityingly. "You'll have to be punished, then."

I could smell ashes about her, something cold. I started to whimper started to say I hadn't done anything wrong, hadn't hurt anything in the house, I had only been exploring—I wouldn't come back again—

She was smiling at me, uncovering her teeth. She could read my thoughts before I could think them.

The skin of her face was in layers like an onion, like she'd been sunburnt, or had a skin disease. There were patches that had begun to peel. Her look was wet and gloating. Don't hurt me, I wanted to say. Please don't hurt me.

I'd begun to cry. My nose was running like a baby's. I thought I would crawl past the woman I would get to my feet and run past her and escape but the woman stood in my way blocking my way leaning over me breathing damp and warm her breath like a cow's breath in my face. Don't hurt me, I said, and she said, "You know you have to be punished—You and your pretty blond sister."

"She isn't my sister," I said.

"And what is her name?"

The woman was bending over me, quivering with laughter.

"Speak up, miss. What is it?"

"I don't know—" I started to say. But my voice said, "Mary Lou."

The woman's big breasts spilled down onto her belly, I could feel her shaking with laughter. But she spoke sternly saying that Mary Lou and I had been very bad girls and we knew it her house was forbidden territory and we knew it hadn't we known all along that others had come to grief beneath its roof?

"No," I started to say. But my voice said, "Yes."

The woman laughed, crouching above me. "Now, miss, 'Melissa' as they call you—your parents don't know where you are at this very moment, do they?"

"I don't know."

"Do they?"

"No."

"They don't know anything about you, do they?—what you do, and what you think? You and 'Mary Lou.'"

She regarded me for a long moment, smiling. Her smile was wide and friendly.

"You're a spunky little girl, aren't you, with a mind of your own, aren't you, you and your pretty little sister. I bet your bottoms have been warmed many a time," the woman said, showing her big tobacco-stained teeth in a grin, ". . . your tender little asses."

I began to giggle. My bladder tightened.

"Hand that here, miss," the woman said. She took the willow switch from my fingers—I had forgotten I was holding it. "I will now administer punishment: take down your jeans. Take down your panties. Lie down on that mattress. Hurry." She spoke briskly now she was all business. "Hurry, Melissa! *And* your panties! Or do you want me to pull them down for you?"

She was slapping the switch impatiently against the palm of her left hand, making a wet scolding noise with her lips. Scolding and teasing. Her skin shone in patches, stretched tight over the big hard bones of her face. Her eyes were small, crinkling smaller, black and damp. She was so big she had to position herself carefully over me to give herself proper balance and leverage so that she wouldn't fall. I could hear her hoarse eager breathing as it came to me from all sides like the wind.

I had done as she told me. It wasn't me doing these things but they were done. Don't hurt me, I whispered, lying on my stomach on the mattress, my arms stretched above me and my fingernails digging into the floor. The coarse wood with splinters pricking my skin. Don't don't hurt me O please but the woman paid no heed her warm wet breath louder now and the floorboards creaking beneath her weight. "Now, miss, now 'Melissa' as they call you—this will be our secret won't it—"

When it was over she wiped at her mouth and said she would let me go today if I promised never to tell anybody if I sent my pretty little sister to her tomorrow.

She isn't my sister, I said, sobbing. When I could get my breath.

I had lost control of my bladder after all, I'd begun to pee even before the first swipe of the willow switch hit me on the buttocks, peeing in helpless spasms, and sobbing, and afterward the woman scolded me saying wasn't it a poor little baby wetting itself like that. But she sounded repentant too, stood well aside to let me pass, Off you go! Home you go! And don't forget!

And I ran out of the room hearing her laughter behind me and down the stairs running running as if I hadn't any weight my legs just blurry beneath me as if the air was water and I was swimming I ran out of the house and through the cornfield running in the cornfield sobbing as the corn stalks slapped at my face *Off you go! Home you go! And don't forget!*

*   *   *

I told Mary Lou about the Minton house and something that had happened to me there that was a secret and she didn't believe me at first saying with a jeer, "Was it a ghost? Was it Hans?" I said I couldn't tell. Couldn't tell what? she said. Couldn't tell, I said. Why not? she said.

"Because I promised."

"Promised who?" she said. She looked at me with her wide blue eyes like she was trying to hypnotize me. "You're a god-damned liar."

Later she started in again asking me what had happened what was the secret was it something to do with Hans? did he still like her? was he mad at her? and I said it didn't have anything to do with Hans not a thing to do with him. Twisting my mouth to show what I thought of him.

"Then who—?" Mary Lou asked.

"I told you it was a secret."

"Oh shit—what kind of a secret?"

"A secret."

"A secret *really*?"

I turned away from Mary Lou, trembling. My mouth kept twisting in a strange hurting smile. "Yes. A secret *really*," I said.

The last time I saw Mary Lou she wouldn't sit with me on the bus, walked past me holding her head high giving me a mean snippy look out of the corner of her eye. Then when she left for her stop she made sure she bumped me going by my seat, she leaned over to say, "I'll find out for myself, I hate you anyway," speaking loud enough for everybody on the bus to hear, "—I always have."

Once upon a time the fairy tales begin. But then they end and often you don't know really what has happened, what was meant to happen, you only know what you've been told, what the words suggest. Now that I have completed my story, filled up half my notebook with my handwriting that disappoints me, it is so shaky and childish—now the story is over I don't understand what it means. I know what happened in my life but I don't know what has happened in these pages.

Mary Lou was found murdered ten days after she said those words to me. Her body had been tossed into Elk Creek a quarter mile from the road and from the old Minton place. Where, it said in the paper, nobody had lived for fifteen years.

It said that Mary Lou had been thirteen years old at the time of her death. She'd been missing for seven days, had been the object of a county-wide search.

It said that nobody had lived in the Minton house for years but that derelicts sometimes sheltered there. It said that the body was unclothed and mutilated. There were no details.

This happened a long time ago.

The murderer (or murderers as the newspaper always said) was never found.

Hans Meunzer was arrested of course and kept in the county jail for three days while police questioned him but in the end they had to let him go, insufficient evidence to build a case it was explained in the newspaper though everybody knew he was the

one wasn't he the one?—everybody knew. For years afterward
they'd be saying that. Long after Hans was gone and the Siskins
were gone, moved away nobody knew where.

Hans swore he hadn't done it, hadn't seen Mary Lou for weeks.
There were people who testified in his behalf said he couldn't
have done it for one thing he didn't have his brother's car any
longer and he'd been working all that time. Working hard out in
the fields—couldn't have slipped away long enough to do what
police were saying he'd done. And Hans said over and over he
was innocent. Sure he was innocent. Son of a bitch ought to
be hanged my father said, everybody knew Hans was the one
unless it was a derelict or a fisherman—fishermen often drove
out to Elk Creek to fish for black bass, built fires on the creek
bank and left messes behind—sometimes prowled around the
Minton house too looking for things to steal. The police had
records of automobile license plates belonging to some of these
men, they questioned them but nothing came of it. Then there
was that crazy man that old hermit living in a tarpaper shanty
near the Shaheen dump that everybody'd said ought to have
been committed to the state hospital years ago. But everybody
knew really it was Hans and Hans got out as quick as he could,
just disappeared and not even his family knew where unless they
were lying which probably they were though they claimed not.

Mother rocked me in her arms crying, the two of us crying,
she told me that Mary Lou was happy now, Mary Lou was in
Heaven now, Jesus Christ had taken her to live with Him and I
knew that didn't I? I wanted to laugh but I didn't laugh. Mary
Lou shouldn't have gone with boys, not a nasty boy like Hans,
Mother said, she shouldn't have been sneaking around the way

she did—I knew that didn't I? Mother's words filled my head flooding my head so there was no danger of laughing.

Jesus loves you too you know that don't you Melissa? Mother asked hugging me, I told her yes. I didn't laugh because I was crying.

They wouldn't let me go to the funeral, said it would scare me too much. Even though the casket was closed.

It's said that when you're older you remember things that happened a long time ago better than you remember things that have just happened and I have found that to be so.

For instance I can't remember when I bought this notebook at Woolworth's whether it was last week or last month or just a few days ago. I can't remember why I started writing in it, what purpose I told myself. But I remember Mary Lou stooping to say those words in my ear and I remember when Mary Lou's mother came over to ask us at suppertime a few days later if I had seen Mary Lou that day—I remember the very food on my plate, the mashed potatoes in a dry little mound. I remember hearing Mary Lou call my name standing out in the driveway cupping her hands to her mouth the way Mother hated her to do, it was white trash behavior.

"'Lissa!" Mary Lou would call, and I'd call back, "O.K. I'm coming!" *Once upon a time.*

DEATH VALLEY

The colors of winter here were dun, a bleached brown, layers of rich cobalt blue. The light fell vertical, sharp as a knife. And there was the wind.

He observed as she shaded her eyes, which were not strong eyes, against the glare. "That looks like water," she said brightly. "Or ice."

"Those are salt flats."

"What?"

"Salt. Salt flats."

"It *looks* like ice."

Her tone was lightly combative. As if sexual banter were her primary mode of discourse.

She said, "I was always wondering about the name. Since I was a little girl."

"The name?"

"Death Valley. It's something you hear about, or see in the movies. The old movies. You know: 'Death Valley.' You sort of wonder."

It was then he realized how young she was. Twenty years younger than he, by a generous estimate. At that age you can still reasonably think death is romance.

*   *   *

It was their second day. He had rented a car, a classy-looking metallic-gray BMW, and driven her out into the desert. She'd never seen the desert, she said; she'd never seen Death Valley. There was an air of mild reproach in her voice, as if he, or others like him, had cheated her of a vision that was her due.

In the big casino, where they'd met, there were no clocks on the walls because the principle of time did not apply. Nor did the principle of day and night apply. Like the interior of a great head, he thought. And even in the desert where the winter light fell sharp and straight and blinding it didn't seem like day, exactly, but like something else.

She was saying, persisting, hair blowing prettily across her face, "Are you sure that isn't water, *really?* It looks so much like water."

"Taste it and see,"

In the casino at Caesars, at the craps table he always played at Caesars, he'd said, smiling, "Pray for me, sweetheart," turning to her as if he'd known absolutely she would be there, or someone very like her. Not a hooker but a small-town girl, a secretary or a beauty salon worker, here in Vegas for a three-day weekend with a girlfriend from the office or the beauty salon, come to play the slots and to test her luck. With her hair cascading in shiny synthetic-looking curls halfway down her back, and her eyes like an owl's with makeup, and glossed lips, wasn't she there to bring him good luck? Her or someone like her.

At craps the play is fast and nerved up and choppy like a wind-whipped sea whose waves crash in one direction, then in another, and then in another. Pray for me honey, he'd said, and twenty minutes later walked away with $14,683, not the very most he'd ever won in Vegas but the most he'd won in a long time. The girl, whose name was Linda, pressed her hand against her heart, saying it was going like crazy from all the excitement; how could people *do* such things, take such risks? He kissed her solemnly on the cheek and thanked her. His lips were cold.

She hadn't prayed for him, she said. She'd had her fingers crossed but she hadn't prayed because God is God no matter who you are or think you are; God is a wrathful God you best did not provoke.

She rolled her almost-pretty owl's eyes as if she knew, as if she'd had a personal run-in with God.

"It's just your special luck," she said, drawing her fingers slow across his sleeve.

"You think I'm a lucky man?" he said happily.

"I *know* you're a lucky man: I just saw."

He kissed her on the lips, smelling her sweet sharp perfume, and through it he saw the bargain-rate motel room she and her girlfriend were renting for the weekend, the beaverboard walls, the stained venetian blinds pulled against the sun, the window air conditioner with its amiable guttural rumble. The girlfriend had a date for the night but Linda was alone. The kind of girl, baby fat in her cheeks, a little pinch of it under her chin, who wouldn't be alone for long and surely knew it.

But she surprised him, the quickness with which she framed his face in her hands, a dozen bracelets jingling, and kissed him, lightly, on the lips, like a woman in a movie when the music comes up.

"Well," he said, smiling his wide white happy smile, his sort of surprised smile, "I guess I *am* a lucky man."

Linda was the kind of girl too, in bright blurry makeup and highlighted ashy hair, chunky legs shaved so smooch they gave off a kind of sheen, like pewter, who has carried with her in secret since the age of sixteen a razor blade sharp as on the day of its purchase, never once used. It is likely to be wrapped in several turns of Kleenex placed carefully against the bottom of her leather shoulder bag. No one knows it is there, and often she too forgets.

An older woman, a friend, advised her to carry the razor blade with her at all times, if not on her actual person (which would be tricky) then within reach. The logic is, If you never have to use it you're in luck, right? If you have to use it and you have it, you're in luck, right? So how can you lose?

So sometimes without knowing what she does her fingers seek out the blade, the shape of the blade, neatly wrapped in its several turns of Kleenex, pressed, there, flat against the bottom of her bag. He guessed it was probably like that.

It was their second day, the first day after their first night; driving out from Vegas into the desert she'd laid her head sleepily against his shoulder, as if she had a right. Perfectly manicured pink-lacquered nails on his thigh, digging lightly into his sharp-pressed chino pants. He told her with the air of one imparting a secret that he drove out into the desert as often as he could, not just to get away from Vegas but to be alone. To listen, he said, to the wind.

"Is it always so windy?" she asked.

"And I like the quiet."

"The *quiet?* But it goes on," she said, her reedy childlike voice beginning to falter, "such a long way."

He'd stopped the car, thinking this was a good place. Back a lane leading off the tourists' loop road, where no one was likely to come. Just this side of Furnace Creek one turn beyond a turnoff for a deserted mine where he'd brought another girl a few months back. There was a dreamy illusion they were the only visitors in this part of Death Valley today, but maybe it wasn't an illusion.

She'd said back in the room she was crazy about him, but now she was holding herself just a little off; he sensed it and liked it, that edge between them, not just the loneliness of the place but the sun did it, the starkness, the sudden wonder why you are here and why with this person, some stranger you hardly know and whose actual name you could not swear to.

"Is that tumbleweed?" she was asking. "I always wondered what tumbleweed was."

"It's something like tumbleweed," he said, "some kind of vegetation that dries out, tumbles in the wind, scatters its seeds that way. It's a weed."

"Everything's a weed, isn't it, in a place like this?"

He laughed; she had him there. "Everything's a weed," he conceded.

She had a way of surprising him now and then. He liked her; he really did. "You have named the secret of the universe," he said, smiling. "*Everything's a weed.*"

He was laughing, and then suddenly he was coughing. She asked was he all right and he said yes, then started in laughing again, or maybe it was coughing. In a kind of paroxysm, like sex. But not always shared, like sex. Not always something you want to see, in others. Like sex.

"Lie down, honey, let's try it here."

He spoke half seriously but teasing too so that she could take it that way if she wanted. Behind the purple-tinted glasses her eyes widened in alarm. She said, "Here? I'd rather go back to Vegas."

He laughed and wiped his mouth with a tissue. He was excited but couldn't keep from yawning; his eyes flooded with tears. "I thought you were a big growed-up girl," he said, winking. He saw that his watch had stopped almost exactly at twelve noon.

She decided he was teasing, maybe he was teasing; she laughed and walked off a little, saying it was a shame she'd left her camera behind, wouldn't you know it, Death Valley and she'd left her camera behind. You could see she was trying. Squinting at these mountains that were not Kodacolor mountains with dazzling snowy peaks but just rock formations lifting out of the earth, weirdly striated.

The striations of the brain, out there. Terrible to see if you saw them.

Vegetation that looked like it was actually mineral.

Rocks, crumbled earth. Dun-colored bleached-looking dead-looking earth.

And the dunes, and the sand in ripples like washboards. And the wind.

She said, licking her lips, uneasy because he'd been silent for so long, hands in his chino pockets, not following her with his eyes as she strolled about, in her tank-top jersey blouse with the spaghetti straps to show she wasn't wearing a bra and the black-and-white striped miniskirt that fitted her hips snug and sweet, as if to set her off the way, say, a model is set off against a dull dun-colored background. "I suppose many people have died out here—pioneers, I mean—crossing the desert? In the old days?"

"I wouldn't doubt it," he said.

"The Donner party—the people who had to eat one another's flesh in order to survive—didn't they cross Death Valley?"

"I don't believe so."

"I thought that was their name. I saw a television show about them once."

"That was the name but I don't think the Donners crossed Death Valley. I think it was Idaho. Somewhere in Idaho."

"It was just heartbreaking, the television show. Once you got to know them, the men and women and the little kids, your heart just went out to them. My God! Turning cannibal!" She spoke vehemently, gesturing with both hands. The wind blew thinly through her hair. "Our ancestors endured so much, it's a miracle we came into being at all."

She looked at him; he was smiling. She shaded her eyes against him and said, "O.K., what's up? Did I say something stupid, or what?"

"You said something wonderful."

"Yeah? What?"

"'It's a miracle we came into being at all.'"

"Yeah?"

"Yeah."

"Just something, you know, nice. I don't like to talk about it, actually."

"But is it strong, is it sweet, is it a little painful, what *is* it? I'm just curious. What women feel."

"I don't like to talk about it actually."

"Why not?"

"I—"

"You said you were married, once. When—when was it?—you were nineteen."

"What's that got to do with it?"

"You're not a kid."

"No. I guess I'm not a kid." She cut her eyes at him, meaning to shift the subject. "You'd maybe prefer a kid?"

"As I said, I'm just curious. How long the sensation lasts, for instance, afterward. Minutes? Hours?"

"Oh, I don't know you know," she said, shy again, not looking at him, a blush starting up from her neck. "A long time sometimes, hours sometimes. I guess it depends."

"On what?"

"How strong it was in the beginning."

"If you love the guy a lot—or don't, much—does that affect the orgasm too?"

"I guess so."

"But don't you *know*?"

She stood mute and resisting, her face, beneath the heavy pancake makeup, decidedly pink. "I guess I don't. I guess it's something that just . . . happens."

"The orgasm, you mean. Can't you say the word?"

She stood smiling, staring at their feet. Sandals with just enough heel to make it unwise for her to have worn them, out here. And if she'd have to run, and kick the shoes off, the sand would be like liquid fire against her feet.

Her purse too, the shoulder bag, left behind in the car. She'd never get to it in time.

"Say it," he said, bending a little to look in her face. Teasing. "Can't you say it? Orgasm."

She laughed nervously, and shook her head, and said, "It makes me feel funny. I don't like it, you looking at me so close."

"Why does it embarrass you?"

"I don't know. I'm not embarrassed."

"A big girl like you."

"I'm not embarrassed, I don't *like* it."

"You look embarrassed. But very sweet too."

"Well."

"You know you're a great-looking girl, don't you? Where did you say you were from? Oh, yes: you and your girlfriend, from Nebraska."

Her face crinkled in childish dislike.

He said, quickly, with an air of apology, "No, I mean Columbus, Ohio. You and two girlfriends from Columbus, Ohio." He was teasing, poking her with a forefinger. In the plump resilient flesh just below her breasts. "The big weekend in Vegas. Right? First time in Vegas, right? And last night you won a hundred and twenty dollars at the slots, you were telling me. Two separate jackpots."

There was a silence. She said, quietly, "I think I'd sort of like to go back now, to Las Vegas. This place is kind of weird."

"I thought you wanted to see the countryside. The 'natural rock formations.'"

"It makes me feel . . . sort of strange, here. Like it's a dream or something."

"A dream of yours or a dream of the landscape?"

She peered at him, suspicious. "What's that mean?"

"What?"

"What you just asked me?"

"*You* were saying it, honey, not me. That it's like a dream here. Where anything can happen."

She laughed again, not exactly frightened yet but on the edge of it. He was thinking how her mouth was her cunt actually, the fat lips glossed up the way they were. The night before he'd taken a wad of toilet paper and was a little rough playing daddy, scolding her to keep it light—he was careful to keep it light—wiping the lipstick off, the apricot makeup, layers of pancake makeup and grainy powder that had caked over her young skin. Without the makeup her skin was doughy and a little coarse but he preferred it to the other. If there was anything he loathed it was female makeup smeared on him, the madman look of lipstick around his mouth, enlarging his mouth.

He kissed her, and whispered some things in her ear, and she slapped at him and said they'd better go back to the car, at least. And he kissed her again, forcing her mouth open, how wet it was, but not really warm, and how he felt, in that instant, the power flow down from his torso into his belly and loins, the first time he'd felt it that day. Last night, he must have felt it too but couldn't remember, he'd been too drunk.

He was thinking, those years he'd worked out every day, lifting weights, keeping himself in condition, he'd had that feeling a lot: you walk in someplace where no one knows you but they glance up in acknowledgment of you, in approval or even admiration, and that does it: sets you up for the rest of the day.

She didn't like him roughhousing; she said, little-girl hurt, "You got the wrong idea about me, mister," and he said, smiling, "You've got an ass, don't you? You've got a cunt. You *are* a cunt. So where's the 'wrong idea'?" But now he'd gone a little too far too fast and she was hurt and beginning to be frightened. Seeing her face he was repentant at once, saying he was sorry, damned sorry. Wouldn't hurt her for the world.

She went ahead of him to the car, swaying a little in the sandals like a drunken woman. He caught up to her, kissed her, apologized another time. He yawned; moisture flooded his eyes. In the car they drank from the bottle he'd brought along, good strong smooth delicious Jim Beam, my pal Jim Beam, don't go anywhere without him. He talked about getting married, it was time for him to settle down, Jesus, it was past the time, he had a hunch he should consolidate his luck and he should do it right now. She lay with her head against his shoulder, just a little uneasy against his shoulder, and he asked if she'd ever heard of the poet Rilke, the great German poet Rilke, and she said she'd maybe heard of the name but couldn't swear to it. Guardedly she said she didn't read much poetry now; used to read it, had to memorize it, back in high school. He was feeling good so he recited what he could remember of one of the *Duino Elegies*, the words pushing through in their startling order which he had not known he still knew but of course there were only snatches, shreds. *"And that is how I have cherished you—-deep inside / the mirror, where you put yourself, far away / from all the world. Why have you come like this / and so denied yourself. . . ."*

His voice trailed off, he sensed her embarrassment, they sat for a while without speaking. Except for the wind it was absolutely silent, but you stopped hearing the wind after a while.

She said, clearing her throat, "It's funny: in the shade it's sort of chilly, but in the sun, out there, it's so hot."

In that instant he hated her. He was very happy. He said, "It's winter, sweetheart. After all."

She was preparing to cry but holding back, thinking was he the kind of man who feels sorry when you cry or was he the kind of man who gets really angry. So he warned her, "I'm getting just a little impatient, honey," and that quieted her fast. He got her into the back of the BMW, and they kissed awhile, he called her honey and sweetheart and said how crazy he was about her, his good luck talisman dropped from the sky. She was still stiff, scared, but he unzipped his trousers anyway, closed his fingers around the nape of her neck; she began to say, "No, hey, no, I don't want to, not here," whimpering like a child, and he said, "Here's as good as anywhere, cunt," so that quieted her, and she did it, she went through with it, in the back seat of the rented car awkward as kids playing in some cramped secret place. And he drifted off thinking of how wild it would be, how no one could stop it from happening; this is the one who's going to lean over quick to get her purse from the front seat and take out the razor blade and unwrap it while his eyes are shut and his face all slack and dreamy like the bones had melted . . . and then she'll bring the blade's edge against his neck, where the big blue artery is throbbing. And there's an immediate explosion of blood and his eyes are open now and he's screaming, he's clutching at his throat with his fingers as if to close the wound, just with his fingers, and she scrambles out of the car, running stumbling in the sand, screaming, How do you like it? How do you like it? Filthy shit-eating bastard, how

do you like it?—running until she's out of the range of his
cries. Until the cries subside.

Then she waits, her heart pounding hard, so scared she's begun
to leak in her panties. But at the same time there's a part of her
brain reasoning. I'm safe here, what can he do to me here? He
can't do anything now.

And she's thinking too, Anything I did to him, it's been done
before by somebody to somebody, not once but many times.

She thinks, shivering, There is that consolation.

When she returns to the BMW, she sees his body on the
ground a few yards from the car where he fell, must have tried
to crawl a little, though there is nowhere his crawling could
have taken him. She sees he isn't breathing, must be dead; and
so much blood in the sand, soaked up in the sand, and in the
back seat of the car, horrible to see. She tries not to look but
has to get the car keys from his pocket, his trousers around
his ankles, unzipped, and his jockey shorts open, everything
looking so tender and exposed like veins on the outside of the
body, and soaked too with blood. The wild thought comes to
her, How will they take photographs of him for the papers,
lying the way he is, how will they manage to show it on the
television news?

Sweet, sweet Linda. God, how sweet.

Back in Vegas, he dropped her off at her motel, said he'd call her
around nine, and she said, "Oh, sure, I'm gonna hang around
here all night in this shithole and wait for you to call, that's
great, thanks a lot, mister," and he said, "If I say I'm going to
call I'm going to call, why are you so angry? Nine P.M. sharp,

or a little after," and she got out of the car, moving stiffly, as if her joints ached; then she leaned in the window, face puffy and mouth bruised-looking. "Fuck you, mister," she said, "in no uncertain terms."

He sat in the car, the engine idling, and watched her walk away and had to give her credit: she didn't once glance back. Holding herself with dignity in that wrinkled miniskirt that barely covered her thighs, walking as steady as she could manage in the tacky fake-leather sandals, as if it mattered, and she mattered, which actually scared him a little—that evidence of the difference between them when he hadn't believed there could be, much.

CRAPS

Just when I thought he'd drifted off to sleep, his head heavy and warm on my shoulder, Hughie says, What's that story you were going to tell me about Vegas? And I tell him quickly, There's lots of stories about Vegas.

Late Sunday morning I'm lying on top of the bed half dressed with Hughie, my ex-husband, sort of cradled in my arms—he'd dropped by earlier just wanting to talk, he said, in one of his moods where he needs consolation and some signs of affection—and lying together like this, just lying still and drowsy, is an old habit of ours but it's Hughie who always requires it, these days. We fit together like a hand and a glove—Hughie's head on my right shoulder and my arm under his neck (where, sometimes, it goes to sleep, gets so numb I can't feel it there), his right arm cradling my breasts from beneath, and his right foot tucked between mine. There are these old habits you slip into no matter how you actually feel about each other, or anything else. Or where your mind drifts, late Sunday morning.

I was seventeen when I met Hughie, who is twenty-two years older than me. I was twenty-seven when I asked him please to leave. The divorce came through in about eighteen months but we're still friends; you could say we are like brother and sister if it was qualified to mean not always getting along with each other but always there; in a small town like this where's there to go? After the divorce, last year, we have actually gotten along better. Hughie is always changing jobs and changing woman friends and stopping drinking (and starting again) and none of what he does is my problem now, though naturally, being the way I am, I take an interest. But I don't let it hurt me, now.

He's away for months and doesn't call and I'm busy with my own life; then suddenly he'll drop by, lonely, depressed, three days' beard and bloodshot eyes and I won't lend him money if that's what he wants (sometimes I think he's just testing me, anyway) but I'll make him supper, or sometimes he has brought something special to eat, or a bottle of wine, sometimes even flowers. Flowers! I can't help laughing when he holds them out to me like a guilty little boy. He was always ready to spend our money on things we didn't need and I saw through that long ago but here's the same Hughie; they don't change. All other things change but they don't change, men like him.

So what's this story about Vegas? Hughie says. I'm waiting.

It isn't any story, I tell him. What's Lynn been telling you behind my back?

Some guy you met at craps. Some millionaire Texan.

I didn't meet him at craps and he wasn't any millionaire Texan and why don't you stay quiet, if you're going to stay here at all. You said you just wanted to nap.

So Hughie draws this long deep breath and burrows his face in my neck and lies very still. You've been to Vegas yourself, I say, you know what it's like. Hughie doesn't answer but I can tell he's waiting for me to go on. Of course it was a real surprise to *me*, I say, walking into the casino with Lynn and already at 9 A.M. there's so many people gambling, at these machines that look like video games. Almost the first people I saw, I swear they looked like your parents: this elderly couple playing the slots side by side, and she's winning some, a few quarters, and he doesn't care to be interrupted, just keeps on playing, leaning real close to the machine like he can't see too well, dropping in a quarter and pulling the lever, dropping in a quarter and pulling the lever, over and over the way they do, and it *is* fascinating, sort of, you can see how people get hooked. Lynn and I spent the morning on the machines and won some, lose some, the way you do. We saw some people Lynn said were probably retired to Vegas just for the slots and some of them, their right hands were actually deformed, like with arthritis, shaped like claws, pulling the lever a thousand times a day. But you could see they were happy, doing what they want to do.

There's lots of Vegas stories we heard just in the brief time we were there, and new ones every day. A man drives across the desert with two suitcases in the car, one empty and one filled with five-hundred-dollar bills; he's got five hundred thousand dollars and places a bet on some heavyweight boxer that the odds are six to one against—and he wins! And they fill the second suitcase for him with thousand-dollar bills and he drives off again and nobody even knows his name. That's a true story, supposed to have happened just a few weeks before. Then there are these millionaire, I mean billionaire, Arab sheiks that fly in for the poker games, these special poker games at some club not open to the general public where there's no limit on bets. I saw some of them, I think, just caught a glimpse. Up at the Sands some man died at blackjack, he'd been at the table for a long time they said and had a coronary for no special reason—I mean, not because he'd won a lot of money, or lost. We were in Vegas at the time but not in that casino, thank God! One thing that did occur, in the Rainbow Casino, it's sort of disgusting, a woman lost control of her bladder, playing the slots and not wanting to take time off, I suppose; people all started walking away fast, as Lynn and I did. Can you imagine! And she wasn't all that old either, around fifty, but a drinker—they must be the worst kind, hooked in with the slots on top of drinking.

Lynn's crazy about the slots but she said we should set ourselves a limit, make it seventy-five apiece, and see how far that would go, which is the only sensible way to approach gambling, and I wasn't playing ten minutes before I won a hundred and sixty dollars, which was one third of a jackpot for that machine. I was excited as a kid, jumping up and down; if it'd been me alone I would have quit right there and gone off and celebrated with a drink and something rich and fancy like a chocolate eclair, but Lynn just laughed and kissed me and said to calm down. Wait till you win a real jackpot, she said. That'll be time to celebrate, then.

I forgot to mention all the conventions being held in the big hotels, and people drinking too much and acting like kids: the National Association of Morticians was one of them, the Fred Astaire Dance Association was another, a bunch of hypnotists, veterinarians—you name it! A lot of them fattish bald guys wearing badges with a look like they're running loose, no wives to crimp their style. I mean *a lot*.

I did see one sight that scared me, a little: that night, late, we were walking with these guys we'd met through Caesars Palace— you know what that place is like, my God!—and there's this nice-looking woman about my age playing the slots, all alone evidently, with her cigarettes and her drink and one of those waxy paper buckets half filled with coins, and all of a sudden she hits the jackpot and it's one of the big jackpots, one thousand silver dollars, and the machine lights up, you know, the way they do, and plays some honkeytonk music, and people come over to watch, especially tourists who've never seen a big jackpot, and all she does is light up a cigarette, her hands are shaking and she doesn't even look at the coins spilling out, she's half turned away from the machine, her face so sad you'd think she was about to cry, and all the while the silver coins are tumbling out and filling the trough and spilling onto the floor and on and on and on! I mean, it keeps *on,* one thousand coins! It's just such a happy sight, the machine lighting up, and the silly music like cartoon music, but she isn't taking the least bit of happiness from it— just tired-looking and so sad it was painful to look at her. This man I was with, Sonny, he said, She's waiting for the jackpot to finish so she can keep on playing. That's all she wants, to keep on playing. A jackpot like that gets in the way.

And that turned out to be the case. At least with that woman— we stood off a ways and watched.

O.K., Hughie says. Now tell me about Sonny.

What I was needing, though, was a new life. Not a new *life,* that sounds sort of extreme, but some new outlook on *this* life. Some new surprise, a set of new feelings. I want a baby but that's not it; I been wanting a baby for a long time. (Which was one of the reasons Hughie and I broke up. He has kids from his first marriage and definitely doesn't want any more.) That might be part of it but that's not it. Some nights, after work, thinking how there's nobody prominent in my affections any longer and nobody I even know of I'd like to be prominent, not in this town at least, where everybody knows everybody else's business and some of them, the men, have the idea I'm still married to Hughie or belong to him at least—some nights I'd start in crying for no reason I could name. Or, not even crying, just my throat closing up, that feeling of some old hurt returning.

So Lynn, my crazy friend Lynn, she comes over and shows me this charter-airline stuff, these brochures about Vegas, how cheap it is to fly there and how the hotels, some of them, aren't really that expensive, considering where you are—the big-name stars playing out there, the quality entertainment. Lynn has been to Vegas a half-dozen times and always enjoyed herself, and she told me if I was feeling bad this was the time to go—mid-January and the holiday season dead and gone and anybody's spirits just naturally need picking up. It didn't matter whether you were sad or not, Lynn said, this time of year would do it.

So I said no, then I heard myself say yes—you know how Lynn is with me. She just winds me around her little finger.

Hughie stirs and says, Oh, yes? And who wants to be wound?

I give him a pinch and tell him be quiet. Does he want to hear this or doesn't he?

Go on, he says. I'm waiting for Sonny, the millionaire Texan.

Anyway, as you know, it was my first time in Vegas. The first time flying over the Rockies like that, and the Grand Canyon— my God, that's beautiful; the whole time in the air was beautiful, sort of like a dream—Lynn hates window seats so I was sitting next to the window and we're flying at thirty thousand feet or whatever the pilot said, over these mountains, these snowy peaks, then over clouds like snow crust—miles and miles of it, I mean *hundreds* of miles of it—and I guess I got sort of hypnotized looking out. It's a funny feeling you have, flying over a big stretch of cloud, like a field piled with snow, but there are people living below it not able to guess how big the field is and how there's other people flying above it. How they're down there hidden and you're up above, flying over.

Hughie is lying heavy against me with his chin sort of sharp on my shoulder. He's breathing hard and steady so I think he might be dropping off to sleep. But he says, a little too loud in my ear to suit me, O.K., O.K., I'm waiting for the high roller. So I tell *him* O.K.: this guy, Sonny Drexel as he introduced himself, from Oklahoma City, a rancher he said he was, him and his buddy were watching Lynn and me at blackjack, where we hadn't any luck—all those damn games go fast, the serious ones; you put your chip down and Christ it's gone before you know what happened. (Which is why some people prefer the slots—you go at your own speed and never lose much.) So these two, Sonny and Brady, said they'd stake us just to keep us in the game, and we all played for a while and got along pretty well, though Lynn and I never did get any luck, me especially. The strange thing is, Sonny said I was luck for him, wearing my turquoise dress, you know that one, and a black velvet ribbon in my hair, that makes me look ten years younger than I am—that's what caught his eye, he told me afterward, the ribbon, reminded him of his little girl. That is, when she was actually little. I guess she's all grown up, now, and then some.

How old was he? Hughie asks.

He *looked* like middle forties, maybe fifty, but I calculated later on he was around sixty—

Sixty!

—but didn't act it at all, good-looking in this cowboy style you see out in Vegas, a suede hat with silver studs, and snakeskin boots, designer jeans, jeweled bracelet on one wrist and wrist-watch on the other, even some rings—the rings all had special meanings. Like one was a birthstone, one used to belong to his great-grandfather, that sort of thing. Lynn says the serious gamblers are all superstitious, they don't do anything by chance. What Sonny reminded me of was one of these cigarette billboard ads, an older man I mean, with pale hair you can't tell is blond or silver, and longish sideburns, and a creased, kindly, slightly puzzled face as if he'd been looking too long into the sun. His voice was higher-pitched than you'd expect. Brady was younger, heavier, with a coarser skin. What the connection was between them I never did learn.

The two of them were taking a break from craps; I got the idea they'd done pretty well judging from the good mood they were in, especially Sonny, buying drinks for Lynn and me and some Japanese tourists we got to talking with at the bar in the Tropicana, then this expensive supper they bought us at the Barbary Coast where we saw some of the floor show, a kind of Ice Capades with singing and rainbow lights and acrobatics—it was beautiful to see, and Lynn and I loved it, but Sonny got restless so we had to leave. Brady was ragging him about not being able to stay away from the craps table for more than an hour or two like he needs his oxygen replenished, and Sonny laughs but you can tell he's annoyed. That kind of a man, you can get intimate with him to a degree and think you know him, but the least hint of familiarity he draws back and chills you out. I picked up on that right away.

Another thing Brady ragged him about was going to the john all the time and washing his hands. He's afraid of germs, Brady said, and Sonny said, You'd be too if you could see them with the naked eye, and we all laughed and Brady said, Can *you* see them with the naked eye? and Sonny laughed too but said in this serious voice, Sometimes. And I don't like it.

And I did notice, the short period of time I was in the man's company, he must have excused himself a dozen times to go to the lavatory. Only when he was shooting craps he didn't, of course—it was like he was another person then. When he was hot, I mean. Really rolling high and nothing could have stopped him.

So we went back to the Dunes and Sonny and Brady got into a game and Sonny was shooting and almost right away got hot. Won eighteen hundred dollars in less time than it takes me to say it! He had me stand on his left-hand side, told me not to move an inch if I could help it. At first he didn't want me to bet, thinking that might go against his own luck, but after a while, when he kept winning and so many other people were betting on the game, he said it might be all right so I started placing little bets on what they called the pass line—the easiest bet. And naturally I won too, though it didn't seem real or right, betting with chips he'd given me and following what he did.

Craps isn't my favorite game, it's so fast and nervous and wild, and so complicated, Christ—like some game that was invented to keep ordinary minds at a distance. All Lynn and I did was bet on the pass line and later on the come line—we wouldn't have wanted to bet no pass and go against Sonny—but these other gamblers got involved, and of course Brady was doing all kinds of things, special bets we couldn't follow. And the smart thing about Sonny was, he knew when to quit for a while—with this big pile of chips he'd built up in half an hour—and let somebody else shoot, so he could bet or nor bet, depending. He told me what to do and I did it and most of the time I won, but if I lost he told me to stop for a while till my luck returned; he said you can feel your luck in you like a pressure in the chest and head but not a cruel pressure, a feeling that's high-wired and happy, and you can feel it drain away, sudden, he said, as water draining out of a sink. A gambler moves by instinct, he said, like a man dousing for water.

I had a granddaddy who could douse for water, I said.

We'll talk about it some other time, he said.

So after Brady shot for a while and did O.K., Sonny took over again and you could tell something would happen: this feeling all around the table, like the air's charged up. Of course we'd all been drinking this while, I don't know how long, Lynn and me excited and giggling like high school girls, arms around each other's waist, saying, This is something different, isn't it! This is something different from the old home routine! And Sonny started his roll and I placed bets on the pass line, which is the only bet I ever felt easy with, that I understood: before the shooter rolls the dice, you place your bet, and if he rolls seven or eleven you and him both win and he keeps the dice to roll again. If he hits two, three, or ten the bet is lost but he keeps his point and goes on rolling until either he makes his point and you both win or he shoots seven and the bet is lost. I *think* that's how the game goes.

That's how it goes, Hughie says. He's wider awake than I thought he would be, which is flattering. Except it's two, three, or twelve on that first roll.

And anyway I won my bets. But like I say it didn't seem real, or exactly right.

Around 4:30 A.M. Sonny quit for the night. He'd been playing in all about fifteen hours, he estimated, in the past twenty-four and needed some rest. As far as I could calculate—they didn't like to talk about these things, like it was in bad taste—he'd won about twenty-five thousand just the time I was with him.

Called me his good luck talisman, said he'd always want me by his side. All the time he was shooting he hadn't touched me, but now he put his arm around me so tight it was hard to walk and sort of leaned on me, calling me pretty girl, pretty Irene, Irene-y, I'll see you in my dreams. He was drunk I guess but not so you'd really notice. Had a way of talking that was a combination of a high-class gentleman and a country boy—a sort of twangy accent, warm and rich like Johnny Cash.

He *was* sweet. Next day down in the promenade—we were staying in the big Hilton, there's all these boutiques and special stores there—he bought me a Japanese kimono, the most beautiful thing, turquoise with a brocade design like a sunburst, gold, red, green: just so beautiful. And some black silk pants to go with the kimono, and some gold lamé sandals with spike heels. And some gold teardrop earrings, and a bottle of perfume. And—

Uh-huh, says Hughie, his leg muscles twitching the way they do when he's asleep but he isn't asleep now, I get the drift of it.

It wasn't *that*, I tell Hughie, I liked him for himself. He was a fine, sweet, generous, thoughtful man. And a gentleman.

Hughie keeps quiet, not wanting to pick a fight and get kicked out of here on his ass as he's in danger of being. My heart's beating hard just at that one thing he said, his sly innuendo that I don't have to swallow any more than I swallowed any of his shit and he knows it—he's the boy who knows it no matter what he goes around town telling his buddies.

He was a gentleman, I say. There aren't many of that kind around.

Hughie doesn't say a word but I know he's fully awake and listening.

I *will* say, though, when we first got to his room—a real nice room in the Hilton Tower, nothing like what Lynn and I were sharing at our motel—I started in feeling very strange and wanted to just say good night and leave. Before, you know, it was too late and Sonny got the wrong idea. I'm just standing there, afraid if I sit down I'll fall asleep—I was more exhausted all of a sudden than I've ever been in my life—and my eyes weren't focusing right, everything sort of swimmy and blurry. I was drunk but that wasn't the only thing. There's this man I don't even know whistling to himself and taking off his shirt and his chest is covered in what looks like actual fur: gray-grizzled, silvery, matted. And his nipples dark as a woman's. And fat loose around his waist though his ribs were showing. And some sort of scar, or burn, on his back that looked just terrible. It's like him and me were married and had been married a long time, he's tossing his things around, whistling loud and happy, has me help him with his boots—these snakeskin boots like nothing you've ever seen, Lynn says something like that would go for five hundred dollars if not a thousand. You don't even see them in any store around here.

So I'm feeling very, very strange, this sickish feeling in my stomach, and Sonny's in the bathroom running the water loud and still whistling. He's happier now than down in the casino, like it was all held in, down there, and now it's coming out—just how happy he is, and how powerful it is, that kind of happiness!—like it would be too much for an ordinary person.

Sonny comes out of the bathroom drying his hands on a towel and when he sees me it's like he's almost forgotten I was there: this big smile comes over his face that looks as if it could stretch his face out of shape. Kisses me, and stands back staring at me, tells me how much I mean to him, how pretty I am, will I be his pretty pretty girl forever, and he takes the velvet bow out of my hair and kisses it solemn and serious and I'm thinking to myself, God, am *I* doing this? This is *me*? In a hotel room with some guy who, nice as he is, I don't know, just met? And I'm laughing too, giggling and scared, 'cause it's so easy, you could see doing this every night, I don't mean for the money or even for the man but just—the fact of how easy it is, once it starts.

Hughie stirs. Irene, he says, and it's the first time I have heard him call me Irene in a long time, this is a hard story to hear.

I told you, be quiet. Or don't you want to hear it?

I *want* to hear it, Hughie says, but I guess I want some parts of it to go by fast.

There's nothing to go by fast, I say, since all that happens is I sort of pass out on one of the beds and Sonny loosens my clothes and takes off my shoes and that's all—he sleeps in his own bed like a gentleman. And that's all.

Then the next morning I wake up pretty late, around eleven, and already he's in the shower, he orders us breakfast from room service which neither one of us can stomach, except for the Bloody Marys, and we go downstairs and pick out those nice things—which were a surprise to me, I swear, completely unexpected. Where Brady and Lynn are, I don't know, and I didn't like to make any inquiries.

Later on we drove over to Vegas World in this special car of
Sonny's, Italian, hand-built, he said, like a custom-made suit,
some sort of Ferrari with a long name, bright red like lipstick
and capable Sonny said of doing 175 miles an hour under the
right road conditions. How'd I like to go for a drive in the desert
maybe the next day? Sonny asked. Out to Death Valley maybe.
I told him I'd like that a lot, but I seemed to know we'd never
get there that something was due to happen; it was like a movie
where things are going so well you know they can't last. Also, it
was only a few blocks to Vegas World but the sunlight hurt our
eyes, even with dark sunglasses. What the actual desert would
be like I didn't want to think.

(It's kind of a startling thing, leaving the inside world and
going to the outside, that you've sort of forgotten is still there.
This ordinary sunshine and ordinary sidewalks and traffic lights
and things, and people in it that didn't seem to have anything
to do with all that was happening in the casinos. It made me
feel sort of sickish, I told Sonny, and he said yes but you get
used to it.)

At Vegas World it's sort of like a circus for adults but Sonny
wasn't interested in any of it, just headed straight for the casino.
And what a crowd packed in! Not just every slot machine taken,
but people waiting for some to open up. Sonny staked me to
some blackjack again, but I didn't do too well, then for a few
turns at roulette, ditto; he didn't play because as he said you get
to know which game is yours and which isn't.

Also, he said, the games were too simple. Didn't command
his fullest concentration.

So it was back at craps, and he had me stand close beside him, on his left, wearing my new outfit, including the shoes, and the black velvet ribbon in my hair. And again Sonny got on a roll, couldn't seem to make a mistake; he doubled his bet, and won, and doubled, and won, and there was this feeling of—it's hard to explain—a kind of excitement at the table, happiness so strong it's scary. That it could go through you like electricity, and kill you, bend your skull out of shape. Some of it's because other people get caught up in the betting, strangers that a few minutes ago didn't know one another but suddenly they're all united, close as old friends or something deeper sisters and brothers—the exact same blood.

So he did real well again but never allowed himself to show what he was feeling. I could never be like that, I guess; I could never be a real gambler! All my feelings show on my face.

So we went back to the Hilton, this is maybe 6 P.M. that day, and Sonny's in a state like I don't believe I have ever seen any person in, giving off heat like a radiator, I swear I could almost feel the waves of it, and I was pretty high too, and we're kissing a little, sort of fooling around, but more like kids, or puppies, than, you know—like he's too worked up for anything to actually happen. His skin is burning like fever, but without sweat. And his eyes, this tawny cat color, the eyeball and the iris or whatever it's called sort of run together, like a man with jaundice, and I notice he's breathing hard, and loud, but don't make much of it. Whatever we're doing he stops all of a sudden and goes into the bathroom to wash his hands—I mean, I guess that's what he was doing—then he comes back and looks at me and says, Get dressed, honey, let's go back to the casino. And I can't believe it.

So we go back out again, this time down to the Sands, and in the car he's talking a mile a minute, to me you'd naturally think but really to himself. I listened hard but I can't remember much of it now. He did want me to marry him, that's for sure—come back with him to Oklahoma City to this new house he planned to build. He didn't ask me anything about myself, such as did I have any children, let alone did I want any children, so I sat there nodding and agreeing but thinking he probably wasn't serious, really. What he said, he meant, but only while he was saying it.

Then at the Sands his luck turned on him after about an hour, I don't know why. I mean—I don't know why he didn't know it was going to turn, the way he'd said he always did. Right in the middle of one of these red-hot rolls—what you would think was a red-hot roll—when he'd made, I calculated, about twenty-two thousand in not much more time than it's taking me to say so, he rolled the wrong numbers and lost the bet; and that was the beginning of the end. The two or three guys that'd been betting don't come won really big, and Sonny just stood there like he couldn't believe he was seeing what he was seeing. And the terrible thing is, the girl just raked in the chips like nothing had gone wrong, or even changed. Not the slightest understanding in her face of what had happened.

Now, *I* seemed to know that poor man should quit right then but he did not pay the least heed to me, and when I put my hand on his arm he pushed away like I was something nasty. Don't touch! he said.

And this feeling came over me like the floor was tilting, and I thought, I know the truth of why we're here on earth, human beings here on earth: it's to love one another if we can, but if we can't—if we try, but can't—we're here to show kindness and gentleness and mercy and respect to one another, and to protect one another. I don't know how I knew but I *knew*.

But would he pay any attention to me? He wouldn't. Saying he wanted to marry me one minute and telling me to go to hell, calling me cunt, the next. For all the good I meant to do him.

So his luck ran out, and I don't know how much he lost, but people made big money betting against him, and in the end nobody wanted to look at him. I should mention he was wearing the suede cowboy hat and the same black silk shirt with one of these little string neckties he'd been wearing the day before, and the fancy boots. And a leather belt with a big silver buckle. And hot as he was he wasn't sweating much. (*I* was the one that was sweating now!)

I recall one final slight the girl in her costume with *Sands* stitched in gold on the back, black jumpsuit and tight belt and black spike heels, hair blonder and puffier than mine, she took this little Plexiglas rake of hers and just raked Sonny's chips away, and took a crumpled-up five-hundred-dollar bill from him the same way except that she pushed it down a little slot in the table like a mail slot. And it just disappeared.

So finally Sonny turned away, his face like paper that's been burnt through but hasn't burst into actual flames yet. Finish up your drink, Blondie, he says to me, smiling. I'm hurt to think the man has forgotten my name.

We went back to the Hilton and he made some calls, then went out, saying he'd be gone awhile. I watched some television and washed my hair and finished this champagne we'd got the night before, and it got late but I was too worked up to sleep. I had the drapes open looking over at Vegas World—that's the tallest building, all colored lights like fireworks. But everywhere on the Strip there's lights: the Sahara, the Oasis, the Golden Nugget, Caesars Palace, all the rest. Off in the distance the mountains you can't see and I never did get to see except from the air and going to and from the airport in the cab.

Around 4 A.M. when I was actually asleep a little, with all the lights on, Sonny came back to the room. He had that look so drunk it might be said to be sober. He sat on the edge of the bed and kneaded his chest with both hands like it hurt him inside. In this calm voice he said, I have led the wrong life. I have done wrong things. At the very time of doing them I knew they were wrong, but I did them nonetheless. I did them *nonetheless*—this word drawn out slow, in a whisper.

He started to cry so it was painful to watch. Begging me not to leave him now his luck had run temporarily out.

I was crying too. I told him I'd stay with him as long as he wanted.

He said, I'm not from where I said. I'm from a different place. Not even Oklahoma. I've been a bad husband and father. There's people back home loved me and gave me their trust, and I let them down. I let them down a lot of times. Right now they don't even know where I am.

I was sort of cradling his head, stooping over him. I said, Don't think about that now, Sonny, and he shot back, Don't think about it *now*? When the fuck *am* I supposed to think about it, then?

But right away he changed his tone back. Said, Dolly. I'm a dead man.

What? I asked.

I'm dying, I'm a dying man, he said. I'm next thing to dead.

Are you serious? Should I call a—

You can't leave me just yet, he said, gripping my arm hard. You know I'm crazy about you; I'd love you if I could.

That didn't make any sense so I said, You can love me, why can't you love me? And he says right away, in this voice like we've been quarreling, Dolly, if I *could*, I *would*.

He grabs me around the hips so hard it hurts and pulls me down onto the bed. Then he's on me pawing and grunting and making this terrible hoarse sobbing noise, and I'm there not helping him much but just waiting for it to get over. I think, He can't do it, he's too drunk, or too sick, or too old, and that's more or less the way it was, I guess, but I wasn't paying close attention, shutting my eyes tight and seeing all kinds of things that had nothing to do with him or what was going on. I could see the wheat field out behind here, the way the wind makes it look like waves. And the Grand Canyon, when the pilot turned the plane for us, explained some things to us, those natural rock formations, what a canyon actually is.

And other things too. Lying there with my eyes shut like they are now, my mind taking me far away from where I was.

Afterward I couldn't wake him. It was almost noon and he was lying on his back with his mouth open and saliva on the pillow and I seemed to know he wasn't just sleeping or even blacked out but something more serious. I tried to wake him,

slapped his face and got a washcloth soaked in cold water, and
that didn't help; oh, Christ, I'm thinking, the man is in a coma,
he's going to die. The loud wheezing breath in a rhythm not like
a normal breath: he's going to die. No matter what I do, shaking
him, shouting in his ear, *I can't wake him up.*

I remembered something I'd read about brain death, a coma
caused by too much alcohol and pills—did I mention Sonny'd
been taking some kind of pills, just popping them now and then,
not too many, and I didn't know if they were for his health, or
what, like my daddy has to take heart pills every day of his life
and glycerin if he gets pains in his chest—but I didn't want to
ask Sonny; I figured it was too personal a question.

I got so scared, I guess I panicked. Thinking if he's going to
die I will be involved. I would be a witness, and maybe arrested.
Called to testify. Or charged with murder like that woman, that
actress, who gave John Belushi a shot of heroin and he died. And
she was tried and found guilty of murder!

So I got dressed and left. I left the kimono behind, and the
jewelry, and even the perfume, and the shoes—it was the only
decent thing to do. I wasn't thinking too clearly but I thought
he could sell them back, maybe, to the stores. Or pawn them.
I found some hundred-dollar bills loose in my purse and left
them too, on the bedside table where he couldn't miss them.

So I went downstairs to the lobby, and in the lobby I called
the house physician and told him Sonny's room number and
hung up quick before he could ask any questions. I went back
to our motel and nobody was there, thank God, and I took a
long bath and tried to keep myself from thinking. I fell asleep
in the bath and sometime that afternoon Lynn helped me out

and dried me and seeing my face she just said, Don't tell me, so
I didn't tell her. I never did tell her much of it.

Before we left Vegas I called Sonny's room but the phone just
rang and rang. I asked at the desk was Sonny Drexel still registered and the girl said there wasn't any Sonny Drexel listed
and had not been, and I said, That can't be right, and the girl
repeated what she'd said, and I asked who was registered in 2023
up in the tower and she said, in the snottiest voice possible, The
Hilton does not give out such information.

And that was the end of that. Like that—it was the end of that.

Hughie? You listening?

But Hughie's asleep by now. Warm moist breath against my
neck like a baby's. Pressing heavy against me, foot twitching
between mine, like always. He's here, then he's gone.

FAMILY

The days were brief and attenuated and the season appeared to be fixed—neither summer nor winter, spring nor fall. A thermal haze of inexpressible sweetness (though bearing tiny bits of grit or mica) had eased into the valley from the industrial regions to the north, and there were nights when the sun set slowly at the western horizon as if sinking through a porous red mass, and there were days when a hard-glaring moon like bone remained fixed in a single position, prominent in the sky. Above the patchwork of excavated land bordering our property—*all* of which had formerly been our property in Grandfather's time: thousands of acres of fertile soil and open grazing land—a curious fibrillating rainbow sometimes appeared, its colors shifting even as you stared, shades of blue, turquoise, iridescent green, russet red, a lovely translucent gold that dissolved to moisture as the thermal breeze stirred, warm and stale as an exhaled breath. As if I'd run excited to tell others of the rainbow, it was likely to have vanished when they came.

"Liar!" my older brothers and sisters said, "—don't promise rainbows when there aren't any!"

Father laid his hand on my head, saying, with a smiling frown, "Don't speak of anything if you aren't certain it will be true for others, not simply for yourself. Do you understand?"

"Yes, Father," I said quietly. Though I did not understand.

This story begins in the time of family celebration—after Father made a great profit selling all but fifteen acres of his inheritance from Grandfather; and he and Mother were like a honeymoon couple, giddy with relief at having escaped the fate of most of our neighbors in the Valley, rancher-rivals of Grandfather's, and their descendants, who had sold off their property before the market began to realize its full potential. ("Full potential" was a term Father often uttered, as if its taste pleased him.) Now these old rivals were without land, and their investments yielded low returns; they'd gone away to live in cities of ever-increasing disorder, where no country people, especially once-aristocratic country people, could endure to live for long. They'd virtually prostituted themselves, Father said, "—and for so little!"

It was a proverb of Grandfather's time that a curse would befall anyone in the Valley who gloated over a neighbor's misfortune but, as Father observed, "It's damned difficult *not* to feel superior, sometimes." And Mother said, kissing him. "Darling—you're absolutely right!"

Our house was made of granite, limestone, and beautiful red-orange brick; the new wing, designed by a famous Japanese architect, was mainly tinted glass, overlooking the Valley, where on good days we could see for many miles and on humid-hazy days we could barely see beyond the fence at the edge of our property. Father, however, preferred the roof of the house: in his white suit (linen in warm weather, light wool in cold), cream-colored fedora cocked back on his head, high-heeled leather-tooled boots, he spent most of his waking hours on the highest peak of the highest roof, observing through high-powered binoculars the astonishing progress of construction in the Valley—for overnight, it seemed, there had appeared roads, expressways, sewers, drainage pipes, "planned communities" with such melodic names as Whispering Glades, Murmuring Oaks, Pheasant Run, Deer Willow, all of them walled to keep our trespassers, and, even more astonishing, immense towers of buildings made of aluminum, and steel, and glass, and bronze, buildings whose magnificent windows winked and glimmered like mirrors, splendid in sunshine like pillars of flame . . . such beauty, where once there'd been mere earth and sky, it caught at your throat like a great bird's talons. "The ways of beauty are as a honeycomb," Father told us mysteriously.

So hypnotized was Father by the transformation of the Valley, he often forgot where he was; failed to come downstairs for meals, or for bed. If Mother, meaning to indulge him, or hurt by his growing indifference to her, did not send a servant to summon him, he was likely to spend an entire night on the roof; in the morning, smiling, sheepishly, he would explain that he'd fallen asleep, or, conversely, he'd been troubled by having seen things for which he could not account—shadows the size of longhorns moving ceaselessly beyond our twelve-foot barbed wire fence and inexplicable winking red lights fifty miles away in the foothills. "Optical illusions!" Mother said, "—or the ghosts of old slaughtered livestock, or airplanes. Have you forgotten, darling, you sold thirty acres of land, for an airport at Furnace Creek?" "These lights more resemble fires," Father said stubbornly. "And they're in the foothills, not in the plain."

There came then times of power blackouts, and financial losses, and Father was forced to surrender all but two or three of servants, but he maintained his rooftop vigil, white-clad, a noble ghostly figure holding binoculars to his eyes, for he perceived himself as a *witness* and believed, if he lived to a ripe old age like Grandfather (who was in his hundredth year when at last he died—of a riding accident), he would be a chronicler of these troubled times, like Thucydides. For, as Father said, "Is there a new world struggling to be born—or only struggle?"

Around this time—because of numerous dislocations in the Valley: the abrupt abandoning of homes, for instance—it happened that packs of dogs began to roam about looking for food, particularly by night, poor starving creatures that became a nuisance and should be, as authorities urged, shot down on sight— these dogs not being feral by birth but former household pets, highly bred beagles, setters, cocker spaniels, terriers, even the larger and coarser type of poodle—and it was the cause of some friction between Mother and Father that, despite his rooftop presence by day and by night, Father nonetheless failed to spy a pack of these dogs dig beneath our fence and make their way to the dairy barn where they tore out the throats—surely this could not have been in silence!—of our remaining few Holsteins, and our last two she-goats, before devouring the poor creatures; nor did Father notice anything unusual the night two homeless derelicts, formerly farmhands of ours, impaled themselves on the electric fence and died agonizing deaths, their bodies found in the morning by Kit, our sixteen-year-old.

Kit, who'd liked the men, said, "—I hope I never see anything like that again in my life!"

It's true that our fence was charged with a powerful electric current, but in full compliance with County Farm and Home Bureau regulations.

Following this, Father journeyed to the state capital with the intention of taking out a sizable loan, and re-establishing, as he called it, old ties with his political friends, or with their younger colleagues; and Mother joined him a few days later for a greatly needed change of scene—"Not that I don't love you all, and the farm, but I need to see other sights for a while!—and I need to be *seen*." Leaving us when they did, under the care of Mrs. Hoyt (our housekeeper) and Cory (our eldest sister), was possibly not a good idea: Mrs. Hoyt was aging rapidly, and Cory, for all the innocence of her marigold eyes and melodic voice, was desperately in love with one of the National Guardsmen who patrolled the Valley in jeeps, authorized to shoot wild dogs, and, when necessary, vandals, arsonists, and squatters who were considered a menace to the public health and well-being. And when Mother returned from the capital, unaccompanied by Father, after what seemed to the family a long absence (two weeks? two months?), it was with shocking news: she and Father were going to separate.

Mother said, "Children, your father and I have decided, after much soul-searching deliberation, that we must dissolve our wedding bond of nearly twenty years." As she spoke Mother's voice wavered like a girl's but fierce little points of light shone in her eyes.

We children were so taken by surprise we could not speak, at first.

Separate! Dissolve! We stood staring and mute; not even Cory, Kit, and Dale, not even Lona who was the most impulsive of us, could find words with which to protest—the younger children began whimpering helplessly, soon joined by the rest. Mother clutched at her hair, saying, "Oh please don't! I can hardly bear the pain as it is!" With some ceremony she then played for us a video of Father's farewell to the family, which drew fresh tears . . . for there, framed astonishingly on our one-hundred-inch home theater screen, where we'd never seen his image before, was Father, dressed not in white but in somber colors, his hair in steely bands combed wetly across the dome of his skull, and his eyes puffy, an unnatural sheen to his face as if it had been scoured, hard. He was sitting stiffly erect; his fingers gripped the arms of his chair so tightly the blood had drained from his knuckles; his words came slow, halting, and faint, like the faltering progress of a gut-shot deer across a field. *Dear children, your mother and I . . . after years of marriage . . . of very happy marriage . . . have decided to . . . have decided . . .* One of the vexatious low-flying helicopters belonging to the National Guard soared past our house, making the screen shudder, but the sound was garbled in any case, as if the tape had been clumsily cut and spliced; Father's beloved face turned liquid and his eyes began to melt vertically, like oily tears; his mouth was distended like a drowning man's, As the tape ended we could discern only sounds, not words, resembling *Help me* or *I am innocent* or *Do not forget me beloved children I AM YOUR FATHER*—and then the screen went dead.

That afternoon Mother introduced us to the man who was to be Father's successor in the household! and to his three children, who were to be our new brothers and sister—we shook hands shyly, in a state of mutual shock, and regarded one another with wide staring wary eyes. Our new father! Our new brothers and sister! So suddenly and with no warning! Mother explained patiently, yet forcibly, her new husband was no mere *stepfather* but a true *father,* which meant that we were to address him as "Father" at all times, with respect, and even in our most private innermost thoughts we were to think of him as "Father": for otherwise he would be hurt, and displeased. And moved to discipline us.

So too with Einar and Erastus, our new *brothers* (not *step*brothers), and Fifi, our new *sister* (not *step*sister).

New Father stood before us smiling happily, a man of our old Father's age but heavier and far more robust than that Father, with an unusually large head, the cranium particularly developed, and small shrewd quick-darting eyes beneath brows of bone. He wore a tailored suit with wide shoulders that exaggerated his bulk and sported a red carnation in his lapel; his black shoes, a city man's shoes, shone splendidly, as if phosphorescent. "Hello Father," we murmured shyly, hardly daring to raise our eyes to his, "—Hello Father." The man's jaws were strangely elongated, the lower jaw at least an inch longer than the upper, so that a wet malevolent ridge of teeth was revealed. As so often happened in those days, a single thought passed like lightning among us children, from one to the other to the other, each of us smiling guiltily as it struck us: *Crocodile! Why, here's Crocodile!* Only little Jori burst into frightened tears and New Father surprised us all by stooping to pick her up gently in his arms and comfort her . . . "Hush, hush little girl! Nobody's going to hurt *you!*" and we others could see how the memory of our beloved former Father began to pass from her, like dissolving smoke. Jori was three years old at this time, too young to be held accountable.

New Father's children were tall, big-boned, and solemn, with a faint greenish-peevish cast to their skin, like many city children; the boys had inherited their father's large head and protruding jaws but the girl, Fifi, seventeen years old, was striking in her beauty, with pale blond fluffy hair as lovely as Cory's, and thickly lashed honey-brown eyes in which something mutinous glimmered. That evening, certain of the boys—Dale, Kit, and Hewett—gathered around Fifi to tell her wild tales of the Valley, how we all had to protect ourselves with Winchester rifles and shotguns, from trespassers, and how there was a mysterious resurgence of rats on the farm, as a consequence of excavation in the countryside, and these tales, just a little exaggerated, made the girl shudder and shiver and giggle, leaning toward the boys as if to invite their protection. Ah, Fifi was so pretty! But when Dale hurried off to fetch her a goblet of ice water at her request, she took the goblet from him, lifted it prissily to the light to examine its contents, and asked rudely, "Is this water *pure*? Is it safe to *drink*?" It was true, our well water had become strangely effervescent, and tasted of rust; after a heavy rainfall there were likely to be tiny red-wriggly things in it, like animated tails; so we had learned not to examine it too closely, just to drink it, and, as our attacks of nausea, diarrhea, dizziness, and amnesia, were only sporadic, we rarely worried but tried instead to be grateful, as Mrs. Hoyt used to urge us, that unlike many of our neighbors we had any drinking water at all. So it was offensive to us to see our new sister Fifi making such a face, handing the goblet back to Dale, and asking haughtily how anyone in his right mind could drink such—*spilth*. Dale said, red-faced, "*How?* This is *how!*" and drank the entire glass in a single thirsty gulp. And he and Fifi stood staring at each other, trembling with passion.

As Cory observed afterward, smiling, yet with a trace of envy or resentment, "It looks as if 'New Sister' has made a conquest!"

"But what will she do," I couldn't help asking, "—if she can't drink our water?"

"She'll drink it," Cory said, with a grim little laugh. "And she'll find it delicious, just like the rest of us."

Which turned out, fairly quickly, to be so.

Poor Cory! Her confinement came in a time of ever-increasing confusion . . . prolonged power failures, a scarcity of all food except canned foods, a scarcity too of ammunition so that the price of shotgun shells doubled and quadrupled; and the massive sky by both day and night was crisscrossed by the contrails of unmarked jet planes (Army or Air Force bombers?) in designs both troubling and beautiful, like the web of a gigantic spider. By this time construction in most parts of the Valley, once so energetic, had been halted; part-completed high-rise buildings punctuated the landscape; some were no more than concrete foundations upon which iron girders had been erected, like exposed bone. How we children loved to explore! The "Mirror Tower" (as we called it: once, it must have had a real, adult name) was a three-hundred-story patchwork of interlocking slots of reflecting glass with a subtle turquoise tint and, where its elegant surface had once mirrored scenes of sparkling natural beauty, there was now a drab scene, or succession of scenes, as on a video screen no one was watching: clouds like soiled cotton batting, smoldering slag heaps, decomposing garbage, predatory thistles and burdocks grown to the height of trees. Traffic, once so congested on the expressways, had dwindled to four or five diesel trucks per day hauling their heavy cargo (rumored to be diseased livestock bound for northern slaughterhouses) and virtually no passenger cars; sometimes, unmarked but official-looking vehicles, like jeeps but much larger than jeeps, passed in lengthy convoys, bound for no one knew where. There were strips of pavement, cloverleafs, that coiled endlessly upon themselves, beginning to be cracked and overgrown by weeds and elevated highways that broke off abruptly in midair, thus, as state authorities warned travelers, they were in grave danger, venturing into the countryside, of being attacked by roaming gangs—but the rumor was, as Father insisted, the most dangerous gangs were rogue Guardsmen who wore their uniforms inside out and gas masks strapped over their faces, preying upon the very citizens they were sworn to protect! None of the adults left our family compound, without being armed and of course we younger children were forbidden to leave at all—when we did, it was by stealth.

All schools, private and public, had been shut down indefinitely. "One long holiday!" as Hewett said.

The most beautiful and luxurious of the model communities, which we called "The Wheel" (its original name was Paradise Hollow), had suffered some kind of financial collapse, so that its well-to-do tenants were forced to emigrate back to the cities from which they'd emigrated to the Valley only about eighteen months before. (We called the complex "The Wheel" because its condominiums, office buildings, shops, schools, hospitals, and crematoria were arranged in spokes radiating outward from a single axis and were ingeniously protected at their twenty-mile circumference not by a visible wall, which the Japanese architect who'd designed it had declared a vulgar and outmoded concept, but by a force field of electricity of lethal voltage.) Though the airport at Furnace Creek was officially closed we sometimes saw, late at night, small aircraft including helicopters taking off and landing there; were wakened by the insectlike whining of their engines, and their winking red lights; and one night when the sun remained motionless at the horizon for several hours and visibility was poor, as if we were in a dust storm yet a dust storm without wind, a ten-seater airplane crashed in a slag heap that had once been a grazing pasture for our cows, and some of the older boys went by stealth to investigate . . . returning with sober, stricken faces, refusing to tell us, their sisters, what they had seen except to say, "Never mind! Don't ask!" Fifteen miles away in the western foothills were mysterious encampments, said to be unauthorized settlements of city dwellers who had fled their cities at the time of the "urban collapse" (as it was called), as well as former ranch families, and various wanderers and evicted persons, criminals, the mentally ill, and victims and suspected carriers of contagious diseases . . . all of these considered "outlaw parties" subject to severe treatment by the National Guardsmen, for the region was now under martial law, and only within family compounds maintained by state registered property owners and heads of families were civil rights, to a degree, still operative. Eagerly, we scanned the Valley for signs of life, passing among us a pair of heavy binoculars, unknown to Father and Mother—like forbidden treasure these binoculars were, though their original owner was forgotten. (Cory believed that this person, a man, had lived with us before Father's time, and had been good to us, and kind. But no one, not even Cory, could remember his name, nor even what he'd looked like.)

Cory's baby was born the very week of the funerals of two of the younger children, who had died, poor things, of a violent

dysentery, and of Uncle Darrah, who'd died of shotgun wounds
while driving his pickup truck along a familiar road in the Valley;
but this coincidence, Mother and Father assured us, was only
that—a coincidence, and not an omen. Mother led us one by
one into the drafty attic room set aside for Cory and her baby
and we stared in amazement at the puppy-sized, florid-faced,
screaming, yet so wonderfully alive creature . . . with its large
soft-looking head, its wizened angry features, its smooth, poreless skin. How had Cory, one of us, accomplished *this*! Sisters
and brothers alike, we were in awe of her, and a little fearful.

Mother's reaction was most surprising. She seemed furious
with Cory, saying that the attic room was good enough for Cory's
"outlaw child," sometimes she spoke of Cory's "bastard child"—
though quick to acknowledge, in all fairness, the poor infant's
parentage was no fault of its own. But it was "fit punishment,"
Mother said, that Cory's breasts ached when she nursed her
baby, and that her milk was threaded with pus and blood . . . "fit
punishment for shameful sluttish behavior." Yet the family's luck
held, for only two days after the birth Kit and Erastus came back
from a nocturnal hunting expedition with a dairy cow: a healthy,
fat-bellied, placid creature with black-and-white-marbled markings similar to those of our favorite cow, who had died long
ago. This sweet-natured cow, named Daisy, provided the family
with fresh, delicious, seemingly pure milk, thus saving Cory's
bastard-infant's life, as Mother said spitefully—"Well, the way
of Providence *is* a honeycomb!"

Those weeks, Mother was obsessed with learning the identity
of Cory's baby's father—Cory's "secret lover," as Mother referred
to him. Cory, of course, refused to say—even to her sisters. She
may have been wounded that the baby's father had failed to come

forward to claim his child, or her; poor Cory, once the prettiest
of the girls, now disfigured with skin rashes like fish scales over
most of her body, and a puffy, bloated appearance, and eyes
red from perpetual weeping. Mother herself was frequently ill
with a similar flaming rash, a protracted respiratory infection,
intestinal upsets, bone-aches, and amnesia; like everyone in the
family except, oddly, Father, she was plagued with ticks—the
smallest species of deer tick that could burrow secretly into the
skin, releasing an analgesic spittle to numb the skin, thus able to
do its damage, sucking blood contentedly for weeks until, after
weeks, it might drop off with a *ping!* to the floor, black, shiny, now
the size of a watermelon seed, swollen with blood. What loathsome things!—Mother developed a true horror of them, for they
seemed drawn to her, especially to her white, wild-matted hair.

By imperceptible degrees Mother had shrunk to a height of
less than five feet, very unlike the statuesque beauty of old photographs, with that head of white hair and pebble-colored eyes as
keen and suspicious as ever, and a voice so brassy and penetrating
it had the power to paralyze any of us where we stood . . . but
even the eldest of her sons, Kit, Hewett, Dale, tall bearded men
who carried firearms even inside the compound, were intimidated by Mother and, like Cory, were inclined to submit to
her authority. When Mother interrogated Cory, "*Who* is your
lover? Why are you so ashamed of him? Did you find him in
the drainage pipe, or in the slag heap?—in the compost?" Cory
bit her lip and said quietly, "Even if I see his face sometimes,
Mother, in my sleep, I can't recall his name. Or who he was, or
is. Or claimed to be."

Yet Mother continued, risking Father's displeasure, for she
began to question *all males* with whom she came into contact,

not excluding Cory's own blood-relations—cousins, uncles, even brothers!—even those ravaged men and boys who made their homes, so to speak, beyond the compound, as she'd said jeeringly, in the drainage pipe, in the slag heap, in the compost. (These men and boys were not official residents on our property but were enlisted by the family in times of crisis and emergency.) But no one confessed—no one acknowledged Cory's baby as his. And one day when Cory lay upstairs in the attic with a fever, and I was caring for the baby, excitedly feeding it from a bottle in the kitchen, Mother entered with a look of such determination I felt a sudden fear for the baby, hugging it to my chest, and Mother said, "Give me the bastard, girl," and I said weakly, "No Mother, don't make me," and Mother said, "Are you disobeying me, girl? *Give me the bastard*," and I said, backing away, daringly, yet determined too, "No Mother, Cory's baby belongs to Cory, and to all of us, and it isn't a bastard." Mother advanced upon me, furious; her pebble-colored eyes now rimmed with white; her fingers—what talons they'd become, long, skinny, clawed!—outstretched. Yet I saw that in the very midst of her passion she was forgetting what she intended to do, and that this might save Cory's baby from harm.

(For often in those days when the family had little to eat except worm-riddled apples from the old orchard, and stunted blackened potatoes, and such game, or wildlife, that the men and boys could shoot, and such canned goods as they could acquire, we often, all of us, young as well as old forgot what we were doing in the very act of doing it; plucking bloody feathers from a quail, for instance, and stopping vague and dreamy wondering what on earth am I doing? here? at the sink? *is* this a sink? what is this limp little body? this instrument—a knife?—in my hands? and naturally in the midst of speaking we might forget the words we meant to speak, for instance *water, rainbow, grief, love, filth, Father, deer tick, God, milk, sky* . . . and Father who'd become brooding with the onset of age worried constantly that we, his family, might one day soon lose all sense of ourselves as a family should we forget, in the same instant, all of us together, the sacred word *family.*)

And indeed, there in the kitchen, reaching for Cory's baby her talonlike fingers, Mother was forgetting. And indeed, within the space of a half minute, she had forgotten. Staring at the defenseless living thing, the quivering, still-hungry creature in my arms, with its soft flat shallow face of utter innocence, its tiny recessed eyes, its mere holes for nostrils, its small pursed mouth set like a manta ray's in its shallow face, Mother could not, simply could not, summon back the word *baby,* or *infant,* nor even the cruel *Cory's bastard,* always on her lips. And at that moment there was a commotion outside by the compound gate, an outburst of gunfire, familiar enough yet always jarring when unexpected, and Mother hurried out to investigate. And Cory's baby returned to sucking hungrily and contentedly at the bottle's frayed rubber nipple; and all was safe for now.

But Cory, my dear sister, died a few days later.

Lona discovered her in her place of exile in the attic, in her bed, eyes opened wide and pale mouth contorted, the bedclothes soaked in blood . . . and when in horror Lona drew the sheet away she saw that Cory's breasts had been partly hacked away, or maybe devoured?—and her chest cavity exposed; she must have been attacked in the night by rats and was too weak or too terrified to scream for help. Yet her baby was sleeping placidly in its crib beside the bed, miraculously untouched . . . sunk in its characteristic sleep to that profound level at which organic matter seems about to revert to the inorganic, to perfect peace. For some reason the household rats with their glittering amaranthine eyes and stiff hairless tails and unpredictable appetites had spared it!—or had missed it altogether!

Lona snatched the baby up out of its crib and ran downstairs screaming for help; and so fierce was she in possession she would not give up the baby to anyone, saying, dazed, sobbing, yet in a way gloating, "This is my baby. This is Lona's baby now." Until Father, with his penchant for logic, rebuked her: "Girl, it is the family's baby now."

And Fifi too had a baby—beautiful blond Fifi; or, rather, the poor girl writhed and screamed in agony for a day and a night before giving birth to a perfectly formed but tiny baby weighing only two pounds that lived only a half hour. How we wept, how we pitied our sister!—in the weeks that followed nothing would give her solace, even the smallest measure of solace, except our musical evenings, at which she excelled. For if Dale tried to touch her, to comfort her, she shrank from him in repugnance; nor would she allow Father, or any male, to come near. One night she crawled into my bed and hugged me in her icy bone-thin arms. "What I love best," she whispered, "—is the black waves that splash over us, endlessly, at night, do you know those waves, sister? and do you love them as I do?" And my heart was so swollen with feeling I could not reply, as I wished to, "Oh *yes*."

Indeed, suddenly the family had taken up music. In the evenings by kerosene lamp. In the predawn hours, roused from our beds by aircraft overhead, or the barking of wild dogs, or the thermal winds. We played such musical instruments as fell into our hands discovered here and there in the house, or by way of strangers at our gate eager to barter anything they owned for food. Kit took up the violin shyly at first and then with growing confidence and joy for, it seemed, he had musical talent—practicing for hours on the beautiful though scarified antique violin that had once belonged to Grandfather, or Great-grandfather (so we surmised: an old portrait depicted a child of about ten posed with the identical violin tucked under his chin) Jori and Vega took up the piccolo, which they shared; Hewett the drums, Dale the cymbals, Einar the oboe, Fifi the piano . . . and the rest of us sang, sang our hearts out.

We sang after Mother's funeral and we sang that week a hot feculent wind blew across the Valley bearing the odor of decomposing flesh and we sang (though often coughing and choking, from the smoke) when fires raged out of control in the dry woodland areas to the east, an insidious wind then too blowing upon our barricaded compound and handsome house atop a high hill, a wind intent upon seeking us out, it seemed, carrying sparks to our sanctuary, our place of privilege, destroying us in fire as others both human and beast were being destroyed . . . and how else for us to endure such odors, such sights, such sounds, than to take up our instruments and play them as loudly as possible, and sing as loudly as possible, and sing and sing and sing until our throats were raw, how else?

Yet, the following week became a time of joy and feasting, since Daisy the cow was dying in any case and might as well be quickly slaughtered, when Father, surprising us all, brought his new wife home to meet us: New Mother we called her, or Young Mother, or Pretty Mother, and Old Mother, that fierce stooped wild-eyed old woman was soon forgotten, even the mystery of her death soon forgotten (for had she like Cory died of household rats? or had she, like poor Erastus, died of a burst appendix? had she drowned somehow in the cistern, had she died of thirst and malnutrition locked away in the attic, had she died of a respiratory infection, of toothache, of heartbreak, of her own rage, or of age, or of Father's strong fingers closing around her neck . . . or had she not "died" at all but passed quietly into oblivion, as the black waves splashed over her, and Young Mother stepped forward smiling happily to take her place).

Young Mother was so pretty!—plump, and round-faced, her complexion rich and ruddy, her breasts like large balloons filled to bursting with warm liquid, and she gave off a hot intoxicating smell of nutmeg, and tiny flames leapt from her when, in a luxury of sighing, yawning, and stretching, she lifted the heavy mass of red-russet hair that hung between her shoulder blades and fixed upon us her smiling-dark gaze. "Mother!" we cried, even the eldest of us, "—oh Mother!" hoping would she hug us, would she kiss and hug us, fold us in those plump strong arms, cuddle our faces against those breasts, each of us, all of us weeping, in her arms, those arms, oh Mother, *there.*

Lona's baby was not maturing as it was believed babies should normally mature, nor had it been named since we could not determine whether it was male or female, or somehow both, or neither; and this household problem, Young Mother addressed herself to at once. No matter Lona's desperate love of the baby, Young Mother was "practical minded" as she said: for why else had Father brought her to this family but to take charge, to reform it, to give *hope?* She could not comprehend, she said,

laughing incredulously, how and why an extra mouth, a useless
mouth, perhaps even a dangerous mouth, could be tolerated
at such a time of near-famine, in violation of certain government edicts as she understood them. "Drastic remedies in drastic
times," Young Mother was fond of saying. Lona said, pleading,
"I'll give it my food, Mother—I'll protect it with my life!" And
Young Mother simply repeated, smiling so broadly her eyes were
narrowed almost to slits, "Drastic remedies in drastic times!"

There were those of us who loved Lona's baby, for it *was* flesh
of our flesh, it *was* part of our family; yet there were others,
mainly the men and boys, who seemed nervous in its presence,
keeping a wary distance when it crawled into a room to nudge
its large bald head or pursed mouth against a foot, an ankle, a
leg. Though it had not matured in the normal fashion, Lona's
baby weighed now about thirty pounds; but it was soft as a slug
is soft; or an oyster, with an oyster's general shape—apparently
boneless; the hue of unbaked bread dough, and hairless. As its
small eyes lacked an iris, being entirely white, it must have been
blind; its nose was but a rudimentary pair of nostrils, holes in
the center of its face; its fishlike mouth was deceptive in that
it seemed to possess its own intelligence, being ideally formed,
not for human speech, but for seizing, sucking, and chewing.
Though it had at best only a cartilaginous skeleton it did boast
two fully formed rows of tiny needle-sharp teeth, which it was
not shy of using, particularly when ravenous for food; and it
was often ravenous. At such times it groped its way around
the house, silent, by instinct, sniffing and quivering, and if by
chance it was drawn by the heat of your blood to your bed it
would burrow beneath the covers, and nudge, and nuzzle, and
begin like a nursing infant to suck virtually any part of the body

though preferring of course a female's breasts . . . and if not stopped in time it would start to bite, chew, *eat* . . . in all the brute innocence of appetite. So some of us surmised, though Lona angrily denied it, that the baby's first mother (a sister of ours whose name we had forgotten) had not died of rat bites after all but of having been attacked in the night and partly devoured by her own baby.

(In this, Lona was duplicitous. She took care never to undress in Mother's presence for fear Mother's sharp eye would discover the numerous wounds on her breasts, belly, and thighs.)

As the family had a time-honored custom of debating issues in a democratic manner—for instance should we pay the exorbitant price a cow or a she-goat now commanded on the open market, or should the boys be given permission to acquire one of these beasts however they could, for instance should we try to feed the starving men, women, and children who gathered outside our fence, even if it was food too contaminated for the family's consumption—so naturally the issue of Lona's baby was taken up too and soon threatened to split the family into two warring sides. Mother argued persuasively, almost tearfully, that the baby was "worthless, repulsive, and might one day be dangerous,"— not guessing that it had already proved dangerous; and Lona argued persuasively, and tearfully, that "Lona's baby," as she called it, was a living human being, a member of the family, one of *us*. Mother said hotly, "It is not one of *us*, girl, if by *us* you mean a family that includes *me*," and Lona said, daringly, "It is one of *us* because it predates any family that includes *you*—'Mother.'"

So they argued; and others joined in; and emotions ran high. It was strange how some of us changed our minds several times, now swayed by Mother's reasoning, and now by Lona's; now by Father who spoke on behalf of Mother, or by Hewett who spoke on behalf of Lona. Was it weeks, or was it months, that the debate raged?—and subsided, and raged again?—and Mother dared not put her power to the vote for fear that Lona's brothers and sisters would side with Lona out of loyalty if not love for the baby. And Father acknowledged reluctantly that however any of us felt about the baby it *was* our flesh and blood and embodied the Mystery of Life: ". . . its soul bounded by its skull, and its destiny no more problematic than the sinewy tubes that connect its mouth and its anus. Who are we to judge!"

Yet Mother had her way, as slyboots Mother was always to have her way . . . one March morning soliciting the help of several of us, who were sworn to secrecy and delighted to be her handmaidens, in a simple scheme: Lona being asleep in the attic, Mother led the baby out of the house by holding a piece of bread soaked in chicken blood in front of its nostrils, led it crawling across the hard-packed wintry earth, to the old hay barn, and, inside, led it to a dark corner where we helped her lift it and lower it carefully into an aged rain barrel empty except for a wriggling mass of half-grown rats, that squealed in great excitement at being disturbed, and at the smell of the blood-soaked bread which Mother dropped with the baby. We then nailed a cover in place; and, as Mother said, her skin warmly flushed and her breath coming fast, "There, girls—it is entirely out of our hands."

And then one day it was spring. And Kit, grinning, led a she goat proudly into the kitchen, her bags primed with milk, swollen pink dugs leaking milk! How grateful we all were, those of us who were with child especially after the privations of so long a winter, or winters, during which time certain words have all but faded from our memories, for instance *she-goat,* and *milk,* and as we realized *rainbow,* for the rainbow too reappeared, one morning, shimmering and translucent across the Valley, a phenomenon as of the quivering of millions of butterflies' iridescent wings. In the fire-scorched plain there grew a virtual sea of fresh green shoots and in the sky enormous dimpled clouds and that night we gathered around Fifi at the piano to play our instruments and to sing. Father had passed away but Mother had remarried: a husky bronze-skinned horseman whose white teeth flashed in his beard, and whose rowdy pinches meant love and good cheer, not meanness. We were so happy we debated turning the calendar ahead to the New Year. We were so happy we debated abolishing the calendar entirely and declaring this the First Day of Year One, and beginning Time anew.

LADIES AND GENTLEMEN:

Ladies and gentlemen: A belated but heartfelt welcome aboard our cruise ship S.S. *Ariel.* It's a true honor and a privilege for me, your captain, to greet you all on this lovely sun-warmed January day—as balmy, isn't it, as any June morning back north? I wish I could claim that we of the *Ariel* arranged personally for such splendid weather, as compensation of sorts for the—shall we say—somewhat rocky weather of the past several days. But at any rate it's a welcome omen indeed and bodes well for the remainder of the cruise and for this morning's excursion, ladies and gentlemen, to the island you see us rapidly approaching, a small but remarkably beautiful island the natives of these waters call the Island of Tranquility or, as some translators prefer, the Island of Repose. For those of you who've become virtual sailors with a keen eye for navigating, you'll want to log our longitude at 155 degrees East and our latitude at 5 degrees North, approximately twelve hundred miles north and east of New Guinea. Yes, that's right! We've come so far! And as this is a rather crucial morning, and your island adventure an important event not only on this cruise but in your lives, ladies and gentlemen, I hope you will quiet just a bit—just a bit!—and give me, your captain, your fullest attention. Just for a few minutes, I promise! Then you disembark.

As to the problems some of you have experienced: let me take this opportunity, as your captain, ladies and gentlemen, to apologize, or at least to explain. It's true for instance that certain of your staterooms are not *precisely* as the advertising brochures depicted them, the portholes are not quite so large; in some cases the portholes are not in evidence. This is not the fault of any of the *Ariel* staff; indeed, this has been a sore point with us for some years, a matter of misunderstandings and embarrassments out of our control, yet I, as your captain, ladies and gentlemen, offer my apologies and my profoundest sympathies. Though I am a bit your junior in age, I can well understand the special disappointment, the particular hurt, outrage, and dismay that attend one's sense of having been cheated on what, for some of you, probably, is perceived as being the last time you'll be taking so prolonged and exotic a trip—thus, my profoundest sympathies! As to the toilets that have been reported as malfunctioning or out of order entirely, and the loud throbbing or "tremors" of the engines that have been keeping some of you awake, and the negligent or even rude service, the overcooked or undercooked food, the high tariffs on mineral water, alcoholic beverages, and cigarettes, the reported sightings of rodents, cockroaches, and other vermin on board ship—perhaps I should explain, ladies and gentlemen, that this is the final voyage of the S.S. *Ariel* and it was the owners' decision, and a justifiably pragmatic decision, to cut back on repairs, services, expenses, and the like. Ladies and gentlemen, I am sorry for your inconvenience, but the *Ariel is* an old ship, bound for dry dock in Manila and the fate of many a veteran seagoing vessel that has outlived her time. God bless her! We'll not see her likes again!

Ladies and gentlemen, may I have some quiet—please, just five minutes more?—before the stewards help you prepare for your disembarkment? Thank you.

Yes, the *Ariel* is bound for Manila next. But have no fear, you won't be aboard.

Ladies and gentlemen, *please*. This murmuring and muttering begins to annoy,

(Yet, as your captain, I'd like to note that, amid the usual whiners and complainers and the just plain bad-tempered, it's gratifying to see a number of warm, friendly, *hopeful* faces and to know that there are men and women determined to enjoy life, not quibble and harbor suspicions. Thank *you*!)

Now to our business at hand: ladies and gentlemen, do you know what you have in common?

You can't guess?

You *can* guess?

No? Yes?

No?

Well, yes sir, it's true that you are all aboard the S.S. *Ariel*; and yes, sir—excuse me, *ma'am*—it's certainly true that you are all of "retirement" age. (Though "retirement" has come to be a rather vague term in the past decade or so, hasn't it? For the youngest among you are in their late fifties—the result, I would guess, of especially generous early-retirement programs—and the eldest among you are in their mid-nineties. Quite a range of ages!)

Yes, it's true you are all Americans. You have expensive cameras, even in some cases video equipment, for recording this South Seas adventure; you have all sorts of tropical-cruise paraphernalia, including some extremely attractive bleached-straw hats; some of you have quite a supply of sun-protective lotions; and most of you have a considerable quantity and variety of pharmacological supplies. And quite a store of paperbacks, magazines, cards, games, and crossword puzzles. Yet there is one primary thing you have in common, ladies and gentlemen, which has determined your presence here this morning, at longitude 155 degrees East and latitude 5 degrees North: your fate, as it were. Can't you guess?

Ladies and gentlemen: *your children.*

Yes, you have in common the fact that this cruise on the S.S. *Ariel* was originally your children's idea and that they arranged for it, if you'll recall. (Though you have probably paid for your own passages, which weren't cheap.) Your children—who are "children" only technically, for of course they are fully grown, fully adult, a good number of them parents themselves (having made you proud grandparents—yes, haven't you been proud!)— these sons and daughters, if I may speak frankly, are *very* tired of waiting for their inheritances.

Yes, and *very* impatient, some of them, *very* angry, waiting to come into control of what they believe is their due.

Ladies and gentlemen, please! I'm asking for quiet, and I'm asking for respect. As captain of the *Ariel,* I am not accustomed to being interrupted.

I believe you did hear me correctly, sir. And you too, sir.

Yes and you, ma'am. And *you.* (Most of you aren't nearly so deaf as you pretend!)

Let me speak candidly. While your children are in many cases, or at least in some cases, genuinely fond of you, they are simply impatient with the prospect of waiting for your "natural" deaths.

Ten years, fifteen? Twenty? With today's medical technology, who knows; you might outlive *them*!

Of course it's a surprise to you, ladies and gentlemen. It's a *shock*. Thus you, sir, are shaking your head in disbelief, and you, sir, are muttering just a little too loudly, "Who does that fool think he is, making such bad jokes?"—and you, ladies, are giggling like teenaged girls, not knowing what to think. But remember: your children have been living lives of their own, in a very difficult, very competitive corporate America; they are, on the face of it, well-to-do, even affluent; yet they want, in some cases desperately need, *your* estates—not in a dozen years but *now*.

That is to say, as soon as your wills can be probated.

For, however your sons and daughters appear in the eyes of their neighbors, friends, and business colleagues, even in the eyes of their own offspring, you can be sure that *they have not enough money*. You can be sure that they suffer keenly certain financial jealousies and yearnings—and who dares calibrate another's suffering? Who dares peer into another's heart? Without betraying anyone's confidence, I can say that there are several youngish men, beloved sons of couples in your midst, ladies and gentlemen, who are nearly bankrupt; men of integrity and "success" whose worlds are about to come tumbling about their heads—unless they get money or find themselves in the position of being able to borrow money against their parents' estates, *fast*. Investment bankers, lawyers, a college professor or two—some of them already in debt. Thus they decided to take severe measures.

Ladies and gentlemen, it's pointless to protest. As captain of the *Ariel*, I merely expedite orders.

And you must know that it's pointless to express disbelief or incredulity, to roll your eyes as if *I* (of all people) were a bit cracked, to call out questions or demands, to shout, weep, sob, beg, rant and rave and mutter—"If this is a joke it isn't a very funny joke!" "As if my son/daughter would ever do such a thing to me/us!"—in short, it's pointless to express any and all of the reactions you're expressing, which have been expressed by other ladies and gentlemen on past *Ariel* voyages to the South Seas.

Yes, it's the best thing, to cooperate. Yes, in an orderly fashion. It's wisest not to provoke the stewards (whose nerves are a bit ragged these days—the crew is only human, after all) into using force.

Ladies and gentlemen, these *are* lovely azure waters—exactly as the brochures promised!—but shark-infested, so take care.

Ah, yes, those dorsal fins slicing the waves, just beyond the surf: observe them closely.

No, we're leaving no picnic baskets with you today. Nor any bottles of mineral water, Perrier water, champagne.

For why delay what's inevitable? Why cruelly protract anguish?

Ladies and gentlemen, maybe it's a simple thing, maybe it's a self-evident thing, but consider: you are the kind of civilized men and women who brought babies into the world not by crude, primitive, anachronistic chance but by systematic deliberation. You planned your futures; you planned, as the expression goes, your parenthood. You are all of that American economic class called "upper middle"; you are educated, you are cultured, you are stable; nearly without exception, you showered love upon your sons and daughters, who knew themselves, practically in the cradle, privileged. The very best—the most exclusive—nursery schools, private schools, colleges, universities. Expensive toys and gifts of all kinds; closets of clothing, ski equipment, stereo equipment, racing bicycles; tennis lessons, riding lessons, snorkeling lessons, private tutoring, trips to the Caribbean, to Mexico, to Tangier, to Tokyo, to Switzerland; junior years abroad in Paris, in Rome, in London; yes, and their teeth were perfect, or were made to be; yes, and they had cosmetic surgery if necessary, or nearly necessary; yes, and you gladly paid for their abortions or their tuition for law school, medical school, business school; yes, and you paid for their weddings; yes, and you loaned them money "to get started," certainly you helped them with their mortgages, or their second cars, or their children's orthodontic bills, nothing was too good or too expensive for them, for what, ladies and gentlemen, would it have been?

And always the more you gave your sons and daughters, the more you seemed to be holding in reserve; the more generous you displayed yourself, the more generous you were hinting you might be in the future. But so far in the future—when your wills might be probated, after your deaths.

Ladies and gentlemen, you rarely stopped to consider your children as other than *your* children, as men and women growing into maturity distinct from you. Rarely did you pause to see how patiently they were waiting to inherit their due—and then, by degrees, how impatiently. What anxieties besieged them, what nightmare speculations—for what if you squandered your money in medical bills? nursing home bills? the melancholic impedimenta of age in America? What if—worse yet!—addle-brained, suffering from Alzheimer's disease (about which they'd been reacting suddenly, it seemed, everywhere) you turned against them, disinherited them, remarried someone younger, healthier, more cunning than they, rewrote your wills, as elderly fools are always doing?

Ladies and gentlemen, your children declare that they want only *what's theirs*.

They say laughingly, *they* aren't going to live forever.

(Well, yes: I'll confide in you, off the cuff, in several instances it was an *in-law* who looked into the possibility of a cruise on the S.S. *Ariel*; your own son/daughter merely cooperated, after the fact as it were. Of course, that isn't the same thing!)

Ladies and gentlemen, as your captain, about to bid you farewell, let me say I *am* sympathetic with your plight. Your stunned expressions; your staggering-swaying gait, your damp eyes, working mouths—"This is a bad joke!" "This is intolerable!" "This is a nightmare!" "No child of mine could be so cruel—inhuman—monstrous" et cetera—all this is touching, wrenching to the heart, altogether *natural*. One might almost say traditional. Countless others, whose bones you may discover should you have the energy and spirit to explore the Island of Tranquility (or Repose), reacted in more or less the same way.

Thus do not despair, ladies and gentlemen, for your emotions, however painful, are time-honored; but do not squander the few precious remaining hours of your life, for such emotions are futile.

Ladies and gentlemen: the Island of Tranquility upon which you now stand shivering in the steamy morning heat is approximately six kilometers in circumference, ovoid in shape, with a curious archipelago of giant metamorphic rocks trailing off to the north, a pounding hallucinatory surf, and horizon, vague, dreamy, and distant, on all sides. Its soil is an admixture of volcanic ash, sand, rock, and peat; its jungle interior is pocked with treacherous bogs of quicksand.

It *is* a truly exotic island, bur fairly quickly most of you will become habituated to the ceaseless winds that ease across the island from several directions simultaneously, air intimate and warmly stale as exhaled breaths, caressing, narcotic. You'll become habituated to the ubiquitous sand flies, the glittering dragonflies with their eighteen-inch iridescent wings, the numerous species of snakes (the small quicksilver orange-speckled *baya* snake is the most venomous, you'll want to know); the red-beaked carnivorous macaw and its ear-piercing shriek; bullfrogs the size of North American jackrabbits; two-hundred-pound tortoises with pouched, intelligent eyes; spider monkeys playful as children; tapirs; tarantulas; and, most colorful of all, the comical cassowary birds with their bony heads, gaily-hued wattles, and stunted wings—these ungainly birds whom millions of years of evolution, on this island lacking mammal predators, have rendered flightless.

And orchids: some of you have already noticed the lovely, bountiful orchids growing everywhere, dozens of species, every imaginable color, some the size of grapes and others the size of a man's head, unfortunately inedible.

And the island's smells, are they fragrances or odors? Is it rampant, fresh-budding life or jungle-rancid decay? Is there a difference?

By night (and the hardiest among you should survive numerous nights, if past history prevails), you'll contemplate the tropical moon, so different from our North American moon, hanging heavy and luminous in the sky like an overripe fruit; you'll be moved to smile at the sport of fiery-phosphorescent fish frolicking in the waves; you'll be lulled to sleep by the din of insects, the cries of nocturnal birds, your own prayers perhaps.

Some of you cling together, like terrified herd animals; some of you will wander off alone, dazed, refusing to be touched, even comforted, by a spouse of fifty years.

Ladies and gentlemen, I, your captain, speak for the crew of the S.S. *Ariel,* bidding you farewell.

Ladies and gentlemen, your children have asked me to assure you that they *do* love you—but circumstances have intervened.

Ladies and gentlemen, your children have asked me to recall to you those years when they were in fact *children*—wholly innocent as you imagined them, adoring you as gods.

Ladies and gentlemen, I now bid farewell to you as children do, waving goodbye not once but numerous times, solemn, reverential. Goodbye, goodbye, goodbye.

WHY DON'T YOU COME LIVE WITH ME, IT'S TIME

The other day, it was a sunswept windy March morning, I saw my grandmother staring at me, those deep-socketed eyes, that translucent skin, a youngish woman with very dark hair as I hadn't quite remembered her, who had died while I was in college, years ago, in 1966. Then I saw—of course it was virtually in the same instant—I saw the face was my own, my own eyes in that face floating there not in a mirror but in a metallic mirrored surface, teeth bared in a startled smile, and seeing my face that was not my face I laughed; I think that was the sound.

You're an insomniac, you tell yourself: there are profound truths revealed only to the insomniac by night like those phosphorescent minerals veined and glimmering in the dark but coarse and ordinary otherwise; you have to examine such minerals in the absence of light to discover their beauty, you tell yourself.

Maybe because I was having so much trouble sleeping at the time, twelve or thirteen years old, no one would have called the problem insomnia, that sounds too clinical, too adult, and anyway they'd said, "You can sleep if you try," and I'd overheard, "She just wants attention—you know what she's like," and I was hurt and angry but hopeful too, wanting to ask, But what am I like, are you the ones to tell me?

In fact, Grandmother had insomnia too—"suffered from insomnia" was the somber expression—but no one made the connection between her and me. Our family was that way: worrying that one weakness might find justification in another and things would slip out of containment and control.

In fact, I'd had trouble sleeping since early childhood but I had not understood that anything was wrong. Not secrecy nor even a desire to please my parents made me pretend to sleep; I thought it was what you do: I thought when Mother put me to bed I had to shut my eyes so she could leave and that was the way of releasing her, though immediately afterward when I was alone my eyes opened wide and sleepless. Sometimes it was day, sometimes night. Often by night I could see, I could discern the murky shapes of objects, familiar objects that had lost their names by night, as by night lying motionless with no one to observe me it seemed I had no name and my body was shapeless and undefined. The crucial thing was to lie motionless, scarcely breathing, until at last—it might be minutes or it might be hours; if there were noises in the house or out on the street (we lived on a busy street for most of my childhood in Hammond) it would be hours—a dark pool of warm water would begin to lap gently over my feet, eventually it would cover my legs, my chest, my face. . . . What adults called "sleep," this most elusive and strange and mysterious of experiences, a cloudy transparency of ever-shifting hues and textures surrounded tense islands of wakefulness, so during the course of a night I would sleep and wake and sleep and wake a dozen times, as the water lapped over my face and retreated from it; this seemed altogether natural, it was altogether desirable, for when I slept another kind of sleep, heavily, deeply, plunged into a substance not water and not a transparency but an oozy lightless muck, when I plunged down into that sleep and managed to wake from it shivering and sweating with a pounding heart and a pounding head as if my brain trapped inside my skull (but "brain" and "skull" were not concepts I would have known, at that time) had been racing feverishly like a small machine gone berserk, it was to a sense of total helplessness and an exhaustion so profound it felt like death: sheer nonexistence, oblivion; and I did not know, nor do I know now, decades later, which sleep is preferable, which sleep is normal, how is one defined by sleep, from where in fact does "sleep" arise.

When I was older, a teenager, with a room at a little distance from my parents' bedroom, I would often, those sleepless nights, simply turn on my bedside lamp and read; I'd read until dawn and day and the resumption of daytime routine in a state of complete concentration, or sometimes I'd switch on the radio close beside my bed—I was cautious of course to keep the volume low, low and secret—and I'd listen fascinated to stations as far away as Pittsburgh, Toronto, Cleveland; there was a hillbilly station broadcasting out of Cleveland, country-and-western music I would never have listened to by day. One by one I got to know intimately the announcers' voices along the continuum of the glowing dial; hard to believe those strangers didn't know *me*. But sometimes my room left me short of breath; it was fresh air I craved: hurriedly I'd dress, pulling on clothes over my pajamas, and even in rainy or cold weather I went outside, leaving the house by the kitchen door so quietly in such stealth no one ever heard, not once did one of them hear—*I will do it: because I want to do it*—sleeping their heavy sleep that was like the sleep of mollusks, eyeless. And outside, in the night, the surprise of the street transformed by the lateness of the hour, the emptiness, the silence; I'd walk to the end of our driveway, staring, listening, my heart beating hard. *So this is—what it is!* The ordinary sights were made strange: the sidewalks, the streetlights, the neighboring houses. Yet the fact had no consciousness of itself except through *me*.

For that has been one of the principles of my life.

And if here and there along the block a window glowed from within (another insomniac?), or if a lone car passed in the street casting its headlights before it, or a train sounded in the distance, or, high overhead, an airplane passed, winking and glittering with lights, what happiness swelled my lungs, what gratitude, what conviction; I was utterly alone for the moment, and invisible, which is identical with being alone.

Come by any time, dear, no need to call first, my grandmother said often. *Come by after school, any time, please!* I tried not to hear the pleading in her voice, tried not to see the soft hurt in her eyes, and the hope.

Grandmother was a "widow": her husband, my step-grandfather, had died of cancer of the liver when I was five years old.

Grandmother had beautiful eyes: deep-set, dark, intelligent, alert. And her hair was a lovely silvery gray, not coarse like others' hair but finespun, silky.

Mother said, "In your grandmother's eyes you can do no wrong." She spoke as if amused but I understood the accusation.

Because Grandmother loved me best of the grandchildren, yes, and she loved me best of all the family; I basked in her love as in the warmth of a private sun. Grandmother loved me without qualification and without criticism, which angered my parents since they understood that so fierce a love made me impervious to their more modulated love, not only impervious but indifferent to the threat of its being withdrawn . . . which is the only true power parents have over their children, isn't it?

We visited Grandmother often, especially now she was alone. She visited us: Sundays, holidays, birthdays. And I would bicycle across the river to her house once or twice a week or drop in after school. Grandmother encouraged me to bring my friends but I was too shy, I never stayed long; her happiness in my presence made me uneasy. Always she would prepare one of my favorite dishes—hot oatmeal with cream and brown sugar, apple cobbler, brownies, fudge, lemon custard tarts—and I sat and ate as she watched, and, eating, I felt hunger; the hunger was in my mouth. To remember those foods brings the hunger back now, the sudden rush of it, the pain. In my mouth.

At home Mother would ask, "Did you spoil your appetite again?"

The river that separated us was the Cassadaga, flowing from east to west, to Lake Ontario, through the small city of Hammond, New York. After I left, aged eighteen, I only returned to Hammond as a visitor. Now everyone is dead, I never go back.

The bridge that connected us was the Ferry Street bridge, the bridge we crossed hundreds of times. Grandmother lived

south of the river (six blocks south, two blocks west), we lived
north of the river (three blocks north, one and a half blocks
east); we were about three miles apart. The Ferry Street bridge,
built in 1919, was one of those long narrow spiky nightmare
bridges; my childhood was filled with such bridges, this one
thirty feet above the Cassadaga, with high arches, steep ramps
on both sides, six concrete supports, rusted iron grillwork, and
neoclassical ornamentation of the kind associated with Chicago
Commercial architecture, which was the architectural style of
Hammond generally.

The Ferry Street bridge. Sometimes in high winds you could
feel the bridge sway. I lowered my eyes when my father drove
us over; he'd joke as the plank floor rattled and beneath the rattling sound there came something deeper and more sinister, the
vibrating hum of the river itself, a murmur, a secret caress against
the soles of our feet, our buttocks, and between our legs, so it
was an enormous relief when the car had passed safely over the
bridge and descended the ramp to land. The Ferry Street bridge
was almost too narrow for two ordinary-sized automobiles to
pass but only once was my father forced to stop about a quarter
of the way out: a gravel truck was bearing down upon us and
the driver gave no sign of slowing down so my father braked
the car, threw it hurriedly into reverse, and backed up red-faced
the way we'd come, and after that the Ferry Street bridge was no
joke to him, any more than it was to his passengers.

The other day, that sunny gusty day when I saw Grandmother's
face in the mirror, I mean the metallic mirrored surface downtown, I mean the face that had seemed to be Grandmother's face
but was not, I began to think of the Ferry Street bridge and since
then I haven't slept well; seeing the bridge in my mind's eye the

way you do when you're insomniac, the images that should be in dreams are loosed and set careening through the day like lethal bubbles in the blood. I had not known how I'd memorized that bridge, and I'd forgotten why.

The time I am thinking of, I was twelve or thirteen years old; I know I was that age because the Ferry Street bridge was closed for repairs then and it was over the Ferry Street bridge I went, to see Grandmother. I don't remember if it was a conscious decision or if I'd just started walking, not knowing where I was going, or why. It was three o'clock in the morning. No one knew where I was. Beyond the barricade and the DETOUR—BRIDGE OUT signs, the moon so bright it lit my way like a manic face.

A number of times I'd watched with trepidation certain of the neighborhood boys inch their way out across the steel beams of the skeletal bridge, walking with arms extended for balance, so I knew it could be done without mishap, I knew I could do it if only I had the courage, and it seemed to me I had sufficient courage; now was the time to prove it. Below, the river rushed past slightly higher than usual; it was October, there had been a good deal of rain; but tonight the sky was clear, stars like icy pinpricks, and that bright glaring moon illuminating my way for me so I thought *I will do it*, already climbing up onto what would be the new floor of the bridge when at last it was completed: not planks but a more modern sort of iron mesh, not yet laid into place. But the steel beams were about ten inches wide and there was a grid of them, four beams spanning the river and (I would count them as I crossed; I would never forget that count) fourteen narrower beams at perpendicular angles with the others, and about three feet below these beams there was a complex crisscrossing of cables you might define as a net of sorts if you wanted to think in such terms, a safety net; there was no danger really, *I will do it because I want to do it, because there is no one to stop me.*

And on the other side, Grandmother's house. And even if its windows were darkened, even if I did no more than stand looking quietly at it and then come back home, never telling anyone what I'd done, even so I would have proven something *because there is no one to stop me,* which has been one of the principles of my life. To regret the principle is to regret my entire life.

I climbed up onto one of the beams, trembling with excitement. But how cold it was! I'd come out without my gloves.

And how loud the river below, the roaring like a kind of jeering applause, and it smelled too, of something brackish and metallic. I knew not to glance down at it, steadying myself as a quick wind picked up, teasing tears into my eyes; I was thinking, *There is no turning back: never,* but instructing myself too that the beam was perfectly safe if I was careful for had I not seen boys walking across without slipping? Didn't the workmen walk across too, many times a day? I decided not to stand, though— I was afraid to stand—I remained squatting on my haunches, gripping the edge of the beam with both hands, inching forward in this awkward way, hunched over, right foot and then left foot and then right foot and then left foot, passing the first of the perpendicular beams, and the second, and the third, and the fourth, and so in this clumsy and painful fashion forcing myself to continue until my thigh muscles ached so badly I had to stop and I made the mistake—which even in that instant I knew was a mistake—of glancing down, seeing the river thirty feet below: the way it was flowing so swiftly and with such power and seeming rage, ropy sinuous coils of churning water, foam-flecked, terrible, and its flow exactly perpendicular to the direction in which I was moving.

"Oh, no. Oh, no. Oh, no."

A wave of sharp cold terror shot up into me as if into my very bowels, piercing me between the legs rising from the river itself, and I could not move; I squatted there on the beam unable to move, all the strength drained out of my muscles, and I was paralyzed, knowing, *You're going to die: of course, die,* even as with another part of my mind (there is always this other part of my mind) I was thinking with an almost teacherly logic that the beam *was* safe, it was wide enough, and flat enough, and not damp or icy or greasy, yes certainly it *was* safe. If this were land, for instance in our back yard, if for instance my father had set down a plank flat in the grass, a plank no more than half the width of the beam, couldn't I, Claire, have walked that plank without the lightest tremor of fear? boldly? even gracefully? even blindfolded? without a moment's hesitation? not the flicker of an eyelid, not the most minute leap of a pulse? *You know you aren't going to die: don't be silly,* but it must have been five minutes before I could force myself to move again, my numbed right leg easing forward, my aching foot; I forced my eyes upward too and fixed them resolutely on the opposite shore, or what I took on faith to be the opposite shore, a confusion of sawhorses and barrels and equipment now only fitfully illuminated by the moon.

But I got there; I got to where I meant to go without for a moment exactly remembering why.

Now the worst of it's done: for now.

*   *   *

Grandmother's house, what's called a bungalow, plain stucco, one-story, built close to the curb, seemed closer to the river than I'd expected. Maybe I was running, desperate to get there, hearing the sound of the angry rushing water that was like many hundreds of murmurous voices, and the streets surprised me with their emptiness—so many vacant lots, murky transparencies of space where buildings had once stood—and a city bus passed silently, lit gaily from within, yet nearly empty too, only the driver and single (male), passenger sitting erect and motionless as mannequins, and I shrank panicked into the shadows so they would not see me; maybe I would be arrested: a girl of my age on the street at such an hour, alone, with deep-set frightened eyes, a pale face, guilty mouth, zip-up corduroy jacket, and jeans over her pajamas, disheveled as a runaway. But the bus passed, turned a corner, and vanished. And there was Grandmother's house, not darkened as I'd expected but lighted, and from the sidewalk staring I could see Grandmother inside, or a figure I took to be Grandmother, but why was she awake at such an hour? How remarkable that she should be awake as if awaiting me, and I remembered then—how instantaneously these thoughts came to me, eerie as tiny bubbles that, bursting, yielded riches of a sort that would require a considerable expenditure of time to relate though there duration was in fact hardly more than an instant!—I remembered having heard the family speak of Grand-mother's sometimes strange behavior, worrisome behavior in a woman of her age or of any age; the problem was her insomnia unless insomnia was not cause but consequence of a malady of the soul. So it would be reported back to my father, her son, that she'd been seen walking at night in neighborhoods unsafe for solitary women, she'd been seen at a midnight showing of a film in downtown Hammond, and even when my step-grandfather was alive (he worked on a lake freighter, he was often gone) she might spend time in local taverns, not drinking heavily but drinking, and this was behavior that might lead to trouble, or so the family worried, though there was never any specific trouble as far as anyone knew, and Grandmother smoked too, smoked on the street, which "looks cheap," my mother said, my mother too smoked but never on the street. The family liked to tell and retell the story of a cousin of my father's coming to Hammond on a Greyhound bus, arriving at the station at about six in the morning, and there in the waiting room was my grandmother in her old fox-fur coat sitting there with a book in her lap, a cigarette in one hand, just sitting there placidly and with no mind for the two or three others, distinctly odd, near-derelict men, in the room with her, just sitting there reading her book (Grandmother was always reading, poetry, biographies of great men like Lincoln, Mozart, Julius Caesar, Jesus of Nazareth), and my father's cousin came in, saw her, said, "Aunt Tina, what on earth are you doing here?" and Grandmother had looked up calmly and said, "Why not? It's for waiting, isn't it?"

Another strange thing Grandmother had done—it had nothing to do with her insomnia that I could see, unless all our strangenesses, as they are judged in others' eyes, are morbidly related—was arranging for her husband's body to be cremated, not buried in a cemetery plot but cremated, which means burnt to mere ash, which means annihilation, and though cremation had evidently been my step-grandfather's wish it had seemed to the family that Grandmother had complied with it too readily, and so immediately following her husband's death that no one had a chance to dissuade her. "What a thing," my mother said, shivering, "to do to your own husband!"

I was thinking of this now, seeing through one of the windows a man's figure, a man talking with Grandmother in her kitchen; it seemed to me that perhaps my step-grandfather had not yet died, thus was not cremated, and some of the disagreement might be resolved; but I must have already knocked at the door since Grandmother was there opening it. At first she stared at me as if scarcely recognizing me; then she laughed, she said, "What are *you* doing here?" and I tried to explain but could not, the words failed to come; my teeth were chattering with cold and fright and the words failed to come, but Grandmother led me inside, she was taller than I remembered and younger, her hair dark, wavy, falling to her shoulders, and her mouth red with lipstick; she laughed, leading me into the kitchen where a man, a stranger, was waiting. "Harry, this is my granddaughter Claire," Grandmother said, and the man stepped forward, regarding me with interest yet speaking of me as if I were somehow not present: "She's your granddaughter?" "She is." "I didn't know you had a granddaughter." "You don't know lots of things."

And Grandmother laughed at us both, who gazed in perplexity and doubt at each other. Laughing, she threw her head back like a young girl, or a man, and bared her strong white teeth.

I was then led to sit at the kitchen table in my usual place, Grandmother went to the stove to prepare something for me, and I sat quietly, not frightened yet not quite at ease though I understood I was safe now, Grandmother would take care of me now, and nothing could happen. I saw that the familiar kitchen had been altered; it was very brightly lit, almost blindingly lit, yet deeply shadowed in the corners; the rear wall where the sink should have been dissolved into what would have been the back yard but I had a quick flash of the back yard, where there were flower and vegetable beds. Grandmother loved to work in the yard, she brought flowers and vegetables in the summer wherever she visited; the most beautiful of her flowers were peonies, big gorgeous crimson peonies, and the thought of the peonies was confused with the smell of the oatmeal Grandmother was stirring on the stove for me to eat. Oatmeal was the first food of my childhood, the first food I can remember, but Grandmother made it her own way, her special way, stirring in brown sugar, cream, a spoonful of dark honey so just thinking of it I felt my mouth water violently; almost it hurt, the saliva flooded so, and I was embarrassed that a trickle ran down my chin and I couldn't seem to wipe it off and Grandmother's friend Harry was watching me, but finally I managed to wipe it off on my fingers, and Harry smiled.

The thought came to me, not a new thought but one I'd had for years, but now it came with unusual force, like the saliva flooding my mouth, that when my parents died I would come live with Grandmother—of course, I would come live with Grandmother—and Grandmother at the stove stirring my oatmeal in a pan must have heard my thoughts, for she said, "Claire, why don't you come live with me, it's time, isn't it?" and I said, "Oh, yes," and Grandmother didn't seem to have heard for she repeated her question, turning now to look at me, to smile, her eyes shining and her mouth so amazingly red, two delicate spots of rouge on her cheeks so my heart caught, seeing how beautiful she was, as young as my mother or younger, and she laughed, saying, "Claire, why don't you come live with me, it's

time, isn't it?" and again I said, "Oh, yes, Grandmother," nodding and blinking tears from my eyes; they were tears of infinite
happiness, and relief: "Oh, Grandmother, *yes*."

Grandmother's friend Harry was a navy radio operator, he said,
or had been; he wore no uniform and he was no age I could
have guessed, with silvery-glinting hair in a crew cut, muscular
shoulders and arms, but maybe his voice was familiar? maybe I'd
heard him over the radio? Grandmother was urging him to tell
me about the universe, distinctly she said those odd words, "Why
don't you tell Claire about the universe," and Harry stared at me
frowning and said, "Tell Claire what about the universe?" and
Grandmother laughed and said, "Oh—anything!" and Harry
said, shrugging, "Hell, I don't know," then, raising his voice,
regarding me with a look of compassion: "The universe goes
back a long way, I guess. Ten billion years? Twenty billion? Is
there a difference? They say it got started with an explosion, and
in a second—well, really a fraction of a second—a tiny bit of
tightness got flung out; it's flying out right now, expanding"—he
drew his hands, broad stubby hands, dramatically apart—"and
most of it is emptiness, I guess, whatever 'emptiness' is. It's still
expanding, all the pieces flying out; there's a billion galaxies like
ours, or maybe a billion billion galaxies like ours, but don't worry,
it goes on forever even when we die—" but at this Grandmother
turned sharply; sensing my reaction, she said, "Oh, dear, don't
tell the child *that*, don't frighten poor little Claire with *that*."
     "You told me to tell her about the—"
     "Oh, just *stop*."
     Quickly Grandmother came to hug me, settled me into my
chair as if I were a much smaller child sitting there at the kitchen

table, my feet not touching the floor; and there was my special
bowl, the bowl Grandmother kept for me, sparkling yellow with
lambs running around the rim; yes, and my special spoon too,
a beautiful silver spoon with the initial C engraved on it which
Grandmother kept polished, so I understood I was safe, nothing
could harm me; Grandmother would not let anything happen
to me so long as I was there. She poured my oatmeal into my
dish; she was saying, "It's true we must all die one day, darling,
but not just yet, you know, not tonight, you've just come to visit,
haven't you, dear? and maybe you'll stay? maybe you won't ever
leave? *now it's time?*"

The words *it's time* rang with a faint echo.

I can hear them now: *it's time: time.*

Grandmother's arms were shapely and attractive, her skin pale
and smooth and delicately translucent as a candied egg, and I
saw that she was wearing several rings, the wedding band that I
knew but others, sparkling with light, and there so thin were my
arms beside hers, my hands that seemed so small, sparrow-sized,
and my wrists so bony, and it came over me, the horror of it, that
meat and bone should define my presence in the universe; the
point of entry in the universe that was *me* that was *me* that was
me, and no other, yet of a fragile materiality that any fire could
consume. "Oh, Grandmother—I'm so afraid!" I whimpered, seeing how I would be burnt to ash, and Grandmother comforted
me, and settled me more securely into the chair, pressed my
pretty little spoon between my fingers, and said, "Darling, don't
think of such things, just *eat.* Grandmother made this for *you.*"

I was eating the hot oatmeal, which was a little too hot,
but creamy as I loved it; I was terribly hungry, eating like an
infant at the breast so blindly my head bowed and eyes nearly

shut, rimming with tears, and Grandmother asked, *Is it good? Is it good?*—she'd spooned in some dark honey too—*Is it good?* and I nodded mutely; I could taste grains of brown sugar that hadn't melted into the oatmeal, stark as bits of glass, and I realized they were in fact bits of glass, some of them large as grape pits, and I didn't want to hurt Grandmother's feelings but I was fearful of swallowing the glass so as I ate I managed to sift the bits through the chewed oatmeal until I could maneuver it into the side of my mouth into a little space between my lower right gum and the inside of my cheek, and Grandmother was watching, asking *Is it good?* and I said, "Oh, yes," half choking and swallowing, "oh, *yes.*"

A while later when neither Grandmother nor Harry was watching I spat out the glass fragments into my hand but I never knew absolutely, I don't know even now, if they were glass and not for instance grains of sand or fragments of eggshell or even bits of brown sugar crystallized into such a form not even boiling oatmeal could dissolve it.

I was leaving Grandmother's house; it was later, time to leave. Grandmother said, "But aren't you going to stay?" and I said, "No, Grandmother, I can't," and Grandmother said, "I thought you were going to stay, dear," and I said, "No, Grandmother, I can't," and Grandmother said, "But why?" and I said, "I just can't," and Grandmother said, laughing so her laughter was edged with annoyance, "Yes, but *why?*" Grandmother's friend Harry had disappeared from the kitchen, there was no one in the kitchen but Grandmother and me, but we were in the street too, and the roaring of the river was close by, so Grandmother hugged me a final time and gave me a little push, saying, "Well, good

night, Claire," and I said apologetically, "Good night, Grandmother," wondering if I should ask her not to say anything to
my parents about this visit in the middle of the night, and she
was backing away, her dark somber gaze fixed upon me half in
reproach. "Next time you visit Grandmother you'll stay, won't
you? Forever?" and I said, "Yes, Grandmother," though I was
very frightened, and as soon as I was out of Grandmother's sight
I began to run.

At first I had a hard time finding the Ferry Street bridge. Though
I could hear the river close by; I can always hear the river close by.

Eventually, I found the bridge again. I know I found the
bridge, otherwise how did I get home? That night?

THE BUCK

This is such a terrible story. It's a story I have told a dozen times, never knowing *why*.

Why I can't forget it, I mean. Why it's lodged so deep in me . . . like an arrow through the neck.

Like that arrow I never saw—fifteen-inch, steel-tipped, razor-sharp—that penetrated the deer's neck and killed him, though not immediately. How many hours, I wonder, till he bled to death, till his body turned cold and grew heavier—they say the weight of Death is always heavier than that of life—how many hours, terrible hours, I don't know.

I was not a witness. The sole witness did not survive.

Each time I tell this story of the wounded buck, the hunter who pursued him, and the elderly woman who rescued him, or tried to rescue him, I think that maybe *this* telling will make a difference. *This* time a secret meaning will be revealed, as if without my volition, and I will be released.

But each telling is a subtle repudiation of a previous telling. So each telling is a new telling. Each telling a forgetting.

That arrow lodged ever more firmly, cruelly. In living flesh.

* * *

I'd take comfort in saying all this happened years ago, in some remote part of the country. *Once upon a time,* I'd begin, but in fact it happened within the past year, and no more than eight miles from where I live, in a small town called Bethany, New Jersey.

Which is in Saugatuck County, in the northwestern corner of the state, bordering the Delaware River.

A region that's mainly rural: farmland, hills, some of the hills large enough to be called mountains. There aren't many roads in this part of New Jersey, and the big interstate highways just slice through, gouge through the countryside, north and south, east and west. Strangers in a rush to get somewhere else.

The incident happened on the Snyder farm. A lonely place, no neighbors close by.

The name "Snyder" was always known in Saugatuck County even though, when I was growing up, the Snyders had sold off most of their land. In the family's prime, in the 1930s, they'd owned three hundred twenty acres, most of it rich farmland; in the 1950s they'd begun to sell, piecemeal, as if grudgingly, maybe with the idea of one day buying their land back. But they never did; they died out instead. Three brothers, all unmarried; and Melanie Snyder, the last of the family. Eighty-two years old when she was found dead in a room of the old farmhouse, last January.

In deer-hunting season. The season that had always frightened and outraged her.

She'd been vigilant for years. She'd acquired a local reputation. Her six acres of land—all that remained of the property—was scrupulously posted against hunters ("with gun, bow and arrow, dog") and trespassers. Before hunting with firearms was banned in Saugatuck County, Melanie Snyder patrolled her property in

hunting season, on foot, fearless about moving in the direction of
gunfire. "You! What are you doing here?" she would call out to
hunters. "Don't you know this land is posted?" She was a lanky
woman with a strong-boned face, skin that looked permanently
wind-burnt, close-cropped starkly white hair. Her eyes were unusually dark and prominent; everyone commented on Melanie
Snyder's eyes; she wasn't a woman any man, no matter his age,
felt comfortable confronting, especially out in the woods.

She sent trespassers home, threatened to call the sheriff if
they didn't leave. She'd stride through the woods clapping her
hands to frighten off deer, pheasants, small game, send them
panicked to safety.

White-tailed deer, or, as older generations called them, Virginia deer, were her favorites, "the most beautiful animals in
creation." She hated it that state conservationists argued in favor
of controlled hunting for the "good" of the deer themselves, to
reduce their alarmingly fertile numbers.

She hated the idea of hunting with bow and arrow—as if it
made any difference to a deer, how it died.

She hated the stealth and silence of the bow. With guns, you
can at least hear the enemy.

His name was Wayne Kunz, "Woody" Kunz, part owner of a
small auto parts store in Delaware Gap, New Jersey, known to
his circle of male friends as a good guy. A good sport. You might
say, a "character."

The way he dressed; his hunting gear, for instance.

A black simulated-leather jumpsuit, over it the regulation
fluorescent-orange vest. A bright red cap, with earflaps. Boots
to the knee, like a Nazi storm trooper's; mirror sunglasses hiding

his pale lashless eyes. He had a large, round, singed-looking face, a small damp mouth: this big-bellied, quick-grinning fellow, the kind who keeps up a constant chatting murmur with himself, as if terrified of silence, of being finally *alone*.

He hadn't been able to talk any of his friends into coming with him, deer hunting with bow and arrow.

Even showing them his new Atlas bow, forty-eight inches, sleek blond fiberglass "wood," showing them the quill of arrows, synthetic-feathered, lightweight steel and steel-tipped and razor-sharp like no Indian's arrows had ever been—he'd been disappointed, disgusted with them, none of his friends wanting to come along, waking in the predawn dark, driving out into Saugatuck County to kill a few deer.

Woody Kunz. Forty years old, five feet ten inches, two hundred pounds. He'd been married, years ago, but the marriage hadn't worked out, and there were no children.

Crashing clumsily through the underbrush, in pursuit of deer.

Not wanting to think he was lost—*was* he lost?

Talking to himself, cursing and begging himself—"C'mon, Woody, for Christ's sake, Woody, move your fat *ass*"—half sobbing as, another time, a herd of deer broke and scattered before he could get into shooting range. Running and leaping through the woods, taunting him with their uplifted white tails, erect snowy-white tails like targets so he couldn't help but fire off an arrow—to fly into space, disappear.

"Fuck it, Woody! Fuck you, asshole!"

Later. He's tired. Even with the sunglasses his eyes are seared from the bright winter sun reflecting on the snow. Knowing he deserves better.

Another time the deer are too quick and smart for him, must be they scented him downwind, breaking to run before he even saw them, only heard them, silent except for the sound of their crashing hooves. This time, he fires a shot knowing it won't strike any target, no warm living flesh. Must be he does it to make himself feel bad.

Playing the fool in the eyes of anybody watching and he can't help but think uneasily that somebody *is* watching—if only the unblinking eye of God.

And then: he sees the buck.

His buck, yes, suddenly. Oh, Jesus. His heart clenches, he *knows*.

He has surprised the beautiful dun-colored animal drinking from a fast-running stream; the stream is frozen except for a channel of black water at its center, the buck with its antlered head lowered. Woody Kunz stares, hardly able to believe his good luck, rapidly counting the points of the antlers—eight? ten?—as he fits an arrow into place with trembling fingers, lifts the bow, and sights along the arrow aiming for that point of the anatomy where neck and chest converge—it's a heart shot he hopes for—drawing back the arrow, feeling the power of the bow, releasing it; and seemingly in the same instant the buck leaps, the arrow has struck him in the neck, there's a shriek of animal terror and pain, and Woody Kunz shouts in ecstatic triumph.

But the buck isn't killed outright. To Woody's astonishment, and something like hurt, the buck turns and runs—flees.

Later he'd say he hadn't seen the NO TRESPASSING signs in the woods, he hadn't come by way of the road so he hadn't seen them there, the usual state-issued signs forbidding hunting, trapping, trespassing on private land, but Woody Kunz would claim he hadn't known it was private land exactly; he'd have to confess he might have been lost, tracking deer for hours moving more or less in a circle not able to gauge where the center of the circle might be; and yes, he was excited, adrenaline rushing in his veins as he hadn't felt it in God knows how long, half a lifetime maybe, so he hadn't seen the signs posting the Snyder property or if he'd seen them they had not registered upon his consciousness or if they'd registered upon his consciousness he hadn't known what they were, so tattered and weatherworn.

That was Woody Kunz's defense, against a charge, if there was to be a charge, of unlawful trespassing and hunting on posted property.

Jesus is the most important person in all our lives!
   Jesus abides in our hearts, no need to see Him!
These joyful pronouncements, or are they commandments, Melanie Snyder sometimes hears, rising out of the silence of the old house. The wind in the eaves, a shrieking of crows in the orchard, and this disembodied voice, the voice of her long-dead fiancé—waking her suddenly from one of her reveries, so she doesn't remember where she is, what year this is, what has happened to her, to have aged her so.

She'd fallen in love with her brothers, one by one. Her tall strong indifferent brothers.

Much later, to everyone's surprise and certainly to her own, she'd fallen in love with a young Lutheran preacher, just her age.

Standing just her height. Smiling at her shyly, his wire-rimmed glasses winking as if shyly too. Shaking her gloved hand. Hello, Miss Snyder. Like a brother who would at late see *her*.

Twenty-eight years old! She'd been fated to be a spinster, of course. That plain, stubborn, sharp-tongued girl, eyes too large and stark and intelligent in her face to be "feminine," her body flat as a board.

In this place in which girls married as young as sixteen, began having their babies at seventeen, were valued and praised and loved for such qualities as they shared with brood mares and milking cows, you cultivated irony to save your soul—and your pride.

Except: she fell in love with the visiting preacher, introduced to him by family friends, the two "young people" urged together to speak stumblingly, clumsily to each other of—what? Decades later Melanie Snyder won't remember a syllable, but she remembers the young man's preaching voice, *Jesus! Jesus is our only salvation!* He'd gripped the edges of the pulpit of the Bethany church, God love shining in his face, white teeth bared like piano keys.

How it happened, how they became officially engaged—whether by their own decision or others'—they might not have been able to say. But it was time to marry, for both.

Plain, earnest, upright young people. Firm-believing Christians, of that there could be no doubt.

Did Melanie doubt? No, never!

She was prepared to be a Christian wife and to have her babies one by one. As God ordained.

There were passionate-seeming squeezes of her hand, there were chaste kisses, fluttery and insubstantial as a butterflies wings. There were Sunday walks, in the afternoon. Jesus is the most important person in my life, I feel Him close beside us—don't you, Melanie?

The emptiness of the country lane, the silence of the sky, except for the crows' raucous jeering cries. Slow-spiraling hawks high overhead.

Oh, yes, certainly! Oh, yes.

Melanie Snyder's fiancé. The young just-graduated seminary student, with his hope to be a missionary. He was an energetic softball player, a pitcher of above-average ability; he led the Sunday school children on hikes, canoe trips. But he was most himself there in the pulpit of the Bethany church, elevated a few inches above the rapt congregation, where even his shy stammering rose to passion, a kind of sensual power. How strong the bones of his earnest, homely face, the fair-brown wings of hair brushed back neatly from his forehead! *Jesus, our redeemer. Jesus, our only salvation.* As if the God love shining in the young man's face were a beacon, a lighthouse beacon, flung out into the night, giving light yet unseeing, blind, in itself.

The engagement was never officially terminated. Always, there were sound reasons for postponing the wedding. Their families were disappointed but eager, on both sides, to comply. His letters came to her like clockwork, every two weeks, from North Carolina, where he was stationed as a chaplain in the U.S. Army. Dutiful letters, buoyant letters about his work, his "mission," his conviction that he was at last where God meant him to be.

Then the letters ceased. And they told Melanie he'd had an "accident" of some kind; there'd been a "misunderstanding" of some kind. He was discharged from his army post and reassigned to a Lutheran church in St. Louis, where he was to assist an older minister. But why? Melanie asked. Why, what has happened? Melanie demanded to know, but never was she told, never would a young woman be told such a thing, not for her ears, not for an ignorant virgin's ears; she'd wept and protested and mourned and lapsed finally into shame, not knowing what had happened to ruin her happiness but knowing it must constitute a rejection of her, a repudiation of the womanliness she'd tried so hard—ah, so shamefully hard!—to take on.

That feeling, that sense of unworthiness, she would retain for years. Studying her face in a mirror, plain, frank, unyielding, those eyes alit with irony, she realized she'd known all along—she was fated to be a spinster, never to be any man's wife.

And didn't that realization bring with it, in truth, relief?

Now, fifty years later, if those words *Jesus! Jesus abides in our hearts, no need to see Him!* ring out faintly in the silence of the old house, she turns aside, unhearing. For she's an old woman who has outlived such lies. Such subterfuge. She has taken revenge on Jesus Christ by ceasing to believe in Him—or in God, or in the Lutheran faith, or in such pieties as meekness, charity, love of one's enemies. Casting off her long-dead fiancé (who had not the courage even to write Melanie Snyder, finally, to release her from their engagement), she'd cast off his religion, as, drifting off from a friend, we lose the friends with whom he or she connected us, there being no deeper bond.

What is it?

She sees, in the lower pasture, almost out of the range of her vision, a movement of some kind: a swaying dun-colored shape, blurred by the frost on the aged glass. Standing in her kitchen, alert, aroused.

An animal of some kind? A large dog? A deer?

A wounded deer?

Melanie hurries to pull her sheepskin jacket from a peg; she's jamming her feet into boots, already angry, half knowing what she'll see.

Guns you could at least hear; now the slaughter is with bow and arrow. Grown men playing at Indians. Playing at killing.

The excuse is, the "excess" deer population in the county has to be kept down. White-tailed deer overbreeding, causing crop damage, auto accidents. As if men, the species of men who prowl the woods seeking innocent creatures to kill, need any excuse.

Melanie Snyder, who has known hunters all her life, including her own brothers, understands: to the hunter, killing an animal is just a substitute for killing another human being. Male, female. That's the forbidden fantasy.

She has never been frightened of accosting them, though, and she isn't now. Running outside into the gusty January air. A scowling wild-eyed old woman sexless leathery face, white hair rising from her head in stiff tufts. She is wearing a soiled sheepskin jacket several sizes too large for her, a relic once belonging to one of her brothers; her boots are rubberized fishing boots, the castoffs of another, long-deceased brother.

Melanie is prepared for an ugly sight but this sight stuns her at first; she hears herself cry out, "Oh. Oh, God!"

A buck, full grown, beautiful, with handsome pointed antlers, is staggering in her direction, thrashing his head from side to side, desperate to dislodge an arrow that has penetrated his neck. His eyes roll in his head, his mouth is opening and closing spasmodically, blood flows bright and glistening from the wound; in fact it is two wounds, in the lower part of his neck near his left shoulder. Behind him, in the lower pasture, running clumsily after him, is the hunter, bow uplifted: a bizarre sight in black jumpsuit, bright orange vest, comical red hat. Like a robot or a spaceman, Melanie thinks, staring. She has never seen any hunter so costumed. Is this a man she should know? a face? a name? He's a hefty man with pale flushed skin, damp mouth, eyes hidden behind sunglasses with opaque mirrored lenses. His breath is steaming in the cold; he's clearly excited, agitated—dangerous. Fitting an arrow crookedly to his bow as if preparing, at this range, to shoot.

Melanie cries, "You! Get out of here!"

The hunter yells, "Lady, stand aside!"

"This land is posted! I'll call the sheriff!"

"Lady, you better gimme a clear shot!"

The buck is snorting, stamping his sharp-hooved feet in the snow. Deranged by terror and panic, he thrashes his antlered head from side to side, bleeding freely, bright-glistening blood underfoot, splattered onto Melanie Snyder's clothes as, instinctively, recklessly, she positions herself between the wounded animal and the hunter. She's pleading, angry, "Get off my land! Haven't you done enough evil? This poor creature! Let him alone!"

The hunter, panting, gaping at her, can't seem to believe what he sees: a white-haired woman in men's clothes, must be eighty years old, trying to shield a buck with an arrow through his neck. He advances to within a few yards of her, tries to circle around her. Saying incredulously, "That's my arrow, for Christ's sake, lady! That buck's a goner and he's *mine*!"

"Brute! Murderer! I'm telling you to get off my land or I'll call the sheriff and have you arrested!"

"Lady, that buck is goddamned dangerous—you better stand aside."

"*You* stand aside. Get off my property!"

"Lady, for Christ's sake—"

"You heard me: *get off my property!*"

So, for some minutes, there's an impasse.

Forever afterward Woody Kunz will remember, to his chagrin and shame: the beautiful white-tailed full-grown buck with the most amazing spread of antlers he'd ever seen—*his* buck, *his* kill, *his* arrow sticking through the animal's neck—the wounded buck snorting, thrashing his head, stamping the ground, blood everywhere, blood-tinged saliva hanging from his mouth in threads, and the crazy old woman shielding the buck with her body, refusing to surrender him to his rightful owner. And Woody Kunz is certain *he* is the rightful owner; he's shouting in the old woman's face, he's pleading with her, practically begging, finally; the fucking deer is *his*, he's earned it, he's been out tramping in the cold since seven this morning, God damn it if he's going to give up! Face blotched and hot, tears of rage and impotence stinging his eyes: oh, Jesus, he'd grab the old hag by the shoulders, lift her clear, and fire another arrow this time into the heart so there'd be no doubt—except, somehow, he doesn't do it, doesn't dare.

Instead, he backs off. Still with his bow upraised, his handsome brand-new Atlas bow from Sears, but the arrow droops useless in his fingers.

In a voice heavy with disgust, sarcasm, he says, "O.K., O.K., lady, you win."

The last glimpse Woody Kunz has of this spectacle, the old woman is trying clumsily to pull the arrow out of the buck's neck, and the buck is naturally putting up a struggle, swiping at her with his antlers, but weakly, sinking to his knees in the snow, then scrambling to his feet again; still the old woman persists; sure, she *is* crazy and deserves whatever happens to her, the front of her sheepskin jacket soaked in blood by now, blood even on her face, in her hair.

It isn't until late afternoon, hours later, that Woody Kunz returns home.

Having gotten lost in the countryside, wandered in circles in the woods, couldn't locate the road he'd parked his goddamned car on, muttering to himself, sick and furious and shamed, in a state of such agitation his head feels close to bursting, guts like a nest of tangled snakes. Never, *never*, is Woody Kunz going to live down this humiliation in his own eyes.

So he's decided not to tell anyone. Not even to fashion it into an anecdote to entertain his friends: Woody Kunz being cheated out of a twelve-point buck by an old lady? Shit, he'd rather die than have it known.

Sure, it crosses his mind he should maybe report the incident to the sheriff. Not to reiterate his claim of the deer—though the deer *is* his—but to report the old woman in case she's really in danger. Out there, seemingly alone, so old, in the middle of nowhere. A mortally wounded full-grown whitetail buck, crazed with pain and terror, like a visitation of God, in her care.

She's begging, desperate: "*Let* me help you, oh, please! Oh, please! Let me—"

Tugging at the terrible arrow, tugging forward, tugging back, her fingers slippery with blood. Woman and beast struggling, the one disdainful, even reckless, of her safety; the other dazed by trauma or loss of blood, not lashing out as ordinarily he would, to attack an enemy, with bared teeth, antlers, sharp hooves.

"Oh, please, you must not die, please—"

It's probable that Melanie Snyder has herself become deranged. All of the world having shrunk to the task at hand, to the forcible removal of this steel bar that has penetrated the buck's neck, fifteen-inch steel-glinting sharp-tipped arrow with white, synthetic quills—nothing matters but that *the arrow must be removed.*

The bulging eyes roll upward, there's bloody froth at the shuddering nostrils, she smells, tastes, the hot rank breath—then the antlers strike her in the chest, she's falling, crying out in surprise.

And the buck has pushed past her, fleeing on skidding hooves, on legs near buckling at the knees, so strangely—were she fully conscious she would realize, *so* strangely—into her father's house.

It won't be until three days later, at about this hour of the morning, that they'll discover her—or the body she has become. Melanie Snyder and the buck with the arrow through his neck.

But Melanie Snyder has no sense of what's coming, no cautionary fear. As if, this damp-gusty January morning, such a visitation, such urgency pressed upon her, has blotted out all anticipation of the future, let alone of danger.

In blind panic, voiding his bowels, the buck has run crashing into the old farmhouse, into the kitchen, through to the parlor; as Melanie Snyder sits dazed on the frozen ground beneath her rear stoop he turns, furious, charges into a corner of the room, collides with an upright piano, making a brief discordant startled music, an explosion of muted notes; turns again, crashing into a table laden with family photographs, a lamp of stippled milk glass with a fluted shade. A renewed rush of adrenaline empowers him; turning again, half rearing, hooves skidding on the thin loose-lying Oriental carpet faded to near transparency, he charges his reflection in a mirror as, out back, Melanie Snyder sits trying to summon her strength, trying to comprehend what has happened and what she must do.

She doesn't remember the buck having knocked her down, thus can't believe he *has* attacked her.

She thinks, Without me, he is doomed.

She hears one of her brothers speaking harshly, scolding: What is she doing there sitting on the ground?—*For the Lord's sake, Melanie!*—but she ignores him, testing her right ankle, the joint is livid with pain but not broken—she can shift her weight to her other foot—a high-pitched ringing in her head as of church bells, and where there should be terror there's determination, for Melanie Snyder is an independent woman, a woman far too proud to accept, let alone solicit, her neighbors' proffered aid since the death of the last of her brothers: she wills herself not to succumb to weakness now, in this hour of her trial.

Managing to get to her feet, moving with calculating slowness. As if her bones are made of glass.

Overhead, an opaque January sky, yet beautiful. Like slightly tarnished mother-of-pearl.

Except for the crows in their gathering place beyond the barns, and the hoarse *uh-uh-uh* of her breathing: silence.

She enters the house. By painful inches, yet eagerly. Leaning heavily against the door frame.

She sees the fresh blood trail, sees and smells the moist animal droppings, so shocking, there on the kitchen floor she keeps clean with a pointless yet self-satisfying fanaticism, the aged linoleum worn nearly colorless, yes, but Melanie has a house owner's pride, and pride is all. The buck in his frenzy to escape the very confines he has plunged into is turning, rearing, snorting, crashing in the other room. Melanie calls, "I'm here! I will help you!"—blindly too entering the parlor with its etiolated light, tasseled shades drawn to cover three quarters of the windows as, decades ago, Melanie Snyder's mother had so drawn them, to protect the furnishings against the sun. Surely she's a bizarre sight herself, drunk-swaying, staggering, her wrinkled face, hands glistening with blood, white hair in tufts as if she hasn't taken a brush to it in weeks, Melanie Snyder in the oversized sheepskin jacket she wears in town, driving a rusted Plymouth pickup truck with a useless muffler—everybody in Bethany knows Melanie Snyder though she doesn't know them, carelessly confuses sons with fathers, granddaughters with mothers, her own remote blood relations with total strangers—she's awkward in these rubberized boots many sizes too large for her shrunken feet, yet reaching out—unhesitantly, boldly—to the maddened buck who crouches in a corner facing her, his breath frothing in blood, in erratic shuddering waves, she is speaking softly, half begging, "I want to help you! Oh—" as the heavy head dips, the antlers rush at her—how astonishing the elegance of such male beauty, and the burden of it, God's design both playful and deadly shrewd, the strangeness of bone growing out of flesh, bone calcified and many-branched as a young apple tree—clumsily he charges this woman who is his enemy even as, with a look of startled concern, she opens her arms to him, the sharp antlers now striking her a second time in the chest and this time breaking her fragile collarbone as easily as one might break a chicken wishbone set to dry on a windowsill for days, and the

momentum of his charge carries him helplessly forward, he falls,
the arrow's quill brushing against Melanie Snyder's face; as he
scrambles in a frenzy to upright himself his sharp hooves catch
her in the chest, belly, pelvis; he has fallen heavily, as if from
a great height, as if flung down upon her, breath in wheezing
shudders and the blood froth bubbling around his mouth, and
Melanie Snyder lies pinned beneath the animal body, legs gone,
lower part of her body gone, a void of numbness, not even pain,
distant from her as something seen through the wrong end of
a telescope, rapidly retreating.

How did it happen, how strange; they were of the same height
now, or nearly: Melanie Snyder and her tall strong indifferent
brothers. Never married, none of them, d'you know why? No
woman was ever quite good enough for the Snyder boys, and
the girl, Melanie—well, one look at her and you know: a born
spinster.

It's more than thirty years after they informed her, guardedly, without much sympathy—for perhaps sympathy would
have invited tears, and they were not a family comfortable with
tears—that her fiancé had been discharged from the army, that
Melanie dares to ask, shyly, without her customary aggressive-
ness, what had really happened, what the mysterious "accident,"
or was it a "misunderstanding," had been. And her brother, her
elder by six years, an aged slope-shouldered man with a deeply
creased face, sighs and passes his hand over his chin and says, in
a tone of mild but unmistakable contempt, "Don't ask."

She lies there beneath the dying animal, then beneath the lifeless
stiffening body, face no more than four inches from the great

head, the empty eyes—how many hours she's conscious, she can't gauge.

At first calling, into the silence, "Help—help me! Help—"

There *is* a telephone in the kitchen; rarely does it ring, and when it rings Melanie Snyder frequently ignores it, doesn't want people inquiring after her, well-intentioned neighbors, good Lutherans from the church she hasn't set foot in, except for funerals, in twenty-odd years.

The dying animal, beautiful even in dying, bleeding to death, soaking Melanie Snyder's cloches with his blood, and isn't she bleeding too, from wounds in her throat and face, her hands?

And he's dead, she feels the life pass from him—"Oh, no, oh, *no*," sobbing and pushing at the body, warm sticky blood by degrees cooling and congealing—the wood-fire stove in the kitchen has gone out and cold eases in from out-of-doors; in fact the kitchen door must be open, creaking and banging in the wind. A void rises from the loose-fitting floorboards as from the lower part of Melanie's body; she's sobbing as if her heart is broken, she's furious, trying to lift the heavy body from her, clawing at the body, raking her torn nails and bleeding fingers against the buck's thick winter coat, a coarse-haired furry coat, but the buck's body will not budge.

The weight of Death, so much more powerful than life.

Later. She wakes moaning and delirious, a din as of sleet pellets against the windows, and the cold has congealed the buck's blood and her own, the numbness has moved higher, obliterating much of what she has known as "body" these eighty-odd years; she understands that she is dying—consciousness like a fragile bubble, or a skein of bubbles—yet she is able still to wish to summon her old strength, the bitter joy of her stubborn strength, pushing at the heavy animal body, dead furry weight, eyes sightless as glass and the arrow, the terrible arrow, the obscene arrow: "Let me *go*. Let me *free*."

Fainting and waking. Drifting in and out of consciousness.

Hearing that faint ringing voice in the eaves, as always subtly chiding, in righteous reproach of Melanie Snyder, mixed with the wind and that profound agelessness of wind as if blowing to us from the farthest reaches of time as well as space—*Jesus! Jesus is our only salvation! Jesus abides in our hearts!*—but in pride she turns aside unhearing; never has she begged, nor will she beg now. Oh, never.

And does she regret her gesture, trying to save an innocent beast? She does not.

And would she consent, even now, to having made a mistake, acted improvidently? She would not.

When after nearly seventy-two hours Woody Kunz overcomes his manly embarrassment and notifies the Saugatuck County sheriff's office of the "incident" on the Snyder farm and they go out to investigate, they find eighty-two-year-old Melanie Snyder dead, pinned beneath the dead whitetail buck, in the parlor of the old farmhouse in which no one outside the Snyder family had stepped for many years. An astonishing sight: human and animal bodies virtually locked together in the rigor of death, their mingled blood so soaked into Melanie Snyder's clothes, so frozen, it is possible to separate them only by force.

THE MODEL

1. The Approach of Mr. Starr

Had he stepped out of nowhere, or had he been watching her for some time, even more than he'd claimed, and for a different purpose?—she shivered to think that, yes, probably, she had many times glimpsed him in the village, or in the park, without really seeing him: him, and the long gleaming black limousine she would not have known to associate with him even had she noticed him: the man who called himself Mr. Starr.

As, each day, her eyes passed rapidly and lightly over any number of people both familiar to her and strangers, blurred as in the background of a film in which the foreground is the essential reality, the very point of the film.

She was seventeen. It was in fact the day after her birthday, a bright gusty January day, and she'd been running in the late afternoon, after school, in the park overlooking the ocean, and she'd just turned to head toward home, pausing to wipe her face, adjust her damp cotton headband, feeling the accelerated strength of her heartbeat and the pleasant ache of her leg muscles: and she glanced up, shy, surprised, and there he stood, a man she had never knowingly seen before. He was smiling at her, his smile broad and eager, hopeful, and he stood in such a way, leaning lightly on a cane, as to block her way on the path; yet tentatively too, with a gentlemanly, deferential air, so as to suggest that he meant no threat. When he spoke, his voice sounded hoarse as if from disuse. "Excuse me!—Hello! Young lady! I realize that this is abrupt, and an intrusion on your privacy, but I am an artist, and I am looking for a model, and I wonder if you might be interested in posing for me? Only here, I mean, in the park—in full daylight! I am willing to pay, per hour—"

Sybil stared at the man. Like most young people she was incapable of estimating ages beyond thirty-five—this strange person might have been in his forties, or well into his fifties. His thin, lank hair was the color of antique silver—perhaps he was even older. His skin was luridly pale, grainy, and rough; he wore glasses with lenses so darkly tinted as to suggest the kind of glasses worn by the blind; his clothes were plain, dark, conservative—a tweed jacket that fitted him loosely, a shirt buttoned tight to the neck, and no tie, highly polished black leather shoes in an outmoded style. There was something hesitant, even convalescent in his manner, as if, like numerous others in this coastal Southern California town with its population of the retired, the elderly, and the infirm, he had learned by experience to carry himself with care; he could not entirely trust the earth to support him. His features were refined, but worn; subtly distorted, as if seen through wavy glass, or water.

Sybil didn't like it that she couldn't see the man's eyes. Except to know that he was squinting at her, hard. The skin at the corners of his eyes was whitely puckered as if, in his time, he'd done a good deal of squinting and smiling.

Quickly, but politely, Sybil murmured, "No, thank you, I can't."

She was turning away, but still the man spoke, apologetically, "I realize this is a—surprise, but, you see, I don't know how else to make inquiries. I've only just begun sketching in the park, and—"

"Sorry!"

Sybil turned, began to run, not hurriedly, by no means in a panic, but at her usual measured pace, her head up and her arms swinging at her sides. She was, for all that she looked younger than her seventeen years, not an easily frightened girl, and she was not frightened now; but her face burned with embarrassment. She hoped that no one in the park who knew her had been watching—Glencoe was a small town, and the high school was about a mile away. Why had that preposterous man approached *her*!

He was calling after her, probably waving his cane after her—she didn't dare look back. "I'll be here tomorrow! My name is Starr! Don't judge me too quickly—please! I'm true to my word! My name is Starr! I'll pay you, per hour—" and here he cited an exorbitant sum, nearly twice what Sybil made babysitting or working as a librarian's assistant at the branch library near her home, when she could get hired.

She thought, astonished, "He must be mad!"

2. The Temptation

No sooner had Sybil Blake escaped from the man who called himself Starr, running up Buena Vista Boulevard to Santa Clara, up Santa Clara to Meridian, and so to home, than she began to

consider that Mr. Starr's offer was, if preposterous, very tempting. She had never modeled of course but, in art class at the high
school, some of her classmates had modeled, fully clothed, just
sitting or standing about in ordinary poses, and she and others
had sketched them, or tried to—it was really not so easy as it
might seem, sketching the lineaments of the human figure; it was
still more difficult, sketching an individual's face. But modeling,
in itself, was effortless, once you overcame the embarrassment
of being stared at. It was, you might argue, a morally neutral
activity.

What had Mr. Starr said—*Only here, in the park. In full daylight. I'm true to my word!*

And Sybil needed money, for she was saving for college; she
was hoping, too, to attend a summer music institute at U.C.
Santa Barbara. (She was a voice student, and she'd been encouraged by her choir director at the high school to get good professional training.) Her Aunt Lora Dell Blake, with whom she
lived, and had lived since the age of two years eight months, was
willing to pay her way—was determined to pay her way—but
Sybil felt uneasy about accepting money from Aunt Lora, who
worked as a physical therapist at a medical facility in Glencoe,
and whose salary, at the top of the pay structure available to her
as a state employee, was still modest by California standards.
Sybil reasoned that her Aunt Lora Dell could not be expected
to support her forever.

A long time ago, Sybil had lost her parents, both of them
together, in one single cataclysmic hour, when she'd been too
young to comprehend what Death was, or was said to be. They
had died in a boating accident on Lake Champlain, Sybil's
mother at the age of twenty-six, Sybil's father at the age of

thirty-one, very attractive young people, a "popular couple" as Aunt Lora spoke of them, choosing her words with care, and saying very little more. *For why ask*, Aunt Lora seemed to be warning Sybil—*you will only make yourself cry*. As soon as she could manage the move, and as soon as Sybil was placed permanently in her care, Aunt Lora had come to California, to this sun-washed coastal town midway between Santa Monica and Santa Barbara. Glencoe was less conspicuously affluent than either of these towns, but, with its palm-lined streets, its sunny placidity, and its openness to the ocean, it was the very antithesis, as Aunt Lora said, of Wellington, Vermont, where the Blakes had lived for generations. (After their move to California, Lora Dell Blake had formally adopted Sybil as her child: thus Sybil's name was "Blake," as her mother's had been. If asked what her father's name had been, Sybil would have had to think before recalling, dimly, "Conte.") Aunt Lora spoke so negatively of New England in general and Vermont in particular, Sybil felt no nostalgia for it; she had no sentimental desire to visit her birthplace, nor even to see her parents' graves. From Aunt Lora's stories, Sybil had the idea that Vermont was damp and cold twelve months of the year, and frigidly, impossibly cold in winter; its wooded mountains were unlike the beautiful snow-capped mountains of the West, and cast shadows upon its small, cramped, depopulated and impoverished old towns. Aunt Lora, a transplanted New Englander, was vehement in her praise of California—"With the Pacific Ocean to the west," she said, "it's like a room with one wall missing. Your instinct is to look out, not back; and it's a good instinct."

Lora Dell Blake was the sort of person who delivered statements with an air of inviting contradiction. But, tall, rangy, restless, belligerent, she was not the sort of person most people wanted to contradict.

Indeed, Aunt Lora had never encouraged Sybil to ask questions about her dead parents, or about the tragic accident that had killed them; if she had photographs, snapshots, mementos of life back in Wellington, Vermont, they were safely hidden away, and Sybil had not seen them. "It would just be too painful," she told Sybil, "—for us both." The remark was both a plea and a warning.

Of course, Sybil avoided the subject.

She prepared carefully chosen words, should anyone happen to ask her why she was living with her aunt, and not her parents; or, at least, one of her parents. But—this was Southern California, and very few of Sybil's classmates were living with the set of parents with whom they'd begun. No one asked.

An orphan?—I'm not an orphan, Sybil would say. I was never an orphan because my Aunt Lora was always there.

I was two years old when it happened, the accident.

No, I don't remember.

But no one asked.

Sybil told her Aunt Lora nothing about the man in the park—the man who called himself Starr—she'd put him out of her mind entirely and yet, in bed that night, drifting into sleep, she found herself thinking suddenly of him, and seeing him again, vividly. That silver hair, those gleaming black shoes. His eyes hidden behind dark glasses. How tempting, his offer!—though there was no question of Sybil accepting it. Absolutely not.

Still, Mr. Starr seemed harmless. Well-intentioned. An eccentric, of course, but *interesting*. She supposed he had money, if he could offer her so much to model for him. There was something *not contemporary* about him. The set of his head and shoulders. That air about him of gentlemanly reserve, courtesy—even as he'd made his outlandish request. In Glencoe, in the past several years, there had been a visible increase in homeless persons and derelicts, especially in the oceanside park, but Mr. Starr was certainly not one of these.

Then Sybil realized, as if a door, hitherto locked, had swung open of its own accord, that she'd seen Mr. Starr before . . . somewhere. In the park, where she ran most afternoons for an hour? In downtown Glencoe? On the street?—in the public library? In the vicinity of Glencoe Senior High School?—in the school itself, in the auditorium? Sybil summoned up a memory as if by an act of physical exertion: the school choir, of which she was a member, had been rehearsing Handel's "Messiah" the previous month for their annual Christmas pageant, and Sybil had sung her solo part, a demanding part for contralto voice, and the choir director had praised her in front of the others . . . and she'd seemed to see, dimly, a man, a stranger, seated at the very rear of the auditorium, his features indistinct but his gray hair striking, and wasn't this man miming applause, clapping silently? *There, at the rear, on the aisle.* It frequently happened that visitors dropped by rehearsals—parents or relatives of choir members, colleagues of the music director. So no one took special notice of the stranger sitting unobtrusively at the rear of the auditorium. He wore dark, conservative clothes of the kind to attract no attention, and dark glasses hid his eyes. But there he was. *For Sybil Blake. He'd come for Sybil.* But at the time, Sybil had not seen.

Nor had she seen the man leave. Slipping quietly out of his seat, walking with a just perceptible limp, leaning on his cane.

3. The Proposition

Sybil had no intention of seeking out Mr. Starr, nor even of looking around for him, but the following afternoon, as she was headed home after her run, there, suddenly, the man was—taller than she recalled, looming large, his dark glasses winking in the sunlight, and his pale lips stretched in a tentative smile. He wore his clothes of the previous day except he'd set on his head a sporty plaid golfing cap that gave him a rakish yet wistful air, and he'd tied, as if in haste, a rumpled cream-colored silk scarf around his neck. He was standing on the path in approximately the same place as before, and leaning on his cane; on a bench close by were what appeared to be his art supplies, in a canvas duffel bag of the sort students carried. "Why, hello!" he said, shyly but eagerly, "—I didn't dare hope you would come back, but—" his smile widened as if on the verge of desperation, the puckered skin at the corners of his eyes tightened, "—I *hoped.*"

After running, Sybil always felt good: strength flowed into her legs, arms, lungs. She was a delicate-boned girl, since infancy prone to respiratory infections, but such vigorous exercise had made her strong in recent years; and with physical confidence had come a growing confidence in herself. She laughed, lightly, at this strange man's words, and merely shrugged, and said, "Well—this *is* my park, after all." Mr. Starr nodded eagerly, as if any response from her, any words at all, were of enormous interest. "Yes, yes," he said, "—I can see that. Do you live close by?"

Sybil shrugged. It was none of his business, was it, where she lived? "Maybe," she said.

"And your—name?" He stared at her, hopefully, adjusting his glasses more firmly on his nose. "—My name is Starr."

"My name is—Blake."

Mr. Starr blinked, and smiled, as if uncertain whether this might be a joke. "'Blake'—? An unusual name for a girl," he said.

Sybil laughed again, feeling her face heat. She decided not to correct the misunderstanding.

Today, prepared for the encounter, having anticipated it for hours, Sybil was distinctly less uneasy than she'd been the day before: the man had a business proposition to make to her, that was all. And the park *was* an open, public, safe place, as familiar to her as the small neat yard of her Aunt Lora's house.

So, when Mr. Starr repeated his offer, Sybil said, yes, she was interested after all; she did need money, she was saving for college. "For college?—really? So young?" Mr. Starr said, with an air of surprise. Sybil shrugged, as if the remark didn't require any reply. "I suppose, here in California, young people grow up quickly," Mr. Starr said. He'd gone to get his sketch pad, to show Sybil his work, and Sybil turned the pages with polite interest, as Mr. Starr chattered. He was, he said, an "amateur artist"—the very epitome of the "amateur"—with no delusions regarding his talent, but a strong belief that the world is redeemed by art— "And the world, you know, being profane, and steeped in wickedness, requires constant, ceaseless redemption." He believed that the artist "bears witness" to this fact; and that art can be a "conduit of emotion" where the heart is empty. Sybil, leafing through the sketches, paid little attention to Mr. Starr's tumble of words; she was struck by the feathery, uncertain, somehow *worshipful* detail in the drawings, which, to her eye, were not so bad as she'd expected, though by no means of professional quality. As she looked at them, Mr. Starr came to look over her shoulder, embarrassed, and excited, his shadow falling over the

pages. The ocean, the waves, the wide rippled beach as seen from
the bluff—palm trees, hibiscus, flowers—a World War II memo-
rial in the park—mothers with young children—solitary figures
huddled on park benches—cyclists—joggers—several pages of
joggers: Mr. Starr's work was ordinary, even commonplace, but
certainly earnest. Sybil saw herself amid the joggers, or a figure
she guessed must be herself, a young girl with shoulder-length
dark hair held off her face by a headband, in jeans and a sweatshirt, caught in midstride, legs and swinging arms caught in
motion—it *was* herself, but so clumsily executed, the profile
so smudged, no one would have known. Still, Sybil felt her
face grow warmer, and she sensed Mr. Starr's anticipation like
a withheld breath.

Sybil did not think it quite right for her, aged seventeen,
to pass judgment on the talent of a middle-aged man, so she
merely murmured something vague and polite and positive; and
Mr. Starr, taking the sketch pad from her, said, "Oh, I *know*—I'm
not very good, yet. But I propose to try." He smiled at her, and
took out a freshly laundered white handkerchief, and dabbed
at his forehead, and said, "Do you have any questions about
posing for me or shall we begin? We'll have at least three hours
of daylight, today."

"Three hours!" Sybil exclaimed. "That long?"

"If you get uncomfortable," Mr. Starr said quickly, "—we'll
simply stop, wherever we are." Seeing that Sybil was frowning, he added, eagerly, "We'll take breaks every now and then,
I promise. And, and—" seeing that Sybil was still indecisive,
"—I'll pay you for a full hour's fee, for any part of an hour."
Still Sybil stood, wondering if, after all, she should be agreeing
to this, without her Aunt Lora, or anyone, knowing: wasn't

there something just faintly odd about Mr. Starr, and about his willingness to pay her so much for doing so little? And wasn't there something troubling (however flattering) about his particular interest in her? Assuming Sybil was correct, and he'd been watching her . . . aware of her . . . for at least a month. "I'll be happy to pay you in advance, Blake."

The name "Blake" sounded very odd, in this stranger's mouth, Sybil had never before been called by her last name only.

Sybil laughed nervously, and said, "You don't have to pay me in advance—thanks!"

So Sybil Blake, against her better judgment, became a model, for Mr. Starr.

And, despite her self-consciousness, and her intermittent sense that there was something ludicrous in the enterprise, as about Mr. Starr's intense, fussy, self-important manner as he sketched her (he was a perfectionist, or wanted to give that impression: crumpling a half-dozen sheets of paper, breaking out new charcoal sticks, before he began a sketch that pleased him), the initial session was easy, effortless. "What I want to capture," Mr. Starr said, "—is, beyond your beautiful profile, Blake—and you *are* a beautiful child!—the brooding quality of the ocean. That look to it, d'you see?—of it having consciousness of a kind, actually thinking. Yes, *brooding*!"

Sybil, squinting down at the white-capped waves, the rhythmic crashing surf, the occasional surfers riding their boards with their remarkable amphibian dexterity, thought that the ocean was anything but *brooding*.

"Why are you smiling, Blake?" Mr. Starr asked, pausing. "Is something funny?—am *I* funny?"

Quickly Sybil said, "Oh, no, Mr. Starr, of course not."

"But I *am*, I'm sure," he said happily. "And if you find me so, please *do* laugh!"

Sybil found herself laughing, as if rough fingers were tickling her. She thought of how it might have been . . . had she had a father, and a mother: her own family, as she'd been meant to have.

Mr. Starr was squatting now on the grass close by, and peering up at Sybil with an expression of extreme concentration. The charcoal stick in his fingers moved rapidly. "The ability to *laugh*," he said, "is the ability to *live*—the two are synonymous. You're too young to understand that right now, but one day you will." Sybil shrugged, wiping at her eyes. Mr. Starr was talking grandly. "The world is fallen and profane—the opposite of 'sacred,' you know, *is* 'profane.' It requires ceaseless vigilance—ceaseless redemption. The artist is one who redeems by restoring the world's innocence, where he can. The artist gives, but does not take away, nor even supplant."

Sybil said, skeptically, "But you want to make money with your drawings, don't you?"

Mr. Starr seemed genuinely shocked. "Oh, my, no. Adamantly, *no*."

Sybil persisted, "Well, most people would. I mean, most people need to. If they have any talent—" she was speaking with surprising bluntness, an almost childlike audacity, "—they need to sell it, somehow."

As if he'd been caught out in a crime, Mr. Starr began to stammer apologetically, "It's true, Blake, I—I am not like most people, I suppose. I've inherited some money—not a fortune, but enough to live on comfortably for the rest of my life. I've been traveling abroad," he said, vaguely, "—and, in my absence, interest accumulated."

Sybil asked doubtfully, "You don't have any regular profession?"

Mr. Starr laughed, startled. Up close, his teeth were chunky and irregular, slightly stained, like aged ivory piano keys. "But dear child," he said, "*this* is my profession—'redeeming the world'!"

And he fell to sketching Sybil with renewed enthusiasm.

Minutes passed. Long minutes. Sybil felt a mild ache between her shoulder blades. A mild uneasiness in her chest. *Mr. Starr is mad. Is Mr. Starr 'mad'?* Behind her, on the path, people were passing by, there were joggers, cyclists—Mr. Starr, lost in a trance of concentration, paid them not the slightest heed. Sybil wondered if anyone knew her, and was taking note of this peculiar event. Or was she, herself, making too much of it? She decided she would tell her Aunt Lora about Mr. Starr that evening, tell Aunt Lora frankly how much he was paying her. She both respected and feared her aunt's judgment: in Sybil's imagination, in that unexamined sphere of being we call the imagination, Lora Dell Blake had acquired the authority of both Sybil's deceased parents.

Yes, she would tell Aunt Lora.

After only an hour and forty minutes, when Sybil appeared to be growing restless, and sighed several times, unconsciously, Mr. Starr suddenly declared the session over. He had, he said, three promising sketches, and he didn't want to exhaust her, or himself. She *was* coming back tomorrow—?

"I don't know," Sybil said. "Maybe."

Sybil protested, though not very adamantly, when Mr. Starr paid her the full amount, for three hours' modeling. He paid her in cash, out of his wallet—an expensive kidskin wallet brimming with bills. Sybil thanked him, deeply embarrassed, and eager to escape. Oh, there *was* something shameful about the transaction!

Up close, she was able—almost—to see Mr. Starr's eyes through the dark-tinted lenses of his glasses. Some delicacy of tact made her glance away quickly but she had an impression of kindness—gentleness.

Sybil took the money, and put it in her pocket, and turned, to hurry away. With no mind for who might hear him, Mr. Starr called after her, "You see, Blake?—Starr is true to his word. Always!"

4. Is the Omission of Truth a Lie, or Only an Omission?

"Well, tell me how things went with *you*, today—Sybil!" Lora Dell Blake said, with such an air of bemused exasperation, Sybil understood that, as so often, Aunt Lora had something to say that really couldn't wait—her work at the Glencoe Medical Center provided her with a seemingly inexhaustible supply of comical and outrageous anecdotes. So, deferring to Aunt Lora, as they prepared supper together as usual, and sat down to eat it, Sybil was content to listen, and to laugh.

For it *was* funny, if outrageous too—the latest episode in the ongoing folly at the Medical Center.

Lora Dell Blake, in her late forties, was a tall, lanky, restless woman; with close-cropped graying hair; sand-colored eyes, and skin; a generous spirit, but a habit of sarcasm. Though she claimed to love Southern California—"You don't know what paradise *is* unless you're from somewhere else"—she seemed in fact an awkwardly transplanted New Englander, with expectations and a sense of personal integrity, or intransigence, quite out of place here. She was fond of saying she did not suffer fools gladly, and so it was. Overqualified for her position at the Glencoe Medical Center, she'd had no luck in finding work elsewhere, partly because she did not want to leave Glencoe, and "uproot" Sybil while she was still in high school; and partly because her interviews were invariably disasters—Lora Dell Blake was incapable of being, or even seeming, docile, tractable, "feminine," hypocritical.

Lora was not Sybil's sole living relative—there were Blakes, and Contes, back in Vermont—but Lora had discouraged visitors to the small stucco bungalow on Meridian Street, in Glencoe, California; she had not in fact troubled to reply to letters or cards since, having been granted custody of her younger sister's daughter, at the time of what she called "the tragedy," she'd picked up and moved across the continent, to a part of the country she knew nothing about—"My intention is to erase the past, for the child's sake," she said, "and to start a new life."

And: "For the child, for poor little Sybil—I would make any sacrifice."

Sybil, who loved her aunt very much, had the vague idea that there had been, many years ago, protests, queries, telephone calls—but that Aunt Lora had dealt with them all, and really had made a new and "uncomplicated" life for them. Aunt Lora was one of those personalities, already strong, that is strengthened, and empowered, by being challenged; she seemed to take an actual zest in confrontation, whether with her own relatives or her employers at the Medical Center—anyone who presumed to tell her what to do. She was especially protective of Sybil, since, as she often said, they had no one but each other.

Which was true. Aunt Lora had seen to that.

Though Sybil had been adopted by her aunt, there was never any pretense that she was anything but Lora's niece, not her daughter. Nor did most people, seeing the two together, noting their physical dissimilarities, make that mistake.

So it happened that Sybil Blake grew up knowing virtually nothing about her Vermont background except its general tragic outline: her knowledge of her mother and father, the precise circumstances of their deaths, was as vague and unexamined in her consciousness as a childhood fairy tale. For whenever, as a little girl, Sybil would ask her aunt about these things, Aunt Lora responded with hurt, or alarm, or reproach, or, most disturbingly, anxiety. Her eyes might flood with tears—Aunt Lora, who never cried. She might take Sybil's hands in both her own, and squeeze them tightly, and, looking Sybil in the eyes, say, in a quiet, commanding voice, "But, darling, *you don't want to know.*"

So too, that evening, when, for some reason, Sybil brought up the subject, asking Aunt Lora how, again, exactly, *had* her parents died, Aunt Lora looked at her in surprise; and, for a long moment, rummaging in the pockets of her shirt for a pack of cigarettes that wasn't there (Aunt Lora had given up smoking the previous month, for perhaps the fifth time), it seemed almost that Lora herself did not remember.

"Sybil, honey—why are you asking? I mean, why *now?*"

"I don't know," Sybil said evasively. "I guess—I'm just asking."

"Nothing happened to you at school, did it?"

Sybil could not see how this question related to her own, but she said, politely, "No, Aunt Lora. Of course not."

"It's just that, out of nowhere—I can't help but wonder *why*," Aunt Lora said, frowning, "—you should ask."

Aunt Lora regarded Sybil with worried eyes: a look of such suffocating familiarity that, for a moment, Sybil felt as if a band were tightening around her chest, making it impossible to breathe. *Why is my wanting to know a test of my love for you?—why do you do this Aunt Lora, every time?* She said, an edge of anger to her voice, "I was seventeen years old last week, Aunt Lora. I'm not a child any longer."

Aunt Lora laughed, startled. "Certainly you're not a child!"

Aunt Lora then sighed, and, in a characteristic gesture, meaning both impatience and a dutiful desire to please, ran both hands rapidly through her hair, and began to speak. She assured Sybil that there was little to know, really. The accident—the tragedy—had happened so long ago. "Your mother, Melanie, was twenty-six years old at the time—a beautiful sweet-natured young woman, with eyes like yours, cheekbones like yours, pale wavy hair. Your father, George Conte, was thirty-one years old—a promising young lawyer, in his father's firm—an attractive, ambitious man—" And here as in the past Aunt Lora paused, as if, in the very act of summoning up this long-dead couple, she had forgotten them; and was simply repeating a story, a family tale, like one of the more extreme of her tales of the Glencoe Medical Center, worn smooth by countless tellings.

"A boating accident—Fourth of July—" Sybil coaxed, "—and I was with you, and—"

"You were with me, and Grandma, at the cottage—you were just a little girl!" Aunt Lora said, blinking tears from her eyes, "—and it was almost dusk, and time for the fireworks to start. Mommy and Daddy were out in Daddy's speedboat—they'd been across the lake, at the Club—"

"And they started back across the lake—Lake Champlain—"

"—Lake Champlain, of course: it's beautiful, but treacherous, if a storm comes up suddenly—"

"And Daddy was at the controls of the boat—"

"—and, somehow, they capsized. And drowned. A rescue boat went out immediately, but it was too late." Aunt Lora's mouth turned hard. Her eyes glistening with tears, as if defiantly. "They drowned."

Sybil's heart was beating painfully. She was certain there must be more, yet she herself could remember nothing—not even herself, that two-year-old child, waiting for Mommy and Daddy who were never to arrive. Her memory of her mother and father was vague, dim, featureless, like a dream that, even as it seems about to drift into consciousness, retreats further into darkness. She said, in a whisper, "It was an accident. No one was to blame."

Aunt Lora chose her words with care. "No one was to blame."

There was a pause. Sybil looked at her aunt, who was not now looking at her. How lined, even leathery, the older woman's face was getting!—all her life she'd been reckless, indifferent, about sun, wind, weather, and now, in her late forties, she might have been a decade older. Sybil said, tentatively, "*No one* was to blame—?"

"Well, if you must know," Aunt Lora said, "—there was evidence he'd been drinking. They'd been drinking. At the Club."

Sybil could not have been more shocked had Aunt Lora reached over and pinched the back of her hand. "Drinking—?" She had never heard this part of the story before.

Aunt Lora continued, grimly, "But not enough, probably, to have made a difference." Again she paused. She was not looking at Sybil. "Probably."

Sybil, stunned, could not think of anything further to say, or to ask.

Aunt Lora was on her feet, pacing. Her close-cropped hair was disheveled and her manner fiercely contentious, as if she were arguing her case before an invisible audience as Sybil looked on. "What fools! I tried to tell her! 'Popular' couple—'attractive' couple—lots of friends—too many friends! That Goddamned Champlain Club, where everyone drank too much! All that money, and privilege! And what good did it do! She—Melanie— so proud of being asked to join—proud of marrying *him*— throwing her life away! That's what it came to, in the end. I'd warned her it was dangerous—playing with fire—but would she listen? Would either of them listen? To Lora?—to *me*? When you're that age, so ignorant, you think you will live forever—you can throw your life away—"

Sybil felt ill, suddenly. She walked swiftly out of the room, shut the door to her own room, stood in the dark, beginning to cry.

So that was it, the secret. The tawdry little secret—drinking, drunkenness—behind the "tragedy."

With characteristic tact, Aunt Lora did not knock on Sybil's door, but left her alone for the remainder of the night.

Only after Sybil was in bed, and the house darkened, did she realize she'd forgotten to tell her aunt about Mr. Starr—he'd slipped her mind entirely. And the money he'd pressed into her hand, now in her bureau drawer, rolled up neatly beneath her underwear, as if hidden. . . .

Sybil thought, guiltily, I can tell her tomorrow.

5. The Hearse

Crouched in front of Sybil Blake, eagerly sketching her likeness, Mr. Starr was saying, in a quick, rapturous voice, "Yes, yes, like that!—yes! Your face uplifted to the sun like a blossoming flower! Just so!" And: "There are only two or three eternal questions, Blake, which, like the surf, repeat themselves endlessly: 'Why are we here?'—'Where have we come from, and where are we going?'—'Is there purpose to the universe, or merely chance?' These questions the artist seems to express in the images he knows." And: "Dear child, I wish you would tell me about yourself. Just a little!"

As if, in the night, some change had come upon her, some new resolve, Sybil had fewer misgivings about modeling for Mr. Starr, this afternoon. It was as if they knew each other well, somehow: Sybil was reasonably certain that Mr. Starr was not a sexual pervert, nor even a madman of a more conventional sort; she'd glimpsed his sketches of her, which were fussy, overworked, and smudged, but not bad as likenesses. The man's murmurous chatter was comforting in a way, hypnotic as the surf, no longer quite so embarrassing—for he talked, most of the time, not with her but at her, and there was no need to reply. In a way, Mr. Starr reminded Sybil of her Aunt Lora, when she launched

into one of her comical anecdotes about the Glencoe Medical
Center. Aunt Lora was more entertaining than Mr. Starr, but
Mr. Starr was more idealistic.

His optimism was simpleminded, maybe. But it *was* optimistic.

For this second modeling session, Mr. Starr had taken Sybil
to a corner of the park where they were unlikely to be disturbed.
He'd asked her to remove her headband, and to sit on a bench
with her head dropping back, her eyes partly shut, her face uplifted to the sun—an uncomfortable pose at first, until, lulled
by the crashing surf below, and Mr. Starr's monologue, Sybil
began to feel oddly peaceful, floating.

Yes, in the night some change had come upon her. She could
not comprehend its dimensions, nor even its tone. She'd fallen
asleep crying bitterly but had wakened feeling—what? Vulnerable, somehow. And wanting to be so. *Uplifted. Like a blossoming
flower.*

That morning, Sybil had forgotten again to tell her Aunt Lora
about Mr. Starr, and the money she was making—such a generous amount, and for so little effort! She shrank from considering
how her aunt might respond, for her aunt was mistrustful of
strangers, and particularly of men. . . . Sybil reasoned that, when
she did tell Aunt Lora, that evening, or tomorrow morning, she
would make her understand that there was something kindly
and trusting and almost child-like about Mr. Starr. You could
laugh at him, but laughter was somehow inappropriate.

As if, though middle-aged, he had been away somewhere,
sequestered, protected, out of the adult world. Innocent and,
himself, vulnerable.

Today, too, he'd eagerly offered to pay Sybil in advance for
modeling, and, another time, Sybil had declined. She would not

have wanted to tell Mr. Starr that, were she paid in advance, she might be tempted to cut the session even shorter than otherwise.

Mr. Starr was saying, hesitantly, "Blake?—can you tell me about—" and here he paused, as if drawing a random, inspired notion out of nowhere, "—your mother?"

Sybil hadn't been paying close attention to Mr. Starr. Now she opened her eyes, and looked directly at him.

Mr. Starr was perhaps not so old as she'd originally thought, nor as old as he behaved. His face was a handsome face, but oddly roughened—the skin like sandpaper. Very sallow, sickly-pale. A faint scar on his forehead above his left eye, the shape of a fish hook, or a question mark. Or was it a birthmark?—or, even less romantically, some sort of skin blemish? Maybe his roughened, pitted skin was the result of teenage acne, nothing more.

His tentative smile bared chunky damp teeth.

Today Mr. Starr was bareheaded, and his thin, fine, uncannily silver hair was stirred by the wind. He wore plain, nondescript cloches, a shirt too large for him, a khaki-colored jacket with rolled-up sleeves. At close range, Sybil could see his eyes through the tinted lenses of his glasses: they were small, deep-set, intelligent, glistening. The skin beneath was pouched and shadowed, as if bruised.

Sybil shivered, peering so directly into Mr. Starr's eyes. As into another's soul, when she was unprepared.

Sybil swallowed, and said, slowly, "My mother is . . . not living."

A curious way of speaking!—for why not say, candidly, in normal usage, *My mother is dead.*

For a long painful moment Sybil's words hovered in the air between them; as if Mr. Starr, discountenanced by his own blunder, seemed not to want to hear.

He said, quickly, apologetically, "Oh—I see. I'm so sorry."

Sybil had been posing in the sun, warmly mesmerized by the sun, the surf, Mr. Starr's voice, and now, as if wakened from a sleep of which she had not been conscious, she felt as if she'd been touched—prodded into wakefulness. She saw, upside down, the fussy smudged sketch Mr. Starr had been doing of her, saw his charcoal stick poised above the stiff white paper in an attitude of chagrin. She laughed, and wiped at her eyes, and said, "It happened a long time ago. I never think of it, really."

Mr. Starr's expression was wary, complex. He asked, "And so—do you—live with your—father?" The words seemed oddly forced.

"No, I don't. And I don't want to talk about this any more, Mr. Starr, if it's all right with you."

Sybil spoke pleadingly, yet with an air of finality.

"Then—we won't! We won't! We certainly won't!" Mr. Starr said quickly. And fell to sketching again, his face creased in concentration.

And so the remainder of the session passed, in silence.

Again, as soon as Sybil evinced signs of restlessness, Mr. Starr declared she could stop for the day—he didn't want to exhaust her, or himself.

Sybil rubbed her neck, which ached mildly; she stretched her arms, her legs. Her skin felt slightly sun- or wind-burnt and her eyes felt seared, as if she'd been staring directly into the sun. Or had she been crying?—she couldn't remember.

Again, Mr. Starr paid Sybil in cash, out of his kidskin wallet brimming with bills. His hand shook just visibly as he pressed the money into Sybil's. (Embarrassed, Sybil folded the bills quickly and put them in her pocket. Later, at home, she would discover that Mr. Starr had given her ten dollars too much: a bonus, for almost making her cry?) Though it was clear that Sybil was eager to get away, Mr. Starr walked with her up the slope, in the direction of the Boulevard, limping, leaning on his cane, but keeping a brisk pace. He asked if Sybil—of course, he called her Blake: "Dear Blake"—would like to have some refreshment with him, in a café near by?—and, when Sybil declined, murmured, "Yes, yes, I understand—I suppose." He then asked if Sybil would return the following day, and, when Sybil did not say no, added that, if she did, he would like to increase her hourly fee in exchange for asking of her a slightly different sort of modeling—"A slightly modified sort of modeling, here in the park, or perhaps down on the beach, in full daylight of course, as before, and yet, in its way—" Mr. Starr paused nervously, seeking the right word, "—experimental."

Sybil asked doubtfully, "'Experimental'—?"

"I'm prepared to increase your fee, Blake, by half."

"What kind of 'experimental'?"

"Emotion."

"What?"

"Emotion. Memory. Interiority."

Now that they were emerging from the park, and more likely to be seen, Sybil was glancing uneasily about: she dreaded seeing someone from school, or, worse yet, a friend of her aunt's. Mr. Starr gestured as he spoke, and seemed more than ordinarily excited. "—'Interiority.' That which is hidden to the outer eye. I'll tell you in more detail tomorrow, Blake," he said. "You *will* meet me here tomorrow?"

Sybil murmured, "I don't know, Mr. Starr."'

"Oh, but you must!—please."

Sybil felt a tug of sympathy for Mr. Starr. He *was* kind, and courteous, and gentlemanly; and, certainly, very generous. She could not imagine his life except to see him as a lonely, eccentric man without friends. Uncomfortable as she was in his presence, she yet wondered if perhaps she was exaggerating his eccentricity: what would a neutral observer make of the tall, limping figure, the cane, the canvas duffel bag, the polished black leather shoes that remind her of a funeral, the fine, thin, beautiful silver hair, the dark glasses that winked in the sunshine . . . ? Would such an observer, seeing Sybil Blake and Mr. Starr together, give them a second glance?

"Look," Sybil said, pointing, "—a hearse."

At a curb close by there was a long sleekly black car with dark tinted, impenetrable windows. Mr. Starr laughed, and said, embarrassed, "I'm afraid, Blake, that isn't a hearse, you know—it's my car."

"Your car?"

"Yes. I'm afraid so."

Now Sybil could see that the vehicle was a limousine, idling at the curb. Behind the wheel was a youngish driver with a visored cap on his head; in profile, he appeared Oriental. Sybil stared, amazed. So Mr. Starr was wealthy, indeed.

He was saying, apologetically, yet with a kind of boyish pleasure, "I don't drive, myself, you see!—a further handicap. I did, once, long ago, but—circumstances intervened." Sybil was thinking that she often saw chauffeur-driven limousines in Glencoe, but she'd never known anyone who owned one before. Mr. Starr said, "Blake, may I give you a ride home?—I'd be delighted, of course."

Sybil laughed, as if she'd been tickled, hard, in the ribs.

"A ride? In that?" she asked.

"No trouble! Absolutely!" Mr. Starr limped to the rear door and opened it with a flourish, before the driver could get out to open it for him. He squinted back at Sybil, smiling hopefully. "It's the least I can do for you, after our exhausting session."

Sybil was smiling, staring into the shadowy interior of the car. The uniformed driver had climbed out, and stood, not quite knowing what to do, watching. He was a Filipino, perhaps, not young after all but with a small, wizened face; he wore white gloves. He stood very straight and silent, watching Sybil.

There was a moment when it seemed, yes, Sybil was going to accept Mr. Starr's offer, and climb into the rear of the long sleekly black limousine, so that Mr. Starr could climb in behind her, and shut the door upon them both; but, then, for some reason she could not have named—it might have been the smiling intensity with which Mr. Starr was looking at her, or the rigid posture of the white-gloved driver—she changed her mind and called out, "No thanks!"

Mr. Starr was disappointed, and hurt—you could see it in his downturned mouth. But he said, cheerfully, "Oh, I quite understand, Blake—I *am* a stranger, after all. It's better to be prudent, of course. But, my dear, I *will* see you tomorrow—?"

Sybil shouted, "Maybe!" and ran across the street.

6. The Face

She stayed away from the park. *Because I want to, because I can.* Thursday, in any case, was her voice lesson after school. Friday, choir rehearsal; then an evening with friends. On Saturday

morning she went jogging, not in the oceanside park but in
another park, miles away, where Mr. Starr could not have known
to look for her. And, on Sunday, Aunt Lora drove them to Los
Angeles for a belated birthday celebration, for Sybil—an art
exhibit, a dinner, a play.

So, you see, I can do it. I don't need your money, or you.

Since the evening when Aunt Lora had told Sybil about her
parents' boating accident—that it might have been caused by
drinking—neither Sybil nor her aunt had cared to bring up the
subject again. Sybil shuddered to think of it. She felt properly
chastised, for her curiosity.

Why do you want to know?—you will only make yourself cry.

Sybil had never gotten around to telling Aunt Lora about Mr.
Starr, nor about her modeling. Even during their long Sunday
together. Not a word about her cache of money, hidden away
in a bureau drawer.

Money for what?—for summer school, for college.

For the future.

Aunt Lora was not the sort of person to spy on a member of her
household, but she observed Sybil closely, with her trained clini-
cian's eye. "Sybil, you've been very quiet, lately—there's nothing
wrong I hope?" she asked, and Sybil said quickly, nervously, "Oh,
no! What could be wrong?"

She was feeling guilty about keeping a secret from Aunt Lora
and she was feeling guilty about staying away from Mr. Starr.

Two adults. Like twin poles. Of course, Mr. Starr was really
a stranger—he did not exist in Sybil Blake's life, at all. Why did
it feel to her, so strangely, that he did?

Days passed, and, instead of forgetting Mr. Starr, and strength-
ening her resolve not to model for him, Sybil seemed to see the
man, in her mind's eye, ever more clearly. She could not understand why he seemed attracted to her, she was convinced it was
not a sexual attraction but something purer, more spiritual, and
yet—why? Why *her*?

Why had he visited her high school, and sat in on a choir
rehearsal? Had he known she would be there?—or was it simply
coincidence?

She shuddered, to think of what Aunt Lora would make of
this, if she knew. If news of Mr. Starr got back to her.

Mr. Starr's face floated before her. Its pallor, its sorrow. That
look of convalescence. Waiting. The dark glasses. The hopeful
smile. One night, waking from a particularly vivid, disturbing
dream, Sybil thought for a confused moment that she'd seen Mr.
Starr, in the room—it hadn't been just a dream! How wounded
he'd looked, puzzled, hurt. *Come with me, Sybil. Hurry. Now.
It's been so long.* He'd been waiting for her in the park for days,
limping, the duffel bag slung over his shoulder, glancing up
hopefully at every passing stranger.

Behind him, the elegantly gleaming black limousine, larger
than Sybil remembered; and driverless.

Sybil?—Sybil? Mr. Starr called, impatiently.

As if, all along, he'd known her real name. And she had known
he'd known.

7. The Experiment

So, Monday afternoon, Sybil Blake found herself back in the
park, modeling for Mr. Starr.

Seeing him in the park, so obviously awaiting her, Sybil had felt almost apologetic. Not that he greeted her with any measure of reproach (though his face was drawn and sallow, as if he hadn't been sleeping well), nor even questioned her mutely with his eyes *Where have you been?* Certainly not! He smiled happily when he saw her, limping in her direction like a doting father, seemingly determined not to acknowledge her absence of the past four days. Sybil called out, "Hello, Mr. Starr!" and felt, yes, so strangely, as if things were once again right.

"How lovely!—and the day is so fine!—'in full daylight'—as I promised!" Mr. Starr cried.

Sybil had been jogging for forty minutes, and felt very good, strengthened. She removed her damp yellow headband and stuffed it in her pocket. When Mr. Starr repeated the terms of his proposition of the previous week, restating the higher fee, Sybil agreed at once, for of course that was why she'd come. How, in all reasonableness, could she resist?

Mr. Starr took some time before deciding upon a place for Sybil to pose—"It must be ideal, a synthesis of poetry and practicality." Finally, he chose a partly crumbling stone ledge overlooking the beach in a remote corner of the park. He asked Sybil to lean against the ledge, gazing out at the ocean. Her hands pressed flat against the top of the ledge, her head uplifted as much as possible, within comfort. "But today, dear Blake, I am going to record not just the surface likeness of a lovely young girl," he said, "—but *memory*, and *emotion*, coursing through her."

Sybil took the position readily enough. So invigorated did she feel from her exercise, and so happy to be back, again, in her role as model, she smiled out at the ocean as at an old friend. "What kind of memory and emotion, Mr. Starr?" she asked.

Mr. Starr eagerly took up his sketch pad and a fresh stick of charcoal. It was a mild day, the sky placid and featureless, though, up the coast, in the direction of Big Sur, massive thunderclouds were gathering. The surf was high, the waves powerful, hypnotic. One hundred yards below, young men in surfing gear, carrying their boards lightly as if they were made of papier-mâché, prepared to enter the water.

Mr. Starr cleared his throat, and said, almost shyly, "Your mother, dear Blake. Tell me all you know—all you can remember—about your mother."

"My mother?"

Sybil winced and would have broken her position, except Mr. Starr put out a quick hand, to steady her. It was the first time he had touched her in quite that way. He said, gently, "I realize it's a painful subject, Blake, but—will you try?"

Sybil said, "No. I don't want to."

"You won't, then?"

"I *can't.*"

"But why can't you, dear?—any memory of your mother would do."

"*No.*"

Sybil saw that as Mr. Starr was quickly sketching her, or trying to—his hand shook. She wanted to reach out to snatch the charcoal stick from him and snap it in two. How dare he! Goddamn him!

"Yes, yes," Mr. Starr said hurriedly, an odd, elated look on his face, as if, studying her so intently, he was not seeing her at all, "—yes, dear, like that. Any memory—any! So long as it's yours."

Sybil said, "Whose else would it be?" She laughed, and was surprised that her laughter sounded like sobbing.

"Why, many times innocent children are given memories by adults; contaminated by memories not their own," Mr. Starr said somberly. "In which case the memory is spurious. Inauthentic."

Sybil saw her likeness on the sheet of stiff white paper, upside down. There was something repulsive about it. Though she was wearing her usual jogging clothes Mr. Starr made it look as if she were wearing a clinging, flowing gown; or, maybe, nothing at all. Where her small breasts would have been were swirls and smudges of charcoal, as if she were on the brink of dissolution. Her face and head were vividly drawn, but rather raw, crude, and exposed.

She saw too that Mr. Starr's silver hair had a flat metallic sheen this afternoon; and his beard was faintly visible, metallic too, glinting on his jaws. He was stronger than she'd thought. He had knowledge far beyond hers.

Sybil resumed her position. She stared out at the ocean—the tall, cresting, splendidly white-capped waves. Why was she here, what did this man want of her? She worried suddenly that, whatever it was, she could not provide it.

But Mr. Starr was saying, in his gentle, murmurous voice, "There are people, primarily women!—who are what I call 'conduits of emotion.' In their company, the half-dead can come alive. They need not be beautiful women or girls. It's a matter of blood-warmth. The integrity of the spirit." He turned the page of his sketch pad, and began anew, whistling thinly through his teeth. "Thus an icy-cold soul, in the presence of one so blessed, can regain something of his lost self. Sometimes!"

Sybil tried to summon forth a memory, an image at least, of her mother. *Melanie. Twenty-six at the time. Eyes . . . cheekbones . . . pale wavy hair.* A ghostly face appeared but faded

almost at once. Sybil sobbed involuntarily. Her eyes stung
with tears.

"—sensed that you dear Blake—*is* your name Blake, really?—
are one of these. A 'conduit of emotion'—of finer, higher things.
Yes, yes! My intuition rarely misguides me!" Mr. Starr spoke as,
hurriedly, excitedly, he sketched Sybil's likeness. He was squatting close beside her, on his haunches; his dark glasses winked
in the sun. Sybil knew, should she glance at him, she would not
be able to see his eyes.

Mr. Starr said, coaxingly, "Don't you remember anything—at
all—about your mother?"

Sybil shook her head, meaning she didn't want to speak.

"Her name. Surely you know her name?"

Sybil whispered, "Mommy."

"Ah, yes: 'Mommy.' To you, that would have been her name."

"Mommy—went away. They told me—"

"Yes? Please continue!"

"—Mommy was gone. And Daddy. On the lake—"

"Lake? Where?"

"Lake Champlain. In Vermont, and New York. Aunt Lora
says—"

"'Aunt Lora'—?"

"Mommy's sister. She was older. Is older. She took me away.
She adopted me. She—"

"And is 'Aunt Lora' married?"

"No. There's just her and me."

"What happened on the lake?"

"—it happened in the boat, on the lake. Daddy was driving the
boat, they said. He came for me too but—I don't know if that was
that time or some other time. I've been told, but I don't *know*."

Tears were streaming down Sybil's face now; she could not maintain her composure. But she managed to keep from hiding her face in her hands. She could hear Mr. Starr's quickened breath, and she could hear the rasping sound of the charcoal against the paper.

Mr. Starr said gently, "You must have been a little girl when—whatever it was—happened."

"I wasn't little to *myself*. I just *was*."

"A long time ago, was it?"

"Yes. No. It's always—there."

"Always where, dear child?"

"Where I, I—see it."

"See what?"

"I—don't *know*."

"Do you see your mommy? Was she a beautiful woman?—did she resemble you?"

"Leave me alone—I don't *know*."

Sybil began to cry. Mr. Starr, repentant, or wary, went immediately silent.

Someone—it must have been cyclists—passed behind them, and Sybil was aware of being observed, no doubt quizzically: a girl leaning forward across a stone ledge, face wet with tears, and a middle-aged man on his haunches busily sketching her. An artist and his model. An amateur artist, an amateur model. But how strange, that the girl was crying! And the man so avidly recording her tears!

Sybil, eyes closed, felt herself indeed a conduit of emotion—she *was* emotion. She stood upon the ground but she floated free. Mr. Starr was close beside her, anchoring her, but she floated free. A veil was drawn aside, and she saw a face—Mommy's face—a pretty heart-shaped face—something both affectionate and petulant in that face—how young Mommy was!—and her hair up, brown-blond lovely hair, tied back in a green silk scarf. Mommy hurried to the phone as it rang, Mommy lifted the receiver, Yes? yes? Oh hel*lo*—for the phone was always ringing, and Mommy was always hurrying to answer it, and there was always that expectant note to her voice, that sound of hope, surprise—oh, hel*lo*.

Sybil could no longer maintain her pose. She said, "Mr. Starr, I am through for the day, I am *sorry*." And, as the startled man looked after her, she walked away. He began to call after her, to remind her that he hadn't paid her, but, no, Sybil had had enough of modeling for the day. She broke into a run, she escaped.

8. A Long Time Ago . . .

A girl who'd married too young: was that it?

That heart-shaped face, the petulant pursed lips. The eyes widened in mock-surprise: Oh, Sybil what have you *done* . . . ?

Stooping to kiss little Sybil, little Sybil giggling with pleasure and excitement, lifting her chubby baby arms to be raised in Mommy's and carried in to bed.

Oh honey, you're too big for that now. Too heavy!

Perfume wafting from her hair, loose to her shoulders, pale golden-brown, wavy. A rope of pearls around her neck. A low-cut summer dress, a bright floral print, like wallpaper. Mommy!

And Daddy, where *was* Daddy?

He was gone, then he was back. He'd come for her, little Sybil, to take her in the boat, the motor was loud, whining, angry as a bee buzzing and darting around your head, so Sybil was crying, and someone came, and Daddy went away again. She'd heard the motor rising, then fading. The churning of the water she couldn't see from where she stood, and it was night too, but she wasn't crying and no one scolded.

She could remember Mommy's face, though they never let her see it again. She couldn't remember Daddy's face.

Grandma said, You'll be all right, poor little darling you'll be all right, and Aunt Lora too, hugging her tight. Forever now you'll be all right, Aunt Lora promised. It was scary to see Aunt Lora crying: Aunt Lora never cried, did she?

Lifting little Sybil in her strong arms to carry her in to bed but it wasn't the same. It would never be the same again.

9. The Gift

Sybil is standing at the edge of the ocean.

The surf crashes and pounds about her . . . water streams up the sand, nearly wetting her feet. What a tumult of cries, hidden within the waves! She feels like laughing, for no reason. *You know the reason: he has returned to you.*

The beach is wide, clean, stark, as if swept with a giant broom. A landscape of dream-like simplicity. Sybil has seen it numberless times but today its beauty strikes her as new. *Your father: your father they told you was gone forever: he has returned to you.* The sun is a winter sun, but warm, dazzling. Poised in the sky as if about to rapidly descend. Dark comes early because, after all, it is winter here, despite the warmth. The temperature will drop twenty degrees in a half hour. *He never died: he has been waiting for you all these years. And now he has returned.*

Sybil begins to cry. Hiding her face, her burning face, in her hands. She stands flat-footed as a little girl and the surf breaks and splashes around her and now her shoes are wet, her feet, she'll be shivering in the gathering chill. *Oh, Sybil!*

When Sybil turned, it was to see Mr. Starr sitting on the beach. He seemed to have lost his balance and fallen—his cane lay at his feet, he'd dropped the sketch pad, his sporty golfing cap sat crooked on his head. Sybil, concerned, asked what was wrong—she prayed he hadn't had a heart attack!—and Mr. Starr smiled weakly and told her quickly that he didn't know, he'd become dizzy, felt the strength go out of his legs, and had had to sit. "I was overcome suddenly, I think, by your emotion!—whatever it was," he said. He made no effort to get to his feet but sat there awkwardly, damp sand on his trousers and shoes. Now Sybil stood over him and he squinted up at her, and there passed between them a current of—was it understanding? sympathy? recognition?

Sybil laughed to dispel the moment and put out her hand for Mr. Starr to take, so that she could help him stand. He laughed too, though he was deeply moved, and embarrassed. "I'm afraid I make too much of things, don't I?" he said. Sybil tugged at his hand (how big his hand was! how strong the fingers, closing about hers!) and as he heaved himself to his feet, grunting, she felt the startling weight of him—an adult man, and heavy.

Mr. Starr was standing close to Sybil, not yet relinquishing her hand. He said, "The experiment was almost too successful, from my perspective! I'm almost afraid to try it again."

Sybil smiled uncertainly up at him. He was about the age her own father would have been—wasn't he? It seemed to her that a younger face was pushing out through Mr. Starr's coarse, sallow face. The hook-like quizzical scar on his forehead glistened oddly in the sun.

Sybil politely withdrew her hand from Mr. Starr's, and dropped her eyes. She was shivering—today, she had not been running at all, had come to meet Mr. Starr for purposes of modeling, in a blouse and skirt, as he'd requested. She was bare-legged and her feet, in sandals, were wet from the surf.

Sybil said, softly, as if she didn't want to be heard, "I feel the same way, Mr. Starr."

They climbed a flight of wooden steps to the top of the bluff, and there was Mr. Starr's limousine, blackly gleaming, parked a short distance away. At this hour of the afternoon the park was well populated; there was a gay giggling bevy of high school girls strolling by, but Sybil took no notice. She was agitated, still; weak from crying, yet oddly strengthened, elated too. *You know who he is. You always knew.* She was keenly aware of Mr. Starr limping beside her, and impatient with his chatter. Why didn't he speak directly to her, for once?

The uniformed chauffeur sat behind the wheel of the limousine, looking neither to the right nor the left, as if at attention. His visored cap, his white gloves. His profile like a profile on an ancient coin. Sybil wondered if the chauffeur knew about her—if Mr. Starr talked to him about her. Suddenly she was filled with excitement, that someone else should *know*.

Mr. Starr was saying that, since Sybil had modeled so patiently that day, since she'd more than fulfilled his expectations, he had a gift for her—"In addition to your fee, that is."

He opened the rear door of the limousine, and took out a square white box, and, smiling shyly, presented it to Sybil. "Oh,

what *is* it?" Sybil cried. She and Aunt Lora rarely exchanged
presents any longer, it seemed like a ritual out of the deep past,
delightful to rediscover. She lifted the cover of the box, and saw,
inside, a beautiful purse; a shoulder bag; kidskin, the hue of rich
dark honey, "Oh, Mr. Starr—thank you," Sybil said, taking the
bag in her hands. "It's the most beautiful thing I've ever seen."
"Why don't you open it dear?" Mr. Starr urged, so Sybil opened
the bag, and discovered money inside—fresh-minted bills—the
denomination on top was a twenty. "I hope you didn't overpay
me again," Sybil said, uneasily, "—I haven't modeled for three
hours yet. It isn't fair." Mr. Starr laughed, flushed with pleasure.
"Fair to whom?" he asked. "What is 'fair'?—*we* do what *we* like."

Sybil raised her eyes shyly to Mr. Starr's and saw that he was
looking at her intently—at least, the skin at the corners of his
eyes was tightly puckered. "Today, dear, I insist upon driving
you home," he said, smiling. There was a new authority in his
voice that seemed to have something to do with the gift Sybil
had received from him. "It will soon be getting chilly, and your
feet are wet." Sybil hesitated. She had lifted the bag to her face,
to inhale the pungent kidskin smell: the bag was of a quality
she'd never owned before. Mr. Starr glanced swiftly about, as if
to see if anyone was watching; he was still smiling. "Please do
climb inside, Blake!—you can't consider me a stranger, now."

Still, Sybil hesitated. Half teasing, she said, "*You* know my
name isn't Blake, don't you, Mr. Starr?—how do you know?"

Mr. Starr laughed, teasing too, "*Isn't* it? What is your name,
then?"

"Don't you know?"

"Should I know?"

"Shouldn't you?"

There was a pause. Mr. Starr had taken hold of Sybil's wrist; lightly, yet firmly. His fingers circled her thin wrists with the subtle pressure of a watchband.

Mr. Starr leaned close, as if sharing a secret. "Well, I did hear you sing your solo, in your wonderful Christmas pageant at the high school; I must confess, I'd sneaked into a rehearsal too—no one questioned my presence. And I believe I heard the choir director call you—is it 'Sybil'?"

Hearing her name in Mr. Starr's mouth, Sybil felt a sensation of vertigo. She could only nod, mutely, yes.

"*Is* it?—I wasn't sure if I'd heard correctly. A lovely name, for a lovely girl. And 'Blake'—is 'Blake' your surname?"

Sybil murmured, "Yes."

"Your father's name?"

"No. Not my father's name."

"Oh, and why not? Usually, you know, that's the case."

"Because—" And here Sybil paused, confused, uncertain what to say. "It's my mother's name. Was."

"Ah, really! I see." Mr. Starr laughed. "Well, truly, I suppose I *don't*, but we can discuss it another time. Shall we—?"

He meant, shall we get into the car; he was exerting more pressure on Sybil's wrist, and, though kindly as always, seemed on the edge of impatience. His grip was unexpectedly hard. Sybil stood flat-footed on the sidewalk, wanting to acquiesce; yet, at the same time, uneasily thinking that, no, she should not. Not yet.

So Sybil pulled away, laughing nervously, and Mr. Starr had to release her, with a disappointed downturning of his mouth. Sybil thanked him, saying she preferred to walk. "I hope I will see you tomorrow, then?—'Sybil'?" Mr. Starr called after her. "Yes?"

But Sybil, hugging her new bag against her chest, as a small child might hug a stuffed animal, was walking quickly away.

Was the black limousine following her, at a discreet distance?

Sybil felt a powerful compulsion to took back, but did not.

She was trying to recall if, ever in her life, she'd ridden in such a vehicle. She supposed there had been hired, chauffeur-driven limousines at her parents' funerals, but she had not attended those funerals; had no memory of anything connected with them, except the strange behavior of her grandmother, her Aunt Lora, and other adults—their grief, but, underlying that grief, their air of profound and speechless shock.

Where is Mommy, she'd asked, where is Daddy, and the replies were always the same: Gone away.

And crying did no good. And fury did no good, Nothing little Sybil could do, or say, or think did any good. That was the first lesson, maybe.

But Daddy isn't dead, you know he isn't. You know, and he knows, why he has returned.

10. "Possessed"

Aunt Lora was smoking again!—back to two packs a day. And Sybil understood guiltily that she was to blame.

For there was the matter of the kidskin bag. The secret gift. Which Sybil had hidden in the farthest corner of her closet, wrapped in plastic, so the smell of it would not permeate the room. (Still, you could smell it—couldn't you? A subtle pervasive smell, rich as my perfume?) Sybil lived in dread that her aunt would discover the purse, and the money; though Lora

Dell Blake never entered her niece's room without an invitation, somehow, Sybil worried, it *might* happen. She had never kept any important secret from her aunt in her life, and this secret both filled her with a sense of excitement and power, and weakened her, in childish dread.

What most concerned Lora, however, was Sybil's renewed interest in *that*—as in, "Oh, honey, are you thinking about *that* again? *Why?*"

That was the abbreviated euphemism for what Lora might more fully call "the accident"—"the tragedy"—"your parents' deaths."

Sybil, who had never shown more than passing curiosity about that in the past, as far as Lora could remember, was now in the grip of what Lora called "morbid curiosity." That mute, perplexed look in her eyes! That tremulous, sometimes sullen, look to her mouth! One evening, lighting up a cigarette with shaking fingers, Lora said, bluntly, "Sybil, honey, this tears my heart out. What *is* it you want to know?"

Sybil said, as if she'd been waiting for just this question, "Is my father alive?"

"What?"

"My father. George Conte. *Is* he—maybe—alive?"

The question hovered between them, and, for a long, pained moment, it seemed almost that Aunt Lora might snort in exasperation, jump up from the table, walk out of the room. But then she said, shaking her head adamantly, dropping her gaze from Sybil's, "Honey, no. The man is not alive." She paused. She smoked her cigarette, exhaled smoke vigorously through her nostrils; seemed about to say something further; changed her mind; then said, quietly, "You don't ask about your mother, Sybil. Why is that?"

"I—believe that my mother is dead. But—"

"But—?"

"My—my father—"

"—isn't?"

Sybil said, stammering, her cheeks growing hot, "I just want to *know*. I want to see a, a—grave! A death certificate!"

I'll send to Wellington for a copy of the death certificate," Aunt Lora said slowly. "Will that do?"

"You don't have a copy here?"

"Honey, why would I have a copy here?"

Sybil saw that the older woman was regarding her with a look of pity, and something like dread. She said, stammering, her cheeks warm, "In your—your legal things. Your papers. Locked away—"

"Honey, no."

There was a pause. Then Sybil said, half sobbing, "I was too young to go to their funeral. So I never saw. Whatever it was—I never *saw*. Is that it? They say that's the reason for the ritual—for displaying the dead."

Aunt Lora reached over to take Sybil's hand. "It's one of the reasons, honey," she said. "We meet up with it all the time, at the medical center. People don't believe that loved ones are dead—they know, but can't accept it; the shock is just too much to absorb at once. And, yes, it's a theory, that if you don't see a person actually dead—if there isn't a public ceremony to define it—you really have difficulty accepting it. You may—" and here Aunt Lora paused, frowning, "—be susceptible to fantasy."

Fantasy! Sybil stared at her aunt, shocked. *But I've seen him, I know. I believe him and not you!*

The subject seemed to be concluded for the time being. Aunt Lora briskly stubbed out her cigarette, and said, "I'm to blame—probably. I'd been in therapy for a couple of years after it happened and I just didn't want to talk about it any longer, so when you'd asked me questions, over the years, I cut you off; I realize that. But, you see, there's so little to say—Melanie is dead, and *he* is dead. And it all happened a long time ago."

That evening, Sybil was reading in a book on memory she'd taken out of the Glencoe Public Library: *It is known that human beings are "possessed" by an unfathomable number of dormant memory-traces, of which some can be activated under special conditions, including excitation by stimulating points in the cortex. Such traces are indelibly imprinted in the nervous system and are commonly activated by mnemonic stimuli—words, sights, sounds, and especially smells. The phenomenon of déjà vu is closely related to these experiences, in which a "doubling of consciousness" occurs, with the conviction that one has lived an experience before. Much of human memory, however, includes subsequent revision, selection, and fantasizing . . .*

Sybil let the book shut. She contemplated, for the dozenth time, the faint red marks on her wrist, where Mr. Starr—the man who called himself Mr. Starr—had gripped her, without knowing his own strength.

Nor had Sybil been aware, at the time, that his fingers were so strong; and had clasped so tightly around her wrist.

11. "Mr. Starr"—or "Mr. Conte"

She saw him, and saw that he was waiting for her. And her impulse was to run immediately to him, and observe, with childish delight, how the sight of her would illuminate his face. *Here! Here I am!* It was a profound power that seemed to reside in her, Sybil Blake, seventeen years old—the power to have such an effect upon a man whom she scarcely knew, and who did not know her.

Because he loves me. Because he's my father. That's why.

And if he isn't my father—

It was late afternoon of a dull, overcast day. Still, the park was populated at this end: joggers were running, some in colorful costumes. Sybil was not among them, she'd slept poorly the previous night, thinking of—what? Her dead mother who'd been so beautiful?—her father whose face she could not recall (though, yes surely, it was imprinted deep, deep in the cells of her memory)?—her Aunt Lora who was, or was not, telling her the truth, and who loved her more than anyone on earth? And Mr. Starr of course.

Or Mr. Conte.

Sybil was hidden from Mr. Starr's gaze as, with an air of smiling expectancy, he looked about. He was carrying his duffel bag and leaning on his cane. He wore his plain, dark clothes; he was bare-headed, and his silvery hair shone; if Sybil were closer, she would see light winking in his dark glasses. She had noticed the limousine, parked up on the Boulevard a block away.

A young woman jogger ran past Mr. Starr, long-legged, hair flying, and he looked at her, intently—watched her as she ran out of sight along the path. Then he turned back, glancing up toward the street, shifting his shoulders impatiently. Sybil saw him check his wristwatch.

Waiting for you. You know why.

And then, suddenly—Sybil decided not to go to Mr. Starr, after all. The man who called himself Starr. She changed her mind at the last moment, unprepared for her decision except to understand that, as she quickly walked away, that it must be the right decision: her heart was beating erratically, all her senses alert, as if she had narrowly escaped great danger.

12. The Fate of "George Conte"

On Mondays, Wednesdays, and Fridays Lora Dell Blake attended an aerobics class after work, and on these evenings she rarely returned home before seven o'clock. Today was a Wednesday, at four: Sybil calculated she had more than enough time to search out her aunt's private papers, and to put everything back in order, well before her aunt came home.

Aunt Lora's household keys were kept in a top drawer of her desk, and one of these keys, Sybil knew, was to a small aluminum filing cabinet beside the desk, where confidential records and papers were kept. There were perhaps a dozen keys, in a jumble, but Sybil had no difficulty finding the right one. "Aunt Lora, please forgive me," she whispered. It was a measure of her aunt's trust of her that the filing cabinet was so readily unlocked.

For never in her life had Sybil Blake done such a thing, in violation of the trust between herself and her aunt. She sensed that, unlocking the cabinet, opening the sliding drawers, she might be committing an irrevocable act.

The drawer was jammed tight with manila folders, most of them well-worn and dog-eared. Sybil's first response was disappointment—there were hundreds of household receipts, financial statements, Internal Revenue records dating back for years. Then she discovered a packet of letters dating back to the 1950s, when Aunt Lora would have been a young girl. There were a few snapshots, a few formally posed photographs—one of a strikingly beautiful, if immature-looking, girl in a high school graduation cap and gown, smiling at the camera with glossy lips. On the rear was written "Melanie, 1969." Sybil stared at this likeness of her mother—her mother long before she'd become her mother—and felt both triumph and dismay: for, yes, here was the mysterious "Melanie," and, yet, *was* this the "Melanie" the child Sybil knew?—or, simply, a high school girl Sybil's own approximate age, the kind who, judging from her looks and self-absorbed expression, would never have been a friend of Sybil's?

Sybil put the photograph back, with trembling fingers. She was half grateful that Aunt Lora had kept so few mementos of the past—there could be fewer shocks, revelations.

No photographs of the wedding of Melanie Blake and George Conte. Not a one.

No photographs, so far as Sybil could see, of her father "George Conte" at all.

There was a single snapshot of Melanie with her baby daughter Sybil, and this Sybil studied for a long time. It had been taken in summer, at a lakeside cottage; Melanie was posing prettily, in a white dress, with her baby snug in the crook of her arm, and both were looking toward the camera, as if someone had just called out to them, to make them laugh—Melanie with a wide, glamorous, yet sweet smile, little Sybil gaping open-mouthed. Here Melanie looked only slightly more mature than in the graduation photograph: her pale brown hair, many shades of brown and blond; was shoulder-length, and upturned; her eyes were meticulously outlined in mascara, prominent in her heart-shaped face.

In the foreground, on the grass, was the shadow of a man's head and shoulders—"George Conte," perhaps? The missing person.

Sybil stared at this snapshot, which was wrinkled and faded. She did not know what to think, and, oddly, she felt very little: for was the infant in the picture really herself, Sybil Blake, if she could not remember?

Or did she in fact remember, somewhere deep in her brain, in memory-traces that were indelible?

From now on, she would "remember" her mother as the pretty, self-assured young woman in this snapshot. This image, in full color, would replace any other.

Reluctantly, Sybil slid the snapshot back in its packet. How she would have liked to keep it!—but Aunt Lora would discover the theft, eventually. And Aunt Lora must be protected against knowing that her own niece had broken into her things, violated the trust between them.

The folders containing personal material were few, and quickly searched. Nothing pertaining to the accident, the "tragedy"?— not even an obituary? Sybil looked in adjacent files, with increasing desperation. There was not only the question of who her father was, or had been, but the question, nearly as compelling, of why Aunt Lora had eradicated all trace of him, even in her own private files. For a moment Sybil wondered if there had ever been any "George Conte" at all: maybe her mother had not married, and that was part of the secret? Melanie had died in some terrible way, terrible at least in Lora Dell Blake's eyes, thus the very fact must be hidden from Sybil, after so many years? Sybil recalled Aunt Lora saying, earnestly, a few years ago, "The only thing you should know, Sybil, is that your mother—and your father—would not want you to grow up in the shadow of their deaths. They would have wanted you—your mother especially—to be *happy*."

Part of this legacy of happiness, Sybil gathered, had been for her to grow up as a perfectly normal American girl, in a sunny, shadowless place with no history, or, at any rate, no history that concerned her. "But I don't want to be *happy*, I want to *know*," Sybil said aloud.

But the rest of the manila files, jammed so tightly together they were almost inextricable, yielded nothing.

So, disappointed, Sybil shut the file drawer, and locked it.

But what of Aunt Lora's desk drawers? She had a memory of their being unlocked, thus surely containing nothing of significance; but now it occurred to her that, being unlocked, one of these drawers might in fact contain something Aunt Lora might want to keep safely hidden. So, quickly, with not much hope, Sybil looked through these drawers, messy, jammed with papers, clippings, further packets of household receipts, old programs from plays they'd seen in Los Angeles—and, in the largest drawer, at the very bottom, in a wrinkled manila envelope with MEDICAL INSURANCE carefully printed on its front, Sybil found what she was looking for.

Newspaper clippings, badly yellowed, some of them spliced together with aged cellophane tape—

WELLINGTON, VT., MAN SHOOTS WIFE, SELF
SUICIDE ATTEMPT FAILS

AREA MAN KILLS WIFE IN JULY 4 QUARREL
ATTEMPTS SUICIDE ON LAKE CHAMPLAIN

GEORGE CONTE, 31, ARRESTED FOR MURDER
WELLINGTON LAWYER HELD IN SHOOTING DEATH OF WIFE, 26

CONTE TRIAL BEGINS

PROSECUTION CHARGES "PREMEDITATION"

FAMILY MEMBERS TESTIFY

So Sybil Blake learned, in the space of less than sixty seconds, the nature of the tragedy from which her Aunt Lora had shielded her for nearly fifteen years.

Her father was indeed a man named "George Conte," and this man had shot her mother "Melanie" to death, in their speedboat on Lake Champlain, and pushed her body overboard. He had tried to kill himself too but had only critically wounded himself with a shot to the head. He'd undergone emergency neurosurgery, and recovered; he was arrested, tried, and convicted of second-degree murder; and sentenced to between twelve and nineteen years in prison, at the Hartshill State Prison in northern Vermont.

Sybil sifted through the clippings, her fingers numb. So this was it! This! Murder, attempted suicide!—not mere drunkenness and an "accident" on the lake.

Aunt Lora seemed to have stuffed the clippings in an envelop in haste, or in revulsion; with some, photographs had been torn off, leaving only their captions—"Melanie and George Conte, 1975," "Prosecution witness Lora Dell Blake leaving courthouse." Those photographs of George Conte showed a man who surely did resemble "Mr. Starr": younger, dark-haired, with a face heavier in the jaws and an air of youthful self-assurance and expectation. *There. Your father. "Mr. Starr." The missing person.*

There were several photographs, too, of Melanie Conte, including one taken for her high school yearbook, and one of her in a long, formal gown with her hair glamorously upswept—"Wellington woman killed by jealous husband." There was a wedding photograph of the couple looking very young, attractive, and happy; a photograph of the "Conte family at their summer home"; a photograph of "George Conte, lawyer, after second-degree murder verdict"—the convicted man, stunned, downlooking, being taken away handcuffed between two grim sheriff's men. Sybil understood that the terrible thing that had happened in her family had been of enormous public interest in Wellington, Vermont, and that this was part of its terribleness, its shame.

What had Aunt Lora said?—she'd been in therapy for some time afterward, thus did not want to relive those memories.

And she'd said, *It all happened a long time ago.*

But she'd lied, too. She had looked Sybil full in the face and lied, lied. Insisting that Sybil's father was dead when she knew he was alive.

When Sybil herself had reason to believe he was alive.

My name is Starr! Don't judge me too quickly!

Sybil read, and reread, the aged clippings. There were perhaps twenty of them. She gathered two general things: that her father George Conte was from a locally prominent family, and that he'd had a very capable attorney to defend him at his trial; and that the community had greatly enjoyed the scandal, though, no doubt, offering condolences to the grieving Blake family. The spectacle of a beautiful young wife murdered by her "jealous" young husband, her body pushed from an expensive speedboat to sink in Lake Champlain—who could resist? The media had surely exploited this tragedy to its fullest.

Now you see, don't you, why your name had to be changed. Not "Conte," the murderer, but "Blake," the victim, is your parent.

Sybil was filled with a child's rage, a child's inarticulate grief—
Why, why! This man named George Conte had, by a violent
act, ruined everything!

According to the testimony of witnesses, George Conte had
been "irrationally" jealous of his wife's friendship with other
men in their social circle; he'd quarreled publicly with her upon
several occasions, and was known to have a drinking problem.
On the afternoon of July Fourth, the day of the murder, the
couple had been drinking with friends at the Lake Champlain
Club for much of the afternoon, and had then set out in their
boat for their summer home, three miles to the south. Midway,
a quarrel erupted, and George Conte shot his wife several times
with a .32 caliber revolver, which, he later confessed, he'd acquired for the purpose of "showing her I was serious." He then
pushed her body overboard, and continued on to the cottage
where, in a "distraught state," he tried to take his two-year-old
daughter, Sybil, with him, back to the boat—saying that her
mother was waiting for her. But the child's grandmother and
aunt, both relatives of the murdered woman, prevented him
from taking her, so he returned to the boat alone, took it out
a considerable distance onto the lake, and shot himself in the
head. He collapsed in the idling boat, and was rescued by an
emergency medical team and taken to a hospital in Burlington
where his life was saved.

Why, why did they save *his* life?—Sybil thought bitterly.

She'd never felt such emotion, such outrage, as she felt for
this person George Conte: "Mr. Starr." He'd wanted to kill
her too, of course—that was the purpose of his coming home,
wanting to get her, saying her mother wanted her. Had Sybil's
grandmother and Aunt Lora not stopped him, he would have

shot her too, and dumped her body into the lake, and ended it all by shooting himself—but not killing himself. A bungled suicide. And then, after recovering, a plea of "not guilty" to the charge of murder.

A charge of second-degree murder, and a sentence of only between twelve to nineteen years. So, he was out. George Conte was out. As "Mr. Starr," the amateur artist, the lover of the beautiful and the pure, he'd found her out, and he'd come for her.

And you know why.

13. "Your Mother Is Waiting for You"

Sybil Blake returned the clippings to the envelope so conspicuously marked MEDICAL INSURANCE, and returned the envelope to the very bottom of the unlocked drawer in her aunt's desk. She closed the drawer carefully, and, though she was in an agitated state, looked about the room, to see if she'd left anything inadvertently out of place; any evidence that she'd been in here at all.

Yes, she'd violated the trust Aunt Lora had in her. Yet Aunt Lora had lied to her too, these many years. And so convincingly.

Sybil understood that she could never again believe anyone, fully. She understood that those who love us can, and will, lie to us; they may act out of a moral conviction that such lying is necessary, and this may in fact be true—but, still, they *lie*.

Even as they look into our eyes and insist they are telling the truth.

Of the reasonable steps Sybil Blake might have taken, this was the most reasonable: she might have confronted Lora Dell Blake with the evidence she'd found and with her knowledge of what the tragedy had been, and she might have told her about "Mr. Starr."

But she hated him so. And Aunt Lora hated him. And, hating him as they did, how could they protect themselves against him, if he chose to act? For Sybil had no doubt, now, her father had returned to her, to do her harm.

If George Conte had served his prison term, and been released from prison, if he was free to move about the country like any other person, certainly he had every right to come to Glencoe, California. In approaching Sybil Blake, his daughter, he had committed no crime. He had not threatened her, he had not harassed her, he had behaved in a kindly, courteous, generous way; except for the fact (in Aunt Lora's eyes this would be an outrageous, unspeakable fact) that he had misrepresented himself.

"Mr. Starr" was a lie, an obscenity. But no one had forced Sybil to model for him, nor to accept an expensive gift from him. She had done so willingly. She had done so gratefully. After her initial timidity, she'd been rather eager to be so employed.

For "Mr. Starr" had seduced her—almost.

Sybil reasoned that, if she told her aunt about "Mr. Starr" their lives would be irrevocably changed. Aunt Lora would be upset to the point of hysteria. She would insist upon going to the police. The police would rebuff her, or, worse yet, humor her. And what if Aunt Lora went to confront "Mr. Starr" herself?

No, Sybil was not going to involve her aunt. Nor implicate her, in any way.

"I love you too much," Sybil whispered. "You are all I have."

To avoid seeing Aunt Lora that evening, or, rather, to avoid being seen by her, Sybil went to bed early, leaving a note on the kitchen table explaining that she had a mild case of the flu. Next morning, when Aunt Lora looked in Sybil's room, to ask her worriedly how she was, Sybil smiled wanly and said she'd improved but, still, she thought she would stay home from school that day.

Aunt Lora, ever vigilant against illness, pressed her hand against Sybil's forehead, which did seem feverish. She looked into Sybil's eyes, which were dilated. She asked if Sybil had a sore throat, if she had a headache, if she'd had an upset stomach or diarrhea, and Sybil said no, no, she simply felt a little weak, she wanted to sleep. So Aunt Lora believed her, brought her Bufferin and fruit juice and toast with honey, and went off quietly to leave her alone.

Sybil wondered if she would ever see her aunt again.

But of course she would: she had no doubt, she could force herself to do what must be done.

Wasn't her mother waiting for her?

A windy, chilly afternoon. Sybil wore warm slacks and a wool pull-over sweater and her jogging shoes. But she wasn't running today. She carried her kidskin bag, its strap looped over her shoulder.

Her handsome kidskin bag, with its distinctive smell.

Her bag, into which she'd slipped, before leaving home, the sharpest of her aunt's several finely honed steak knives.

Sybil Blake hadn't gone to school that day but she entered the park at approximately three forty-five, her usual time. She'd sighted Mr. Starr's long elegantly gleaming black limousine parked on the street close by, and there was Mr. Starr himself, waiting for her.

How animated he became, seeing her!—exactly as he'd been in the past. It seemed strange to Sybil that, somehow, to him, things were unchanged.

He imagined her still ignorant, innocent. Easy prey.

Smiling at her. Waving. "Hello, Sybil!"

Daring to call her that—"Sybil."

He was hurrying in her direction, limping, using his cane. Sybil smiled. There was no reason not to smile, thus she smiled. She was thinking with what skill Mr. Starr used that cane of his, how practiced he'd become. Since the injury to his brain?—or had there been another injury, suffered in prison?

Those years in prison, when he'd had time to think. Not to repent—Sybil seemed to know he had not repented—but, simply, to think.

To consider the mistakes he'd made, and how to unmake them.

"Why, my dear, hello!—I've missed you, you know," Mr. Starr said. There was an edge of reproach to his voice but he smiled to show his delight. "—I won't ask where *were* you, now you're *here*. And carrying your beautiful bag—"

Sybil peered up at Mr. Starr's pale, tense, smiling face. Her reactions were slow at first, as if numbed; as if she were, for all that she'd rehearsed this, not fully wakened—a kind of sleepwalker.

"And—you *will* model for me this afternoon? Under our new, improved terms?"

"Yes, Mr. Starr."

Mr. Starr had his duffel bag, his sketch pad, his charcoal sticks. He was bareheaded, and his fine silver hair blew in the wind. He wore a slightly soiled white shirt with a navy blue silk necktie and his old tweed jacket; and his gleaming black shoes that put

Sybil in mind of a funeral. She could not see his eyes behind the dark lenses of his glasses but she knew by the puckered skin at the corners of his eyes that he was staring at her intently, hungrily. She was his model, he was the artist, when could they begin? Already, his fingers were flexing in anticipation.

"I think, though, we've about exhausted the possibilities of this park, don't you, dear? It's charming, but rather common. And so *finite*," Mr. Starr was saying, expansively. "Even the beach, here in Glencoe. Somehow it lacks—amplitude. So I was thinking—I was hoping—we might today vary our routine just a bit, and drive up the coast. Not far—just a few miles. Away from so many people, and so many distractions." Seeing that Sybil was slow to respond, he added, warmly, "I'll pay you double, Sybil—of course. You know you can trust me by now, don't you? Yes?"

That curious, ugly little hook of a scar in Mr. Starr's fore-head—its soft pale tissue gleamed in the whitish light. Sybil wondered if that was where the bullet had gone in.

Mr. Starr had been leading Sybil in the direction of the curb, where the limousine was waiting, its engine idling almost sound-lessly. He opened the rear door. Sybil, clutching her kidskin bag, peered inside, at the cushioned, shadowy interior. For a moment, her mind was blank. She might have been on a high board, about to dive into the water, not knowing how she'd gotten to where she was, or why. Only that she could not turn back,

Mr. Starr was smiling eagerly, hopefully. "Shall we? Sybil?"

"Yes, Mr. Starr," Sybil said, and climbed inside.

EXTENUATING CIRCUMSTANCES

Because it was a mercy. Because God even IN His cruelty will sometimes grant mercy.

Because Venus was in the sign of Sagittarius.

Because you laughed at me, my faith in the stars. My hope. Because he cried, you do not know how he cried.

Because at such times his little face was so twisted and hot, his nose running with mucus, his eyes so hurt.

Because in such he was his mother, and not you. Because I wanted to spare him such shame.

Because he remembered you, he knew the word *Daddy*.

Because watching TV he would point to a man and say, *Daddy—?*

Because this summer has gone on so long, and no rain. The heat lightning flashing at night, without thunder.

Because in the silence, at night, the summer insects scream.

Because by day there are earthmoving machines and grinders operating hour upon hour razing the woods next to the playground. Because the red dust got into our eyes, our mouths.

Because he would whimper *Mommy?*—in that way that tore my heart.

Because last Monday the washing machine broke down, I heard a loud thumping that scared me, the dirty soapy water would not drain out. Because in the light of the bulb overhead he saw me holding the wet sheets in my hand crying *What can I do? what can I do?*

Because the sleeping pills they give me now are made of flour and chalk, I am certain.

Because I loved you more than you loved me even from the first when your eyes moved on me like candleflame.

Because I did not know this yet; yes I knew it but cast it from my mind.

Because there was shame in it. Loving you knowing you would not love me enough.

Because my job applications are laughed at for misspellings and torn to pieces as soon as I leave.

Because they will not believe me when listing my skills. Because since he was born my body is misshapen, the pain is always there.

Because I see that it was not his fault and even in that I could not spare him.

Because even at the time when he was conceived (in those early days we were so happy! so happy I am certain! lying together on top of the bed the corduroy bedspread in that narrow jiggly bed hearing the rain on the roof that slanted down so you had to stoop being so tall and from outside on the street the roof with its dark shingles looking always wet was like a lowered brow over the windows on the third floor and the windows like squinty eyes and we would come home together from the University meeting at the Hardee's corner you from the geology lab or the library and me from Accounting where my eyes ached because of the lights with their dim flicker no one else could see and I was so happy your arm around my waist and mine around yours like any couple, like any college girl with her boy friend, and walking *home*, yes it was *home*, I thought always it was *home*, we would look up at the windows of the apartment laughing saying who do you think lives there? what are their names? who are they? that cozy secret-looking room under the eaves where the roof came down, came down dripping black runny water I hear now drumming on this roof but only if I fall asleep during the day with my clothes on so tired so exhausted and when I wake up there is no rain, only the earthmoving machines and grinders in the woods so I must acknowledge *It is another time, it is time*) yes I knew.

Because you did not want him to be born.

Because he cried so I could hear him through the shut door, through all the doors.

Because I did not want him to be *Mommy*, I wanted him to be *Daddy* in his strength.

Because this washcloth in my hand was in my hand when I saw how it must be.

Because the checks come to me from the lawyer's office not from you. Because in tearing open the envelopes my fingers shaking and my eyes showing such hope I revealed myself naked to myself so many times.

Because to this shame he was a witness, he saw.

Because he was too young at two years to know. Because even so he knew.

Because his birthday was a sign, falling in the midst of Pisces.

Because in certain things he *was* his father, that knowledge in eyes that went beyond me in mockery of me.

Because one day he would laugh, too, as you have done.

Because there is no listing for your telephone and the operators will not tell me. Because in any of the places I know to find you, you cannot be found.

Because your sister has lied to my face, to mislead me. Because she who was once my friend, I believed, was never my friend.

Because I feared loving him too much, and in that weakness failing to protect him from hurt.

Because his crying tore my heart but angered me too, so I feared laying hands upon him wild and unplanned.

Because he flinched seeing me. That nerve jumping in his eye.

Because he was always hurting himself, he was so clumsy falling off the swing hitting his head against the metal post so one of the other mothers saw and cried out *Oh! oh look your son is bleeding!* and that time in the kitchen whining and pulling at me in a bad temper reaching up to grab the pot handle and almost overturning the boiling water in his face so I lose control slapping him shaking him by the arm *Bad! bad! bad! bad!* my voice rising in fury not caring who heard.

Because that day in the courtroom you refused to look at me, your face shut like a fist against me and your lawyer too, like I was dirt beneath your shoes. Like maybe he was not even your son but you would sign the papers as if he was, you are so superior.

Because the courtroom was not like any courtroom I had a right to expect, not a big dignified courtroom like on TV just a room with a judge's desk and three rows of six seats each and not a single window and even here that flickering light that yellowish-sickish fluorescent tubing making my eyes ache so I wore my dark glasses giving the judge a false impression of me, and I was sniffing, wiping my nose, every question they asked me I'd hear myself giggle so nervous and ashamed even stammering over my age and my name so you looked with scorn at me, all of you.

Because they were on your side, I could not prevent it.

Because in granting me child support payments, you had a right to move away. Because I could not follow.

Because he wet his pants, where he should not have, for his age.

Because it would be blamed on me. It *was* blamed on me.

Because my own mother screamed at me over the phone. She could not help me with my life she said, no one can help you with your life, we were screaming such things to each other as left us breathless and crying and I slammed down the receiver knowing that I had no mother and after the first grief I knew *It* is *better, so.*

Because he would learn that someday, and the knowledge of it would hurt him.

Because he had my hair coloring, and my eyes. That left eye, the weakness in it.

Because that time it almost happened, the boiling water overturned onto him, I saw how easy it would be. How, if he could be prevented from screaming, the neighbors would not know.

Because yes they would know, but only when I wanted them to know.

Because you would know then. Only when I wanted you to know.

Because then I could speak to you in this way, maybe in a letter which your lawyer would forward to you, or your sister, maybe over the telephone or even face to face. Because then you could not escape.

Because though you did not love him you could not escape him.

Because I have begun to bleed for six days quite heavily, and will then spot for another three or four. Because soaking the blood in wads of toilet paper sitting on the toilet my hands shaking I think of you who never bleed.

Because I am a proud woman. I scorn your charity.

Because I am not a worthy mother. Because I am so tired.

Because the machines digging in the earth and grinding trees are a torment by day, and the screaming insects by night.

Because there is no sleep.

Because he would only sleep, these past few months, if he could be with me in my bed.

Because he whimpered, *Mommy!—Mommy don't!*

Because he flinched from me when there was no cause.

Because the pharmacist took the prescription and was gone such a long time, knew he was telephoning someone.

Because at the drugstore where I have shopped for a year and a half they pretended not to know my name.

Because in the grocery store the cashiers stared smiling at me and at him pulling at my arm spilling tears down his face.

Because they whispered and laughed behind me, I have too much pride to respond.

Because he was with me at such times, he was a witness to such.

Because he had no one but his Mommy and his Mommy had no one but him. Which is so lonely.

Because I had gained seven pounds from last Sunday to this, the waist of my slacks is so tight. Because I hate the fat of my body.

Because looking at me naked now you would show disgust.

Because I was beautiful for you, why wasn't that enough?

Because that day the sky was dense with clouds the color of raw liver but yet there was no rain. Heat lightning flashing with sound making me so nervous but no rain.

Because his left eye was weak, it would always be so unless he had an operation to strengthen the muscle.

Because I did not want to cause him pain and terror in his sleep.

Because you would pay for it, the check from the lawyer with no note.

Because you hated him, your son.

Because he was *our* son, you hated him.

Because you moved away. To the far side of the country I have reason to believe.

Because in my arms after crying he would lie so still, only one heart beating between us.

Because I knew I could not spare him from hurt.

Because the playground hurt our ears, raised red dust to get in our eyes and mouths.

Because I was so tired of scrubbing him clean, between his toes and beneath his nails, the insides of his ears, his neck, the many secret places of filth.

Because I felt the ache of cramps again in my belly, I was in a panic my period had begun so soon.

Because I could not spare him the older children laughing.

Because after the first terrible pain he would be beyond pain.

Because in this there is mercy.

Because God's mercy is for him, and not for me.

Because there was no one here to stop me.

Because my neighbors' TV was on so loud, I knew they could not hear even if he screamed through the washcloth.

Because you were not here to stop me, were you.

Because finally there is no one to stop us.

Because finally there is no one to save us.

Because my own mother betrayed me.

Because the rent would be due again on Tuesday which is the first of September. And by then I will be gone.

Because his body was not heavy to carry and to wrap in the down comforter, you remember that comforter, I know.

Because the washcloth soaked in his saliva will dry on the line and show no sign.

Because to heal there must be forgetfulness and oblivion.

Because he cried when he should not have cried but did not cry when he should.

Because the water came slowly to boil in the big pan, vibrating and humming on the front burner.

Because the kitchen was damp with steam from the windows and so tight, the temperature muse have been 100°F.

Because he did not struggle. And when he did, it was too late.

Because I wore rubber gloves to spare myself being scalded.

Because I knew I must not panic, and did not.

Because I loved him. Because love hurts so bad.

Because I wanted to tell you these things. Just like this.

THE GIRL WHO WAS TO DIE

The girl who was to die wasn't a girl any longer but a young woman of twenty-four, with a small, shapely, perky body and a china-doll face that, to Beverly Crystal's eye, was almost too small, the perfect features too squeezed together, like a midget's. She was a nurse at Yewville General Hospital and in her trim, white nylon uniform, gauzy white stockings and spotless white lace-up shoes, her honey-brown curly hair shaken loose from her nurse's cap, she looked striking, out of place in the Crystals' gloomy living room, sitting on the old Italian Provincial sofa, toes just touching the carpet, speaking in an earnest, breathless, little-girl voice. Her name was Audrey McDermitt and she was a friend of Beverly Crystal's stepdaughter Ednella from high school, though Beverly hadn't known the girls were so close.

It was late afternoon of November 6, two nights before her death, that Audrey McDermitt dropped by the Crystals' to visit with Ednella. Beverly, who observed the girls in the living room, uncertain at first whether to come out and say hello, hadn't known whether Ednella had invited Audrey to stop by after her hospital shift or whether Audrey had invited herself. Beverly's relations with her deceased husband's twenty-five-year-old daughter were amicable and warm, for the most part, but not intimate; Beverly could chat companionably with Ednella about many things, then offend her with the most inadvertent innocent question, if it touched upon something private. So Beverly wouldn't have asked about Audrey McDermitt for fear of drawing some quick, quiet, coldly hurtful rebuff from Ednella. She was never to ask.

That day, a Wednesday, it was dark by 5:45 P.M. Beverly, upstairs, had heard someone come in the front door, had been hearing voices, muffled laughter, assumed it was Ednella and a visitor; and so came downstairs by the back way. (The Crystals' house, in which Beverly and her stepdaughter now lived by themselves, without Wally Crystal, Beverly's husband and Ednella's father, to connect them, was one of the old, spacious, well-kept Victorian houses on Church Street. It had a broad staircase off the front foyer and a narrow, steep, almost ladderlike staircase at the rear, off the kitchen.) Beverly in flannel slacks and a strawberry-pink hand-knitted cardigan appeared at the doorway of the dining room, smiling hesitantly in the direction of Ednella and her friend in the nurse's uniform that looked so dazzlingly white. Beverly wondered, Would the girls like some coffee? tea? something sweet? It was like Ednella not to have thought to offer her visitor anything. But neither took the slightest notice of Beverly, they were so intent upon their conversation. Audrey McDermitt was saying in her hushed, little-girl voice, "—so I said to him, I was crying, but I was damned mad, too! I said, 'Mister, if you think so low of me, maybe I just better give you this back right now,'" making a weak tugging gesture at the ring on her left hand, and Ednella asked something in a soft, wondering voice that Beverly couldn't hear, and Audrey said, with a nervous giggle, "Well, then, *he* started crying! Said he'd kill himself, blast his head off with a shotgun, if—"

What on earth were the girls talking about, Beverly wondered. There was the McDermitt girl fluttering her hands, her small face heated and self-important, like a face on afternoon television prettily made-up for some dramatic purpose, and there was Ednella Crystal who usually scorned her former high-school classmates, as she scorned most Yewville residents, dismissing them as provincial, narrow-minded, dull—Ednella in a chair facing Audrey, leaning far forward, elbows on knees, chin resting on clasped hands, staring at her friend. Ednella was a lean knife-blade of a girl with dark ironic eyes and dry, sallow skin. She was between jobs at the moment, and had not been out of the house all day; she wore the shapeless beige corduroy slacks she'd been wearing for weeks and a much-laundered, shrunken sweatshirt that emphasized her gaunt, flat torso. Beverly winced, seeing that damned sweatshirt on Ednella: it was steel-gray with an insipid, faded image of Mickey Mouse on its front and the letters VASSAR COLLEGE fanning beneath. A memento, and a ridiculous one, of Ednella's undergraduate college where, for all the girl's intelligence and talent, she'd come close to not graduating with her class. (Poor Wally, still alive at the time, had to make several urgent telephone calls to the college president, to get things straight. Beverly never learned just what the problem was.) Ednella was, in Beverly's eyes, a beautiful young woman, far more striking in appearance than the little McDermitt girl who resembled a Kewpie doll; but she wore no makeup, neglected her limp, fine black hair, seemed more naturally inclined to frown than to smile, and was unpredictable in her moods. For instance, Beverly could never have predicted that she would come downstairs to find Ednella in an intense conversation with Audrey McDermitt, of all people.

Audrey was saying, breathlessly, wiping at her eyes, "Damn it, he *knows* there isn't the least reason to be jealous. Of Ron Carpenter, of all people! What girl would look twice at Ron, if Harvey Mercer was in the room! My goodness, Ron and I have known each other since fifth grade, and now that Ron's mother has chemotherapy at the hospital, and Ron brings her, we just naturally see each other, and if I have time we talk. Ron's worried sick about his mother, and—"

Ednella leaned farther forward. She had taken acting lessons at Vassar and had had a year of law school at Albany; there was often something histrionic and coiled about her. "That's all?" she interrupted. "Just 'talk'?"

"Well—we've had coffee in the cafeteria together, once or twice," Audrey said. She crinkled her little-girl's face in appeal. "And, I guess, he drove me out to Piketown"—Piketown, named for a local road, was the area's largest mall—"once, after my shift. But—"

"Did someone tell Harvey?"

"I guess so! Goddamn it! You know Yewville—such a damned small town." Audrey paused, wiping at her eyes with a tissue. Her pretty face shimmered with tears as if about to dissolve. "The thing is, he scares me. Harv, I mean. I love him and I can't live without him and that's never going to change no matter what my parents say, but—"

Ednella said, nodding, "Harv doesn't mean it really, he's just a hot-headed guy. I could talk to him, maybe. I could explain."

"Oh, Ednella, I don't know!" Audrey said. "He respects you, I know that, but if he even guessed I was talking about him behind his back, saying I was scared of him, he'd—well, maybe take it as betrayal. That's a word he says all the time now—'betrayal.'"

Ednella continued in a low, intense voice, as if she hadn't heard. "He just needs someone to *explain*. Someone he can *trust*." Ednella had run her fingers through her hair so that it looked spiky and electrified, as if with the urgency of her thought. "Harvey isn't superficial like most people, he's *deep*. Passionate, and *deep*."

At this moment, just when Beverly had decided she had better not intrude, and might just retreat quietly back into the kitchen, Audrey McDermitt glanced up and saw her. Immediately she cried, "Oh, Mrs. Crystal! Hello!" like the sweet, good, uncomplicated Yewville girl she was; her smile seemed genuine, though her eyes glittered with tears. Beverly, who had been feeling so critical about the girl, now felt a rush of affection for her—my goodness, she *was* pretty, and quite winning in her nurse's uniform. Ednella, turning to squint at Beverly, did not smile, at first, at all—blinked and stared at her stepmother, the handsome, softspoken, easily wounded fifty-three-year-old woman with whom she shared the house, as if, for a long pained moment, she failed to recognize her.

Then, with coolly forced animation, "Hello, Beverly! Come in! You know Audrey, of course?"

So Beverly, blushing, had no choice but to come forward and join the girls. She smiled warmly, graciously, hopefully. (If she'd been stung by Ednella's greeting, the dissonant sound of "Beverly" where, at another time, Ednella might have murmured, "Mother," she gave not the slightest sign.) She switched on a second lamp. "You girls, sitting in the dark!" She asked them, putting the question to Audrey in particular, would they like some coffee? tea? something sweet? "It wouldn't take me but a minute to get things ready."

There was such appeal in Beverly's voice, her eyes behind her new mother-of-pearl glasses so hopeful, Audrey McDermitt hesitated a moment before saying apologetically, "Oh, thank you, Mrs. Crystal—but I'm just on my way. In fact—" a quick glance at the wristwatch on her child-sized wrist, "—I'm *late*."

And she jumped up, with a high-school cheerleader's energy, and was on her way.

After the girl had gone Beverly asked Ednella what was wrong, for of course it was only natural for her to ask under the circumstances; even as she dreaded her stepdaughter's probable response. But Ednella surprised Beverly by saying, thoughtfully, "You can see why she's a nurse, can't you—just as, in high school, she was a cheerleader. That bounce. That optimism." Ednella shook her head, as if mildly disapproving, yet in wonder. "Even with her life at risk—Audrey is what she *is*."

Beverly was astonished. "'Life at risk'? What on earth do you mean, Ednella?"

Ednella shrugged, headed for the stairs. "I can't say, Beverly. I can't violate Audrey's confidence. Anyway, probably I'm exaggerating—you know me."

"But, Ednella—"

Beverly stared after Ednella as, lithe and springy on her feet as a wild creature, she bounded up the stairs, taking them two at a time. She called back over her shoulder, almost gaily, "You know *me*."

In fact, Beverly didn't.

She knew that she admired her stepdaughter, yes, and she felt a strong if inchoate emotion for her, with which Beverly's hope of being accepted at last in Yewville was naively bound up—but she would not have said she knew Ednella Crystal, really. Nine years ago, brought to the house on Church Street, Yewville, as Wally Crystal's new wife (his second wife, the first, Ednella's mother, had died when Ednella was four years old), Beverly had told Wally, "Your daughter is a special person—I can see it in her eyes!" But Wally, gruff, good-natured, vaguely embarrassed, had turned the compliment back upon Beverly. "Ednella? Hell, she's just spoiled."

Which was true, Beverly supposed. But only a fraction of the truth.

When Beverly was first introduced to Ednella, by Wally, it was only a week before the wedding. The girl was sixteen, but looking much younger. Her skin was fair, but mildly blemished; her eyes were clear, dark, beautiful, but marred by an expression of subtle derision. Her hand in Beverly's was cool, limp, unresisting; her cheek, kissed, was cool too, impassive as marble. In bleached jeans and a black turtleneck sweater, Ednella had stood straight and tall, as tall as Beverly, gazing at her imperturbably, as Beverly nervously chattered. Then she'd interrupted, as if gently. "You know, all this isn't necessary—really."

"What isn't necessary?" Beverly asked.

"All this *trying* so hard."

Beverly stared at the girl, speechless. She had never been so hurt. So cut to the quick. So found out. So helpless. Forty-four years old, a woman of some independence; never married; shortly to be the bride of a well-to-do small-city banker whose name she had not known twelve weeks before. But how to reply to his daughter? How to define herself to this eerily composed child who seemed to be looking not at, but through her? Beverly stammered, "I—don't know what you mean, Ednella. '*Trying*?'"

Still imperturbed, the girl said, as calmly as if she'd memorized the words, "You're here to be my father's wife, Beverly. Not my mother. My mother has been dead a long time and everyone has adjusted."

But I love you, Beverly wanted to plead. *I want to love you.*

It seemed the most improbable, in a way the most mysterious culmination of her life as a woman—to discover herself, in middle age, anxiously courting the moody daughter of a woman she had never known.

How clumsy it was, how supremely mawkish! Like an oversized package Beverly had to carry everywhere with her, fearful of setting it down and misplacing it.

She was to be Wallace Crystal's wife for only five years, but those five years would alter the course of her life irrevocably. Now, years after his death, she was known in Yewville as Wally Crystal's *widow*; as, while he'd lived, one of the town's most prominent citizens, she'd been Wally Crystal's *second wife*.

Not that Beverly minded, of course. She was very happy in Yewville, if lonely. Her life before marrying and coming here had not been a happy one, nor even clearly defined.

Yewville was curious about Wally Crystal's *second wife,* but not really interested in her. Even the women Beverly wished to count as friends. "Where's your family?" "Where're you from?" "*How* did you and Wally meet?" Their questions were prying, but never deep. Beverly answered them simply and honestly, knowing herself on trial. (But for what?) Virtually every answer she gave misrepresented her, for her marriage to Wally Crystal had been anything but calculated; in fact, it had come about sheerly by chance.

They had met on a Caribbean cruise, of all unlikely places; the first Wally had ever taken, and so very reluctantly, in his life. (As he would confide in Beverly, he'd had a heart attack the year before, not a serious one but a heart attack nonetheless, and it had "scared the bejesus" out of him. He'd wanted to do something romantic, extravagant, before it was too late.) Beverly herself was on the cruise in the role of "social director"—her first voyage too, and in a position she'd accepted in desperation for a job. (On this issue, Beverly blurred the precise facts in speaking about herself. She'd been trained as a teacher of high-school French but, somehow, through the course of humbling, exhausting years, had never found a teaching position that was suitable; or, if suitable, permanent. Where a school board was eager to hire a teacher of her qualifications, she was reluctant to be hired; where she would have wished to be hired, budgets suddenly evaporated, and French-teaching jobs. But how to explain this, without sounding defensive? self-pitying? a failure?) On the tackily expensive cruise ship amid the over-bright days and the balmy, calypso nights, enjoying a distinct advantage because of her age (Beverly, at forty-four, was perhaps the youngest woman on the cruise), she'd somehow cultivated a bubbly outgoing personality, at odds with her real personality; she was the ship's "social director," after all. With stylish frost-tipped hair, chic new glasses, an ascending laugh of sheer uncomplicated gaiety, Beverly had won over, within a few hours, the lonely, homesick, brooding, slightly dyspeptic Wally Crystal, who hadn't understood, he confided in Beverly afterward, how badly he wanted to be married again, until he'd seen her.

Which was flattering, wasn't it? Of course it was.

Wally Crystal was a man of evident means, if little formal education, in his early fifties: near-bald, heavy, though not fat; with a weatherworn, lined, ugly-attractive face, a froggish sort of face, slack-jowled, but shrewd about the eyes, intelligent. (That intelligence, an unmistakable ironic sharpness of the eye, Beverly would note in Ednella. But little else of Wally.) He had the gruffly shy manner of a man accustomed to ordering employees about, but uneasy in social situations involving women. His most common expletive was a nervous expulsion of breath, "Well!—*well!*" and a wide, strained helpless smile.

Beverly had known at once, seeing him: *widower*.

Beverly was an attractive woman whose youth had passed rapidly by, like scenery glimpsed from a speeding car. Where it had gone, she did not want to think. Yes, she'd had romances in her life ("romances" being a kinder word than "affairs"), but she had never married; she had never had a child. It was too late for the child but not too late to marry and, mildly drunk, Beverly accepted Wally Crystal's proposal not with an air of startled gratitude, which might have alarmed him, but with that newly acquired ascending laugh that sounded like crushed ice being dropped into a glass. It bespoke marital good times, uncomplicated bliss. It bespoke a future.

True, Beverly was not in love with Wally Crystal. The man was not—had he ever been?—the kind of man with whom a woman might be in love. But she grew to like him, very much. In time, she grew to love him. And then, after a second heart attack, in their sixth year together, Wally died.

So Wally Crystal's *second wife* became Wally Crystal's *widow*.

At that time, after having dropped out of law school, Ednella was living in New York and working as an assistant stage manager at a small theater in SoHo. She was twenty-two years old and had stayed away from Yewville since her father's remarriage, except for brief visits at holidays and during the summers. (At which times she was unfailingly polite, if rather cool, with her father's new wife. The three syllables of "Bev-er-ly" sounded in her mouth like a droll foreign word, each syllable equally stressed.) When Beverly telephoned Ednella with the news of her father's death, Ednella screamed at her and slammed down the receiver. Later, when Beverly managed to speak with her, Ednella did not cry but was raving, incoherent; as it happened, Ednella herself was ill, had been seriously ill for days, with what would be diagnosed as mononucleosis. In the midst of funeral preparations, Beverly flew to New York to bring Ednella home. She nearly fainted, seeing her beautiful stepdaughter skeleton-thin, with enormous scared eyes in a ravaged face. (Beverly's first panicked thought was that the girl had AIDS.) On the plane coming home, Ednella leaned weakly into Beverly's arms, calling her "Mother."

The shock and the pleasure of the word passed through Beverly like an electric current.

Afterward, yes, and fairly frequently, the two quarreled; or, rather, Ednella quarreled with Beverly. But that was all right. That was to be expected. Beverly consoled herself, *I can wait.*

Several times during the day following Audrey McDermitt's visit to the house, Beverly was aware of Ednella on the telephone, not that she eavesdropped on the extension, of course. (Beverly was too respectful of Ednella's privacy to do such a thing. Besides, quick-witted Ednella would have detected her at once.) In the early afternoon, lifting the receiver to make a call of her own,

Beverly happened to overhear a man's voice, a snatch of some slurred, sarcastic words: "—expect me to believe that shit? I—" Beverly replaced the receiver at once, as if it burnt her fingers.

So far as Beverly knew, her stepdaughter was seeing no man, or men, at the present time. There had been no one in Yewville in recent memory. Ednella had remarked to Beverly that she'd long ago outgrown her contemporaries in Yewville; in New York, she'd "overdosed." Her wan, ironic, rather wistful smile suggested that the situation was not ideal, but Beverly had not felt welcome to inquire.

In high school, Ednella had had no boyfriends, but she had cultivated passionate friendships with two or three boys. To Beverly's surprise, the boys hadn't been the kind one might have expected Ednella Crystal to associate with—boys who, like Ednella, were taking college-entrance courses—they were rough, coarse, problematic types, prototypical dropouts, losers. Aggressive, masculine. From backgrounds very different from her own. One of them, Beverly suddenly remembered, was named Harvey Mercer—whom Audrey McDermitt had mentioned the previous day. A tall, blond, hulking boy with unkempt hair and Presley-style sideburns and a stubbled chin, good-looking in that way of swaggering adolescence that so quickly loses its edge. Ednella had spent weeks, or had it been months, helping Harvey Mercer rebuild a car after school and on weekends: she'd chattered excitedly of two cars to "wreck" and one to "build" and "V-8 engines" and "hot-wiring" and "stripping" and "sanding" and "painting with primer" and the "pick-up" the car would have when finished. Wally had been annoyed that Ednella seemed so willing to devote her energies to an effort of the kind, but he'd supposed it was harmless as long as the garage was well ventilated (Ednella assured him it was: she knew better than to breathe in stripper fumes); Beverly worried about Ednella, so naive for all her surface sophistication and intelligence, being gang-raped one terrible day by Harvey Mercer and his buddies. But to confront a girl of seventeen with one's wishes for her well-being, still less her future, was, Beverly knew, ill-advised. Of Harvey Mercer, Ednella would say, with a defiant, mysterious smile, "We get along. There's no bullshit with *him*."

Nothing came of such friendships, in the end. Not so far as Beverly knew. There must have been a day, an hour, when Ednella Crystal realized that she wasn't—finally, ultimately—wanted; when a car having been test driven, and brought to its highest level of performance, it was used to impress other girls, a vehicle for romance, passion, sex. The swaggering boys with sideburns went out with girls very different from Ednella Crystal: if they were lucky, girls like Audrey McDermitt.

At six o'clock on November 7, a drizzly dusk smelling of winter, Beverly heard a car pull up in front of the house, and saw Ednella, bareheaded, run out and get inside. The car's headlights were on, its windshield wipers in operation. Wasn't that Audrey McDermitt's little VW? Perplexed, Beverly watched out the vestibule window for some minutes; then, unable to resist, she clumsily draped a raincoat over her head, hurried out to the car, rapped on a window, smiling, admonitory, hopeful—"Girls! Please come inside! It's so nasty out here." The young women stared blinking at her as if she were a fantastical apparition. Ednella's expression was severe, and Audrey seemed to be crying, a lighted cigarette in her fingers. The interior of the little car was hazy with smoke.

Ednella rolled down her window a grudging inch or two. "Beverly," she said, her voice trembling, "Audrey and I are having a private conversation. *Please.*"

"Oh, I know, I'm sorry, but I thought—"

"*Please.*"

So, her cheeks burning, Beverly retreated to the house.

Thinking, *Why don't they need me? I'm a woman, too.*

Thinking, *Nurses of all people shouldn't smoke.*

It was to be the last time Beverly Crystal would see Audrey McDermitt alive.

That evening, though Beverly prepared dinner as usual, Ednella refused to sit down at the table with her. She was much too excited, distracted. When, at 10:20 P.M., the telephone rang, she hurried to get it (downstairs: Beverly sitting in the television room, staring without interest at a BBC-made rebroadcast of one or another English-style soap opera of the monied classes, heard her rapid, surprisingly heavy footsteps overhead); minutes later, to Beverly's astonishment, she hurried down the rear stairs, and would surely have rushed out of the house without a word of explanation, or even a shouted "Goodbye!" if Beverly, breathless, had not hurried after her. "Ednella, what on earth? Where are you going?" she cried.

Ednella turned to her as if, indeed, she'd forgotten that she shared the house with another person. Beverly saw that Ednella was flush-faced, and breathless; she'd shampooed and brushed her hair so that it shone, and she was wearing trim black wool trousers and a scarlet Shetland pullover. How severe, yet how attractive, she looked! Carelessly she said, "I'm going to talk with him—Audrey's fiancé. The one who's so jealous. They need me, it's urgent, I won't be long. Don't wait up for me, Beverly? Please?" She was already at the back door, car keys rattling in her hand. Beverly called after her, "Ednella, dear, who? Who are you going to talk to?"

Ednella called back over her shoulder, annoyed, but elated too, "Just don't wait up. *Please.*"

Beverly did not dare wait up for Ednella, but, of course, she was unable to sleep. Where had the girl gone, what danger might she be in! The ghostly luminous dials of Beverly's bedside clock, the slow hands circling the face, exerted a morbid fascination upon her. Midnight, 1:05 A.M., 2:40 A.M. . . . at last, car headlights swung across the bedroom ceiling, Ednella's car turned into the drive. Beverly had been in such a state of apprehension that, released, she nearly wept.

"Ednella. Thank God."

She heard Ednella enter the house by the rear, quietly. Heard footsteps in the kitchen. Quiet. As if in stealth.

It would occur to her later that Ednella must have refrained from slamming her car door shut. To spare waking her. To spare disturbing her any further.

Beverly rose from bed, slipped on her bathrobe, went soundlessly to the rear stairs. Then, seeing that Ednella had not switched on the stairway light, and that the only light was at the foot of the stairs where the kitchen door had been left ajar, Beverly realized that she must not intrude; must not let Ednella know that she was awake at this hour, and so clearly waiting for her. Yet she could not resist descending the stairs, as quietly as she could. Her heart was beating painfully hard. She would tell herself afterward that she had not been spying on her stepdaughter: she had only wanted to see, with her own eyes, that Ednella was all right.

I loved her . . . love her. Where was the harm.

As Beverly cautiously neared the foot of the stairs, she was puzzled to hear Ednella murmuring to herself; she heard the girl's quickened breath, the opening and closing of the refrigerator door. A rattling as of ice cubes? Then, abruptly, Ednella was speaking over the phone, in a low, urgent voice, "Audrey? It's me. Yes. Yes, it is. Listen!—*he* is." A pause. Beverly listened, fascinated. She drew closer, peering through the doorway at a slant. Where was Ednella? The kitchen telephone was a wall phone, and Ednella was leaning against the sink, the cord stretched almost horizontal. "I've been there all this time. Sobered him up—made him drink black coffee—talked him out of—you know." Another pause. A deep, exhilarated breath, Then, more animated, as if she were trying to talk reason into a stubborn child, "Give him a call, say you're coming over. He's waiting. He keeps saying he isn't 'worthy.' We won't ever know how serious he was, I guess—'Blowing his head off.' My God! He was crying off and on. Said he was so ashamed! Didn't know what in hell came over him, hurting you like he did, but he knew—" here there was another pause, a quick intake of breath as if Ednella were suppressing a sob, or laughter, "—knew he loves *you*. Wants to marry you. If—"

Part in fascination, part in dread, Beverly drew closer to the doorway, seeing, then, an extraordinary sight: even as Ednella was speaking so passionately to Audrey McDermitt over the telephone, the receiver gripped tight between her shoulder and her chin, she was leaning back against the sink, spine arched, head dropped back and eyes shut in a pained sort of euphoria; she'd drawn her bright-colored sweater up, baring her breasts, small, hard, faintly bluish breasts with childlike nipples, and she was rubbing several ice cubes against them, in slow languorous circular motions. As the ice melted in contact with her heated skin it ran in glistening rivulets down her midriff.

Beverly stared, shocked and uncomprehending.

The thought came to her, unbidden, *Has Ednella had sex with that girl's young man!*—even as she knew this was not likely. No, it was not likely.

Beverly shrank back from the doorway, anxious now not to be seen. Quickly turned, retreated up the stairs as silently as she'd come down. Returning to her bed, exhausted, dazed, ready for sleep. Seeing the time on her bedside clock: a few minutes before three.

She's safe! She's in the house! That's all that matters.

Next day, by noon, word had spread through Yewville: Audrey McDermitt had been killed by Harvey Mercer, who had then apparently (so eyewitnesses claimed) killed himself by deliberately smashing his car against a concrete abutment a few miles north of Yewville.

Even as local television and radio stations were issuing news bulletins of the "tragedy"—variously known as the "double tragedy" and the "lovers' tragedy"—Yewville residents, acquainted with the young people, were telephoning one another, stopping one another on the street, in stores. The sheriff's office was beginning its investigation. It had not been until Harvey Mercer's death at 9:20 A.M., that a search was made for Audrey McDermitt, who had failed to arrive at the hospital for her shift that morning, and who had not been home the previous night. Audrey often stayed with her fiancé Harvey Mercer in his rented house on the south side of Yewville, according to her family, and it was there, amid the wreckage of Mercer's bedroom, that her badly bruised naked body was found.

The coroner's report would list strangulation as the official cause of death. The young woman had died sometime between 4:00 A.M. and 5:30 A.M.

Audrey McDermitt, nurse, twenty-four years old, 1985 graduate of Yewville High School.

Harvey Mercer, employed by Valley Lumber, twenty-seven years old, attended Yewville High School without graduating.

Both had been born in Yewville. Both were survived by numerous relatives.

Both had been drinking for some time before their deaths.

The young couple had become engaged the previous April. The engagement, despite "disagreements," had not been broken.

Audrey McDermitt was wearing her engagement ring, a one-carat diamond, at the time of her death.

Police were investigating reports that Mercer, jealous of his fiancée's alleged friendships with other men, had acted violently in the past and had made threats against her life, before witnesses.

Anyone who could help with the police investigation was urged to come forward.

Beverly, hearing the first news on her kitchen radio, at noon, was overcome with shock and disbelief. Aloud she whispered, "My God. No. That little girl. It can't be." She turned the radio volume up higher, listened. She was paralyzed, she could not think. Then, beginning to tremble, she shut off the radio. Thinking, *Ednella must not know, just yet.*

Thinking, Does Ednella know?

Of course, Ednella had not known. When Beverly told her the news, Ednella stared at her uncomprehendingly; even, so very queerly, smiling slightly, as if she suspected a joke. "Beverly, what? What are you saying?" Beverly, her own eyes filling with tears, repeated what she'd said, supplying what details she knew from the news bulletin, and Ednella interrupted, panicked. "What? What? What? You're crazy!" she cried. In an instant the blood was draining rapidly out of her face. Her lips, already pale, were turning a ghastly sickish blue.

Beverly made a gesture as if to hold Ednella, to help her to a chair (they were in the kitchen: Ednella had just come downstairs, sallow-faced and groggy), but Ednella pushed away as if in terror. She turned, ran out of the room. Up the stairs, her footsteps heavy, pounding. Her voice lifted like a child's wail— aggrieved, incredulous.

No. Ednella had not known.

That afternoon, Yewville police, two detectives, came to the Crystal home at 8 Church Street, to question Ednella Crystal about the murder-suicide. Ednella had telephoned in, to volunteer the information that she'd seen Harvey Mercer the previous night; it was possible that she was the last person (except, of course, for Audrey McDermitt) to have seen the young man alive.

Yes, and she'd seen the young murdered woman, too. Earlier in the evening. Audrey had been desperate to talk with her, to enlist her help with Harvey; she'd driven over, and Ednella had sat out in her car with her, talking. For about an hour.

The detectives asked, gently, had Ednella been a friend of both?

"I was. I was a friend of—both."

Ednella's voice was soft, faint, toneless. Her face was mottled, her eyes threaded with blood. She wore black—a long black wool skirt, a black silk blouse with an elaborate lace collar. (A beautiful blouse, which Beverly had not seen before: bought, perhaps, at an antique clothing store in New York?) Her hair, shining still, had been brushed back severely from her face, emphasizing her sharp cheekbones and the angular thinness of her face. As she answered the detectives' questions her eyes moved restlessly over them, to Beverly; and back. (Beverly, of course, had insisted upon being present. She had a strong impulse to grip her stepdaughter's hand, tight.) The detectives were middle-aged, solid men, the elder resembling Wally Crystal—bald, with a lined, jowly, kindly face and a habit of sighing audibly. In fact, both police officers had known, or had known of, Wally Crystal. They spoke of him, respectfully, as "Mr. Crystal."

Ednella was telling the detectives, with an air of choosing her words precisely, that she had been asked by Audrey—by both Audrey and Harvey, but Audrey first—to help smooth over their difficulties. She'd known Harvey in high school, just as a friend—"We got along, understood each other"—but had been closer to Audrey since coming back to Yewville: it was strange, how friendships evolved. You couldn't predict.

The detectives asked if Ednella had gone to Harvey Mercer's house at Audrey McDermitt's request?

Ednella nodded. Her eyes were bright with tears. "Yes, I did. Audrey was so upset, crying, almost hysterical—I couldn't say no."

Had she intervened between the two in the past?

"No! Oh, no," Ednella said quickly. "I didn't feel comfortable in such a position. I—have my own life. I only did it because Audrey begged me, and I wanted her to be happy. Her, and Harvey."

Audrey McDermitt had been upset? Worried for her life?

"No, I think—I think she was worried that, because Harvey was so jealous, and tended to exaggerate when he drank, he would stop loving her and break off their engagement. She was always saying, 'I can't live without him.'"

But hadn't Audrey McDermitt been frightened, too, that Mercer might seriously injure her? kill her? According to her family—

Ednella interrupted, shaking her head. As if this were an old issue, she said, "Audrey had to know Harvey loved her, was crazy for her. He'd gone out with other girls—there was even some married woman in town he'd see—but he was in love with Audrey, and that was that. He wouldn't have hurt her—I mean, under ordinary circumstances."

These hadn't been ordinary circumstances, last night? Why?

"I—really don't know. I—" Ednella paused, wiping at her eyes. She spoke slowly, falteringly, "—don't *know*. They'd always had a stormy relationship. Harvey is—was—well, passionate. Hot-headed. And he'd gotten a drinking problem, I guess you'd have to say. And Audrey was so pretty, flighty—she didn't always know the effect she was having on him, how jealous she could make him." Ednella paused. Then said, almost bitterly, "She knew, but didn't know. Didn't let on."

Had Audrey McDermitt been going out with other men? Had there been any basis for Mercer's jealousy?

"No! Not really. And I told him so. I tried to kid him, I said, 'Don't be stupid, Audrey loves *you*. These other guys don't mean anything—to a girl like her, friends are a dime a dozen.'" Ednella laughed sharply. Then, more soberly, "At any rate, he seemed to believe me. By the time I left—"

But hadn't Ednella been worried, meeting Mercer like that? At his house? Alone? When he'd been drinking? When he'd already knocked Audrey McDermitt around, and threatened her life?

Ednella shook her head, annoyed. "Of course I wasn't worried. Not *me*."

But why not?

Ednella said impatiently, "Because he was my friend! My buddy. We got along." A pause. Ednella's lips twitched. She glanced over at Beverly, with a look of confusion and grief. "My God. I can't believe I'll never see him again! Either of them! *I can't believe it*."

Yet the detectives persisted: Ednella hadn't been afraid of Mercer, last night, only a few hours before he was to murder Audrey McDermitt, and take his own life?

"I said, *no*! Not *me*. Harvey would never have killed *me*—he didn't love me." Ednella smiled ironically. As if baiting the detectives, she said, "A man has to love you to kill you—right?"

But the detectives merely snorted with quick laughter, an obligatory and fleeting mirth.

They persisted: when Ednella had left Mercer's house, he was showing no signs, so far as Ednella could detect, of potential violence? He'd calmed down?

"Yes! Definitely. I'd swear."

So Ednella's intervention had helped, she'd thought?

Ednella gnawed at a thumbnail. Her eyes were clouded with doubt, fear. "That's what is so—horrible! So—unbelievable. I'd told Harvey just to get some sleep, he looked terrible, really strung-out, he should get some sleep and see Audrey the next day—call her in the morning. I'm wondering now if somebody else got to him—some of his friends, maybe. Poisoning him against her. You know how guys can be. When I left him, he shook my hand and thanked me. He really did. There were tears in his eyes. My God! Poor Harvey! And I was feeling pretty good about it! My God!"

And when had Ednella left Mercer?

At this, Ednella blinked. She was sitting very straight and poised in her black wool skirt, her black silk blouse with the exquisite lace collar. The faint bruised crescents beneath her eyes gave her an air of ravaged dignity. Ednella met the detectives gazes levelly, and said, "Let's see; Harvey telephoned around 10:30, sounding desperate, and I drove out to his place right away afterward; I was talking to him for, maybe, an hour; maybe a little more." Ednella paused. She was breathing quickly, almost eagerly. She said, "I—was back here by about midnight, I guess. I—went to bed. I'd gotten Harvey to promise he'd call Audrey in the morning. *I* didn't want to call her, I didn't want to be involved any further in such a private, intimate matter, so—I went home, and I went to bed. I guess—around midnight. I was so exhausted—" Ednella's voice trailed off, childlike and forlorn.

There was a moment's silence, Then, as the detectives were about to continue, Beverly said, quickly, "Yes—it was around midnight." She had been sitting unobtrusively to one side, hands clasped in her lap, head racked with pain, and now she spoke, helpfully, yet with an air of apology for interrupting. "I'd been asleep, but Ednella's car turning in the driveway woke me. Five minutes after twelve; I think."

The detectives nodded, and smiled, and believed her, for why should they not?

She was Wally Crystal's second wife, Wally Crystal's widow: a handsome middle-aged woman in a good magenta jersey dress, mother-of-pearl eyeglasses, black patent leather shoes. She was immaculately if fussily well-groomed. Her silver-blond hair was permed; her just perceptibly softening face was lightly powdered; she wore a pale coral lipstick. The detectives, smiling at her, saw this woman, Ednella, staring, might have seen someone else.

When the detectives rose to leave. Beverly was the one to see them to the door; Ednella remained in the living room, sobbing bitterly. The detectives thanked Beverly and apologized for disturbing her and Ednella: it was simply routine, part of their investigation, which would probably be completed in another day or two. The case, after all, was open and shut—cases of murder-suicide usually were.

Beverly winced, and managed a weak smile. "Oh, yes! I can see how they would be."

Just don't wait up for me, Beverly. Please!

This time Ednella had run out of the house in silence. Beverly, hearing her pounding feet on the stairs, had not called out after her, had not so much as glanced out a window at Ednella's car as it was backed, swiftly, recklessly, out of the driveway.

*   *   *

Prowling the house, the empty house. Not waiting, nor even thinking of the fact that she was not waiting. There was a glass of tart red wine in her unsteady hand and perhaps, after the two massive headache pills she'd swallowed down, that was unwise?

How swiftly dusk had come, and then night. November was gusty and damp. Leaves were blown against her windows with a sound suggesting giddiness, hilarity. Already, the girl had been dead more than twelve hours.

"It doesn't seem possible."

Where had Ednella gone, well, she did not know, nor care, where Ednella had gone, that was none of her business. Shortly after the detectives left, Ednella had fled (possibly to visit with the McDemitts? to share their grief? Offer commiseration? Or was she, more likely, simply driving into the country, into the night?) and it was none of Beverly Crystal's business. They were not related by blood, nor by sentiment. That was a fact, an implacable fact, Beverly had not wanted to know.

A life consists of many facts, implacable facts, you do not want to know.

Beverly Crystal, a widow, prowling a strange house in the dark. As if she feared putting on lights. Feared what she might see.

Just don't wait up for me. Please!

She had not had so blinding a headache since Wally Crystal's heart attack. Finding him groaning in the upstairs bathroom, telephoning for an ambulance, trying to keep the hysteria out of her voice. They'd come for him within five minutes, taken him away. Brief, brave, doomed hours in the intensive care ward of Yewville General Hospital.

Beverly, who are you? I'm just curious.

Who am—?

Who are you, beside my father's widow?

Why, what a thing to—ask!

And in the hired limousine, bringing them back to Church Street from the cemetery.

Beverly, stunned, had blinked at her fierce, cruel, beautiful stepdaughter not knowing whether the girl's question was sincere or meant, simply, to hurt. She'd managed a smile, she'd drawn a deep breath. *Do I have to be anyone? Anyone special?*

Her head was throbbing, the capillaries heated, swollen! Yes, surely it was a mistake to be drinking (was this Beverly's third glass?) after taking such powerful medication—but who would know?

"No witnesses."

She was going to go to bed, but, somehow, she did not go to bed. Somehow, another time, to her disgust, there she was, in the television room, watching, again, local television coverage of the deaths. It was 11:00 P.M. So late. Mesmerized, watching. The empty creaking house and a woman in nightgown, bathrobe, watching. What?—images of the dead. Familiar images at which one stared in the hope of—what?—that they might come alive, refute the fact of their deaths? These were mainly reruns of tapes shown earlier, yet they exerted an irresistible spell. Blurred with tears. "Oh, damn!"—the wineglass tilting, spilling. Beverly was too dizzy to pick it up, staring another time at pretty Audrey McDemitt in her blue-and-gold cheerleader's costume, in her gravely black high school graduation costume, now, so proudly, in her crisp, white nurse's costume, a cap smartly set on her honey-brown curly hair. Smiling her dazzling smile for the camera, for a television audience she could not see. Not hearing, either, the newscaster's solemn voice-over speaking of funeral arrangements.

And here were images of the "murderer-suicide" Harvey Mercer. None so formal or posed as those of the victim, none in any kind of uniform. In one snapshot, the husky young man, dirty-blond hair worn long, stood leaning against the hood of a car with oversized tires (was this the car Ednella Crystal had helped Mercer rebuild? Sanding, stripping, painting, polishing? As if her young life had depended upon it?), grinning at the camera. In another snapshot a close-up, Mercer smiled almost shyly, his arms tightly folded across his muscular chest. A handsome young man, but with something too intense about him. Furrowed forehead, heavy eyebrows, blond-glinting stubble on his jaws. *A man has to love you to kill you—right?*

In fact, Beverly did remember Harvey Mercer. Not by name, but by appearance. She'd seen him occasionally in Yewville, on the street, in a store; she seemed to recall he'd worked for a while at one of the local service stations where she went for gas. Of course, he had not known her as Ednella Crystal's stepmother. He hadn't even seen her, probably.

Beyond the excited buzz of the television set, there was the sound of a door quietly opening, shutting. Footsteps?

"No. Never again."

Beverly shut her eyes. It was a way of keeping the tears from running down her cheeks. She wasn't drunk, she was just very sad. She *was* crying, but no one would see. Having grabbed from somewhere (the hall closet? but much larger than she recalled the closet being) that heavy, soiled, quilted L.L. Bean coat of Ednella's the girl hadn't worn for years, and she was walking swiftly, half running, along the alley behind the house, the darkened alley where Church Street residents or their servants set out garbage and trash cans for the twice-weekly pickup, snowflakes melting against her heated skin and *Where am I? why am I here?* panting staring frightened at the shadows surrounding her, she was a girl of eleven or twelve again, in a distant city, returning home from school at dusk, wintry dusk, in lightly falling snow peering into the lighted houses of strangers, catching glimpses of unknown, inaccessible lives, warm-lit kitchens, parlors with their shades not yet drawn (sometimes, even as Beverly stood on the sidewalk staring, a man or a woman would come to pull the blind: so casually excluding her!), she was not crying but she was staring in resentful longing, yes, in envy, yes, in a kind of bitter love, for her own home was not a happy home—*Don't! don't think of that!*—so she would not think of it, for she was also a mature woman, an adult, staring-astonished into the rear of a kitchen where a young girl, breasts bared, was leaning back ecstatically, eyes closed, rubbing something glistening against her heated skin, and Beverly knew she should look away; but could not.

What did you tell him? Did you let that girl die? Did you let that girl die?

"Beverly?"

The voice was so faint and hoarse, Beverly would not have recognized it.

She opened her eyes, disoriented. Her headache was blinding. For a moment she did not know where she was. In the doorway stood Ednella, staring at her. The girl's hair was disheveled, her face pale, ravaged, ugly, eyes bloodshot with crying. Simulated laughter sounded raucous and demented from the television set.

This, then, confusedly, was what happened.

By a gesture of grief and repugnance, Beverly indicated that she did not wish to speak with, no nor even look at, her distraught stepdaughter. Ednella, stung, turned away at once, and retreated back along the darkened corridor, to the kitchen. For some minutes Beverly remained where she was, seated on the sofa, trying to get the better of the throbbing pain in her head. Aloud she murmured, "No. I won't. I don't have to." Elsewhere in the house there was silence. Had Ednella run out again? Beverly saw that there was nothing else to be done, she found herself already in motion, though moving unsteadily, back to the kitchen where, looking as if she'd been slapped hard in the face, Ednella was sitting at the table. Seeing Beverly, however, Ednella rose, came eagerly forward, whispering, "I—didn't mean—I never meant—Oh, Mother!" She burst into tears. She was shivering convulsively. Beverly found herself embracing Ednella, comforting her, even as the girl gripped her tight, tight, to the point of pain. She was murmuring, "It's all right, dear, it will be all right, I love you." For that was the one thing she knew, amid all that she didn't.

POOR BIBI

Were you ever awakened from a deep satisfying sleep to the sound of another's hoarse, strangulated breathing? It isn't a very pleasant experience, I can tell you!

My husband and I were so awakened, one night not long ago, by Bibi, poor thing—and when we discovered him, (not in his pile of rags in the warmest snuggest corner of the cellar but in a far, dark corner) it seemed we were already too late, and Bibi was dying.

Poor thing!—he'd been ailing for weeks. Since he first came to live in our house Bibi had been susceptible to respiratory infections, a genetic weakness for which some ancestor was to blame, but what good are accusations at such a time?

Bibi himself was very much to blame. One of us, my husband or I, would notice that Bibi was behaving oddly, coughing, wheezing, pushing his food aside in a gesture of revulsion, and say, Maybe we should take Bibi to be examined?—and the other would agree, Yes, we should. But cunning Bibi overheard, and understood, and managed to improve, for a few days. And since it was disruptive to the entire household to force Bibi to do anything against his will—I still have a scar, on the back of my left hand, from one such episode, last spring!—we kept postponing the task.

And it did seem, for weeks I swear—Bibi *was* holding his own.

Of course, with Bibi, it was easy to be deceived. That had been one of the problems with Bibi from the start.

In the beginning, though it was long ago, I can remember we were very happy. It had been promised to my bridegroom and me that we would be very happy all the days of our lives. I believe this would be so, still, had we not weakened, and out of loneliness brought Bibi home to live with us. We were *two* then, and with the recklessness of youth thought we would expand our happiness to *three*.

How many years ago has it been, since Bibi first came to live in our household?—the happiest, most energetic, most innocent and delightful creature imaginable! All marveled at his frisky antics, his unflagging high spirits. Many were frankly envious. Darling Bibi!—the miraculous flame of life itself danced in him, unquenchable. In those early days his eyes were dear and shining; lovely, faintly iridescent, shifting shades of amber. His pert little "button" nose was pink, damp, and cool—how I shivered, when he nuzzled it against my bare legs! His ears pricked up erect, his pelt crackled with static electricity when we brushed it, his small, sharp teeth were glistening and white—no, you would not want to tease Bibi too roughly, in the vicinity of those teeth.

Bibi! Bibi! we would cry, clapping as Bibi raced around the lawn yipping and squealing like a maddened creature. (How we laughed, though perhaps it was not always amusing!) Inside the house, though it was forbidden, Bibi made a game of scrambling up the staircase and rumbling head-first down again, his sharp nails clicking and scraping against the polished parquet. Bibi, naughty boy!—oh, aren't you *darling*!

We forgave him, we had not the heart to seriously discipline him, as our wise elders urged us; when he pushed his heated little face against us, frantic to know how we loved him, and only him.

As, of course, in those early years, we did.

Then, it seemed with cruel abruptness, Bibi was no longer young, and no longer in good health. And no longer our darling naughty boy.

If he snapped at us—if his teeth caught in our flesh, drawing blood—forgiveness didn't come so readily.

If he refused his food, or, indeed, gobbled it down in a way disgusting to see, and vomited it, in dribbles, through the house—are we to be blamed for relegating him more and more to the cellar, and out of our sight?

(Not that the cellar was a dank, damp, unhealthy place. In the warm snug corner near the furnace, where Bibi's bed of rags lay, it was really most comfortable. It was really quite nice.)

We did not neglect him, even so. Indeed it was impossible to ignore him!—with his whining, whimpering, and clawing at the cellar door, and the loathsome messes he made which one of us (more often, I) would have to clean up each morning.

Yet it was impossible to be angry with Bibi for long. When he lay on his back and rolled awkwardly over, showing his belly, as if in a memory of play, when he gazed up at us, his master and mistress, with eyes rimmed in mucus, that look of mute animal sorrow, animal hurt, animal terror—we saw that, yes, we loved him still.

And how painful, such love!

For it became ever more obvious, Bibi's time had come.

We can't let him suffer, one of us said. And the other, We can't, may God have mercy we *can't*.

And wept in each other's arms, as Bibi gazed mutely and fearfully up at us.

So it happened that, on that night we were awakened so rudely from our sleep, my husband and I made our decision. Stealing silently into the cellar before the sun had fully risen, to surprise Bibi where he lay, out of spite I believe, in his dark, cold corner. Quickly, we wrapped him in an old blanket, binding his limbs to keep him from struggling. Fortunately, he'd grown too feeble to put up much resistance.

We then carried him out to the car, and I held him in my lap as my husband drove to Family Pet Veterinary Hospital and Emergency Clinic several miles away. This was an establishment we had passed numerous times, noting that it boasted 24-HOUR EMERGENCY SERVICE.

Bibi, good Bibi, sweet Bibi, I murmured, everything will be all right! Trust us! But Bibi was whining, and whimpering, and growling, and drooling; and his mucus-dotted eyes rolled in his head in a way distressful to see.

When we arrived at Family Pet Veterinary Hospital and Emergency Clinic we were astonished to see that the large parking lot, so very unexpectedly for this early hour (not yet seven A.M.), was nearly full. Inside, the barnlike waiting room was so crowded, not a single seat was free! Fortunately, as we gave our names to the receptionist, a couple was called into the waiting room, and two seats became available.

How disagreeably busy it was in the pet hospital!—how warm, airless, and oppressive the atmosphere. Bibi began to whimper and squirm, but was too weak to cause any mischief.

Nor, apparently, had he eaten for some time; a blessing since, in panic, or out of spite, he might have vomited on us—or worse!

So we sat, and waited. I had had the foresight to wrap Bibi in his blanket so that only the very rips of his ears showed. I meant to protect the poor, dying thing against the prurient stares of strangers—how I loathed them, staring at my husband and me, with our feebly squirming burden.

So many men and women, married couples like ourselves, were seated in the waiting room, with their ailing, fretting creatures. What a din! Yips, barks, whining, cries, groans, shrieks, pitiful to hear. There was a feverish pulse to the air, and such a combination of smells! The waiting room was vast, larger than one might have predicted from the outside; in the unwinking fluorescent glare, rows of seats stretched virtually out of sight.

My husband whispered, Shall I hold Bibi for a while? and I assured him, Oh no, the poor thing isn't heavy any longer. My husband wiped at his eyes, and said, He's being very brave, isn't he? and I said, carefully, for I was on the verge of bursting into tears, We are all being very brave.

Finally our names were called. As we rose, Bibi put up a last, faint struggle, but I gripped him tight. Everything will be all right, Bibi, soon!—I promised. Have faith in us!

Strangers' eyes followed us as we went into the examining room. But I had made certain that Bibi was wrapped up snug in his blanket, and shielded from them. Poor darling! And so *brave*!

*   *   *

A young female assistant in a blood- or excrement-smeared uniform led us briskly into the examination room, which was windowless, with grim, gray, unadorned concrete walls and floor; a high ceiling; harsh fluorescent lighting; and a searing odor of disinfectant. This young woman behaved with bright, mechanical efficiency, instructing us to lay Bibi—"your patient"—on a metal table in the center of the room, which we did; and to remove his blanket, which we did. At that moment, the doctor appeared, entering the room whistling thinly, and I thought rudely, through his teeth; he was wiping his hands on a paper towel which he crumpled and tossed carelessly in the direction of an overflowing trash basket. He was young, and the assessing look he gave us, my husband and me, before turning to Bibi, was one of shocking impertinence.

By this time, my husband and I were exhausted, and our tempers wearing thin. We explained to the doctor that we'd been waiting for hours to see him; we'd hurried to this place in the hope that Bibi might be granted a quick, merciful end to his suffering, but, so far, he'd only suffered more.

Bibi was lying, quivering, on the cold metal table, his slack, hairless belly exposed; ribs and pelvic bones protruding obscenely. I had not realized the poor thing had lost so much flesh, and felt a twinge of shame—as if I were to blame. His eyes were encrusted with dried mucus, yet shifted nervously in their sockets, so it was clear that the poor thing heard, and surely understood, everything that was being said about him.

Doctor, my husband and I pleaded—just look at him! Will you help us?

The young doctor had been staring at Bibi, rooted to the spot. His whistling had ceased abruptly.

Doctor—?

Still, the doctor stood staring at Bibi. Yes, it was true that Bibi looked piteous, but surely a doctor has seen worse, far worse? Why did he stare at Bibi so—incredulously?

At last, turning to my husband and me, he said, his voice trembling, Is this some sort of joke?

My husband, who is a forthright man, faltered beneath the doctor's glare. Joke?—what on earth do you mean, Doctor?

The doctor said, regarding us with an expression of disbelief and revulsion, What do *you* mean, coming to me with *this*? Are you mad?

My husband and I were utterly baffled, and becoming desperate. We said, Why, Doctor, we would like a—merciful end to poor Bibi's suffering. Can't you see, he's suffering terribly, he's past all hope—

But the doctor said rudely. My God! I can't believe this!

Doctor?—what do you mean? Can't you put him to—to sleep?

All this while, it breaks my heart to report that poor Bibi was lying helpless before us on the table. Panting, shivering, a frothy line of drool on his discolored lips. I saw with a shock that his eyes were not amber any longer, but a sickly yellow, as with jaundice. The insides of his ears, that had once been so pink and clean, were yellow too, and encrusted with scum. How unspeakably cruel, that he should be a witness to such a scene!

The doctor and his assistant were conferring together, in whispers. The young woman too had been staring aghast at Bibi—as if she had any right to judge.

My husband dared interrupt, for he was losing his patience. Doctor?—what on earth is wrong? We're going to pay you, after all. You do this simple procedure for others all the time—*why not far us?*

But the doctor had turned resolutely away from Bibi, as from my husband and me, as if he could not bear our presence another moment. Impossible, he said. Just take it—him—out of here, at once. Of course we don't do such things.

Stubbornly, angrily, my husband repeated, You do this for others, Doctor—*why not for us?*

And I joined in, my eyes flooded with tears, Oh Doctor yes, please—*why not for us?*

But the young doctor had had enough of us. He simply strode out of the room, and shut the door behind him. Our words hung in the air like shameful gaseous odors. How could anyone in a position of authority, to whom others have come begging for help, behave so cruelly?—so unprofessionally?

My husband and I stared at each other, and at Bibi. We *two* who had lost all innocence by becoming *three*. What was wrong? Was there some error?—some terrible misunderstanding?

But there was only Bibi there on the cold metal table, in mortal agony, beneath the unwinking fluorescent lights, watching us, hearing every word.

The doctor's assistant handed us Bibi's soiled blanket as if it were contaminated, and said, with an air of righteous disgust, You may leave by this door, into the parking lot. Please.

And so (I know you are preparing to judge us harshly, too) we did it ourselves. We did what had to be done.

For, after all, society failed us. What choice had we!

Fifty feet behind the pet hospital was a deep drainage ditch filled with brackish, ill-smelling water, in which there floated, like shards of dreams, threads of detergent scum. Trembling, sick at heart, blinking back tears, my husband and I carried Bibi to the ditch, resolved to put the poor thing out of his misery.

We hadn't needed, even, to confer. No, there was no possibility of our bringing Bibi back home with us. We simply couldn't go through all that again!

For we, too, have grown, if not old, older. We, too, have lost our hope and high spirits, along with our youth.

We, too, to whom it was promised we would live happily forever have had quite enough of suffering.

And yet: not in our very worst dreams could we have anticipated such an ending to our beloved Bibi. So heartbreaking a task, yes and physically demanding and repulsive an ordeal—forcing poor Bibi into that cold, foul water, and pushing his head under! And how fiercely, how savagely he fought us!—he, who had pretended to be so feeble!—he, our darling Bibi, who had lived with us for so many years, transformed into a stranger, an enemy—a beast! Causing us to think afterward that *Bibi had been hiding his deepest, most secret self from us.* Never had we truly known him.

Bibi, no! we cried.

Bibi, *obey!*

Naughty Bibi! Bad boy! *Obey!*

The appalling struggle lasted at least ten minutes. I will never, never forget. I, who'd loved Bibi so, was forced to become his executioner, in the interest of mercy. And my poor, dear husband, the most refined and civilized of men, imagine him suddenly provoked to rage—for Bibi would not die for the longest time—grunting, cursing, ugly veins standing out in his forehead as he held the thrashing, squirming, frantic creature beneath the surface of ditch water in a suburban field, one weekday morning. Imagine!

For we soon forget what we do, in the human desperation of doing it.

And you, you damned hypocrites—what will you do with yours?

THE UNDESIRABLE TABLE

With mumbled apologies, the maître d' seated us at an undesirable table in our favorite restaurant Le Coq d'Or. The men in our party protested. But there was nothing to be done. It was a Saturday night in the holiday season, the more desirable tables had been booked weeks in advance. Our reservation had been made practically at the last minute, what could we expect? Even though we were—are—frequent patrons of Le Coq d'Or, and had imagined ourselves on special terms with the management.

As we took our seats, reluctantly, at the undesirable table, in a front bay window of the dining room, one of our party remarked, bemused, yet serious, that perhaps the maître d' had expected a twenty-dollar bill to be slipped surreptitiously to him. Was *that* it?

Seated at the undesirable table, in a front bay window of the dining room of Le Coq d'Or, we discussed this possibility in lowered, incensed voices. We are highly verbal people and much of dispute in our lives is resolved, if not satisfied, by speech. The more cynical among our party believed that yes, this might be so; though, in the past, and we'd dined in this restaurant innumerable times, the maître d' had not behaved like an extortionist.

The more optimistic among our party believed that, no, that wasn't it, at all; surely not; our reservation had been made late, just the day before, the holiday season was frenzied this year, it *was* a Saturday night. And so why not enjoy ourselves? As we'd come out to do?

Even if it was something of a disappointment, and a rude surprise in a way, to be seated at an undesirable table in Le Coq d'Or.

And so, seated at the undesirable table, in a front bay window of the dining room of Le Coq d'Or, with an unwanted view of the street outside, we gave our drink orders to the waiter; we smiled gamely, and took up our hefty Le Coq d'Or menus (parchment-bound, gilt-printed, gold-tasseled, with elegantly scripted French, and English translations below) and perused the familiar categories of appetizers, first courses, entrees, desserts, wines. We chattered to one another discussing the dishes we might order, recalling previous meals at Le Coq d'Or, previous evenings in one another's company that had been both intellectually stimulating and emotionally rewarding, evenings that had had *meaning* of a kind, precious to consider. For food consumed in the presence of dear friends is not mere food but sustenance; a sustenance of the soul. A formal meal, with excellent wines, in a restaurant of the quality of Le Coq d'Or, in the right company, is a celebration. Yes?

So it was, we smiled gamely. We chattered happily. We were not to be cheated of our evening's pleasure—for most of us, a well-deserved reward for the rigors of the previous week—by the accident of being seated at an undesirable table. We gave our orders to the waiter, who was all courtesy and attentiveness. We handed back our hefty menus. When our drinks arrived, we lifted them to drink with pleasure and relief. We were almost successfully ignoring two facts: that the undesirable table in the bay window of the dining room was even more undesirable than the most pessimistic of us had anticipated; and that those of us unfortunate enough to be seated facing the bay window were particularly afflicted. Yet such was our courtesy with one another, even after years of friendship, and so awkward was the situation, that no one, not even those facing the bay window and the street, chose to speak of it. For to *name* a problem is *to invest it with too much significance.*

We, who are so highly verbal, whose lives, it might be said, are ingeniously amassed cities of words, understand the danger as few others do. Ah, yes!

There followed then, with much animation, a discussion of wines—in which several of our company, male, participated with great gusto and expertise, while others listened with varying degrees of attentiveness and indulgence. Which wines, of the many wines of Le Coq d'Or's excellent list, were to be ordered?—considering that the party was to dine variously on seafood, fish, poultry, and meat. Our conversations about wine are always lengthy and passionate, and touched with a heartfelt urgency; even pedantry; yet there is an undercurrent of bemused self-consciousness, too—for the wine connoisseurs are well aware of the absurdity of their almost mystical fanaticism even as they unapologetically indulge in it. After all, if there is a simple, direct, unalloyed ecstasy to be taken by the mouth, savored by the tongue like a liquid communion wafer, how can it be denied to those with the means to purchase it?—and by whom?

So, the usual spirited talk of wine among our party. And some argument. Where there is passion there *is* argument. Not that the wine connoisseurs dominated completely, despite their loud voices. Conversation became more general, there were parenthetical asides, the usual warm queries of health? recent trips? family? work? gossip of mutual acquaintances, colleagues? If there was a distracting scene outside the window, on the street (which was in fact an avenue, broad, windy, littered, eerily lit by street lamps whose light seemed to withhold, not give, illumination) or even on the sidewalk a few yards away from those of our company with our backs stolidly to the window *we knew nothing of it: saw nothing.*

At last, our appetizers were brought to us. And the first of the wines. The ceremonial uncorking, the tasting—exquisite!

Red caviar, and arugula salads. Giant shrimp delicately marinated. Pâté maison, Escargots. Coquilles St. Jacques. Consommé a la Barigoule. Steak tartare. And of course the thick crusty brown bread that is a specialty of Le Coq d'Or. As we talked now of politics. Foreign, national, state, local. We talked of religion—is there any *demonstrable difference* between the actions of "believers" and "nonbelievers"? We asked after our friends' children in the hope and expectation that they would ask after ours.

(One of our party, her gaze drawn repeatedly to something outside the window, which, facing it as she was, at this undesirable table in the dining room of Le Coq d'Or, seemed to possess a morbid attraction for her, suddenly laid her fork down. Shut her eyes. As conversation swirled around her. But she said nothing, and nothing was said to her, and after a pause of some seconds she opened her eyes and, gazing now resolutely at her plate, picked up her fork and resumed eating.)

(Another of our party weakened. Laid his fork down too, pressed the back of his hand against his forehead. Again, conversation continued. Our eyes were firmly fixed on one another. And after a minute or so he, too, revived, with steely resolution lifting his wineglass to his mouth and draining it in a single swallow.)

Boeuf Stroganoff. Pompano à la Meunière. Bouillabaisse. Sweetbreads à la York. Chateaubriand. Blanquette of veal, coq au vin, sole Lyonnaise, and an elegantly grilled terrapin with black mushrooms. And julienne vegetables, lightly sauteed in olive oil. And another generous basket of crusty brown bread. And another bottle of wine, this time a Bordeaux.

One of our party, a woman with widened moist eyes, said, Oh!—what are they doing—? staring out the window in an attitude of disbelieving horror. But adding quickly, a hot blush mottling her face, No really—*don't look.*

No one of us having looked, nor even heard. In any case.

(Yes, certainly it crossed the minds of those gentlemen of our party with their backs to the offending scene to offer to exchange seats with the women facing it. Yet we hesitated. And finally, as if by mutual consent, said nothing. For to *name* a problem, in particular an upsetting and demoralizing problem over which none of us has any control, is *to invest it with too much significance.*)

How popular Le Coq d'Or is!—a region, an atmosphere, an exquisite state of the soul rather than merely a *restaurant.* In such surroundings, amid the glitter of flashing cutlery, expensive glassware, and crystal chandeliers, animal gluttony is so tamed as to appear a kind of asceticism.

At Le Coq d'Or, a perfectly orchestrated meal—which, we were determined, ours would be, even at an undesirable table—is rarely a matter of less than two hours.

Casting our eyes resolutely *not* in the direction of the window, the avenue, the luckless creatures outside. But, rather, with some envy at parties seated at desirable tables. Impossible not to feel resentment, bitterness, rancor. Even as we smiled, smiled. Even as the maître d' hovered guiltily near, inquiring after the quality of our food and drink and service, which we assured him, with impeccable politeness, and a measure of coolness, was excellent as always. Yet: *Why are these other patrons favored with desirable tables, while we, equally deserving, possibly more deserving, are not?*

Perennial questions of philosophy. The mystery of good, evil. God, devil. More wine?—a final bottle uncorked. Through the plate glass bay window an occasional unwelcome, unheard stridency of sound. Keening wails, or sirens? No, mere vibrations. All sound *is* vibrations, devoid of meaning. Coffee, liqueurs. Desserts so delicious they must be shared: Sorbet à la Bruxelles, profiteroles au chocolate, meringue glacé, zabaglione frappé, strawberries flambé. And those luscious Swiss mints. It was observed that the rose-tinted wax candles in the center of the table had burned low, their flames had begun to flicker. A romance of candlelight. The circular table, draped in a fine oyster-white linen cloth—the rose-patterned cushioned chairs—were floating in a pool of darkness. Staring intensely at one another, friends, dear friends, the fever of our love for one another, our desperate faith in one another, transfixed by one another's faces. For there lies *meaning*. Yes?

You expected me to weaken. To surrender to an instinctive narrative momentum. In which the *not-named* is suddenly, and therefore irrevocably, *named*. Following the conventions of narration,

I might have proceeded then to Events B, C, D, the horror of disclosure increasing in rhythm with the courses of our elaborate meal. By the climax—the emptying of the very last bottle of wine, the paying of the check, our rising to leave—a revelation would have occurred. *We would never be the same again after our experience at the undesirable table*. You expected that.

But that was not my way, because it did not happen that way. There was no *naming*, thus no *narrative*.

The check was paid, we rose to leave. One of us, fumbling for her handbag, dropped it and it fell onto a chair and from the chair to the floor spilling some of its contents with a startled little cry.

We walked through the dining room of Le Coq d'Or without a backward glance at the undesirable table.

(Let the maître d', who wished us happy holidays with a forced smile, worry that we'll never return to his damned restaurant. Let him worry he's insulted us, and we'll spread the word to others. Our revenge!)

Fortunately, there is a high-rise parking structure directly accessible from Le Coq d'Or so that patrons are spared walking along the windswept, littered avenue, and the possible danger of this walk. We'd parked our cars there, on Level A, and in the cooler air felt a sudden giddy sense of release, like children freed from confinement. We were talking loudly, we were laughing. We shook hands warmly saying goodnight, we hugged one another, we kissed. Old friends, dear friends. Now the ordeal of the undesirable table was behind us it was possible to forget it. In fact, we were rapidly forgetting it. We would retain instead the far more meaningful memory of another superb shared meal at Le Coq d'Or, another memorable evening in one another's company. Of course we'll be back—many times.

For Le Coq d'Or is, quite simply, the finest restaurant available to us. It might be said we have no choice.

THE HAND-PUPPET

How strangeness enters our lives. The mother had known that her eleven-year-old daughter Tippi had had an interest in puppets, and in ventriloquism, since fourth grade, but she'd had no idea that Tippi had been working in secret, upstairs in her room, on a hand-puppet of her own invention; nor that the child, by nature a shy, somewhat withdrawn child, planned to surprise her with it in quite so dramatic a way—thrusting the ugly thing into her face when she stepped into the kitchen one Monday morning to prepare breakfast, and wriggling it as frantically as if it were alive.

"H'LO MISSUS! G'MORNIN' MISSUS! WHAT'S TO EAT MISSUS!"—the voice was a low guttural mocking drawl, the mother would have sworn a stranger's voice.

The mother was of course taken totally by surprise. She'd had no idea that her daughter had come downstairs before her, and so stealthily! It was all so premeditated, seemingly rehearsed, like theater.

"Oh God!"—the mother responded in the way the daughter must have wished, giving a little shriek and pressing her hand against her heart; staring, for an instant uncomprehending, at the big-headed baby-faced puppet cavorting a few inches from her face. Afterward she would recall that, in that first startled instant, the puppet had seemed somehow familiar, the close-set black-button eyes, the leering red-satin mouth, but in fact she'd never seen anything like it before. It had a misshapen body made of stiff felt that was mainly shoulders and arms; the head was bald and domed, like an embryo's; the nose was a snubbed little piece of cotton made prehensile by a strip of wire. How obscene, the mother thought.

"Tippi, how—clever," the mother said, seeing that the child was hiding clumsily behind a part-opened closet door, her arm, in the flannel sleeve of her pajama top, tremblingly extended. "But you shouldn't scare the life out of your poor mother, that isn't very nice."

"SORRY MISSUS! SORRY MISSUS!" The puppet squirmed in exaggerated delight, stretching its red mouth, making a series of mock bows.

The mother tried to interrupt but the low guttural drawl continued—"MISSUS I BEEN HERE BEFORE YA! AN' I GONNA BE HERE WHENYA GONE!" There came then a crackling lunatic laugh the mother would have sworn issued, not from her daughter's mouth, but from the puppet's.

"Tippi, really!"—the mother, now annoyed, but smiling to conceal her annoyance, pushed the closet door open, to reveal the daughter there, mere inches away, breathing quickly, eyes shining, flush-faced with excitement as a small child caught in mischief. "Isn't it a little early in the morning for this sort of thing?"

Boldly, Tippi kept the puppet between her mother and herself, the big domed head and antic face still cavorting—"DID I SCARED YOU MISSUS! SOOO SOORRY MISSUS!"

"Tippi, please. That's enough."

"TIPPI AIN HERE MISSUS TOO BAD! BYEBYE!"

"Tippi, damn—!"

Exasperated, beginning to be a little frightened, the mother took hold of the puppet, grasping her daughter's antic fingers inside the cloth torso. For a moment the fingers resisted—and surprisingly strong they were. Then, abruptly, Tippi gave in, ducking her head. Rarely disobedient or rebellious, even as a toddler, she seemed embarrassed by this display; her sallow skin blotched red and her pale myopic eyes, framed by milky-blue plastic frames, seemed to dim in retreat. She mumbled, "Sorry Mom," adding in an undertone, "It's just some silly thing I made!"

"Tippi, it *is* amazing. It's . . . ingenious."

Now she'd regained some measure of control, the mother complimented the daughter on the hand-puppet. What was surprising, unexpected, was that the daughter had been so creative—fashioning a professional-looking puppet out of household odds and ends, pieces of felt, strips of satin, ribbons, buttons, thumbtacks—she who seemed so frequently overwhelmed by school, and whose grades were only average; she whose creative efforts, guided by one or another teacher, and always on assignment, had seemed in the past touchingly derivative and conventional. The mother warmly noted the clever floppy rabbit ears, the drollery of five prehensile fingers and a lumpy thumb on each hand. The slightly asymmetrical domed head with a prominent crooked seam like a cracked egg. "When on earth did you make this, Tippi? And your voice—how on earth did you do *that*?"

The daughter shrugged, not meeting the mother's eye. Mumbled again a vague apology; disparaging words about the

puppet—"silly, dumb, didn't turn out right"—then she was hurrying out of the kitchen, the puppet carelessly crumpled in her
hand. She ran upstairs to get ready for school, a soft-bodied
child in flannel pajamas, barefoot, her heels coming down hard
on the stairs. The mother, hand still pressed against her heart,
stared after her in perplexed silence.

How strangeness enters our lives.

It was in fact, it would remain in memory, an ordinary schoolday
morning. The Monday following the weeklong Easter recess in
the public schools. Lorraine Lake, Tippi's mother, usually came
downstairs at about 7:30 A.M. weekdays to prepare breakfast
for her husband and daughter, but on this morning, the morning of the hand-puppet, Mr. Lake, sales manager for a local
electronics company, was in Dallas at a convention. So there
was just Lorraine and Tippi, whose school bus would arrive at
about 8:10 A.M., stopping at a corner up the road. Mr. Lake
traveled frequently; so his absence on this morning would not
be disturbing; in fact, such mornings, mother and daughter
at the breakfast table, mother and daughter exchanging casual
remarks as the radio on the windowsill played cheery-bright
morning music and chickadees fluttered about the bird feeder
outside the window, were routinely pleasant, companionable. It
might be said that Lorraine Lake looked forward to them. And
now, her nerves jangling from the surprise, the oddity, of the
hand-puppet, felt subtly betrayed by her daughter.

It was deliberate, she thought. Premeditated. Because I'm
alone. She would never have done that to her father.

Staring out the window above the sink, as into a void. The
Lakes lived in a rural-suburban landscape where, in summer, the

foliage of crowded trees created a dark screen, like a perpetual cloud ceiling; in winter and early spring, before the trees budded, the sky was predominant, pressing. Yet it seemed always the same sky—opaque, dully white, layers of stained cumulus clouds like ill-fitting flagstones.

Lorraine Lake stared, and, by degrees, into focus came the needle-thin red column of mercury in the thermometer outside the window: 41 degrees Fahrenheit. This too was a familiar fact.

Briskly then Lorraine Lake prepared breakfast. Hot oatmeal with raisins and sliced bananas for Tippi, toast and black coffee for herself. A ritual, and pleasure in it. I am the mother, Lorraine Lake was thinking. I am not "*Missus*"! She was a fully mature woman of forty-two and she was not a woman who believed she might have cultivated another, more worthy, more mysterious and sublime life elsewhere, a life without husband, child; a "true" life without the trappings of the identity that accrued to her in this shining kitchen, this rural-suburban brick-and-stucco colonial house on a curving cul-de-sac lane. If Lorraine Lake had had a life preceding this April morning, this nerve-jangled moment, she did not recall it with any sense of loss, nor any particular sentiment.

I do these things because I am the mother.

Because I am the mother, I do these things.

Remembering how, the previous week, Tippi had stayed home, most of the time upstairs in her room. A quiet child. A shy child. A good child who seemed, at a casual glance, younger than eleven—lacking a certain exuberance, a spark, an air of resistance. MISSUS I BEEN HERE BEFORE YA! AN' I GONNA BE HERE WHENYA GONE! Tippi seemed to have few friends at school, or, in any case, rarely spoke of them; but there was a girl named Sonia, also a sixth grader, who lived in the neighborhood, who'd sometimes invited Tippi over . . . but had not, recently; nor had Tippi asked if she might invite Sonia over. The realization was alarming. I don't want my daughter to be left behind, Lorraine Lake thought. I don't want my daughter to be unhappy.

Recalling how, as a small child, Tippi had chattered incessantly to herself, sometimes, it had seemed, preferring her own solitary company to that of her loving, doting parents'. Thank God she'd grown out of that stage! In later years too the child talked to herself, but usually in private; in her room, or in the bathroom; which isn't uncommon, after all. Now, Lorraine Lake recalled with dismay having heard, just last week, a low guttural voice in the house, a radio or TV voice she'd assumed it must be . . . she'd been on the telephone the other day when she'd heard it, at a distance, and had thought nothing of it. She realized now with a sick sensation that this had been the puppet-voice, the "thrown" voice of Tippi's ventriloquism.

How had the child, practicing in secret, grown so adept? So quickly?

Could one be born with a natural gift for—such a thing?

When Tippi came back downstairs, her face washed, her limp fawn-colored hair combed, she carried herself stiffly, as if she'd been wounded. Her appetite for the oatmeal, and her usual glass of fruit juice, was conspicuously restrained. She wants praise for that ugly thing, Lorraine Lake thought, incensed. Well, she's getting none from me. It was almost 8 A.M. Except for the cheery-bright radio music and the excited tittering of chickadees outside the window, there was a strained silence. Finally Lorraine said, with a sudden smile, "Your puppet is very . . . clever, Tippi. And the *voice*, how on earth did you do that?" Tippi seemed scarcely to hear, spooning oatmeal slowly, chewing with apparent distaste. She was a child who loved sweets and often over-ate, even at breakfast, but this morning her very mouth was sullen. "I had no idea you were making anything like that," Lorraine persisted, enthusiastically. "Was it a secret? A project for school?"

Tippi shrugged her shoulders. Her milky-blue glasses were sliding down her nose and Lorraine had to resist the impulse to push them back up.

Tippi mumbled something not quite audible. The puppet was "silly." Hadn't "turned out right."

Like all the other girls at her school, Tippi wore jeans, sneakers, a cotton-knit sweater over a shirt; Tippi's sweater was so baggy as to resemble a maternity smock. Such clothes should have disguised the child's plumpness, but did not. Tippi's plain prim moon-shaped face seemed to Lorraine to be stiffened in opposition, and in the newly tasted strength of opposition. Lorraine asked, with her bright, eager smile, "But is it a project? Are you taking it to school?"

Tippi sighed, messing with her oatmeal; her pale eyes, lifting reluctantly to Lorraine's, were obdurate, opaque. "No, Mom. It isn't a *project*." Her lips twisted scornfully. "And I'm not taking it to dumb old school, don't worry."

Lorraine protested, "Tippi, I wasn't worried. I was just—" She hesitated over the word "concerned." Saying instead, "—curious."

"No, Mom. I'm not taking it to dumb old school, don't worry."

"I said, Tippi, I *wasn't worried*."

Which was not the truth, but Tippi could not know. So much of what a mother must say in a household is not true, yet it is always in the interests of other members of the household not to know.

On these mornings, the arrival of the yellow school bus with its invasive sound of brakes was always imminent, awaited. If a child, of the six who boarded the bus at the corner, was late, the driver sounded the horn, once, twice, a third time; waited a beat or two; then drove off, with an invasive shifting of gears. Lorraine Lake had not realized how she'd come to hate the yellow school bus until a dream she'd had one night of its careening off a bridge?—sinking into a river?—a confused, muddled dream, a nightmare best unexamined. When Tippi had been younger, Lorraine had taken her hand in hand out to the corner to catch the bus; Tippi was one of those tearful-sullen children reluctant to go to school, and many mornings a good deal of cajoling, coaxing, kissing, admonishing was required, Now, Tippi was older; Tippi could get to the bus by herself, however reluctantly, and however inclined she was to dawdle. But by custom in the Lake household it fell to Lorraine, the mother, to take note of the time when the time moved dangerously beyond 8 A.M.; it fell to Lorraine to urge Tippi to finish her breakfast, brush her teeth, get on her outdoor clothes and get outside before the bus moved on. Weeks ago, in the dead of February, in an uncharac-teristic mood of maternal impatience, Lorraine had purposefully remained silent as if unaware of the time, and of course Mr. Lake, skimming computer printouts at the breakfast table while Tippi ate her cereal, took not the slightest notice, and Tippi had in fact missed the bus that morning. But the upset to the household, the flurry of accusations and refutations and hurt feelings, the unleashed anger, had hardly been worth it; and the result had been that Lorraine had had to drive Tippi four miles into town, to school—as she might have predicted.

This morning, however, solemn-faced, pouty-mouthed, in her bulky quilted jacket looking like a mobile fire hydrant, Tippi Lake left the house in time to catch the bus. Lorraine called goodbye after her as always but Tippi scarcely glanced back, and her voice was flat, almost inaudible—"Bye, Mom."

"TIPPI AIN HERE MISSUS TOO BAD! BYEBYE!"

The ugly jeering words echoing in Lorraine Lake's head.

And what else had the hand-puppet said, his stunted arms flailing and his mouth working lewdly—"MISSUS I BEEN HERE BEFORE YA! AN' I GONNA BE HERE WHENYA GONE!"

It was not possible to believe that Tippi had said such things. That she'd been able to disguise her thin, childish voice so effectively, and "throw" it into the puppet, that she'd had the manual skills to create the puppet, let alone the concept. No, it just wasn't possible. Someone else, an older student, perhaps a teacher, had put her up to it.

I know my daughter, Lorraine thought. And that isn't *her*.

After Tippi left on the school bus, the house was so unnaturally empty. There was the relief of the sullen child's departure, but there was the strained absence as well. The radio wasn't enough to fill the void, so the mother switched it off. "I know my own daughter," she said aloud, with an angry laugh.

The urge to search Tippi's room was very strong. Yet she resisted. If Tippi said she wasn't bringing the hand-puppet to school, then that was so. Lorraine would not violate her daughter's trust by seeming to doubt her, even if she doubted her. And if she found the obscene little puppet in Tippi's room, what then? "DID I SCARED YOU MISSUS! SOOO SOORRY MISSUS!" Lorraine had a vision of tearing it to bits. "BYEBYE!"

Later that morning, Lorraine drove to town. She had an appointment with a gynecologist which she'd several times postponed since an examination of a year ago had gone badly. This morning's appointment was a secret from Mr. Lake and Tippi. (Not that Tippi would have been much concerned: when health or medical matters were mentioned, Tippi seemed simply not to hear. Her eyes glazed, her pert little mouth remained shut. This is a trait fairly common in children of her age and younger, Lorraine had been told. A form of denial.) Lorraine Lake was not a superstitious person but she had a dislike of sharing with others private matters that might turn out happily after all.

As she drove the several miles to town, her eyes moved over the eroding countryside without recognition. More woodland being razed for a new shopping mall, another housing subdivision, Sylvan Acres, rising out of a swamp of frozen mud. Mustard-yellow excavating vehicles were everywhere. Grinding, beeping. Flutter of wind-whipped banners advertising a new condominium complex. When Lorraine and her husband had first moved to their home, ten years before, most of this area had been farmland. Now, even the memory of that farmland was confused, eroded. A trust had been betrayed. This is America, the mother thought. Her mouth twisting. Don't tell me what I already know.

Dr. Fehr's waiting room was companionably crowded as usual. Several of the women were hugely pregnant. Lorraine began to feel stabs of panic like early contractions. But when her name was called—"Lorraine Lake?"—she rose obediently, with a small eager smile.

Undressing as she was bidden in an examination room, clumsy in her nakedness, a woman no longer young, embarrassed by flesh. Rolls of it, raddled and pinched. Drooping breasts oddly yellow-tinged as if with jaundice; the nipples raw-looking, scaly. As if something had been suckling her without her knowledge. How strangeness enters our lives.

A cheerful blond nurse, very young, weighed Lorraine Lake as she stood barefoot, rigid on an old-fashioned scale, weight one hundred twenty-two, then took her blood pressure as she sat, self-conscious in her flimsy paper smock, on the edge of the examining table. Something was wrong with the instrument, or with Lorraine Lake, so the nurse took another reading and entered the data on a sheet of paper attached to a clipboard. Lorraine said with a nervous laugh that she was always a little nervous at such times, so perhaps her blood pressure was a little high, and the nurse said yes, that happens sometimes, we can wait awhile and take another reading later. There was a gentle rap of knuckles on the door and Dr. Fehr entered brisk ruddy-faced and smiling as Lorraine recalled him, a man of vigorous youngish middle age, glittering round glasses and goatish ears in which graying-red hairs sprouted. Asking his frightened patient in the paper smock how she was, nodding and murmuring, "Good, good!" at whatever the answer, looming over her beneficent as a midday sun. Forcing rubber gloves onto his capable hands he said, just slightly reproachfully, "You've been postponing this awhile, Mrs. Lake"—a question posed as a statement.

The examination, familiar as a recurring nightmare, was conducted through a confused roaring in Lorraine Lake's ears. The curious localized pain in the uterus, the physician's invasion to be endured stoically, like a rape by Zeus. The patient was lying rigid on the examining table, head back, jaws clenched, eyes shut; fingers gripping the underside of the table so desperately she would discover afterward that several of her nails had cracked. The Pap smear swab, the chilly speculum, the deep probing of Dr. Fehr's strong fingers . . . seeking the spongy tumor, grown to the size of, what?—a nectarine, perhaps. After all these months.

Whatever words Dr. Fehr was saying, kindly or chiding or merely factual, Lorraine Lake did not hear. Blood roared in her ears like a crashing surf. She was blinking enormous hot tears from her eyes, that rolled down her cheeks onto the tissue paper that covered the examining table. She was thinking of the pregnancy that had inhabited her body nearly twelve years ago. The enormous swelling weight of the baby. The pressure, the billowing radiant pain. They praised her, who had not after all been a young mother, not *young* as such things are measured. They insisted she'd been brave, tireless, pushing! pushing! pushing! for more than eighteen hours. Giving birth. As if birth were something given, and given freely. In truth, Lorraine Lake had wanted to say that the birth had been taken from her. The baby forced itself from her. A vessel of violence, of hot unspeakable rage. And the terror of such knowledge, which she could share with no other person, certainly not the man who was her husband, the baby's "father." And the forgetfulness afterward, black wash of oblivion. *God never sends us more than He knows we can bear* one of Lorraine's older female relatives assured her. Lorraine laughed, remembering.

Dr. Fehr, vigorously palpating uterine tissue, seeking the perimeters of the spongy tumor, must have been surprised. The laugh became a cough, the cough a fit of sobbing, unless it was laughing, a gut-wrenching laughter, for in addition to experiencing pain the patient was being roughly tickled, too.

Through a teary haze the alarmed faces of doctor and nurse stared. Then ordered to lie flat, the weeping patient was quieted; no longer hyperventilating; the mad pulse in her left wrist deftly taken by a man's forceful thumb. "It's just that my body isn't my own," Lorraine Lake was explaining, now calmly. "I'm in it, I'm trapped in it, but it isn't my own. Someone makes me speak, too—not these words, but the others. But I'm terrified to leave my body, because where would I go?" This question so earnest Lorraine began to laugh again, and the laughter became helpless hiccuping that lasted for several minutes.

It was decided, then, when Lorraine Lake was herself again, and upright, able to look Dr. Fehr unflinchingly in the eye, that, yes, of course, she would have the operation she'd been postponing—a hysterectomy. The fibroid tumor was nonmalignant, but steadily growing; it was in fact the size of a nectarine, soon to be a grapefruit; not dangerous at the present time, but of course it must come out. Lorraine Lake was a reasonable woman, wasn't she. She had no phobias about hospitals, surgery, did she. "A hysterectomy is a common medical procedure," Dr. Fehr said gently.

"Common as death?" his patient inquired.

Frowning as he scribbled something onto the sheet attached to the clipboard, Dr. Fehr seemed not to have heard.

"No. I guess nothing is as common as death," his patient said, with an awkward laugh. She may have believed herself a person with a reputation for drollery and wit, in some other lifetime.

In any case, the examination was over. Dr. Fehr in his white
physician's costume, his round eyeglasses glittering, got to his
feet. The patient would call his office, make arrangements with
his nurse, for the next step preparatory to surgery. "Thank you,
Doctor," Lorraine said, stammering, "—I—I'm just so sorry
that I broke down—" Dr. Fehr waved away her apology as if it
were of no more significance than the female hysteria that had
preceded it, and was gone. Left by herself, Lorraine wiped her
eyes on a tissue, wiped her entire face which stung as if sunburnt.
She whispered, "I *am* sorry, and it won't happen again." She
crumpled the tissue, along with the ridiculous baby-doll paper
smock, and dropped both into a gleaming metallic wastebasket.

"A common medical procedure."

Driving then, not home, for she could not bear the prospect
of *home*, but in the direction of Tippi's school. The midday sky
had lightened somewhat but was still stippled with clouds, a
pale luminous sun like a worn-out penny.

It was noon recess. Boys and girls everywhere in the vicinity
of John F. Kennedy Elementary School—in the playground,
on the school's steps, milling about on the sidewalks. Traffic
moved slowly here, monitored by crossing guards. Lorraine
looked quickly for Tippi, but did not see her; no doubt, Tippi
was inside the school building, in the cafeteria or in her home-
room. How gregarious these children were! Lorraine braked her
car, moving slowly along the curb, avidly watching the children,
strangers to her, who were her daughter's classmates. Were any
of those girls Tippi's friends?—did any of them even know Tippi
Lake?—or care about her? Lorraine felt a mother's dismay, seeing
how pretty, how assured, how like young teenagers many of the

girls seemed, hardly Tippi's age at all. Some of the girls appeared to be wearing makeup—was that possible? At the age of eleven? Poor Tippi! No wonder she disliked school and was reluctant to discuss it, if these girls were her sixth-grade classmates.

It was as she passed the playground that she saw Tippi.

There was the quilted jacket, there the familiar fawn-colored hair and short plump shape, at the edge of the playground not more than ten yards away. At first, it looked as if Tippi was in a group of children; then it became clear that Tippi was by herself, though advancing aggressively toward the children, who were younger than she; she was unaware of her mother, of course, or of anyone watching. The several children, all girls, shrank from Tippi as she thrust something toward them—*was it the hand-puppet?* Lorraine stared in disbelief. Tippi's face was fierce and contorted as Lorraine had never seen it, and her body was oddly hunched, tremulous with concentration, appalling to witness. The younger children moved away from Tippi, not amused by the puppet, but staring at it, the object animated on Tippi's right hand, with looks of alarm and confusion. *What was the puppet saying? What foul threatening words issued from its lewd red-satin mouth?* Two older girls, witnessing Tippi's behavior, approached her and seemed to be challenging her, and Tippi whirled upon them savagely, wielding the puppet like a weapon. Lorraine could see the very cords in her daughter's throat work convulsively as Tippi "threw" her voice into the big-headed baby-faced bald creature on her hand.

"Tippi!—my God."

Lorraine would have shouted out the window of her car, but by this time she'd driven by; traffic bore her along the narrow street, and there was nowhere to park. Her heart was beating so rapidly she was terrified she might faint. The panic of the physical examination washed back over her. *That child is mad. That is the face of madness.*

No, it's harmless, just a game. Tippi gets carried away by games.

Lorraine drove through an intersection—blindly through a red light—a car horn sounded in annoyance—she was trying to think what she should do. Drive around the block, approach Tippi a second time, call out her name and break up the incident—my God, it was unthinkable, her own shy, sensitive daughter bullying and frightening smaller children! But at once Lorraine changed her mind, no of course not, no she could not, dared not confront Tippi in the playground of her school, in such a way, so public—Tippi would be humiliated, and Tippi might be furious. Tippi would think Lorraine was spying on her—she would never trust Lorraine again.

The profound shock was: Tippi had taken the hand-puppet with her to school, after all.

Tippi had lied to her. Deliberately, shamelessly, looking her mother in the eye.

Still, Lorraine could not confront her daughter, not now. Better to think of it later. Another, calmer time. She decided to continue with her errands in town, as if nothing out of the ordinary had occurred, for perhaps nothing had. In any case she was damned if she was going to cry again, become hysterical a second time within an hour—no thank you, not Lorraine Lake.

That afternoon, waiting for Tippi to come home from school, she prowled the house, restless, agitated. A cigarette burned in her fingers. Several times she believed she heard, in the distance, the sound of the school bus grinding its ugly brakes—then nothing. She steeled herself against the intrusion. Her aloneness would soon be violated by the child's noisy entry.

She was smoking again—the first time in twelve years. Her husband and her daughter would be shocked, disapproving; as she herself would have been, in different circumstances. The sharp nicotine charge in her lungs was like a thrust of love, imperfectly but passionately recalled. Why not?—we don't live forever, the mother thought. Except, mouthing the words to herself, what she actually said was, "We don't love forever." She heard this, and laughed.

She was passing by Tippi's closed door. She had not entered before, and she would not, now.

Instead, she climbed to the third floor, to the attic. Where rarely she went and then only on an errand of strict necessity; never for such purpose—simply to stand, heart beating quickly, before a grimy window. Not knowing where she was exactly except it was a place or sanctuary, solitude. The sky was closer here, drawing the eye upward. She smoked her cigarette with a lover's abandon, coughing a little, wiping at her eyes. She was free here, she was safe here, wasn't she!—when Tippi came home, Tippi would not know where she was. Tippi would want to hurry to her room to hide the hand-puppet and she, the mother, would not be a witness to the child's stealth; each would be spared. But really she did not care. She was not thinking of Tippi, or of the loathsome hand-puppet, at all.

How beautiful! The gray impacted clouds had begun to separate, like gigantic boulders, shot fiercely with flame. There was to have been an afternoon thunderstorm, but the northeast wind out of Canada had blown it past. The mother stared, in a trance.

She knew there was something behind her, below her; something imminent, threatening; a grinding of brakes, a jeering nasal child-voice . . . But, no: she was alone here, and she was safe. She leaned forward breathlessly: she saw herself climbing into the sky of boulders. As a girl, so long ago, she'd been wonderfully physical—athletic, self-assured. What buoyancy to her step, what jubilation, like that of a soul coming home! Her tall erect figure receded into the distance, and never a backward glance.

VALENTINE

In upstate New York in those years there were snowstorms so wild and fierce they could change the world, within a few hours, to a place you wouldn't know. First came the heavy black thunderheads over Lake Erie, then the wind hammering overhead like a freight train, then the snowflakes erupting, flying, swirling like crazed atoms. If there'd been a sun it was extinguished, gone. Night and day were reversed, the fallen snow emitted such a radium-glare.

I was fifteen years old living in the Red Rock section of Buffalo with an aunt, an older sister of my mother's, and her husband who was retired from the New York Central Railroad with a disability pension. My own family was what you'd call "dispersed"—we were all alive, seven of us, I believed we were all alive, but we did not live together in the same house any longer. In fact, the house, an old rented farmhouse twenty miles north of Buffalo, was gone. Burned to the ground.

Valentine's Day 1959, the snowstorm began in midafternoon and already by 5 P.M. the power lines were down in Buffalo. Hurriedly we lit kerosene lamps whose wicks smoked and stank as they emitted a begrudging light. We had a flashlight, of course, and candles. In extra layers of clothes we saw our breaths steam as we ate our cold supper on plates like ice. I cleaned up the kitchen as best I could without hot water, for that was always my task, among numerous others, and I said "Goodnight, Aunt Esther" to my aunt who frowned at me seeing someone not-me in my place who filled her heart with sisterly sorrow and I said "Goodnight, Uncle Herman" to the man designated as my uncle, who was no blood-kin of mine, a stranger with damp eyes always drifting onto me and a mouth like a smirking scar burn. "Goodnight" they murmured as if resenting the very breath expelled for my sake. *Goodnight don't run on the stairs don't drop the candle and set the house on fire.*

Upstairs was a partly finished attic narrow as a tunnel with a habitable space at one end—my "room." The ceiling was covered in strips of peeling insulation and so steep-slanted I could stand up only in the center. The floorboards were splintery and bare except for a small shag rug, a discard of my aunt's, laid down by my bed. The bed was another discard of my aunt's, a sofa of some mud-brown prickly fabric that pierced sheets laid upon it like whiskers sprouting through skin. But this was *a bed of my own* and I had not *own, a door to shut against others* even if, like the attic door, it could not be locked.

By midnight the storm had blown itself out and the alley below had vanished in undulating dunes of snow. Everywhere snow! Glittering like mica in the moonlight! And the moon—a glowing battered-human face in a sky strangely starless, black as a well. The largest snowdrift I'd ever seen, shaped like a right-angled triangle, slanted up from the ground to the roof close outside my window. My aunt and her husband had gone to bed downstairs hours ago and thought came to me unbidden *I can run away, no one would miss me.*

Along Huron Street, which my aunt's house fronted, came a snowplow, red light flashing atop its cab; otherwise there were few vehicles and these were slow-moving with groping headlights, like wounded beasts. Yet even as I watched there came a curiously shaped small vehicle to part at the mouth of the alley; and the driver, a long-legged man in a hooded jacket, climbed out. To my amazement he stomped through the snow into the alley to stand peering up toward my window, his breath steaming. Who? Who was this? *Mr. Lacey, my algebra teacher?*

My Valentine's Day that morning I had brought eight homemade valentines to school made of stiff red construction paper edged with paper lace, in envelopes decorated with red-ink hearts; the valentine TO MR. LACEY was my masterpiece, the largest and most ingeniously designed, interlocking hearts fashioned with a ruler and compass to resemble geometrical figures in three dimensions. HAPPY VALENTINE'S DAY I had neatly printed in black ink. Of course I had not signed any of the valentines and had secretly slipped them into the lockers of certain girls and boys and Mr. Lacey's onto his desk after class. I had instructed myself not to be disappointed when I received no valentines in return, not a single valentine in return, and I was not disappointed when at the end of the school day I went home without a single one: *I was not.*

Mr. Lacey seemed to have recognized me in the window where I stood staring, my outspread fingers on the glass bracketing my white astonished face, for he'd begun climbing the enormous snowdrift that lifted to the roof. How assured, how matter-of-fact, as if this were the most natural thing in the world. I was too surprised to be alarmed, or even embarrassed—my teacher would see me in a cast-off sweater of my brother's that was many sizes too large for me and splotched with oil stains, he would see my shabby little room that wasn't really a room, just part of an unfinished attic. He would know I was the one who'd left the valentine TO MR. LACEY on his desk in stealth not daring to sign my name. *He would know who I was, how desperate for love.*

Once on the roof, which was steep, Mr. Lacey made his way to my window cautiously. The shingles were covered in snow, icy patches beneath. There was a rumor that Mr. Lacey was a skier, and a skater, though his lanky body did not seem the body of an athlete and in class sometimes he seemed distracted in the midst of speaking or inscribing an equation on the blackboard; as if there were thoughts more crucial to him than tenth-grade algebra at Thomas W. Dewey High School which was one of the poorest schools in the city. But now his footing was sure as a mountain goat's, his movements agile and unerring. He crouched outside my window tugging to lift it—*Erin? Make haste!*

I was helping to open the window which was locked in ice. It had not been opened for weeks. Already it seemed I'd pulled on my wool slacks and wound around my neck the silver muffler threaded with crimson yarn my mother had given me two or three Christmases ago. I had no coat or jacket in my room and dared not risk going downstairs to the front closet. I was very excited, fumbling, biting my lower lip, and when at last the window lurched upward the freezing air rushed in like a slap in the face. Mr. Lacey's words seemed to reverberate in my

ears *Make haste, make haste!—not a moment to waste!* It was his
teasing-chiding classroom manner that nonetheless meant business. Without hesitating, he grabbed both my hands—I saw that
I was wearing the white angora mittens my grandmother had
knitted for me long ago, which I'd believed had been lost in the
fire—and hauled me through the window.

Mr. Lacey led me to the edge of the roof, to the snowdrift,
seeking out his footprints where he knew the snow to be fairly
firm, and carefully he pulled me in his wake so that I seemed
to be descending a strange kind of staircase. The snow was so
fresh-fallen it lifted like powder at the slightest touch or breath,
glittering even more fiercely close up, as if the individual snowflakes, of such geometrical beauty and precision, contained
minute sparks of flame. *Er-in, Er-in, now your courage must
begin* I seemed to hear and suddenly we were on the ground
and there was Mr. Lacey's Volkswagen at the mouth of the
alley, headlights burning like cat's eyes and tusks of exhaust
curling up behind. How many times covertly I'd tracked with
my eyes that ugly-funny car shaped like a sardine can, its black
chassis speckled with rust, as Mr. Lacey drove into the teachers' parking lot each morning between 8:25 A.M. and 8:35 A.M.
How many times I'd turned quickly aside in terror that Mr.
Lacey would see *me*. Now I stood confused at the mouth of
the alley, for Huron Street and all of the city I could see was
so changed, the air so terribly cold like a knifeblade in my
lungs; I looked back at the darkened house wondering if my
aunt might wake and discover me gone, and what then would
happen?—as Mr. Lacey urged *Come, Erin, hurry! She won't
even know you're gone* unless he said *She won't ever know you're*

gone. Was it true? Not long ago in algebra class I'd printed in
the margin of my textbook

MR.

L.

IS

AL

WA

YS

RI

GH

T!

which I'd showed Linda Bewley across the aisle, one of the popular tenth-grade girls, a B+ student and very pretty and popular,
and Linda frowned trying to decipher the words which were
meant to evoke Mr. Lacey's pole-lean frame, but she never did
get it and turned away from me annoyed.

Yet it was so: Julius Lacey was always always right.

Suddenly I was in the cramped little car and Mr. Lacey was
behind the wheel driving north on icy Huron Street. *Where are
we going?* I didn't dare ask. When my grades in Mr. Lacey's class
were less than 100 percent I was filled with anxiety that turned
my fingers and toes to ice for even if I'd answered nearly all the
questions on a test correctly *how could I know I could answer the
next question? solve the next problem? and the next?* A nervous passion drove me to comprehend not just the immediate problem
but the principle behind it, for behind everything there was an
elusive and tyrannical principle of which Mr. Lacey was the sole
custodian; and I could not know if he liked me or was bemused
by me or merely tolerated me or was in fact disappointed in me
as a student who should have been earning perfect scores at all

times. He was twenty-six or -seven years old, the youngest teacher at the school, whom many students feared and hated, and a small group of us feared and admired. His severed, angular face registered frequent dissatisfaction as if to indicate *Well, I'm waiting! Waiting to be impressed! Give me one good reason to be impressed!*

Never had I seen the city streets so deserted. Mr. Lacey drove no more than twenty miles an hour passing stores whose fronts were obliterated by snow like waves frozen at their crests and through intersections where no traffic lights burned to guide us and our only light was the Volkswagen's headlights and the glowering moon large in the sky as a fat navel orange held at arm's length. We passed Carthage Street that hadn't yet been plowed—a vast river of snow six feet high. We passed Templeau Street where a city bus had been abandoned in the intersection, humped with snow like a forlorn creature of the Great Plains. We passed Sturgeon Street where broken electrical wires writhed and crackled in the snow like snakes crazed with pain. We passed Childress Street where a water main had burst and an arc of water had frozen glistening in a graceful curve at least fifteen feet high at its crest. At Ontario Avenue Mr. Lacey turned right, the Volkswagen went into a delirious skid, Mr. Lacey put out his arm to keep me from pitching forward—*Erin, take care!* But I was safe. And on we drove.

Ontario Avenue, usually so crowded with traffic, was deserted as the surface of the moon. A snowplow had forged a single lane down the center. On all sides were unfamiliar shapes of familiar objects engulfed in snow and ice—parking meters? mailboxes? abandoned cars? Humanoid figures frozen in awkward, surprised postures—hunched in doorways, frozen in midstride on the sidewalk? *Look! Look at the frozen people!* I cried in a raw loud girl's voice that so frequently embarrassed me when Mr. Lacey called upon me unexpectedly in algebra class; but Mr. Lacey shrugged saying *Just snowmen, Erin—don't give them a second glance.* But I couldn't help staring at these statue-figures for I had an uneasy sense of being stared at by them in turn, through chinks in the hard-crusted snow of their heads. And I seemed to hear their faint despairing cries *Help! help us!*—but Mr. Lacey did not slacken his speed.

(Yet: who could have made so many "snowmen," so quickly after the storm? Children? Playing so late at night? And where were these children now?)

Mysteriously Mr. Lacey said *There are many survivors, Erin. In all epochs, just enough survivors.* I wanted to ask should we pray for them? pressing my hands in the angora mittens against my mouth to keep them from crying, for I knew how hopeless prayer was in such circumstances, God only helps those who don't require His help.

Were we headed for the lakefront?—we crossed a swaying bridge high above railroad tracks, and almost immediately after that another swaying bridge high above an ice-locked canal. We passed factories shut down by the snowstorm with smokestacks so tall their rims were lost in mist. We were on South Main Street now passing darkened shuttered businesses, warehouses, a slaughterhouse; windowless brick buildings against whose walls snow had been driven as if sandblasted in eerie, almost legible patterns

$$\int \, \chi \, \nearrow \, \frown \, \searrow \, \daleth \, \gimel \, \diagup \, \measuredangle \, \int$$

These were messages, I was sure!—yet I could not read them.

Out of the corner of my eye I watched Mr. Lacey as he drove. We were close together in the cramped car; yet at the same time I seemed to be watching us from a distance. At school there were boys who were fearful of Mr. Lacey yet, behind his back, sneered at him muttering what they'd like to do with him, slash his car tires, beat him up, and I felt a thrill of satisfaction *If you could see Mr. Lacey now!* for he was navigating the Volkswagen so capably along the treacherous street, past snowy hulks of vehicles abandoned by the wayside. He'd shoved back the hood of his wool jacket—how handsome he looked! Where by day he often squinted behind his glasses, by night he seemed fully at ease. His hair was long and quill-like and of the subdued brown hue of a deer's winter coat; his eyes, so far as I could see, had a luminous coppery sheen. I recalled how at the high school Mr. Lacey was regarded with doubt and unease by the other teachers, many of whom were old enough to be his parents; he was considered arrogant because he didn't have an education degree from a state teachers' college, like the others, but a master's degree in math from the University of Buffalo where he was a part-time Ph.D. student. *Maybe I will reap where I haven't had any luck sowing* he'd once remarked to the class, standing chalk in hand at the blackboard which was covered in calculations. And this remark too had passed over our heads.

Now Mr. Lacey was saying as if bemused *Here, Erin—the edge. We'll go no farther in this direction.* For we were at the shore of Lake Erie—a frozen lake drifted in snow so far as the eye could see. (Yet I seemed to know how beneath the ice the water was agitated as if boiling, sinuous and black as tar.) Strewn along the beach were massive ice-boulders that glinted coldly in the moonlight. Even by day at this edge of the lake you could see only an edge of the Canadian shore, the farther western shore was lost in distance. I was in terror that Mr. Lacey out of some whim would abandon me here, for never could I have made my way back to my aunt's house in such cold.

But already Mr. Lacey was turning the car around, already we were driving inland, a faint tinkling music seemed to draw us, and within minutes we were in a wooded area I knew to be Delaware Park—though I'd never been there before. I had heard my classmates speak of skating parties here and had yearned to be invited to join them as I had yearned to be invited to visit the homes of certain girls, without success. *Hang on! Hang on!* Mr. Lacey said, for the Volkswagen was speeding like a sleigh on curving lanes into the interior of a deep evergreen forest. And suddenly—we were at a large oval skating rink above which strings of starry lights glittered like Christmas bulbs, where dozens, hundreds of elegantly dressed skaters circled the ice as if there had never been any snowstorm, or any snowstorm that mattered to *them.* Clearly these were privileged people, for electric power had been restored for their use and burned brilliantly, wastefully on all sides. *Oh, Mr. Lacey I've never seen anything so beautiful* I said, biting my lip to keep from crying. It was a magical, wondrous place—the Delaware Park Skating Rink! Skaters on ice smooth as glass—skating round and round to gay, amplified music like that of a merry-go-round. Many of the skaters were in brightly colored clothes, handsome sweaters, fur hats, fur muffs; beautiful dogs of no breed known to me trotted alongside their masters and mistresses, pink tongues lolling in contentment. There were angel-faced girls in skaters' costumes, snug little pearl-buttoned velvet jackets and flouncy skirts to midthigh, gauzy knit stockings and kidskin boot-skates with blades that flashed like sterling silver—my heart yearned to see such skates for I'd learned to skate on rusted old skates formerly belonging to my older sisters, on a creek near our farmhouse, in truth I had never really learned to skate, not as these skaters were skating, so without visible effort, strife, or anxiety. Entire families were skating—mothers and fathers hand in hand with small children, and older children, and white-haired elders who must have been grandparents!—and the family dog trotting along with that look of dogs laughing. There were attractive young people in groups, and couples with their arms around each other's waist, and solitary men and boys who swiftly threaded their way through the crowd unerring as undersea creatures perfectly adapted to their element. Never would I have dared join these skaters except Mr. Lacey insisted. Even as I feebly protested *Oh but I can't, Mr. Lacey—I don't know how to skate* he was pulling me to the skate rental where he secured a pair of skates for each of us; and suddenly there I was stumbling and swaying in the presence of real skaters, my ankles weak as water and my face blotched with embarrassment, oh what a spectacle—but Mr. Lacey had closed his fingers firmly around mine and held me upright, refused to allow me to fall. *Do as I do! Of course you can skate! Follow me!* So I had no choice but to follow, like an unwieldy lake barge hauled by a tugboat.

How loud the happy tinkling music was out on the ice, far louder than it had seemed on shore, as the lights too were brighter, nearly blinding. *Oh! Oh!* I panted in Mr. Lacey's wake, terrified of slipping and falling; breaking a wrist, an arm, a leg; terrified of falling in the paths of swift skaters whose blades flashed sharp and cruel as butcher knives. Everywhere was a harsh hissing sound of blades slicing the surface of the ice, a sound you couldn't hear on shore. I would be cut to ribbons if I fell! All my effort was required simply to stay out of the skaters' paths as they flew by, with no more awareness of me than if I were a passing shadow; the only skaters who noticed me were children, girls as well as boys, already expert skaters as young as nine or ten who glanced at me with smiles of bemusement, or disdain. *Out! Out of our way! you don't belong here on our ice!* But I was stubborn too, I persevered, and after two or three times around the rink I was still upright and able to skate without Mr. Lacey's continuous vigilance, my head high and my arms extended for balance. My heart beat in giddy elation and pride. I was skating! At last! Mr. Lacey dashed off to the center of the ice where more practiced skaters performed, executing rapid circles, figure eights, dancerlike and acrobatic turns, his skate blades flashing, and a number of onlookers applauded, as I applauded, faltering but regaining my balance, skating on. I was not graceful—not by any stretch of the imagination—and I guessed I must have looked a sight, in an old baggy oil-stained sweater and rumpled wool slacks, my kinky-snarly red-brown hair in my eyes—but I wasn't quite so clumsy any longer, my ankles were getting stronger and the strokes of my skate-blades more assured, sweeping. How happy I was! How proud! I was beginning to be warm, almost feverish inside my clothes.

Restless as a wayward comet a blinding spotlight moved about the rink singling out skaters, among them Mr. Lacey as he spun at the very center of the rink, an unlikely, storklike figure to be so graceful on the ice; for some reason then the spotlight abruptly shifted—to me! I was so caught by surprise I nearly tipped, and fell—I heard applause, laughter—saw faces at the edge of the rink grinning at me. Were they teasing, or sincere? Kindly, or cruel? I wanted to believe they were kindly for the rink was such a happy place but I couldn't be sure as I teetered past, arms flailing to keep my balance. I couldn't be certain but I seemed to see some of my high school classmates among the spectators; and some of my teachers; and others, adults, a caseworker from the Erie County family services department, staring at me disapprovingly. The spotlight was tormenting me: rushing at me, then falling away; allowing me to skate desperately onward, then seeking me out again swift and pitiless as a cheetah in pursuit of prey. The harshly tinkling music ended in a burst of static as if a radio had been turned violently up, then off. A sudden vicious wind rushed thin and sharp as a razor across the ice. My hair whipped in the wind, my ears were turning to ice. My fingers in the tight angora mittens were turning to ice, too. Most of the skaters had gone home, I saw to my disappointment, the better-dressed, better-mannered skaters, all the families, and the only dogs that remained were wild-eyed mongrels with bristling hackles and stumpy tails. Mr. Lacey and I skated hastily to a deserted snowswept section of the rink to avoid these dogs, and were pursued by the damned spotlight; here the ice was rippled and striated and difficult to skate on. An arm flashed at the edge of the rink, I saw a jeering white face, and an ice-packed snowball came flying to strike Mr. Lacey between his shoulder blades and shattered in pieces to the ground. Furious, his face reddening, Mr. Lacey whirled in a crouch—*Who did that? Which of you?* He spoke with his classroom authority but he wasn't in his classroom now and the boys only mocked him more insolently. They chanted something that sounded like *Lac-ey! Lace-ey! Ass-y! Assy-Asshole!* Another snowball struck him on the side of the head, sending his glasses flying and skittering along the ice. I shouted for them to *stop! stop!* and a snowball

came careening past my head, another struck my arm, hard.
Mr. Lacey shook his fist daring to move toward our attackers
but this only unleashed a barrage of snowballs; several struck
him such force he was knocked down, a starburst of red at his
mouth. Without his glasses Mr. Lacey looked young as a boy
himself, dazed and helpless. On my hands and knees I crawled
across the ice to retrieve his glasses, thank God there was only a
hairline crack on one of the lenses. I was trembling with anger,
sobbing. I was sure I recognized some of the boys, boys in my
algebra class, but I didn't know their names. I crouched over
Mr. Lacey asking was he all right? was he all right? seeing that
he was stunned, pressing a handkerchief against his bleeding
mouth. It was one of his white cotton handkerchiefs he'd take
out of a pocket in class, shake ceremoniously open, and use to
polish his glasses. The boys trotted away jeering and laughing.
Mr. Lacey and I were alone, the only skaters remaining on the
rink. Even the mongrel dogs had departed.

It was very cold now. Earlier that day there'd been a warning—
temperatures in the Lake Erie–Lake Ontario region would drop
as low that night, counting the windchill factor, as −30 degrees
Fahrenheit. The wind stirred snake-skeins of powdery snow as
if the blizzard might be returning. Above the rink most of the
lightbulbs had burnt out or had been shattered by the rising
wind. The fresh-fallen snow that had been so purely white was
now trampled and littered; dogs had urinated on it; strewn
about were cigarette butts, candy wrappers, lost boots, mittens,
a wool knit cap. My pretty handknit muffler lay on the ground
stiffened with filth—one of the jeering boys must have taken
it from me when I was distracted. I bit my lip to keep from
crying, the muffler had been ruined and I refused to pick it up.

Subdued, silent, Mr. Lacey and I hunted our boots amid the litter, and left our skates behind in a slovenly mound, and limped back to the Volkswagen that was the only vehicle remaining in the snowswept parking lot. Mr. Lacey swore seeing the front windshield had been cracked like a spider's web, very much as the left lens of his glasses had been cracked. Ironically he said *Now you know, Erin, where the Delaware Park Skating Rink is.*

The bright battered-face moon had sunk nearly to the treeline, about to be sucked into blankest night.

In the Bison City Diner adjacent to the Greyhound bus station on Eighth Street, Mr. Lacey and I sat across a booth from each other, and Mr. Lacey gave our order to a brassy-haired waitress in a terse mutter—*two coffees, please.* Stern and frowning to discourage the woman from inquiring after his reddened face and swollen, still bleeding mouth. And then he excused himself to use the men's room. My bladder was aching, I had to use the restroom too, but would have been too shy to slip out of the booth if Mr. Lacey hadn't gone first.

It was 3:20 A.M. So late! The electricity had been restored in parts of Buffalo, evidently—driving back from the park we saw streetlights burning, traffic lights again operating. Still, most of the streets were deserted; choked with snow. The only other vehicles were snowplows and trucks spewing salt on the streets. Some state maintenance workers were in the Bison Diner, which was a twenty-four-hour diner, seated at the counter, talking and laughing loudly together and flirting with the waitress who knew them. When Mr. Lacey and I came into the brightly lit room, blinking, no doubt somewhat dazed-looking, the men glanced at us curiously but made no remarks. At least, none that we could hear. Mr. Lacey touched my arm and gestured with his head for me to follow him to a booth in the farthest corner of the diner—as if it was the most natural thing in the world, Mr. Lacey and me, sliding into that very booth.

In the clouded mirror in the women's room I saw my face strangely flushed, eyes shining like glass. This was a face not exactly known to me; more like my older sister Janice's, yet not Janice's, either. I cupped cold water into my hands and lowered my face to the sink grateful for the water's coolness for my skin was feverish and prickling. My hair was matted as if someone had used an eggbeater on it and my sweater, my brother's discard, was more soiled than I'd known, unless some of the stains were blood—for maybe I'd gotten Mr. Lacey's blood on me out on the ice. *Er-in Don-egal* I whispered aloud in awe, amazement. In wonder. Yes, in pride! I was fifteen years old.

Inspired, I searched through my pockets for my tube of raspberry lipstick, and eagerly dabbed fresh color on my mouth. The effect was instantaneous. *Barbaric!* I heard Mr. Lacey's droll voice for so he'd once alluded to female "makeup" in our class *painting faces like savages with a belief in magic.* But he'd only been joking.

I did believe in magic, I guess. I had to believe in something.

When I returned to the booth in a glow of self-consciousness there was Mr. Lacey with his face freshly washed too, and his lank hair dampened and combed. His part was on the left side of his head, and wavery. He squinted up at me—his face pinched in a quick frowning smile signaling he'd noticed the lipstick, but certainly wouldn't comment on it. Pushed a menu in my direction—*Order anything you wish, Erin, you must be starving* and I picked up the menu to read it, for in fact I was light-headed with hunger, but the print was blurry as if under water

and to my alarm I could not decipher a word. In regret I shook
my head no, no thank you. *No Erin? Nothing?* Mr. Lacey asked
surprised. Elsewhere in the diner a jukebox was playing a sentimental song—"Are You Lonesome Tonight?" At the counter,
amid clouds of cigarette smoke, the workmen and the brassy-
haired waitress erupted in laughter.

It seemed that Mr. Lacey had left his bloody handkerchief in
the car and, annoyed and embarrassed, was dabbing at his mouth
with a wadded paper towel from the men's room. His upper lip
was swollen as if a bee had stung it and one of his front teeth
was loose in its socket and still leaked blood. Almost inaudibly
he whispered *Damn. Damn. Damn.* His coppery-brown eye
through the cracked left lens of his glasses was just perceptibly
magnified and seemed to be staring at me with unusual intensity.
I shrank before the man's gaze for I feared he blamed me as the
source of his humiliation and pain. In truth, I was to blame: these
things would never have happened to Julius Lacey except for me.

Yet when Mr. Lacey spoke it was with surprising kindness.
Asking *Are you sure you want nothing to eat, Erin? Nothing,
nothing—at all?*

I could have devoured a hamburger half raw, and a plate of
greasy French fries heaped with ketchup, but there I was shaking
my head *no, no thank you Mr. Lacey.*

Why?—I was stricken with self-consciousness, embarrassment. To eat in the presence of this man! The intimacy would
have been paralyzing, like stripping myself naked before him.

Indeed it was awkward enough when the waitress brought
us our coffee, which was black, hotly steaming in thick mugs.
Once or twice in my life I'd tried to drink coffee, for everyone
seemed to drink it, and the taste was repulsive to me, so bitter!

But now I lifted the mug to my lips and sipped timidly at the steaming hot liquid black as motor oil. Seeing that Mr. Lacey disdained to add dairy cream or sugar to his coffee, I did not add any to my own. I was already nervous and almost at once my heart gave odd erratic beats and my pulse quickened.

One of my lifetime addictions, to this bitterly black steaming-hot liquid, would begin at this hour, in such innocence.

Mr. Lacey was saying with an air of reluctance, finality *In every equation there is always an x-factor, and in every x-factor there is the possibility, if not the probability, of tragic misunderstanding.* Out of his jacket pocket he'd taken, to my horror, a folded sheet of paper—red construction paper!—and was smoothing it out on the tabletop. I stared, I was speechless with chagrin. *You must not offer yourself in such a fashion, not even in secret, anonymously* Mr. Lacey said with a teacher's chiding frown. *The valentine heart is the female genitals, you will be misinterpreted.*

There was a roaring in my ears confused with music from the jukebox. The bitter black coffee scalded my throat and began to race along my veins. Words choked me *I'm sorry. I don't know what that is. Don't know what you're speaking of. Leave me alone, I hate you!* But I could not speak, just sat there shrinking to make myself as small as possible in Mr. Lacey's eyes staring with a pretense of blank dumb ignorance at the elaborate geometrical valentine TO MR. LACEY I had made with such hope the other night in the secrecy of my room, knowing I should not commit such an audacious act yet knowing, with an almost unbearable excitement, like one bringing a lighted match to flammable material, that I was going to do it.

Resentfully I said *I guess you know about me, my family. I guess there aren't any secrets.*

Mr. Lacey said *Yes, Erin. There are no secrets. But it's our preroga-tive not to speak of them if we choose.* Carefully he was refolding the valentine to return to his pocket, which I interpreted as a gesture of forgiveness. He said *There is nothing to be ashamed of, Erin. In you, or in your family.*

Sarcastically I said *There isn't?*

Mr. Lacey said *the individuals who are your mother and father came together out of all the universe to produce you. That's how you came into being, there was no other way.*

I couldn't speak. I was struck dumb. Wanting to protest, to laugh but could not. Hot tears ran down my cheeks.

Mr. Lacey persisted, gravely *And you love them, Erin. Much more than you love me.*

Mutely I shook my head *no.*

Mr. Lacey said, with his air of completing an algebra problem on the blackboard, in a tone of absolute finality *Yes. And we'll never speak of it again after tonight. In fact, of any of this*—making an airy magician's gesture that encompassed not just the Bison Diner but the city of Buffalo, the very night—*ever again.*

And so it was, we never did speak of it again. Our adventure that night following Valentine's Day 1959, ever again.

Next Monday at school, and all the days, and months, to come, Mr. Lacey and I maintained our secret. My heart burned with a knowledge I could not speak! But I was quieter, less ner-vous in class than I'd ever been; as if, overnight, I'd matured by years. Mr. Lacey behaved exactly, I think, as he'd always behaved toward me: no one could ever have guessed, in any wild flight of imagination, the bond between us. My grades hovered below 100 percent, for Mr. Lacey was surely one to wish to retain the power of giving tests no student could complete to perfection.

With a wink he said *Humility goeth in place of a fall, Erin.* And in September when I returned for eleventh grade, Julius Lacey who might have been expected to teach solid geometry to my class was gone: returned to graduate school, we were told. Vanished forever from our lives.

All this was far in the future! That night, I could not have foreseen any of it. Nor how, over thirty years later, on the eve of Valentine's Day I would remove from its hiding place at the bottom of a bureau drawer a bloodstained man's handkerchief initialed *JNL*, fine white cotton yellowed with time, and smooth its wrinkles with the edge of my hand, and lift it to my face like Veronica her veil.

By the time Mr. Lacey and I left the Bison Diner the light there had become blinding and the jukebox music almost deafening. My head would echo for days *lonely? lonely? lonely?* Mr. Lacey drove us hurriedly south on Huron Street passing close beneath factory smokestacks rimmed at their tops with bluish-orange flame, spewing clouds of gray smoke that, upon impact with the freezing wind off Lake Erie, coalesced into fine gritty particles and fell back to earth like hail. These particles drummed on the roof, windshield, and hood of the Volkswagen, bouncing and ricocheting off, denting the metal. *God damn* Mr. Lacey swore softly *will you never cease!*

Abruptly then we were home. At my aunt's shabby woodframe bungalow at 3998 Huron Street, Buffalo, New York, that might have been any one of dozens, hundreds, even thousands of similar woodframe one-and-a-half-story bungalows in working-class neighborhoods of the city. The moon had vanished as if it had never been and the sky was depthless as a black paper cutout, but a streetlamp illuminated the mouth of the snowed-in alley and the great snowdrift in the shape of a right-angled triangle lifting to the roof below my window. *What did I promise, Erin?—no one knows you were ever gone.* Mr. Lacey's words seemed to reverberate in my head without his speaking aloud. With relief I saw that the downstairs windows of the house were all darkened but there was a faint flickering light up in my room—the candle still burning, after all these hours. Gripping my hand tightly, Mr. Lacey led me up the snowdrift as up a treacherous stairs, fitting his boots to the footprints he'd originally made, and I followed suit, desperate not to slip and fall. *Safe at home, safe at home!* Mr. Lacey's words sounded close in my ears, unless it was *Safe alone, safe alone!* I heard. Oh! The window was frozen shut again! So the two of us tugged, tugged, tugged, Mr. Lacey with good-humored patience until finally ice shattered, the window lurched up to a height of perhaps twelve inches. I'd begun to cry, a sorry spectacle, and my eyelashes had frozen within seconds in the bitter cold so Mr. Lacey laughed kissing my left eye, and then my right eye, and the lashes were thawed, and I heard *Goodbye, Erin!* as I climbed back through the window.

THE COLLECTOR OF HEARTS

Funny! You never met me, don't know my name but you're holding me in your hand. Turning me in your fingers, peering at what remains of me saying *This is—ivory? Carved? It's so beautiful.*

Old man must've been fifty, dyed muskrat-color mustache and a bald head clean and shiny as chrome, quiet-spoken but you know you wouldn't want to mess with him; that strong Daddy-type that's been my weakness. There he was showing me into his house. His family house he said. But his family was deceased. He was the only survivor—"Unmarried, and without heirs. A classic story." I wasn't listening, my eyes were darting every which way taking in this big old mildew-smelling house with high-ceiling rooms going off in all directions and a staircase off the front vestibule rising up to—what? I swear, there wasn't nothing beyond the landing but shadows. Like somebody'd been drawing it in, got impatient and erased it with a dirty eraser so it's all smudged.

I thought I'd better say something so I said, making a joke, "Well. There's a whole lot of kids, nobody needs more." I got this nervous habit giggling after practically every remark I make whether funny or otherwise and cracking my gum. Usually I get some response like "Cool" or if it's a guy, laughing loud and appreciative.

This old Judge Whosis made some mumble like he was trying not to scold me for the gum. Touching my shoulder just with his fingertips like he was fearful of burning himself. Saying, "My collection of hearts." We were in a room of dark carved-wood walls, a black marble fireplace taking up half of one wall, a stained old mirror above the fireplace where my head floated like that was all it was—a head, no shoulders or body beneath. I liked my wet-looking red lips and my hair was an Afro so pale and soft you almost couldn't say what color it was, but I was surprised how crisscrossed my forehead was from frowning (which I hadn't realized I'd been doing) and I couldn't seem to see my eyes, it was weird.

"Wow." I giggled, and cracked my gum. "Wow. Cool."

It *was* cool: these glittery things, more than I could've counted, on the fireplace mantel, on a long skinny table of some fine old wood that's a little warped, on a round table where there's a fringe-shaded lamp the old guy switches on, all over. Not like valentine hearts—that kind of heart-shape, nor like the gold (maybe it's fake-gold) locket I wear for good luck on a thin chain swinging between my bare breasts in my little zebra-stripe purple tank top, but artistic-shaped hearts you could say, more like what you'd imagine a real heart to look like. For isn't a heart an actual muscle? There was a crystal heart on the fireplace mantel with facets so gleaming-bright you almost couldn't figure out what it was. There was a shiny grape-colored ceramic heart with a hint of actual veins or arteries. Some baked clay earthy-colored hearts, beautiful shades of dark red, rust-brown, mahogany-brown streaked with pale green. There was one spiky iron heart.

There was one delicately engraved silver heart (but the engraved words were in some language I didn't know, ODI ET AMO) and there was one heavy gold heart gleaming like a little sun. On a table, eight same-sized hearts carved of some cold-looking stony material I guess must've been marble—cream-colored, powder-gray, dark-purple, midnight-blue, white streaked with gray, pink like the inside of a wet mouth, milky-black and pure pitch-black. There was a heart so beautiful, dusty-rose-brown like my skin and glittering with mica like gold dust or sparks, I drew in my breath and stood staring for the longest time. All I could think to say was, "Wow. Cool." And cracked my gum real thoughtful.

Most of these hearts, as the old guy called them, you wouldn't probably identify as hearts if he hadn't said. They were about the size and shape of a man's clenched fist. I wondered where he got them, some special art store? antique store? I seemed to know you couldn't just walk into a department store like say Macy's and make such a purchase. Some of them must've been real expensive, too.

I'd been thinking (I mean, you always think in such ways, invited into a stranger's house) there might be something for me to pocket, the right-size item that can find its way into your pocket without you even knowing, exactly, but for sure these items of "the heart collection" were too heavy and clunky-size, but I didn't feel too disappointed, I was so curious and it's my natural nature to ask questions. "Does this open? Is that how it was made, in fit-together halves?" I lifted this coppery shining heart using both hands, it was heavier than you'd expect, and would've examined the underside where there was a fine seam, but Judge Whosis says real quick and kind of scared, "Please!

Don't touch." And takes it from me with his trembly fingers and sets it back exactly on the spot it'd been on the table—in the very dust-outline where you could figure it'd been sitting for a long time.

But he was smiling.

We'd met in his courtroom just that morning. He was Judge—of the county criminal court. (I have to admit I'd forgot his name almost as soon as I heard it. Always I had this bad habit, names sailed past me if they were the names of somebody old, ugly, boring or what you'd call official like teachers, church people, social workers, public defenders, judges.) A straggly troop of us, six or seven females, the youngest being me, was brought over from the women's detention next door to the third floor of the moldy old county courthouse which was one of the places on this Earth I hated almost as bad as I hated the shitty detention house. But Judge —— was a surprise. Not that he wasn't stern. He was. But not mean and nasty like most. Not like a certain female judge where if you're young, pretty and almost-white she'll fuck you over as best she can. Judge —— was sort of scary-looking at first, wrinkled-homely as a toad with that shiny bald head and dyed-brown mustache like something painted on and he was wearing this judge's robe that fitted him like a shower curtain would, but he was alert and listening to the reports, asked serious questions about those of us hauled before him so it wasn't like some assembly line or something. He impressed me he was O.K. for an old guy so weird-looking. He treated the older girls, hookers and crack addicts, O.K., though they all had to serve some time; and with me, I'm next to last, brought up in front of his bench with the shakes, not that I'm actually scared but I get the shakes easy, and I hadn't had a smoke in eighteen hours so my voice is so low and trembling he has to ask me to repeat what I said more than once. I'm here for shoplifting and a bench warrant for some bad checks from last Christmas; also I'd gotten in a scuffle with the security guard at the Discount King where he'd insulted me with a racial epithet so I went a little wild and bit the fucker in the hand and they're charging me for that, too—assault, for Christ's sake. The D.A.'s assistant is laying it on like I'm a public menace and need to be incarcerated for a long time, also she's pissed this is my third offense as an adult, and my attorney's arguing some crap I'm not much listening to. I see Judge ——— regarding me in that frowning-kindly way like I might've been his daughter or granddaughter almost. I had the hope he'd give me a suspended sentence so I told my attorney I changed my plea to *guilty* and I got to say in this breathy little voice, "Guilty, Your Honor," which gave me a shiver and made the old guy's yellowish droopy eyes shine like somebody'd goosed him. So it was O.K. It was terrific. I wasn't bullshitting for once, I was serious for I'd seen in the old man's eyes something that had to do with *me.* Not some court number on a piece of paper. And Judge ——— says, "Eight months, suspended sentence, counseling at County Health suggested." And that was it! "Thank you, Your Honor," I said, wiping at my eyes, and this was no bullshit, either. "I'm r-real grateful."

I figured that was that, Jesus was I lucky. Then back at this place where I and a girlfriend (that I hadn't actually seen in over a week, I believe she'd gone off with some guy to Atlantic City), rented a room, there came a call for me at 6 P.M. I figured it was one of my boyfriends I wasn't in any hurry to hook up with—but it was this gravelly toad-voice I recognized right away.

Judge —— saying he was concerned with my case, a young woman of my age, with my history of arrests, etc. He believed I was "clearly under a malevolent influence" and "malnourished both physically and spiritually." He said he would like to speak with me to discuss my case that evening. He was personally involved in sending certain deserving young people to training schools (business, barbering and hairdressing, restaurant work) and perhaps I would be eligible. I said O.K. it sounded good so he sent a car for me to bring me to his big old place on the River Road where there's mansions on a ridge overlooking the Delaware River, a section of the city remote to me as the far side of the moon though I knew of it, of course, and probably had had some dates from this neighborhood though for sure they'd never have identified themselves as such. The car pulled up this drive and I got out of breath just staring at the big old maroon-brick house with the pointy roof and half dozen chimneys. I laughed saying, "Hey. Wow," to myself, and cracked my gum. Have to admit I believed every word Judge —— told me and even some he'd only hinted at, like there was this special understanding between us *because I was special.* Which we all know or wish to believe in our hearts.

There was Judge —— at the side door of the big old house. He sent away the driver. He asked me please to come inside. He wasn't wearing his black judge's robe of course and looked more like an ordinary oldish man with a sizable gut riding his belt and a streak of something flushed and excited in his face. Right away he was saying he wanted to show me his "collection of hearts—which it requires a sensitive eye to appreciate." His own droopy-lidded eyes sort of eating me up like he wasn't aware, or couldn't help it, I'm wearing my zebra-stripe purple jersey tank top (just bare titties beneath) and my little gold-heart locket on a chain around my neck and a black vinyl miniskirt to practically just my crotch and I'd picked out my hair so it was fine and airy and exploded-looking as dandelion fluff. And platform shoes of spangle-blue plastic, with ankle straps. Inside, it smelled of mildew and maybe old newspapers and something sweetish-sharp like in a dentist's office (not my favorite smell in the world!) and sure not romantic (if that was what the old white guy was thinking) but I was smelling pretty good myself with this spray-on Chanel No. 5 I'd pocketed at Macy's a few weeks ago so it was O.K. I mean, no immediate danger I'd puke.

For I did have a kind of sensitive stomach. From a long time of stress where I'd forgot to eat regular, kept going on cigarettes, black coffee and what I could get on the street.

Judge Whosis saying, leading me along some hall, few people realize how lonely it is being a judge if you don't wish to belong to the "ruling elite" and I giggled and said, "Yeah, I bet. Must be weird," and cracked my gum. And Judge Whosis wiping at his damp lardy forehead with a pure-white cotton handkerchief somebody must've laundered and ironed for him, "It *is* . . . weird."

And he laughed too, and made a wet clicking sound with tongue like that was his way, an old-daddy, grandpappy way you had to laugh fondly at, of cracking his gum.

The judge observed in silence as I blinked and grinned and marveled over the collection of hearts. Which was like no other display of anything I'd ever seen before, that I could recall. I said, "Your Honor, this is fan-tas-tic. Like a museum." I was maybe becoming a little uneasy, prickles on my bare arm and that side of my neck nearest the judge, for he was watching me all this while. But I believed (I don't know why!) the man could not be living alone in that house, not such a big old house where you'd need to have lots of servants; also I'd overheard him mumble something (I thought!) out in the hall on our way into the room with the hearts, such as you might say to a maid or somebody. So I was just a little uneasy, not panicked or anything, lighting up a cigarette without asking permission. But Judge Whosis said not a word of scolding, only frowned and said, "You'll anesthetize your taste buds, dear. And I have a little surprise for you."

To this I didn't know how to reply except to giggle again, and shift my shoulders in that nervous habit I had, and exhale smoke as gracefully as I could through my nostrils.

By this time I'd seen about all there was to see of the heart collection at least in this room. I was hoping there wasn't any more, I was hoping there'd be something to eat, it was almost 9 P.M. and I hadn't eaten since breakfast at women's detention at 7 A.M. But the old guy had a few more hearts to show me, one of ruby-red glass he said was a "recent acquisition." And there was a fancy gentleman's cane, shiny black lacquer with a carved wooden heart-handle that was almost too big for me to wrap my fingers around though he was pushing it into my hand. "This is a new venture for me," he said, sort of puffing. "I intend to continue with the series. Next, an exquisitely carved ivory heart. On a cane exactly like this. What do you think? Do you approve of ivory?" Smiling at me with teeth like white enamel so I had to smile back, to be polite. "Yeah. It's O.K. Cool, I guess," I said. Ivory? What're we talking about? There was this old bald dyed-mustache white man, judge of the county criminal court, asking my advice about ivory? And puffing like he'd been climbing stairs. I said, "Where'd you get such a nice cane, your honor?" and Judge Whosis said, like he was proud, "I didn't. It's always been in my family. There are more in the attic. Originally, this came from India. My great-grandfather was a magistrate in India, under British rule." Lifting the cane like a sword the way a kid might, to scare you, and I gave a jump, guess I was more scared than I knew, but he seemed not to mean anything by it, just a clumsy way of moving. Again had me try to wrap my fingers around the handle of wood (fine-carved to resemble an actual heart with veins, etc.), and his fingers over mine, securing them on the handle, which made me uneasy, like I say the handle was too big and of an awkward shape. It was then I had a weird sensation almost like . . . God. I don't know! . . . inside the carved wood heart it was warm, and there was a weak pulsebeat. *A heart. An actual heart. There is an actual heart trapped inside here.* But this was crazy, I put such a notion out of my head the way you'd brush away a fly.

The judge led me at last into another room. Parlor? Old-fashioned velvet drapes, a velvet sofa to sit on. Bottles of champagne and sparkling water on a silver tray, shiny crystal glasses and some little sandwiches without crusts, chopped shrimp he said, turkey, ham, goat-cheese, a "miscellany" he'd ordered he said, also sticky walnut pastries. I was so hungry my mouth watered and I was trembling but made myself hold back for I'd always had good manners, I'd been ridiculed for my prissy-prissy ways by some companions, in fact. Judge Whosis made a fuss pouring champagne for me, but for himself he poured only the sparkling water, with a slice of lemon, saying he rarely drank even champagne, he had a "congenital condition." I drank down the champagne in about one swallow. He poured more, and I drank that down. My mouth was full with the little sandwiches. I was pretty happy now. I said, swallowing, "I'm sorry to hear that, Your Honor." Though I hadn't been listening all that closely. I bit into a walnut pastry, which was what the judge was eating, it was so sugary my mouth stung but, yes, it was delicious, so I ate it all. I drank down another glass of champagne. Wow! I was feeling fantastic. Like snorting coke. Nah, smoking crack. But this was legal, and this was good for me, this was "nutrition" which I had to accept I needed so my bones wouldn't hollow out and snap. The judge was asking me in a kindly voice like in the courtroom that morning about my background, my birth-mother and foster families, and I said real quick I didn't know, didn't believe in dwelling upon the past and he said, nodding, his second chin creasing against his chest, "That's wise, dear. That's wisdom. I, too, don't believe in dwelling upon the past. Except as the past is contained, preserved, in the present. As personal, private, prized history. For there you have the past in the present; but it's your selection of the past, it has become your work of art." I wasn't following this, but I nodded real vigorously. The judge was saying, smiling at me, crouched forward on the sofa with his big sticky-fingered hands clasped on his knees, "Not many times in my professional life has a young woman like yourself, or a young man, made a strong impression on me. I have wanted then to know her, or him, more intimately. To bring her, or him, into my life." I was eating, and I mumbled something with a full mouth. I was hoping he'd move on next to the subject of the training school, I intended to speak of the Trenton School of Beauty Culture where I'd started a nail-and-hair course just out of high school but never completed, maybe I could return to that, I had reason to believe I had a natural talent for such work, skillful hands and a winning personality and if my own God-damned nails keep breaking off I can wear fakes, nobody can tell the difference. But I was feeling kind of drowsy from the champagne I guess, which was a taste new to me, and that good food, peaceful like I wanted to curl up right there on the judge's sofa like a cat. Judge —— smiled kindly at me. He'd poured still another glass of champagne for me, more sparkling water for himself he'd been drinking down like a thirsty dog, and I reached for that final glass, already so sleepy I could hardly keep my eyes open. A thought came to me. I giggled, saying, "Hey, Your Honor? This isn't a love potion, is it?"

Says the old guy clicking his glass against mine, "I hope so, dear."

THE SONS OF ANGUS MACELSTER

A true tale of Cape Breton Island, Nova Scotia, 1923.

This insult not to be borne. Not by the MacElster sons who were so proud. From New Glasgow to Port Hawkesbury to Glace Bay at the wind-buffeted easternmost tip of Cape Breton Island, where the accursed family lived, it was spoken of. All who knew of the scandal laughed, marveled, shook their heads over it. The MacElsters!—that wild crew! Six strapping sons and but a single daughter no man dared approach for fear of old Angus and his sons, heavy drinkers, tavern brawlers, what can you expect? Yet what old Angus MacElster did, and to his own wife, you'd scarcely believe: he'd been gone for three months on a coal-bearing merchant ship out of Halifax, returning home to Glace Bay on a wet-dripping April midday, his handsome ruin of a face windburnt and ruddy with drink, driving with two other merchant seamen who lived in the Bay area, old friends of his, and at the tall weatherworn woodframe house on Mull Street overlooking the harbor he dropped his soiled gear, freshened up and spent a brief half hour in the company of Mrs. MacElster; and the nervous daughter Katy now twenty years old and still living at home, Angus stood before the icebox devouring cold meat loaf with his fingers, breaking off morsels with his stubby gnarled fingers, and washing down his lunch in haste with ale he'd brought with him in several clinking bottles in the pockets of his sheepskin jacket, then it was off to the Mare's Neck as usual, and drinking with his old companions, how like old times it was, and never any improvement in the man's treatment of his wife. Returned to Glace Bay for three weeks before he'd ship out again and already there was a hint of trouble, it was Katy put the call to Rob, the eldest son, and Rob drove over at once from Sydney in an automobile borrowed from his employer at the pulp mill under the pretext of a family emergency, and Cal in his delivery van drove over from Briton Cove, and there was Alistair hurrying from New Skye, and John Rory and John Allan and I, the youngest, live here in Glace Bay where we'd been born, freely we admit we'd been drinking too, you must drink to prepare yourself for the hurtful old man we loved with a fierce hateful love, the heated love of boys for their father, even a father who has long betrayed them with his absence, and the willful withholding of his love, yet we longed like craven dogs to receive our father's blessing, any careless touch of his gnarly hand, we longed to receive his rough wet despairing kisses on the lips of the kind he'd given us long ago when we were boys, before the age of ten, so the very memory of such kisses is uncertain to us, ever shifting and capricious as the fog in the harbor every morning of our waking lives. *Even at that late hour, our hearts might yet have been won.*

Except: unknown to us at the time our mother had gone in reckless despair to the Mare's Neck to seek our father, and the two quarreled in the street where idlers gathered to gawk, at the foot of New Harbor Street in a chill glistening wind, and we would be told that he'd raised a hand to her and she'd cried *Disgusting! How can you!—disgusting! God curse you!* tears shining on her cheeks, and her hair the color of tarnished silver loosened in the wind, and she'd pushed at the old man which you must never do, you must never touch the old man for it is like bringing a lighted match to straw, you can witness the wild blue flame leaping up his body, leaping in his eyes, his eyes bulging like a horse's and red-veined with drink, the flame in his graying red hair the color of fading sumac in autumn, and in a rage he seizes the collar of her old cardigan sweater she'd knitted years ago, seizes it and tears it, and as idlers from the several pubs of New Harbor Street stare in astonishment he tears her dress open, cursing her, *Cow! Sodden cow! Look at you, ugly sodden cow!* ripping her clothes from her, exposing our cringing mother in the halterlike white cotton brassiere she must wear to contain her enormous breasts, milk-pale flaccid breasts hanging nearly to her waist she tries to hide with her arms, our mother publicly shamed pleading with our father *Angus, no! Stop! I beg you, God help you—no!* Yet in his drunken rage Angus MacElster strips his wife of thirty-six years near-naked, as the poor woman shrieks and sobs at the foot of New Harbor Street, and a loose crowd of beyond twenty men has gathered to watch, some of them grinning and laughing but most of them plainly shocked, even the drunks are shocked by a man so publicly humiliating his wife, and his wife a stout middle-aged woman with graying hair, until at last Angus MacElster is persuaded to leave his wife alone, to back off and leave the poor hysterically weeping woman alone, one or two of the men wrap her in their jackets, hide her nakedness, even as old Angus turns aside with a wave of his hand in disgust and stumbles off to Mull Street three blocks away yet not

to the tall weatherworn woodframe house, but instead the old
barn at the rear, muttering and cursing and laughing to himself
Angus sinks insensible into the straw; like a horse in its stall in a
luxuriance of sleep where, when we were small boys, he'd spent
many a night even in winter, returning late to the house and not
caring to blunder into our mother's domain not out of fear of her
wrath nor even of his own wrath turned against her but simply
because he was drawn to sleeping in the barn, in his clothes, in
his boots, luxuriant in such deep dreamless animal sleep as we,
his sons, waited inside the house shuddering and shivering in
anticipation of his return, his heavy footsteps on the stairs, yet
yearning for his return as a dog yearns for the return of the very
master who will kick him, praying he would not cuff us, or beat
us, or kick us, or yank at our coarse red curls so like his own in
that teasing tenderness of our father's that seemed to us far cruel-
ler than actual cruelty for at such times you were meant to smile
and not cringe, you were meant to love him and not fear him,
you were meant to obey him and not turn mutinous, you were
meant to honor your father and not loathe him, still less were
you meant to pray for his death, steeped in sin as you were, even
at a young age, even in childhood touched by the curse of the
MacElsters, emigrated from the wind-ravaged highlands north
of Inverness to the new world with blood, it was rumored, on
their hands, and murder in their hearts. And there at the house
when we arrived was our mother weeping deranged with shock
and humiliation, her mouth bloodied, and Katy tending to her
white-faced and shaking as if she too had been stripped naked
in the street, and would be the scandalized talk of all who knew
the MacElsters and countless others who did not, from Glace
Bay to Port Hawkesbury to New Glasgow and beyond, talk to

endure for years, for decades, for generations to this very day;
and seeming to know this as a fact, Angus's six sons wasted no
time, we strode into the barn known to us as a dream inhabited
nightly, that place of boyhood chores, of boyhood play, badly
weatherworn, with missing boards and rotted shingles loosened
by wind, glaring-eyed Rob has taken up the double-edged ax
where it was leaning against the doorframe, and Cal the resource-
ful one has brought from home a twelve-inch fish-gutting knife,
Alistair has a wicked pair of shears, John Rory and John Allan
have their matching hunting knives of eight-inch stainless steel,
and I have a newly honed butcher knife from my own house,
from out of my own kitchen where my young wife will miss it,
and the six of us enter the barn to see the old man snoring in
the twilight, in a patch of damp straw, and panting we circle
him, our eyes gleaming like those of feral creatures glimpsed
by lamplight in the dusk, and Rob is the first to shout for him
to *Wake! wake up, old man!*—for it seems wrong to murder a
sixty-one-year-old man snoring on his back, fatty-muscled torso
exposed, arms and legs sprawled in a bliss of drunken oblivion,
and at once old Angus opens his eyes, his bulging red-veined
horse's eyes, blinking up at us, knowing us, naming us one by
one his six MacElster sons as damned as he, and yet *even at this
late hour our hearts might yet be won.* Except, being the man he
is, old Angus curses us, calls us young shits, spits at us, tries
to stumble to his feet to fight us, even as the first of our blows
strikes. Rob's double-edged ax like electricity leaping out of the
very air, and there's the flash of Cal's fish-gutting knife, and
Alistair's shears used for stabbing, and the fine-honed razor-
sharp blades of John Rory and John Allan's and mine, blades
sharp enough and strong enough to pierce the hide of the very

devil himself, and in a fever of shouts and laughter we strike, and tear, and lunge, and stab, and pierce, and gut, and make of the old man's wind-roughened skin a lacy-bloody shroud and of his bones brittle sticks as easily broken as dried twigs, and of his terrible eyes cheap baubles to be gouged out and ground into the dirt beneath our boots, and of his hard skull a mere clay pot to be smashed into bits, and of his blood gushing hot and shamed onto the straw and the dirt floor of the barn a glistening stream bearing bits of cobweb, dust, and straw as if a sluice were opened, and we leap about shouting with laughter for this is a game, is it?—will the steaming poison-blood of Angus MacElster singe our boots?—sully our boots?—will some of us be tainted by this blood and others, the more agile, the more blessed, will not?

This old family tale came to me from my father's father Charles MacElster, the eldest son of Cal.

(after Ovid)

ACKNOWLEDGMENTS

"The Death of Mrs. Sheer" originally appeared in *MSS Magazine* (1964); *Upon the Sweeping Flood and Other Stories*, Vanguard (1966).

"In the Warehouse" originally appeared in *Transatlantic Review* (1967); *The Goddess and Other Women*, Vanguard (1974).

"By the River" originally appeared in *December Magazine* (1968); *Marriages and Infidelities: Short Stories*, Vanguard (1972).

"Queen of the Night" was originally published by Lord John Press (1979); *A Sentimental Education: Stories*, Dutton (1981)

"The Revenge of the Foot, 1970" originally appeared in *Salmagundi* (1970); *Will You Always Love Me? And Other Stories*, Dutton (1996).

"The Doll" originally appeared in *Epoch* (1980); *Haunted: Tales of the Grotesque*, Dutton (1994).

"Little Wife" originally appeared in *Kenyon Review* (1986); *Raven's Wing: Stories*, Dutton (1986).

"Yarrow" originally appeared in *TriQuarterly* (1987); *Heat and Other Stories*, Dutton (1991).

"Haunted" originally appeared in *The Architecture of Fear*, Arbor House (1987); *Haunted: Tales of the Grotesque*, Dutton (1994).

"Death Valley" originally appeared in *Esquire* (1988); *Heat and Other Stories*, Dutton (1991).

"Craps" originally appeared in *Boulevard* (1989); *Heat and Other Stories*, Dutton (1991).

"Family" originally appeared in *Omni* (1989); *Heat and Other Stories*, Dutton (1991).

"Ladies and Gentlemen:" originally appeared in *Harper's Magazine* (1990); *Heat and Other Stories*, Dutton (1991).

"Why Don't You Come Live With Me, It's Time" originally appeared in *Tikkun* (1990); *Heat and Other Stories*, Dutton (1991).

"The Buck" originally appeared in *Story* (1991); *Heat and Other Stories*, Dutton (1991).

"The Model" originally appeared in *Ellery Queen's Mystery Magazine* (1992); *Haunted: Tales of the Grotesque*, Dutton (1994).

"Extenuating Circumstances" originally appeared in *Sisters in Crime 5*, Berkley Books (1992); *Haunted: Tales of the Grotesque*, Dutton (1994).

"The Girl Who Was to Die" originally appeared in *Gettysburg Review* (1993); *Will You Always Love Me? And Other Stories*, Dutton (1996).

"Poor Bibi" originally appeared as "Poor Thing" in *Tikkun* (1992); *Haunted: Tales of the Grotesque*, Dutton (1994).

"The Undesirable Table" originally appeared in *Raritan* (1994); *Will You Always Love Me? And Other Stories*, Dutton (1996).

"The Hand-Puppet" originally appeared in *Tales of the Impossible*, Harper Prism (1995); *The Collector of Hearts: New Tales of the Grotesque*, Dutton (1998).

"Valentine" originally appeared in *Michigan Quarterly Review* (1996); *The Collector of Hearts: New Tales of the Grotesque*, Dutton (1998).

"Collector of Hearts" originally appeared in *Seventeen* (1998); *The Collector of Hearts: New Tales of the Grotesque*, Dutton (1998)

"The Sons of Angus MacElster" originally appeared in *Conjunctions* (1998); *The Collector of Hearts: New Tales of the Grotesque*, Dutton (1998).